In loving memory of Emily Redmond,
a real Lancashire Bomb Girl.
You always said you could write a
book, Mummy . . . well, now you have!

Acknowledgements

I'd like to thank Jacky Hyams for *Bomb Girls* and Russell Miller for *Behind The Lines*. Both books provided invaluable background material, as did the BBC World War 2 Archives. Thanks to Diane Banks' Agency, which led me to the wonderful editorial team at Penguin: Clare Bowron, Maxine Hitchcock and Eve Hall. I'm especially grateful to Jon Styles, for his patience and time spent on endless research, to Sebastian Neave, for his fascinating and detailed knowledge of military history, and to Isabella, my youngest daughter and a writer too, for her constructive criticism on all the drafts I wrote. Thank you, Kate Wheale, for the hot brandy and pep talks, Theresa Plummer-Andrews, for giving me the confidence to take the plunge, my older children, Tamsin and Gabriel, for their excitement and support, and my sister, Kathryn, who shares the same memories as me. And last of all to the real Bomb Girls who helped win the war and give us our freedom.

Chapter 1: Emily

The sun shining through the canteen window illuminated the cloud of flour that Emily had created as she pounded the pastry for her lunchtime meat pies. Blowing stray auburn curls out of her eyes, Emily smiled to herself. Butter might be rationed but there was more than one way to skin a cat when it came to culinary ingenuity. She'd been collecting wartime cookery tips from various magazines and newspapers, discovering alternatives to the real things, like cheese, eggs and milk, that were as rare as hen's teeth these days. Because pastry and pies were big on her canteen menu (and cheap too) she couldn't keep knocking out tasteless flour-and-water-based pastry tops for the poor sods working ten-hour shifts in the cotton sheds. She knew better than most that mill workers needed something to get their teeth into at dinner time.

Emily herself had worked at the looms before she got her lucky break in the canteen. She'd always hated mill work, which was seen as her destiny along with that of every other female in the small Lancashire town of Pendle. She hated the grease and the fluff, the cotton fibres that went everywhere, up your nose, in your hair and clogged your lungs.

'I want to run a canteen,' she told her mother. 'I want to cook food, be a chef!'

Mrs Yates shook her head in despair. How did she and

her even-tempered, steady husband ever manage to produce a firecracker like their Emily? What with her blazing hair, wide sky-blue eyes and generous mouth, she didn't even resemble her parents. Her spirit and laughter, her exuberance for life and her energy were boundless; nothing and nobody ever got in Emily's way. When she started walking out with Bill Redmond, Mrs Yates breathed a sigh of relief. Bill was a lovely boy, the good-looking eldest son of a nice, respectable family, and she'd known him since the day he was born. Bill would soon calm Emily down, Mrs Yates thought. Not so. Love and romance sent Emily into overdrive! Kissing and cuddling, whispering sweet nothings to Bill up on the moonlit moors, made Emily realize there was even more to life than she'd previously thought.

With the coming of the war Emily's major concerns were for her twenty-year-old sweetheart, who, handsome in his soldier's uniform, had left Pendle to fight in northern France with the Lancashire Fusiliers. With the exodus of hundreds of local men, apart from the old and medically exempt, the mill became a predominantly female place. It didn't take canny Emily long to clock that Mr Greenhalgh, the canteen manager, an affable but lazy man who disliked hard work, was in need of an extra pair of hands. Smiling and sweet-talking Mr Greenhalgh, Emily wheedled her way into an interview for canteen cook, a position that Mr Greenhalgh had been planning on giving to his brother.

'But he's no qualifications,' Emily reasoned at the interview while Mr Greenhalgh sat smoking roll-ups with his feet on the scoured kitchen table.

'Neither have you!' barked Mr Greenhalgh.

'I can cook,' Emily protested.

'That's as may be but I'm used to working wi' lads not lasses,' Mr Greenhalgh replied.

Emily smothered a snort of irritation. What planet was this man on? Only a few months ago over three hundred thousand troops had battled it out on the beaches of Dunkirk. Did Mr Greenhalgh really think there were spare men around to peel spuds and wash up kitchen pots?

'There's a war on, sir,' Emily said. 'Needs must.'

Mr Greenhalgh blew out a cloud of smoke as he waxed philosophical.

'Women are funny buggers . . .' he mused. 'I've got one at home,' he said, as if he was talking about his cat. 'She's either waiting for "you know what" to happen or getting over it.'

Assuming 'you know what' was a period, Emily briskly said, 'My "you know whats" won't cause you any trouble.'

Her cryptic comment sealed the deal. Mr Greenhalgh swung his big feet off the table and stubbed out his cigarette in an overflowing ashtray.

'I'll give you a week's trial. Start at seven tomorrow morning – and bring your own overalls.'

Now here she was, six months into the job and loving it. Rationing might be hard and getting harder but that shouldn't stop a cook from experimenting in times of need. Of course it wasn't easy, but it was satisfying to get a result like the pastry she was busily rolling out. She'd kept the dripping back from the weekly roast – it was only a shin of beef but there was enough fat to create dripping – and this she'd combined with thick white lard. Broken up and worked into the flour it worked a treat, making the pie crust light, fluffy and remarkably buttery. Emily expertly spun the large sheet of pastry then cut it into wide strips for topping the meat pies. She'd made three trays of mince, carrot and onion stew, spiced up with a handful of wild herbs and a generous dollop of gravy browning. After sealing the pastry around the trays she bent down and opened the door of the huge industrial oven. Popping the pies inside she quickly closed the door and turned around to find Mr Greenhalgh admiring her shapely backside.

'Nice bit of rump!' he joked.

'Enough of that, Mr Greenhalgh,' she scolded.

'Only talking about the pies, lovie, nowt else!' he chuckled.

The jolly strains of the *Workers' Playtime* theme tune faded away on the Bakelite radio sitting on a wide shelf in pride of place at the front of the canteen. Joe Loss and his popular swing band were replaced by Ernest Bevin, the Minister for Labour, urgently appealing to all women between the ages of twenty and thirty to volunteer for war work.

Emily caught her breath as she incredulously repeated the words she'd just heard.

'We have to report to the local Labour Exchange and register for work in farming or in shelling factories,' she gasped.

Mr Greenhalgh nodded his approval.

'I suppose somebody's got to stand on the production line and make the bullets for our lads at the front,' he said lugubriously.

4

Emily bit back the angry words that sprang to her lips: Somebody . . . ? Anybody but *you*!

Her boss rambled on.

'Who'd a thowt it'd come to this, eh? Lasses manning factories.'

In a rage, Emily turned her back on the radio and opened the heavy oven door to check her meat pies. With heat steaming around her already red face she looked fit to burst.

'It's taken me three years to get out of the weaving shed and into this canteen. Three years!' she seethed. 'And for what? To be conscripted as a land girl or work in a dirty munitions factory!'

'It's that or breaking the law,' her boss answered flatly.

Banging three pans full of peeled potatoes onto the gas rings, Emily lit the burners beneath them as she muttered under her breath, 'I might just do that!'

Serving dinner to over a hundred hungry mill workers soothed Emily's spirits; chatting and joking with her customers was the second best thing to cooking for them.

'What's for pud, love?' asked her mum's sister, who was covered in cotton flecks and, like the rest of the workers, smelled of the oil they greased the machines with.

'Apple fritters for you, Auntie Anne,' Emily replied with a wink. 'Steamed jam pudding for't rest.'

'You're a little lovie,' her auntie said fondly. Dropping her voice to a whisper she added, 'Heard the news on female conscription?'

Emily nodded grimly.

'It had to come,' said Auntie Anne. 'We'll never win this blasted war otherwise.'

Emily knew her auntie was speaking the truth; she knew she was behaving unpatriotically thinking only of herself. She knew she should feel ashamed, but all she felt was frustration. Just as things were looking up it was back to square one for her.

'I'll go and make your fritters, Auntie,' she said brusquely.

'Plenty of custard, lovie!'

As Mr Greenhalgh puffed on a Woodbine whilst reading the early edition of the local evening newspaper, Emily washed up the lunchtime pans and crockery in the vast double sink that had a fine view of Pendle moors. With the windows thrown wide open to the pale spring sunshine she breathed in the cool air drifting over from the high tops still specked with the last of the winter snow and wondered if she could plead illness or insanity, or both? No doctor would back her up with a sick note. At twenty, Emily was the picture of health, youth and beauty. Tall and strong with fine legs, a narrow waist, full breasts and a lovely face, Emily was unquestionably fit for work.

As she scoured the pans with a worn-out piece of Brillo, another thought worse than the first entered her mind: would she be forced to leave home and work in another part of England? Mr Bevin had said conscripted women would be deployed where they were needed. Her blue eyes roved across the familiar line of moorland rolling upwards towards the high, blustery Pennines. She'd lived all her life in Pendle, a small quiet town nestled in the folds of a valley, its skyline spiked with mill chimneys and plumes of factory smoke that coloured the sunsets deep crimson and purple. She didn't want to leave home and she desperately didn't want to be far away from Bill. Emily's stomach lurched at the thought of him. She didn't even know when his next leave would be, and what would happen if she was posted to Aberdeen and Bill turned up in Pendle with a night pass?

Mr Greenhalgh interrupted her chaotic thoughts with a wheezy cough and a loud burp.

'Put kettle on, cock, mi stomach thinks mi throat's cut!'

Chapter 2: Alice

Listening to the tunes on *Music While You Work*, Emily polished down the canteen tables and swept the floor to Anne Shelton's 'Yours Till the Stars Lose Their Glory'. It was their song, the one she and Bill danced to and sang to each other at the end of every leave. Tears sprang to Emily's eyes as she thought of her sweetheart's gentle promises and tender loving words.

'One day when all of this is over I'll make you mine for ever.'

That day couldn't come soon enough, but before then they'd got to get through this bloody war that was turning her comparatively happy world upside down!

Emily wrote out the following day's lunchtime menu on the canteen blackboard.

Potato hash, carrots and turnips
Jam tart and custard

Then, after peeling what seemed like a sackful of spuds, she stripped off her dirty overall and turban, shook out her now unrestrained auburn curls and pulled on her coat.

'See you in the morning, Mr Greenhalgh!' she called as she skipped out of the canteen.

'Don't forget to sign on at the Labour Exchange on your way home,' Mr Greenhalgh shouted after her.

Emily didn't answer. She'd got somebody to see before she allowed Winston Churchill to redefine the rest of her life.

She ran down the hill into the town, which was bright with bursts of yellow daffodils and spring blossom that lent a softness to the grey stone the town was built of. Not wanting to be delayed by neighbours who always stopped for a lengthy natter, Emily threaded her way through the narrow back streets desperate to find her best friend and ally, Alice. There was never a question about where Alice could be found; she was always in Tonge Moor Library, in the quiet reading room, with her nose in a book. She'd taken a temporary job in the local chemist's shop as she prepared for the French degree she was hoping to start at Manchester University in the autumn, but that didn't stop her nipping into the library whenever she had a spare minute.

Alice had always been brainy, but that didn't stop her from being a tearaway and a tomboy too. She'd attended the same local primary school as Emily and played out with her in the back streets, but after the eleven-plus examination everything suddenly changed. Alice left the school where she'd sat beside Emily through long, hot, stuffy days, raffia-weaving on the back row, swapping answers and flicking ink bombs at each other. Alice was the only kid in the street, no, the entire town (and a girl at that!) who went to grammar school.

'A posh kids' education she'll be having,' Emily's mum said tartly as twelve-year-old Alice self-consciously hurried down the street in her brand-new school uniform.

Though Emily and several other children, including young Bill, passed the eleven-plus exam they weren't allowed to go to grammar school. Their parents were unable to afford the compulsory and very expensive school uniform, nor could they pay the bus fares and school dinner money. Alice was the rare exception courtesy of her late dad's pension plan and a generous bequest from her paternal grandmother. Her doting mother poured all of her savings into her only child. Alice was a small, delicate-framed girl with fine blonde hair, usually caught up in a blue ribbon, that brought out the paleness of her dreamy silver-grey eyes.

Their paths may have diverged but Emily and Alice remained very best friends; they shared their secrets, their cigarettes, their hopes and dreams. Spotting Alice in her usual corner, bowed over a book, making notes on a sheet of paper, Emily made a beeline for her.

'Have you heard the news?' she yelped, shattering the silence of the library and causing several old men to look up from their newspapers.

'What news?' Alice whispered.

'Churchill's calling up women!'

Alice was so shocked she burst into tears.

'It hit me just like that too,' Emily said as she handed Alice her rather grubby handkerchief.

'Can you two bugger off and do your skriking outside?' a grouchy old man in a flat cap snapped at them.

'Sorry,' said Alice sweetly as she gathered up her pile of books. 'We've just had a bit of a shock.'

'Yeah . . . well, life's like that,' the old man grumbled.

*

Outside the two friends sat at the top of the flight of municipal steps that led up to the library entrance and glumly smoked cigarette after cigarette.

'I don't believe it!' groaned Alice. 'After all that studying, bang goes my French degree if I'm working in a factory.'

'We could be sent anywhere,' Emily pointed out. 'Scotland, Wales, anywhere!'

'We're not exactly patriotic, are we?' Alice said guiltily. 'Moaning about conscription when there are boys younger than us on the front line.'

Emily flushed with shame. One of those boys on the front line was her fiancé, Bill, so what right had she to complain? Stubbing out her cigarette, she stood up and squared her shoulders.

'You're right. Come on, kid, let's do our bit for King and country.'

Pendle was a small town and when Emily and Alice arrived to sign on they knew most of the women queuing at the Labour Exchange.

'Churchill's done me a favour,' one woman in front of them said. 'Mi dad was all for sending me off to th' army. Didn't fancy being an officer's comforter,' she said with a knowing wink. 'So I grabbed mi chance at munitions.'

'A word of advice, ladies,' an older woman whispered. 'Be careful what group you sign up for.'

Emily and Alice, who had no idea what the woman was talking about, stared at her blankly.

'What do you mean?' Alice asked.

'We've heard that some sections are more prone to explosions than others,' she answered.

'You mean there's a chance we could be blown up?' Alice gasped.

'Well, we're not being conscripted to wrap toffees, are we, cock?' the older woman chuckled.

'How do we know which sections are safer than others?' Emily asked.

The older woman burst into loud raucous laughter.

'You'll know soon enough if you get blown up!'

As they got nearer the desk, Emily muttered to Alice, 'Maybe working on the land would be safer?'

Alice shook her long silver-blonde hair as she indignantly replied, 'I'm not signing up just to shovel cow shit!'

After they'd signed on at the Labour Exchange Emily and Alice returned to Emily's house with a copy of the local newspaper that they'd picked up from the paper shop.

'They're opening up the old Phoenix Mill as a munitions factory,' Emily told her mum as she poured the girls a cup of tea.

'That owd place on't moors,' mused Mrs Yates. 'It's been closed for years.'

'It'll soon be open by the looks of things,' Alice said as she gratefully took the offered tea. 'They're moving munitions factories out of the cities, away from the bombing, and locating them in secret locations like sleepy old Pendle.'

'It says here,' said Emily, tapping the newspaper, 'that the government's sending girls from the London arsenal up here next month.'

'London girls, fancy!' exclaimed Mrs Yates.

Emily's wide blue eyes peered over the top of the paper.

'Can you believe it? There'll be living accommodation right next to the factory.'

'They'll never get hostels built that fast,' scoffed Mrs Yates.

Emily threw down the paper and accepted her tea.

'The Phoenix will open on time, Mam, no danger,' she said. 'The lads working the Howitzer guns on the front line are running out of ammo. Mr Churchill urgently needs shells and bombs and he doesn't care who makes 'em!'

'If you're right, I reckon you local lasses will be first at the Phoenix,' said Mrs Yates.

Emily and Alice looked at each other and grimaced.

'First on the bomb line,' said Alice with a little shiver. 'That's scary!'

Chapter 3: Elsie

A hundred and fifty miles away in Gateshead, Elsie Hogan sat riveted beside the wireless set in the cramped back kitchen where she'd just served up mashed potatoes and fried meatless sausages to her whingeing stepsisters.

'YUK!' squawked the ungrateful girls as they stabbed at the grey sausages that had more bounce than a tennis ball.

'Is this the best you can do?' Elsie's stepmother asked. When she got no reply she raised her voice. 'Turn off that damn radio, girl, and listen to what I'm saying.'

Elsie jumped in fright and quickly turned off the radio.

'Sorry, Mam,' she stammered humbly.

'She's our mam not yours,' sneered Ivy, the elder of the two girls.

Elsie corrected herself.

'Sorry, Mrs Hogan, I tried mi best. It's the rationing allowance, like.'

'You'd best try harder next time,' her stepmother grumbled. 'Your dad would have them so-called sausages on the wall if you served them up to him.'

Aye . . . and he'd have me in a stranglehold halfway up the wall alongside them, Elsie thought knowingly.

Nobody knew her dad's temper better than her. He never laid a hand on his new wife or her peevish girls; her stepmother would have killed him if he so much as even

14

thought of it. But Mr Hogan spared his only daughter nothing. If anything went wrong, from a bad day at work to bad news on the radio, she'd get a belt or kick to ease his filthy mood. He'd been bad enough when her own mam was alive but once she'd died and he'd remarried there was no hope for Elsie, who the entire household treated as their unpaid servant. Elsie longed to get away but where could she go? She had no other living relations, no money, and she was hardly allowed out apart from going to the shops to pick up their meagre war rations. Her life was a round of endless misery and fear, but the radio news she'd just heard inspired her with a rush of hope. Grabbing her shopping basket and a coat, she headed for the back door.

'I'm just popping out to the shops before they close,' she called behind her.

'What about the washing-up?' her stepmother yelled after her.

'I'll only be half an hour or so,' came Elsie's breathless reply as she closed the door behind her.

Down at the local Labour Exchange, gripping her basket handle tightly, Elsie stared intently at the lady behind the desk, who felt sorry for the slip of a girl in front of her. She was barely five foot tall and a bag of bones. Lank brown hair framed a delicate heart-shaped face that would have been lovely if it hadn't been so bruised and tired.

'I heard the news just now,' Elsie started nervously. 'Mr Bevin asking lasses to register for war work.'

The lady behind the desk nodded and smiled.

'What did you have in mind, pet, farm work or filling shell cases?'

'Will I have to go away?' Elsie asked in a tight, tense voice.

'If it's a problem, pet, I'm sure we can find work for you locally.'

'NO!' Elsie almost shouted. 'I want to get away from . . .' She blushed and stopped short as heads turned in her direction. 'Send me as far away as possible,' she pleaded in a whisper.

'Sign on the dotted line, pet,' the lady said as she pushed a form and a pencil across the desk. 'There's some bonny munitions factories a wee way down south.'

Elsie's feet barely touched the ground as she walked away from the Labour Exchange.

'I'm going away, I'm going away! Thank you, Mr Bevin; thank you, Mr Churchill; thank you, God!' she chanted under her breath as she skipped towards her front door, where she stopped dead in her tracks. Taking a deep breath she pushed open the door. Next time she walked out of here, she thought to herself, she would either be in a coffin or carrying a suitcase.

Mr Hogan got his daughter in a stranglehold and all but throttled her when she broke the news.

'You're going bloody nowhere!' he roared. Slamming her slight frame against the kitchen wall, he hit Elsie repeatedly around the head until she saw stars.

Terrified she'd lose consciousness, Elsie cried out: 'Dad! Dad! It's the law. Churchill wants women workers.'

Mr Hogan stopped his hand mid-punch.

'CHURCHILL!' he bellowed. 'What the 'ell's he to do wi' owt?'

Not daring to open her mouth, Elsie cowered on the

stone floor with blood trickling from her nose. Amazingly her stepmother had saved her from another swipe, not because she had an ounce of human kindness in her but just because she enjoyed showing off her knowledge to her slow, doltish husband.

'Female conscription,' she announced. 'There's not enough men left to work, apart from the likes of you,' she added with a sneer. Mr Hogan always claimed he was exempt from active service because of his miner's lungs but his wife knew he'd bribed somebody to fix his papers. 'Lasses are being put to work; it's good money, mind, anything up to four pound a week.'

Mr Hogan's bullish eyes all but rolled out of his head.

'That's bleedin' more than I earn!' he roared.

Elsie slipped into the wash house where, as she wiped blood off her face, she strained her ears to listen to the conversation in the next room.

'It'd be one less mouth to feed and she can send her earnings home every week,' her stepmother said.

Elsie nodded in agreement; she might get a few more slaps and kicks before she left home but she was leaving all right, that was *the law*. As she dabbed the last of the blood away, she smiled slowly to herself. What neither her father nor her stepmother knew was that she was *never* coming back!

Chapter 4: Agnes

Sitting on the lower deck of a London bus with her long dark hair plaited tightly under a thick net and a thin coat pulled around her tall angular frame, Agnes scowled at the April shower that battered the bus bouncing over the rutted road to Greenwich. Exhausted after a twelve-hour shift supervising a line of Bomb Girls all aged under twenty, Agnes grimly pondered her options. She could stay in London and get blown up or she could move to Lancashire where she stood less of a chance of getting blown up. It was a lose/lose situation apart from the singular fact that by moving north she would be in the adjoining county to Esther.

Just thinking of her little daughter brought tears to Agnes's eyes. She'd been separated from her in the autumn of 1940, which was only six months ago but it already seemed like a lifetime. Even though her heart was breaking there'd been no choice but to let Esther go; evacuees were on the move up and down the land and a little girl suffering from polio was considered a priority case for a move out of London. Agnes had just about held it together as she was parted from hysterical Esther, who ripped at her clothes and clung onto her, screaming her little heart out.

The nurses looking after the sick children on the train heading north to Penrith were kind, firm and determined.

Esther's nurse unwound the child's little fingers from her mother's grip, stopped her mouth with a jelly baby then slammed the carriage door on Agnes. The last sight she had of sobbing Esther was swallowed up by a thick cloud of smoke as the train pulled out of Euston station. Wiped out by grief, Agnes had all but fallen to the ground. She had no memory of how she got home but she would never forget the sight of the empty flat when she did return. There on the lino floor was Esther's little dolly with one leg shorter than the other. Agnes had knitted it herself and used it as a tool to explain to Esther why one of her legs was strong and healthy whilst the other remained limp and twisted. Clutching the dolly, Agnes crumpled into an armchair where she finally allowed herself to cry until her chest hurt.

She hadn't seen Esther at Christmas time, though she had received a charming card and photograph of her daughter from the old couple in Keswick who looked after Esther when she wasn't having treatment at the local cottage hospital. Her little girl looked taller and stronger, though the sight of her daughter's leg strapped into an iron calliper shocked Agnes.

All winter she'd tried to get a few days off from the Woolwich Arsenal where she worked but nobody was granted leave, especially a mature, trained supervisor on a vital bomb line. It was the Luftwaffe who'd eventually done Agnes a favour. Their nightly bombing of the Woolwich Arsenal had become a cause of huge national concern. If the arsenal should blow the blast could reach the West End, leaving a crater over half a mile long and untold casualties. It was essential that bomb plants and Bomb Girls were moved swiftly to places of safety outside London, places like Cardiff, Aberdeen, Poole, Glamorgan, Ellesmere Port and Lancashire. Agnes smiled as she dismounted from the bus swinging her gas mask.

Lancashire, she thought to herself, the next county to Cumberland, that has to be a move for the better – only one county away from Esther.

The foreman told Agnes that she'd be moved to Pendle by the beginning of May.

'Could I take a few days off before, to visit Esther?' Agnes enquired.

The foreman shook his head.

'Sorry, no dispensations for leave,' he said with a guilty look.

'You've been saying that since Esther left last year,' Agnes said bitterly.

'It's your fault for being such a first-rate supervisor,' he replied. 'It was you who spotted that witless Vera wearing hair grips and earrings last week. One spark off them and the whole cordite line would have blown!'

Agnes gave a grudging nod. Vera just couldn't get it into her empty head that metal in a bomb factory was banned because of its sparking potential. It had taken Agnes some time to make Vera wear a turban; she said it flattened her permawave! Nobody argued with Agnes for long. Her dark brooding eyes behind her black bottle-top glasses and her determined jaw brooked no nonsense, and anyway the workers had big respect for their supervisor. It was common knowledge that her husband had been reported missing at the start of the war.

Agnes would never forget that sunny, sultry morning,

Sunday, 3 September 1939. Everybody knew war was coming: Hitler had unleashed air and ground forces across Poland in direct response to Neville Chamberlain's ultimatum.

Sitting side by side, she and Stan had listened to the fateful radio bulletin which announced to the world that Britain was at war with Germany.

As he listened, Stan frowned and shook his head.

'Hitler doesn't give a bugger about Chamberlain when he's got his eye on the whole of Europe.'

Agnes gripped his hand.

'What will we do?' she said quietly so as not to upset baby Esther, sleeping in her crib.

Stan stared at her with his honest brown eyes as he replied, 'We'll fight, that's what we'll do, Agnes. We have no choice, not if our little Esther's going to grow up a free Englishwoman.'

Without saying a word to Agnes, fearless, loyal Stan enlisted with the Royal Engineers within days of the outbreak of war.

'I've joined the Sappers,' he told his wife that night as he bathed his baby daughter in a tin bath in front of the fire.

Agnes, stirring a mutton stew over a flaring gas ring, gasped in shock.

'Why so soon?'

'It has to be done, Agnes,' Stan replied. 'Hitler's a maniac and he has to be stopped.'

Within months of Stan's first and only leave Esther fell ill with polio, shortly after which she was evacuated to Keswick in the Lake District. It was no wonder the workforce had a lot of time for Agnes, who never complained or invited sympathy; she just kept focused on her belief that one day Stan would come home, one day they would be a family again and one day her little girl would run unaided into her mother's arms.

As April warmed into May and blossom bloomed on stumps of trees that had missed the bombing raids, Agnes collected together the few things she'd need for her imminent move north. The cherished tin of family snaps, Stan's call-up papers and Esther's birth certificate, her ration book and overalls, the few clothes she had in her wardrobe and Esther's little dolly. Looking around the half-empty flat, Agnes realized she'd be glad to get away from London, the Luftwaffe and the Woolwich Arsenal. She'd had enough. A new start far away, one with no memories, was what she needed and she was counting down the days to a new beginning.

Chapter 5: Lillian

Lillian sang to the tune of 'Little Brown Jug' blasting out on the radio as she mixed hair colour in a glass dish.

'With a bit of luck I'll be dancing to this at Bradford Palais tonight,' she said chattily to her customer, who was sitting staring woefully at her hair in the salon mirror.

'God, I look ninety,' she groaned.

'You'll be fine once I've got this lot on your roots!' Lillian assured her.

In between applications Lillian couldn't help but admire herself in the salon mirror. She'd never have let her mousy roots show a three-inch re-growth like her client. As soon as she'd started in the hairdressing business she'd taken great trouble choosing exactly the same hair dye as her favourite film star, Olivia de Havilland. Lillian was proud of her long, dark, curling locks. They brought out the sultriness of her big brown eyes, especially when she wore the same-coloured, crimson-red lipstick as Olivia de Havilland, which accentuated her soft pouty mouth. Lillian's figure was good too: thirty-four inches up and down, she had a teeny waist, fantastic legs and a sexy swing to her shapely hips.

Lillian took great care of herself; she knew that her face and her body were her fortune and had decided early on in life that she was going to do 'well', whatever it cost. She knew she could do better than Reg, the randy landlord of her shop, but Reg was a man who could lay his hands on anything. In return for black-market knickers, nylons, cigarettes, gin and chocolates, plus a room upstairs rent-free, Lillian put up with Reg's fumbling wet kisses. They were a price worth paying, especially as he had a car and could drive her around the Bradford clubs where she entertained the boozy clientele.

'It was a great night last week with that swing band up from Sheffield,' Lillian enthused. 'I could've sung till dawn.'

'Regular little songbird, you are,' chuckled her client.

Seeing her scruffy younger sister approaching the shop door, Lillian swiftly lowered the noisy hairdryer over her client's head and set it to full so that she wouldn't be able to eavesdrop on their conversation.

'You look like you need a good wash,' she said to her sister.

'I haven't got a fancy man to keep me,' her sister cheekily retorted.

'If it's money you're after, I've got none. I just paid Reg the rent.'

'And there was I thinking you paid him by other means,' her sister said slyly.

Lillian rolled her eyes.

'Tell me what you've come for and get lost.'

'I've come to take you down to the Labour Exchange,' her sister answered.

'I've got a job! If you smarten yourself up they might find one for you cleaning the public lavatories.'

The woman under the hairdryer yelped as the machine began to overheat.

'Turn this bloody thing off, will you, Lillian?' she called out.

As soon as Lillian raised the hairdryer her sister addressed the woman, who was cautiously tapping her hot rollers.

'I was just telling our Lillian about compulsory female conscription,' she said with undisguised glee. 'I said she might have to close down the shop and go and work in a munitions factory.'

The last thing Lillian wanted was to give her gloating sister any satisfaction.

'You've said what you came to say, now push off,' she snapped.

Edging towards the salon door, her sister said, 'While I'm down there shall I tell them to send you a letter as you're too busy to sign on in person?'

Before Lillian could hurl a brush at her sister she skipped out of the door, slamming it loudly behind her. Seeing her client's shocked expression, Lillian started to busily unwind the rollers in her hair.

'Cheek!' she said with a laugh. 'I've got a job, why do I need another one?'

Lillian's sister made sure she got a call-up letter from the Labour Exchange, which Lillian immediately burned. When Reg came round later Lillian was unusually responsive to his advances.

'Let's not get too carried away,' Reg said as he broke into a sweat. 'The missus is expecting me home for tea in ten minutes.'

Normally Lillian thanked her lucky stars for Reg's domineering, hugely overweight wife. He jumped at her call, which meant his amorous encounters with Lillian were mercifully brief and always around his domestic timetable. Tonight, though, Lillian needed reassurance and Reg was the only person she could turn to.

'You know this female-conscription malarkey?' she started.

'I heard a bit about it on't radio t'other day.'

'Well, is there any way out of it . . . ?'

Reg glanced at Lillian's pleading face and burst out laughing.

'So that's your game, eh?'

Stung by his mocking words Lillian leaped away from him.

'I don't want to go traipsing all over England filling bloody shell cases!' she cried. 'I've got a good job right here in Bradford.'

'You can't buy your way out of this one with a bit of slap and tickle,' Reg retorted. 'It's compulsory for lasses your age.'

'I bet your missus will find a loophole,' Lillian raged.

'She's over the age limit,' he replied.

'Lucky cow!' mumbled Lillian.

A policeman (probably sent by her evil slag of a sister) came knocking on Lillian's salon door the next morning.

'I'm here to ask you to fill out your conscription papers,' he boomed, loud enough for the whole street to hear.

'I've lost them,' she replied sulkily.

'I thought you might so I've brought some more,' the policeman replied as he waved a fresh set of papers in her face. 'I'll wait here, if you like, and take 'em back to the Labour Exchange miself.'

Cornered and humiliated, Lillian snatched the papers from his hands.

'How kind!' she snarled as she scrawled her name and handed the papers back to the grinning policeman.

'Is it farming or factory work you fancy?' he asked, as if she was booking her holidays.

Knowing the fight was over, Lillian shrugged her shoulders.

'What do I care? Either way it's a prison sentence.'

Chapter 6: The Phoenix

Mrs Yates's words proved right. By May, local girls from Pendle, Nelson, Colne and Darwin were the first at the Phoenix, arriving in buses or on the backs of trucks. Emily and Alice, who had spent most of their lives running wild over Pendle moors, decided to walk the few miles to the new munitions factory. Carrying their flimsy suitcases, they set off over the hills, recalling memories as they came across their favourite haunts. They knew exactly where to pick the first ripe, juicy winberries, the best slopes to sledge down after a heavy snowfall and the quickest crossing places over the numerous streams and brooks. As children, they'd tracked down the old ruin where the witches of Pendle had held their covens, frightening themselves to death and muttering macabre incantations on stormy Hallowe'ens. They'd played out romantic Brontë scenarios on the high tops with the wind howling around them, taking it in turn to be Anne, Charlotte and tragic Emily.

'There won't be much fun and games where we're going,' Emily moaned as the Phoenix loomed into sight.

'We're not here for laughs, Em,' Alice teased as she ran ahead of her friend. 'We're here to blast Hitler to kingdom come!'

Alice and Emily were astonished at the amount of work going on at the Phoenix and the surrounding moorland. Builders and heavy machinery were everywhere, and as they ducked between tractors and earth movers Emily spotted one of her dad's friends laying a cement foundation. Making their way through a throng of wolf-whistling builders, Emily and Alice approached him.

'Come to admire the Phoenix complex?' he joked.

'It's much, much bigger than I thought,' Emily said as she surveyed the sprawl of low, camouflaged buildings close to the factory.

'Orders from the top, young Emily,' he replied. 'We've got to get you lasses filling shell cases or we might catch the end of a bullet from Mr Churchill! All mod cons too, hot and cold water in every bedroom and indoor privies.'

Recalling the outdoor privy in their back yard at home, Emily burst out laughing.

'That's more than I'm used to.'

Alice's silver-grey eyes were wide with wonder.

'It's like a town within a town,' she said.

The builder nodded.

'Everything's got to be on site, no running up and down the moors to't nearest pub in Pendle!' He turned and pointed to various scattered buildings, some finished, some half complete. 'Over yonder's the married quarters, there's a nursery there for them with babbies. To your right are the shops and a post office, a laundry, a cinema, a pub too, even a chapel to remind you how to behave yourselves.'

'Hard to imagine misbehaving up here miles away from anywhere!' Emily joked.

'You lasses will find a way,' the builder chuckled. 'You always do!'

*

The new munitions girls were greeted in the canteen by the factory manager, Mr Featherstone, a little man with a twirly moustache and a nervous twitch.

'Welcome, ladies,' he started. 'On behalf of Mr Churchill and Mr Bevin, I want to thank you all for your quick response to conscription work.'

'Not like we had any choice,' Emily muttered under her breath.

'Shh!' said Alice as she gave mutinous Emily a quick sideways kick.

'You'll be working round the clock in shifts, six in the morning till two in the afternoon, two till ten, then the night shift, ten till six in the morning. For this you'll be paid between two pounds and four pounds a week, with overtime and bonuses your pay packet could amount to eight pounds.'

A few excited wolf whistles interrupted Mr Featherstone, who ploughed briskly on with his speech.

'You'll be issued with white overalls and turbans. The colour of your turban will indicate which shift you're working on. All jewellery, grips, slides and clips are banned.' He was interrupted again by loud groans from some of the women.

'What about us that're wed?' somebody called out.

'Weddings rings can be worn but they must be covered with a strip of Elastoplast,' Mr Featherstone replied. 'I cannot emphasize enough, ladies, how a tiny spark could trigger an explosion that could take out the entire factory.' He paused before he added, 'Such explosion happened recently in Glamorgan; the crater left behind was nearly half a mile long.' A heavy silence from the workforce followed his sombre announcement. 'London Bomb Girls with experience of shell-filling will be joining us this week, and please make them welcome as we need their expertise up here at the Phoenix. In conclusion, you'll find a list of your shifts and your section and the name of your hostel pinned to the canteen noticeboard.' Bowing abruptly, he ended with a terse, 'Thank you for your cooperation.'

Emily and Alice scanned the board for their names.

'Looks like we've been allocated a hostel off site,' Alice said.

As more than a hundred women started to peel away to their lodgings, Emily and Alice trudged up a cobbled lane to the top of a hill where they saw their new quarters tinted yellow and orange by the sun sinking slowly over the Pennines. For a few stunned seconds they were speechless then Alice burst out laughing.

'It's a cowshed!'

Emily shook her thick auburn curls in despair.

'Wouldn't you know it?' she groaned.

In truth, when they looked around they discovered it was an upmarket cowshed with a good roof, stone floors, hot water, indoor toilet, bathroom and three bedrooms, two double and one single. There was also an old wood burner which the farmer must have used to boil the kettle that was still stuck on top of the stove.

'At least it doesn't smell of cow muck!' laughed Alice.

They both jumped as the door swung open, revealing little Elsie, cringing and self-conscious, blinking at them like a terrified rabbit caught in the headlights.

'H-h-how do you do, like?' she stammered.

Emily and Alice felt desperately sorry for the new girl, who was wearing clothes hardly better than rags. Pulling Elsie gently inside they made her welcome.

'Come in, come in. I'm Emily.'

'And I'm Alice. Let's put the kettle on.'

Tea and toast brought a warm glow to Elsie's emaciated cheeks.

'Ta very much,' she mumbled gratefully. 'I haven't eaten all day,' she said, though in truth she hadn't eaten for twenty-four hours as her stepmother had refused to feed her the day before she left Gateshead.

After finishing their tea the girls explored their digs.

The double bedrooms were surprisingly spacious with high ceilings and timber-framed roofs. In each room there were two single beds side by side, two chests of drawers, a shared wardrobe and a sink with hot and cold water. Elsie gaped at the shiny new sink as if it was an alien object from another planet.

'Does it really work?' she asked as she tested the hot and cold taps, which instantly gushed water.

'Well, I don't think it's there for flower arrangements,' Emily joked.

'A sink in the bedroom is a real luxury,' enthused Alice as she studied her pretty face in the mirror just over the sink.

'All we've got at home is a rusty pump in't back yard,' Elsie exclaimed. Smiling in sheer delight, she added, 'We can even wash our undies indoors!'

Emily was walking around the room thoughtfully tapping the external walls.

'I bet this place is freezing in winter.'

Elsie, who seemed to find everything a joy, said, 'There's hot-water bottles, like.'

'And that old wood-burning stove,' said Alice as she walked back down the corridor into the sitting room. 'We can clean it out and burn wood from the moors. I bet we could keep a kettle permanently on the boil once we've got a fire going.'

The single room was furnished in the same way as the doubles, and its only window, built into the gable end of the cowshed, gave out onto a delightful view of the rolling moors dappled in sunlight.

'It's a proper pretty room,' said Elsie. 'But I fancy sharing with another lass, if that's okay with you two?'

So it was decided that Alice and Emily would take the front double room whilst Elsie took the back double, which she'd share with whoever joined them next.

'I wonder who will join us next?' said Alice.

'Mebbe one of the lasses from London . . . ?' Elsie suggested.

In answer to their speculations the door was thrown open again and Lillian walked in, smartly dressed in a tight-fitting tweed suit, black felt hat and a fox fur slung over one shoulder. Alice's and Emily's first impression of Elsie was that of a lost, neglected child who needed looking after. Their impression of Lillian was that of a film star who'd walked into the wrong room.

Lillian flung off her jacket, revealing her low-cut blouse and soft, full cleavage. Scanning the room, she rolled her big brown eyes in total disgust.

'God! What a shit hole!'

Chapter 7: Canary Girls

Lillian made them laugh nearly all night long. In her smart leather suitcase she had more clothes than the other three girls put together, plus a bottle of black-market brandy, cigarettes and chocolates. Elsie's eyes grew wide in delight as she tasted the first coffee cream of her life.

'Mmm, gorgeous!' she drooled.

'Help yourself, lovie,' said generous Lillian. 'I'll stick with the booze and fags.'

Well after midnight they made up their beds, leaving the single room to the woman who had yet to arrive.

'I can't tell you how hard I tried to get out of war work,' Lillian confessed as she tucked sheets under her narrow mattress. 'I was doing just fine with my little hair salon in Bradford, singing in the local clubs and putting up with my sleazy boyfriend.'

'I felt just the same,' Emily exclaimed. 'Apart from the sleazy boyfriend,' she added with a laugh.

'Mine had desert's disease,' Lillian joked.

Elsie's hazel-green eyes grew wide in concern.

'Ooh, what's that?'

'Wandering palms!' Lillian teased.

As Emily and Alice burst out laughing, Elsie innocently said, 'I've never heard of wandering palms.'

Lillian shook her head, making her dangly earrings jangle.

'We've got a little innocent here,' she said fondly. 'It's when a fella can't stop pawing you, lovie!'

As the penny dropped, Elsie's face blazed crimson with embarrassment.

'Oh!' she gasped as she covered her mouth to stop herself from giggling.

'Don't worry, Elsie, you'll soon get used to me,' Lillian teased.

The following day, slightly bleary-eyed from lack of sleep, they went to the Phoenix canteen for their breakfast. As they settled around a metal table, Elsie sniffed the air appreciatively.

'Toast and chip butties!' she exclaimed.

'And as much tea as you can drink,' Emily added.

Swing music blared out from the canteen radio and it was hard to hear yourself speak over the babble of two hundred women and the booming strains of Glen Miller and his orchestra.

Elsie wolfed back her toast, a pint mug of tea and a chip butty, then looked embarrassed as she saw her friends had barely started their breakfast.

'Don't you like it?' she asked self-consciously.

'It's all right,' said Emily grudgingly. 'I was a canteen cook not long ago and I cooked a lot better than this.'

'It's hard making food interesting with the rationing, like,' Elsie pointed out.

'There's nothing wrong with using your imagination even when times are hard. I'll show you how, one day soon, Elsie,' Emily promised.

Alice gave blushing Elsie a gentle shove.

'We've got a long twelve-hour shift ahead of us; go and help yourself to seconds,' she urged.

'Won't I get told off?' Elsie asked timidly.

'No,' Alice replied. 'Anybody can see you need feeding up.'

As Elsie, clutching her plate, walked shyly away to get more food Emily, Alice and Lillian looked meaningfully at each other.

'She's a sweet kid,' Lillian said.

'She looks like she's been half starved,' whispered Alice.

'We'll keep an eye on her,' said Emily loyally.

'I wonder who Girl Number Five might turn out to be?' Alice asked as she sipped her scalding tea.

'As long as it's not my cow of a sister I don't care,' Lillian chuckled.

'With all them southern girls due up here they're bound to fill it soon,' Emily said as she lit up her first cigarette of the day.

Lillian's thoughts were elsewhere. In between nibbling her chips she carefully scanned the male contingent in the canteen. 'Not exactly spoilt for choice when it comes to local talent,' she lamented. 'It's old, bald and fat or fat, bald and old.'

A dapper, middle-aged man wearing a suit and a bow tie winked at Lillian as he swung by carrying a tray.

'Looks like you've made a conquest,' Alice giggled.

'If he knows a good spiv on the black market he'll do for starters,' Lillian answered with a saucy wink.

*

After breakfast Emily, Alice, Elsie and Lillian donned their white overalls and the big boots that reduced friction on the stone factory floor.

'We look like fellas!' laughed Lillian.

'No jewellery, pins, grips or slides!' yelled a male voice.

As the girls turned to see who their overseer was, they were surprised to recognize the man who'd winked at Lillian in the cafeteria.

Lillian gave him a sulky look but she'd already removed her earrings and watch. As they scrunched their hair into turbans, Lillian purposefully flicked her fringe onto her face.

'Haven't we got to cover all of our hair?' Elsie asked nervously.

Lillian winked.

'Haven't you heard of Canary Girls, Elsie?' she asked.

'Stop teasing me, Lillian,' Elsie giggled.

'I'm not teasing, it's the truth,' Lillian insisted. 'The cordite we're working with bleaches exposed hair yellow-blonde – just like a canary!' Wagging her loose fringe, she added, 'What's wrong with a bit of free hair colour when you're miles away from a beauty salon?'

Elsie smiled shyly as she too released a bit of her fringe . . . If only her dad could see her now!

As the girls approached their section, Alice noticed the floor was wet through.

'Has a pipe burst?' she asked.

The overseer, Malc, shook his head.

'We keep the air moist and the floor damp to reduce the chance of explosions,' he replied.

Emily, Alice, Elsie and Lillian looked at each other, all

laughter and banter gone. This was their war work, dangerous at every turn. There was no going back now.

To the accompaniment of *Workers' Playtime* and *Music While You Work*, Emily, Alice, Elsie and Lillian worked their section monitored by a temporary supervisor. Bomb cases, ninety-nine to a pallet, came rolling down the conveyor belt towards the girls, who filled them to a specified level with cordite then inserted an empty tube for the detonator. Further down the line the detonators were loaded in the tube then the bomb cases were hooked onto an overhead conveyor belt that carried them around the factory floor.

'Where do they go now?' Alice asked Malc, the overseer.

'They're loaded into ammunition boxes and flown out to our lads working the Howitzers on the front line,' he replied.

Alice's heart skipped a beat; she'd already packed cordite into nearly thirty shell cases, bombs that could take out a family, a home, a life. She knew there were German women packing cordite into identical shell cases in Berlin, Hamburg, Munich and other places all over Germany, just like British Bomb Girls assembling explosives in munitions factories all over her own country. Alice sighed. How many thousands of women would pack how many millions of bombs before this hideous war was over?

That first shift was long, exhausting and repetitive.

'I know I've got the attention span of a gnat,' groaned Lillian. 'But this has got to be the most boring job in the world.'

Without stopping shovelling cordite into the bomb cases passing before her on the conveyor belt, Elsie answered happily, 'It's interesting!'

'INTERESTING!' Lillian screeched. 'Depends what you were doing previously, love.'

'Cooking, cleaning, cooking, cleaning, getting belted if I weren't cooking and cleaning,' Elsie replied with remarkable cheerfulness.

Lillian exchanged a look with Emily and Alice on either side of her and quickly backtracked.

'Well, if you put it that way I can see that this would be a bundle of laughs, Elsie,' she laughed.

The government-backed shows on the radio and regular breaks in the canteen, where they could help themselves to endless mugs of sweet tea and free food, lifted the workers' spirits but by 10 p.m. Emily, Alice, Elsie and Lillian were on their knees.

'I just want to go home and sleep,' groaned Emily.

Alice, who hated to be dirty or untidy, scowled at the yellow stains on her slender fingers.

'We've got to get this stinking cordite off our hands first,' she insisted.

'A woman on another section told me to scrub milk and cold tea onto the yellow,' Lillian said.

Emily yawned and shook her head.

'Right now, I don't care – I'm going to bed.'

'If you go without cleaning it off you'll stain your sheets yellow,' Lillian warned.

Emily laughed as she said, 'Maybe I'll sing like a canary and keep you awake all night!'

It was nearly eleven by the time they made their way up

the cobbled track to their digs, where they found all the lights on. Inside Agnes, who was exhausted by her journey north, was curled up fast asleep on the sofa. She jumped up when her room mates entered and blinked at them in surprise.

'Hello,' she mumbled. 'I'm Agnes. I've been transferred from the Woolwich Arsenal.'

Emily, Elsie, Lillian and Alice were visibly taken aback. Agnes was a good ten years older than them; she was sallow-skinned and thin; her clothes resembled the style of the thirties rather than the forties, and her black-metal, bottle-top glasses hid the beauty of her large eyes.

Alice was the first to remember her manners.

'You must be exhausted,' she said as she poked the embers in the wood burner and filled the kettle. 'I'll make some tea.'

Elsie opened the tin that contained Emily's delicious carrot and coconut buns.

'We've got some cake,' she said with relish. 'Proper good cake, home-made, like.'

Agnes gratefully accepted their generosity but there was an awkwardness in the room, especially when she announced she might be their line supervisor.

'Oh, that's good,' said Emily flatly.

'Great!' muttered Lillian under her breath. 'Nothing like living with the boss.'

Alice glared at her whilst Emily gave her a kick. Sensing their discomfort, Agnes rose.

'I think I'll go to bed,' she said tiredly.

Kind, sensitive Elsie leaped to her feet.

'You've got the single room,' she told Agnes as they made their way down the corridor. 'It's got a belting view, like, when it's not raining.'

Lillian scowled as she lit a Woodbine.

'Bloody hell,' she seethed. 'Now we'll have to be on our best sodding behaviour all the time!' She blew out some smoke before adding scornfully, 'And where did she get those terrible clothes from?'

'You can't always go by looks,' sweet little Elsie chided as she returned to her friends gathered round the crackling warm stove. 'I looked like a rag and bone man when I arrived,' she added with a giggle.

'Well, at least we gave her the single room,' Lillian remarked. 'It'd be a nightmare waking up to the bloody boss every morning!'

Elsie, in awe of Agnes's age and experience, kept a respectful distance whilst Alice was curious, especially when she caught sight of a framed photograph on Agnes's bedside table with a little knitted dolly propped up beside it. The picture was of a little girl, aged about two or three years old, with long, dark silky hair, a wide happy smile and big brown eyes fringed with thick dark lashes.

'She's beautiful,' Alice told Emily. 'She must be related. She has the same dark looks as Agnes.'

'She never talks about her family,' Emily said.

'Maybe something terrible happened to them,' Alice replied.

'Best not to mention them until she does,' Emily warned.

Agnes was strict and tight-lipped on the factory floor too; she worked her section hard whilst keeping an eye out for their safety. During her second week, Agnes approached Elsie.

'Can I have a word with you?' she asked.

Elsie's eyes grew wide as she was escorted off the factory floor.

'Have I done something wrong? Am I in trouble? Please don't send me home,' she gabbled in terror.

In a quiet corner of the canteen, Agnes assured Elsie, who was by this time almost hysterical, that all was well.

'It's nothing to panic about,' she said gently. 'I'm just concerned that you're working too hard.'

Elsie wiped away her tears and smiled, and when she did so her lovely green eyes were filled with happiness. Grabbing Agnes's hands, she squeezed them tightly.

'I love my work,' she cried. 'I love the Phoenix and all my friends in the digs.'

Agnes patted Elsie's chapped hands.

'At the rate you're going, I'm afraid you'll burn yourself out.'

'I'm not frightened of hard work,' Elsie insisted. 'If the truth be known, I've never been so happy in my whole life!'

Intrigued by her reply, Agnes asked, 'And why's that, Elsie? Munitions work isn't exactly a picnic.'

Elsie replied with her usual innocent candour.

'I love not living at home and I love my new friends. I couldn't ask for more.'

Agnes smiled gently as she gazed into Elsie's earnest face. What kind of previous life could she have had if relentless hard work at the Phoenix made her so very happy?

Giving her a reassuring pat on the shoulder, Agnes

simply said, 'You're a good girl, Elsie, and you've nothing at all to worry about.'

On a free night off, all five room mates decided to go and see Laurence Olivier in *Rebecca* at the Phoenix picture house.

'I can't wait to see all the posh frocks,' Lillian whispered as she passed around a bag of nut brittle.

As they settled down in their seats, the lights dimmed and the Pathé News preceding the main feature film flashed up. A hush descended over the packed picture house as the narrator spoke.

'Secret footage of British POWs in German concentration camps has been released to the War Office. It is clear that Hitler's officers have thrown aside the rules laid down by the Geneva Convention.'

There was a collective gasp of horror as stark images of skeletal men staggering half naked around a prison yard appeared larger than life on the wide screen.

'Oh, my God!' a woman behind them murmured.

Some of the cinema-goers had to cover their eyes at the sight of British soldiers crawling on the ground and begging for food, but it was Agnes who reacted the most dramatically. Stifling a cry of agony, she literally jumped over the top of her cinema seat.

'NO! Please, God, I can't bear it!' she cried as she ran out of the building.

Emily, Alice, Elsie and Lillian looked at one another, shocked. Then they left their seats and ran after their distressed friend.

'Maybe she recognized somebody in that terrible film,' Alice gasped as they hurried up the steep hill back to their digs.

'Poor girl,' murmured Emily. 'She sounded like she was in agony.'

They found Agnes lying white-faced on her bed.

'Is there anything we can do?' Alice gently asked, perching on the end of the bed.

'There's nothing anybody can do,' Agnes whispered as slow tears rolled unstopped down her cheeks. 'My Stan might be in one of those camps . . . He could be dead for all I know.'

Emily, Elsie and Lillian quietly approached the bed.

Elsie stroked Agnes's limp hands.

'Why didn't you tell us?'

'Talking doesn't help,' she replied bitterly.

'How long's he been gone?' Alice asked.

'Almost two years; he was reported missing right at the beginning of the war.' She took a deep ragged breath then sobbed, 'If he is alive I can't bear to think of him being treated like those poor men, like an animal.'

There was a long pause as Emily, Alice, Lillian and Elsie, all totally lost for words, wondered how any one person could bear so much.

Seeing Elsie peeking at the photograph on her bedside table, Agnes whispered, 'That's my daughter, Esther. She's got polio. She was evacuated to a hospital in the Lake District just after Stan was reported missing. She doesn't know anything about her daddy,' she added sadly.

Filled with pity, Emily said, 'So your whole family was taken from you at the same time?'

Agnes nodded.

'I'm hoping to see more of Esther now I'm working in the north.'

'Well, that sounds a step in the right direction. Look, I'll make you some tea, lovie,' Elsie said softly.

'I need a drink too,' muttered Lillian. 'And I don't mean tea!'

Alice stayed with Agnes while the others crept into the sitting room, where they whispered together as they made tea for Agnes and mixed it with a dash of brandy.

'What with a daughter in hospital and a husband in a concentration camp, it's a wonder she's not topped herself,' Emily murmured.

'She's so brave,' Elsie added quietly.

Lillian nodded grimly. 'Bloody tough too,' she said as she took a deep pull at the brandy bottle.

'Well, we've certainly seen a different side to our boss tonight,' Emily remarked.

'There was I thinking she was a tight-lipped, toffee-nosed southerner,' said Lillian self-deprecatingly. 'How wrong can you be!'

'From now on we're going to look after Agnes,' Emily said firmly.

'Cheers to that!' said Lillian as she took another swig from the brandy bottle.

Things changed after that. On the factory floor Emily, Alice, Elsie and Lillian were civil and obedient with their line supervisor; but once back in their digs Agnes was their dear friend who they treated with love and kindness. Apart from the respect and affection they had for Agnes, they all shared a secret desire to reunite her with her little girl, Esther, as soon as possible.

Chapter 8: Evacuee

The Bomb Girls had arrived at the Phoenix in time to enjoy a mild spring followed by a warm, wet summer.

'Does it ever stop raining up here?' Agnes asked.

'Moanin' southerner!' Lillian teased.

'Rain's good for the complexion,' Emily added.

Agnes stared at the rain belting against the factory windowpanes and clattering down onto the metal roof.

'A bit of sunshine wouldn't go amiss.'

'I wouldn't worry about it, pet, it's not like we get out much,' said Elsie, who put a positive spin on everything.

A damp and misty autumn gave way to a hard winter in the Phoenix, and what with the constantly damp floors and the blustery Pennine winds whistling round the factory, the workers were chilled to the bone from dawn till dusk. There were, however, the welcome breaks in the warm canteen, where Emily had made great friends with the cooks. They had welcomed her help and her new ideas with open arms.

'Mek yourself at home, lass, the more the merrier!'

Emily's flaky pastry, improvised from shin-beef dripping and reconstituted lard, had gone down a storm, so had her herb dumplings, and nobody in Lancashire could cook fish and chips like Emily. Spuds grown locally were in abundance but fish was scarce so, as ever, Emily improvised, making scallops from thick slices of potato deep-fried in a light golden batter.

Elsie nearly fainted with ecstasy when she tasted her first crispy golden scallop.

'Mmm!' she groaned in pleasure. 'How do you do it, our Em?'

'Desperation!' Emily replied. 'If I have to eat any more boring canteen food I might start gnawing my elbows,' she added in a low voice so her new friends in the canteen wouldn't hear her. 'The cooks try their best but they don't think outside the box. Rationing makes cooking a challenge not a drag.'

'Is there owt else you can deep-fry, cock,' a big woman from packing asked. 'Them bloody scallops were a treat!'

The workers' unabashed enthusiasm for 'good grub', as they called it, drove Emily on. There was only one thing Emily liked more than pleasing her friends, and that was cooking, so when the two were combined she was in her element.

Emily knew that the local farm grew plenty of root crops, and one morning, after batting her beautiful blue eyes at the farmer, she walked away with a sack of parsnips which she peeled and boiled then mashed with margarine, salt, pepper, dried sage and thyme. With Elsie's help she rolled the cooled mashed parsnips into little balls then deep-fried them in a big pan of lard and the shin-beef dripping that she kept exclusively for her own purposes.

As the parsnip fritters crackled in the sizzling hot fat, Elsie was anxious.

'Won't we get told off for being in't canteen, like?'

Emily confidently shook her head.

'It gives the cooks time off. Look at them,' she added, as she nodded in the direction of the canteen ladies, who were sitting at one of the tables reading the papers with their feet up. 'Plus, we're doing this out of the goodness of our hearts in our spare time,' she pointed out.

'If you ever open a chip shop, Em, can I work for you?' Elsie said with a sweet shy smile.

'For sure, on condition you don't eat everything in the shop!' Emily replied.

The parsnip fritters were served with an improvised Spam hash that Emily concocted with onions, carrots, blobs of marg and potatoes. She topped the meal with bread pudding, which she spiced up with cinnamon and bulked out for the hungry workers with prunes and apples.

'Eeh, lovie, I wish we could eat like this every day,' an appreciative Bomb Girl said as she hurried back for seconds.

'You could, if they took me off the bomb line and put me in't canteen,' Emily said with a chuckle.

On cold winter days Emily made warm nourishing food to keep the workers going through their long hard shifts: a rich broth from pearl barley and mutton, or soup from dried peas and a pig's head, which she boiled up for stock and meat she could slice out of the cheeks.

Malc, the overseer, had to take Emily on one side to remind her she was a Bomb Girl not a cook.

'I'm not paid to cook, I just love it – and I do it in my free time,' she reminded him.

'I quite understand,' Malc hurriedly replied. 'Just wanted to remind you of your priorities.'

Pretending innocence, Emily stared up at him with her big blue eyes. 'I can stop if you want . . . ?' she added mischievously.

Malc paused for a few seconds. No way did he want Emily to stop; there'd be a riot if her fritters, scallops, soups and broths weren't on the menu.

'We don't have to go that far,' he prevaricated. 'Just don't make it obvious when Mr Featherstone's around.'

There was great camaraderie among the two hundred-strong women at the Phoenix. It wasn't as if they all liked each other, far from it, there were rows and differences every day. People got tired and grumpy, the repetitive hard work, long shifts and relentless cold weather ground the workers down. The fact that most of the women were far away from their loved ones caused spats of anger or tears of sadness. Agnes was always good when these situations erupted. She never offered platitudes because she knew from experience that sort of talking was a waste of time. She had a calm way of addressing problems and asking the right questions, and she always remained focused and strong.

'*Never* give up!' was her unequivocal advice to all.

The increase in the number of deaths, casualties and reports of 'missing in action' had a profound effect on the workforce. A young girl on the next section to the cordite line collapsed when she heard her kid brother had died of septicaemia in a lifeboat. He'd been a young sailor on a minesweeper that had been torpedoed by German U-boats, and the lifeboat he was in had drifted in the freezing North Sea for days before it was picked up by a merchant ship.

Life was unbelievably hard and getting harder by the

day, but the best the Bomb Girls could do was work harder, stay cheerful – and pray.

The need for more and more bombs put pressure on the munitions factories; stringent targets were set and had to be achieved on each shift.

'I know the new targets are going to make things even tougher than they already are,' Agnes said to her over-worked team. 'But the boys we love need a lot more bombs, and that's why we have to do it.'

Conscientious Elsie's green eyes opened wide with anxiety.

'We can't fill the bomb shells any faster,' she said. 'If we did we'd end up spilling cordite then God knows what would happen.'

Lillian rolled her eyes.

'We all know exactly what would happen – BOOM!'

Agnes quickly interrupted.

'I'm not saying take chances; health and safety come first.'

'What you're really saying,' said clever Alice, 'is that you want us to work longer hours?'

Agnes smiled apologetically.

'That's what it boils down to, Al,' she replied. 'It really is the only way we can reach the production target.'

Though weary from their twelve-hour shifts the girls did put in an extra hour a shift when called for.

'I'd love to tell Mr Featherstone where to stick his bloody targets,' grumbled Lillian as they took a brief cigarette break.

'You do get into a rhythm of work,' said the ever-philosophical Alice.

'So do mad rats in a run!' laughed Lillian.

'What I mean is that even though you're tired to the bone your brain's on automatic pilot: shell, cordite, detonator, shell, cordite, detonator. Sometimes I say it in mock French,' she said as she pronounced the words in a French accent. 'Case, detonateur, cordite, case, detonateur, cordite.'

'Sounds sexier in French!' laughed Lillian.

As the girls' friendship deepened and their trust and confidence grew, Agnes talked increasingly about Esther, especially when they settled around the wood burner in their digs, swapping Woodbines and drinking tea.

'I know the extra hours and the increase in productivity are in a good cause but there's always something that gets in the way of me seeing my Esther. At the Woolwich Arsenal it was impossible; they said they couldn't spare an experienced supervisor to go gadding about the countryside visiting relatives.'

'I wouldn't call visiting a sick child gadding about,' Emily protested.

Agnes continued angrily, 'Now their excuse is that time off is impossible because of the blasted targets. I tell you, I can't win!' she exclaimed as she threw her hands in the air with sheer frustration.

'It's a right bugger,' Lillian agreed.

'Maybe we could have a word with Mr Featherstone,' Alice suggested.

'And what good would that do?' Agnes asked.

'Compassionate grounds,' Alice quickly replied.

Agnes was silent for at least a minute then she said, 'Maybe I should go and have a word with Mr Featherstone myself?'

Elsie vehemently nodded her head.

'Thems that doesn't ask doesn't get,' she said solemnly.

Agnes smiled at her intense, loving face.

'You're right, Elsie, them that doesn't ask never gets!'

A few weeks after her meeting with Mr Featherstone Agnes got her much-deserved compassionate leave. When she found a leave pass sitting in her pigeonhole she was so stunned she couldn't stop shaking.

'Two days! TWO DAYS!' she gasped incredulously.

'That's all we can spare,' Lillian teased. 'Then we want you back, bossing us about on the bomb line!'

Agnes threw her arms about Lillian.

'I'm so, so happy,' she said on the verge of tears.

Lillian hugged her tightly. How could she have ever thought Agnes was stern and miserable? She was one of the best and kindest women she had ever met. But there was no doubt about her dress sense; it was unquestionably the worst Lillian had ever seen!

Disentangling herself from Agnes's embrace, Lillian said firmly, 'Now, Agnes, we've got to get you smartened up. We don't want you arriving in Keswick looking like you work down a coal mine, do we?'

Agnes took off her glasses to wipe tears of laughter from her eyes.

'Honestly, Lillian, only you would think of clothes at a moment like this!'

'She might be thinking frocks but I'm thinking food,' Emily said with a secret smile. 'Chocolate truffles for Esther.'

'CHOCOLATE TRUFFLES!' hooted Elsie. 'How do you plan to magic them up?'

Emily smiled as she gave a knowing wink.

'Mock chocolate,' she replied. 'All I need is a bit of marzipan, golden syrup and cocoa powder, some breadcrumbs – and all your sugar rations!' she ended with a peal of laughter.

'And maybe a little book you could read to Esther at bedtime,' Alice suggested. 'I'm sure I've got an old copy of Grimms' fairy tales at home.'

'I've got nowt to give the wee bairn,' Elsie said candidly. 'But when she gets here I could teach you a right bonny lullaby.'

Smiling, Agnes held out her arms to embrace all her friends.

'I promise you Esther will love you all as much as I do!' she cried.

On a chilly December morning Agnes stood at Clitheroe station looking quite unlike she'd ever looked before. Wearing a borrowed pale blue hat and coat of Alice's and carrying Lillian's best leather handbag, she looked a good ten years younger.

'Don't forget to wear your glasses when you're on the train,' Emily said. 'You don't want to miss the view of the mountains.'

Agnes winked as she patted her glasses tucked away in her coat pocket.

'They're right here. Lillian said they ruined my new image. I'll put them on the minute she's out of sight,' she said with a low chuckle.

Emily and Alice handed over their gifts for Esther: Emily's home-made mock-chocolate truffles which they'd spent all their sugar allowance on, wrapped in pretty paper and decorated with coloured string, and Alice's old battered copy of Grimms' fairy tales.

'I hope the big bad wolf doesn't frighten her to death!' Alice giggled.

'Give Esther our love!' Elsie said.

A blast of black engine smoke sent the train shunting sharply forward.

'Get in, be quick,' urged Lillian as she hustled Agnes up the steps and into the train. 'Enjoy yourself!'

'Don't forget to come back!' joked Emily.

'Take care,' cried Alice.

Agnes hung out of the open window and waved good-bye to Emily, Alice, Elsie and Lillian standing on the platform. Before she disappeared from view around a twist in the railway track Agnes blew them kisses.

'THANK YOU!' she cried as the train gathered momentum.

Sitting back against her scratchy upholstered seat, Agnes put on her glasses and gazed out of the window. Joy bubbled like a fizzy drink all the way through her. After months and months of waiting she was only two hours away from her beloved daughter. But now their meeting was a reality what would Agnes tell her little girl if she asked about her father? Esther had still been a baby, not even two years old when Stan had joined up and even then, at such an early age, she adored her father. Images of the horrific Pathé News footage floated into Agnes's mind: walking dead men beaten into submission like dogs, hopeless and unloved. As the train hurtled north,

Agnes gritted her teeth; she had to keep believing that none of them could be her Stan.

The view from the window changed radically once they were past Preston and Chorley, the fertile Lancashire farmlands giving way to the first soft roll of the Cumbrian mountains which grew steeper as they passed Kendal then soared high and majestic as the train chuffed its way around Windermere. Agnes, who'd barely travelled outside of London, had never seen mountains so high or lakes so vast, and when she stepped off the train at the quaint Keswick station she gasped at the purity of the air. Esther could only thrive in such an environment. Following directions to the cottage hospital, Agnes hurried through the market town with its charming Moot Hall, then turned right towards Derwentwater; there she found the hospital surrounded by lawns that ran down to the edge of the lake.

With her pulse racing with excitement and trepidation, Agnes found Esther's ward, where she introduced herself to the doctor.

'I have to be honest, Mrs Sharpe,' the doctor said after the initial formalities. 'Esther's progress is slow and she's distinctly timid about trying out anything new.'

'She's very young,' Agnes replied defensively.

The doctor smiled sympathetically.

'We understand that, plus Esther was parted abruptly from both parents in a very short space of time. She's been through a lot.'

Agnes nodded as she bit back tears.

'We're hoping this long-awaited visit from you might

increase Esther's confidence,' he said as he led Agnes to a window through which she could observe Esther working with her physiotherapist.

Agnes's heart skipped a beat as she watched her little girl intently working on exercising her left leg, which was strapped in a heavy metal calliper that caused her to walk with an uneven hopping gait. Agnes was surprised to see how much Esther had grown since she last saw her, though she was shocked at how thin and pale she was. Tears stung Agnes's eyes as Esther kept anxiously reaching out for her stick, but the physiotherapist was discouraging her from using it. Esther valiantly struggled on but she wobbled nervously as she tried to balance her body weight against the calliper.

She's so young, so small and vulnerable, thought Agnes.

Unable to wait a minute longer, she hurried to the treatment room.

'Esther . . . darling,' she whispered as she pushed open the door and held out her arms to her daughter.

Esther let out a cry of pure joy as she fell into her mother's open arms.

'Mummy, Mummy!' she sobbed.

Weeping with joy, Agnes buried her face in Esther's tumbling dark hair, inhaling for the first time for over a year the sweet young smell of her. Her hands travelled down the child's back where she could feel every bony vertebra. God, she really was thin!

Unable to believe her eyes, Esther said, 'Mummy! You've come at last.'

Agnes, brimming with love and happiness, stroked Esther's hair and kissed away the tears on her damp cheeks.

'It's all right, darling,' she soothed. 'Everything's all right . . . Mummy's here.'

When both of them finally stopped crying Agnes borrowed a wheelchair from the ward. Esther instantly hopped into it.

'Come on, cherub, let's go for a walk,' said Agnes with a radiant smile.

Even though it was a cold winter's day Agnes pushed Esther in her wheelchair around the shores of Derwentwater until it went dark. Neither of them wanted the day to end. Every time Agnes asked Esther if she was cold or hungry her daughter just laughed.

'Keep on walking, Mummy, keep on talking.'

Starved of each other's company for so long, they laughed as they sang Esther's favourite nursery rhymes from her baby days.

'Bye, baby bunting, daddy's gone a-hunting,' Esther chanted. 'Has Daddy really gone hunting, Mummy?' she asked, her dark eyes big with anxiety.

'Yes,' Agnes replied staunchly. 'He's gone hunting but he's a big strong Daddy so he'll come back soon, safe and sound,' she reassured her daughter.

As Agnes and Esther stood by the shore of Derwentwater watching the sun go down, Mr Featherstone sat in his office at the Phoenix scowling at a bomb-assembly manual that was written entirely in French.

'And what exactly are we expected to do with this?' he snapped at Marjorie, his secretary, as he irritably flicked the manual she'd presented to him. 'Who in God's name speaks French round here?'

'We could make a tannoy announcement in the factory and see if we can find somebody who does,' Marjorie replied.

'Make it right away, Marjorie,' said Mr Featherstone. 'The longer we take to find a translator the longer the delay on the bomb line.'

Five minutes later Marjorie's prim tones boomed up and down the assembly lines.

'If there is anybody fluent in the French language could they please make themselves known to Mr Featherstone immediately.'

Emily, standing next to Alice at the conveyer belt, gave her friend a dig in the ribs. 'You speak French. Off you go!' she laughed.

Having got permission from the temporary supervisor to leave her section, Alice hurried to the manager's office, wiping her yellow cordite-stained hands on her white overalls as she did so.

'I'm fluent in French,' she told her boss nervously as she stood before his desk eyeing the manual he was pushing towards her.

Mr Featherstone nodded; he liked the look of this elegant little lass with her bright smile and stunning silver-grey eyes.

'Don't ask me how we finished up with a French manual for English shell cases,' he said with a chuckle. 'Somebody somewhere got their wires crossed. Sure you can manage it?'

Alice turned the pages of the hefty manual and nodded.

'It's mostly technical and has a lot of English words, so

it shouldn't be too complicated,' she replied confidently. 'I'll work on it when I've finished my shift tonight,' she added.

'No, you won't!' Mr Featherstone replied forcefully. 'You'll work on it right now, right here in my office. Marjorie!' he called. 'Tea and biscuits for Alice – right away.'

It was pleasant sitting in the manager's warm office with a fire crackling in the black grate and a big brass clock ticking away on the wall. Alice quickly forgot about Mr Featherstone and Marjorie bustling in the background as she lost herself in the French text. It wasn't just a question of translating the document; she had to make absolutely sure that she accurately understood the intricacies of the bomb-assembly instructions so she chose her words with great care. One wrong word could lead to an explosion on the assembly line or, worse still, an incorrectly assembled bomb that failed to go off when fired on the front line.

When Marjorie and Mr Featherstone bade her a good night Alice stayed on.

At the end of their ten o'clock shift Elsie, Lillian and Emily came to take Alice back to their digs.

'Come on, bedtime,' Emily urged but Alice shook her head.

'I've got to get this done by the morning,' she said. 'It's really important.'

Dawn found Alice slumped over the fully translated text. She awoke with a start as the brass clock struck six, and shivered; with the fire out the office was cold and chilly. Leaving the translated text on Mr Featherstone's desk, Alice hurried back to her digs where she had a hot bath, a mug of sweet tea, then a few hours' sleep before she was back on the assembly line.

In his office Mr Featherstone read through Alice's English assembly instructions and smiled.

'With skills like this,' he said to his secretary as he tapped the hefty pile of papers Alice had so efficiently translated, 'that little lass is wasted down on the factory floor. I tell you, Marjorie, that young Alice Massey is made for much finer things!'

During her whirlwind visit Agnes spent a lot of time boosting Esther's confidence when she worked with her physiotherapist. As little Esther wobbled and swayed without the support of her stick, Agnes had an idea.

'Let's do it with Dolly.'

Holding Esther's little knitted doll, Agnes placed her feet on a flat surface.

'Look how clever she is, she can lift her good leg, then when that's nice and steady she can swing her poorly leg and she won't fall over because her strong leg is keeping her upright.'

As Agnes demonstrated the exercise several times, Esther smiled.

'Clever Dolly!' she said as she picked her up and kissed her.

'Now you show Dolly how to walk without wobbling,' Agnes urged.

The physiotherapist winked at Agnes as she said, 'I'll leave you to it.'

When they were on their own Esther put Dolly through her paces.

'But her polio leg is still thin and poorly,' she said sadly.

Agnes hunkered down to be on the same level as Esther.

'I promise you it will get better and stronger with the hospital medicine and the physiotherapy.' She helped Esther to her feet. 'Let's all do the exercises together with Dolly.'

By the end of the session they were laughing at each other as Agnes hopped on one leg and Esther walked with some significant improvement.

'You're hopping, Mummy. Use both legs, no cheating,' Esther giggled as she repeated the words her mother had said to her.

'You're doing better than me because you've got clever Dolly,' Agnes replied.

Esther rubbed the woollen toy against her pale cheek.

'Can Dolly stay and do physiotherapy with me?' she said softly.

'Of course, darling,' Agnes replied with a catch in her voice. 'You can both help each other to get better.'

All too soon Esther and Agnes were enjoying their last day together, they'd hired a boat and were rowing out to the island in the middle of Derwentwater where they planned to have a picnic, even though it was icy cold and there was snow in the air. Over fish paste sandwiches and a flask of hot tea they talked about the future.

'Will Daddy come home soon,' Esther asked.

'He might do, sweetheart, God willing,' Agnes replied. 'We just have to keep hoping and praying he's safe and well.'

'Will God let you stay here with me, Mummy?' Esther asked sadly.

Feeling like her heart would burst with grief, Agnes gathered her daughter into her arms and kissed her soft dark curls.

'Not yet, darling, but soon, I promise. Mummy will see you more often now and you can come and visit her at the factory where she works; it's not that far away.'

Seeing Esther's dark eyes fill with tears of disappointment, Agnes tried to lighten her load with a joke.

'And guess what?' she said. 'I have *four* best friends: Emily, Alice, Elsie and Lillian.'

Intrigued, Esther said, 'Tell me about them.'

'Well there's Emily, she's a great cook; she made those chocolate truffles for you,' said Agnes with a smile. 'Then there's Alice, she's the clever one, and she can speak French nearly as well as she can speak English. Elsie is the sweetest, kindest lady in the world, and Lillian is funny and *really* cheeky!'

Esther burst out laughing at her mother's lively description of her friends.

'Where do you all live, Mummy?' she asked.

Agnes smiled as she replied, 'A cowshed on the moors!'

Esther's eyes opened wide with amazement.

'A cowshed!' she laughed. 'With pooh?'

Agnes shook her head.

'No! We had to kick the cows out so me and my friends could move in!' she joked.

'I want to meet your new friends, Mummy,' Esther said eagerly.

Agnes kissed her daughter, then said, 'And they can't wait to meet you, sweetheart!'

Though Agnes had been staying with Mr and Mrs

Sugden, the old couple who housed Esther in between her hospital visits, she hadn't had as much time with them as she would have liked. Before Agnes packed her bag and left for the station Mrs Sugden suggested they had a cup of tea together. Agnes immediately accepted then suggested to Esther that she introduced Dolly to her other toys, which she kept in her bedroom.

As soon as Agnes was settled, Mrs Sugden said, 'She stopped wetting the bed whilst you were here.'

Agnes nodded; she'd noticed the thick rubber undersheet on the single bed she'd shared with Esther during her stay.

'She seems very thin.'

'We have trouble getting food down her,' Mrs Sugden replied. 'They say she doesn't eat much of the hospital food either.'

Agnes's heart dropped. During her time with Esther the little girl happily ate the meals and picnics they shared.

'She's pining,' the old lady answered knowingly. 'And there's nothing anybody can do about that.'

'Not unless Hitler and Mr Churchill have a peace parley,' said Mr Sugden, speaking for the first time.

'And that's not likely to happen, not with the way things are going,' retorted Agnes, who'd just been reading in the morning papers of the growing tension in the Pacific.

'We do our best, lovie, even though we know the little lass only wants her mam,' Mrs Sugden assured her

'I'm grateful to you both,' Agnes quickly said. 'You've given my daughter a safe home, and at least she's out of the blitz,' she added, determined to sound upbeat.

'We'll keep her safe,' the old lady promised.

Agnes sighed heavily.

'I'm dreading leaving her,' she murmured.

Mrs Sugden patted her hand.

'We're dreading it too, pet.'

Esther had to be wrenched out of her mother's arms at Keswick railway station.

'Take care of her,' Agnes begged the old couple as she climbed onto the train, which was slowly starting to pull away from the platform.

Sobbing in the woman's arms, Esther waved Dolly in the air.

'Bye, Mummy. I love you!' she cried.

'Bye, darling,' Agnes called back, grateful for the engine smoke that hid from Esther the tears pouring unchecked down her cheeks.

The journey back was nothing like the happy, expectant journey to Keswick. The weather had changed and the bleak December chill settled on the countryside, clothing it in a clinging dank mist. There were endless stops and starts on the journey, with tired troops pushing their way up and down the packed corridors with their loaded kitbags. Knowing she was on an early shift the next morning, Agnes tried to catch some sleep, but her last memory of Esther sobbing her heart out as she waved Dolly in a final farewell drove sleep right out of her mind. When would she see her again? Would Esther remember what she had to do in her next physiotherapy class? Would the poor child start to wet the bed again? How could she persuade her to eat more when she was eighty miles away in another county?

As all these thoughts swirled around her fevered brain, Agnes became aware of a rush of excited laughter and jubilant cries outside in the packed corridor.

'Bloody great news!'

'About time too!'

Baffled, she turned to her companion, a soldier not much older than a boy, who was balancing several kitbags on his lap.

'What's happening?' she asked anxiously.

'Bloody Japs have bombed Pearl Harbor – the Pacific War's on!' he replied, grinning from ear to ear.

Agnes looked at the boy soldier incredulously.

'REALLY?' she gasped.

'Really, missus! With the Yanks on our side we'll soon have this bugger of a war over!'

Agnes slumped back against her seat and smiled.

'Thank God for the Americans!' she exclaimed.

Maybe she'd be reunited with Esther sooner than she thought, and, God willing, Stan too.

Chapter 9: Overpaid,
Oversexed and Over Here

Seeing the huge potential for female conscription Churchill extended the call-up to all women, married or single, between the ages of eighteen and fifty. Only the old, the very young, the infirm and the pregnant slipped through his net. At the war's peak over seven million married women were engaged in full-time or part-time work in Britain, taking on roles that would never previously have been considered appropriate for women. They were on the land, working gruelling seventy-hour weeks; they worked in aircraft factories, building and repairing planes; they were helping to build ships; they were driving fire engines and ambulances; they were working day and night as air-raid wardens. But nowhere was this growing army of women more noticeable than in the munitions factories, which expanded as the desperate need for more bombs grew.

As soon as the conscription age was raised many more women arrived for work at the Phoenix.

'We're bound to get more toffee-nosed southerners coming here now, and none of them'll know their arses from their elbows!' Lillian groaned.

Agnes laughed. 'Oh, you mean like me?' she teased.

Lillian's myth of 'posh southerners', as she called folks from south of Manchester, had been blown away by Agnes, who she unconditionally adored.

'You're different, cock,' she said as she gave her a kiss.

'And so are the other southerners,' Alice reminded Lillian. 'So stop being such a bigot.'

'What's a bigot?' Elsie asked.

'Somebody what doesn't like southerners!' Lillian laughed.

There was a sense of increased hope now that the US had entered the war. Britain finally had a loyal and powerful ally. The Bomb Girls were thrilled when they heard that American forces were being flown into the UK.

'Over here, overpaid and hopefully oversexed!' laughed Lillian in delight.

'We'll probably never see them,' said Alice.

Agnes nodded.

'They'll be stationed in secret locations until Churchill and Roosevelt agree on a plan of action,' she said.

'So much talent – what a waste!' groaned Lillian.

Nothing prepared the girls at the Phoenix for the sudden arrival of a squadron of Canadian airmen, who were billeted in an old airfield down in the valley, a location that completely baffled Alice.

'Why come here?' she puzzled.

'Who cares why so long as they're here!' Lillian replied.

'Seriously,' said Alice thoughtfully. 'Why billet them in an old airfield?'

'I suppose they have to go somewhere,' Elsie replied.

'And it's close to Manchester, Liverpool, even Birmingham,' Agnes added.

'When we've done with the geography lesson,' Lillian

interrupted impatiently, 'can we go and take a peek at the newcomers, just in case somebody's pulling our leg!'

'Count me out!' laughed Agnes. 'I've got better things to do.'

'Like cracking the whip on the factory floor?' Lillian teased.

'I'm not going chasing after foreign fellas I've not been properly introduced to,' Elsie said primly.

'I'm up for it,' giggled Emily.

'Me too,' added Alice.

So the next day, before their afternoon shift started, Emily, Alice and Lillian set off in the softly falling snow, each of them carrying a tin tray borrowed from the canteen.

'There's got to be an explanation for these trays,' Lillian said as they threaded their way over the frozen tracks.

'You'll see soon enough,' Alice assured her.

Emily and Alice led the way across the moors that they knew like the back of their hands, but the going was tough and slow in the deep snow.

'One step forward and three back,' Lillian gasped as she tried to keep up with her friends.

At the top of a steep summit, with a fine view of the valley below, Emily and Alice tucked their coats around their legs then settled themselves firmly on their trays.

'What're you two up to?' Lillian asked as she watched the girls in amazement.

'Going down the quick way!' Alice laughed as she pushed herself off.

With a yelp of excitement, Emily quickly followed.

'Come on, Lil, go for it!'

'S'pose there's always a first time for everything,' Lillian giggled as she hitched her dress into her knickers. 'Here goes!'

The three girls whooshed down the icy hillside, laughing and screaming with excitement as they tried to stay upright on the wobbling trays which, as they gathered speed, veered sideways at their every movement. Lillian was the first to lose her balance; with a scream she bounced off and rolled down hill, where she landed safely in a soft drift of snow. Experienced 'tray surfers', Alice and Emily kept on going, and as the ground flattened out they steered their trays to a stop then ran over to Lillian, hauling her to her feet.

'You two certainly know how to live!' Lillian laughed as she spat snow out of her mouth.

'Are you ladies okay?'

Lillian, Emily and Alice jumped in surprise and turned around to see a Canadian airman curiously eyeing them.

'We're fine,' Emily assured him.

'We always travel on trays in this part of the world!' Lillian joked, putting the other girls at their ease as always with her quick humour.

'You must teach me how to,' the handsome Canadian replied. Giving a smart salute, he quickly added, 'Lieutenant Freddie Bilodeau at your service.'

Lillian winked.

'The eagle has landed!'

The girls introduced themselves to Freddie, who told them that his squadron had flown in from Ontario only that week. 'More of our guys will be joining us soon.'

Lillian smiled in pure delight.

'The more the merrier!' she laughed.

'I say, wanna tour, ladies?' Freddie asked with a heart-stoppingly handsome smile.

'Yes, please!' Emily and Lillian chorused in unison.

'Shouldn't we be making our way back?' Alice asked.

Lillian and Emily turned to her in amazement, and again they spoke in unison as they asked the same question.

'*Why?*'

'Clocking on,' Alice reminded them.

Keen not to lose them, Freddie quickly said, 'I won't keep you too long, ladies,' and with a swagger he helped them into the open-topped jeep, where he purposefully sat Emily in the front passenger seat. 'You cosy down there, sweetheart,' he murmured caressingly.

Lillian, in the back seat with Alice beside her, muttered into Emily's ear.

'Cow! He's making a play for you.'

Alice frowned as she whispered a warning.

'Watch out for him, Em.'

Emily shook her mass of auburn curls now burnished gold by the angle of the winter sun.

'It's only a bit of fun, Al,' she replied as Freddie got in the car.

In the back Lillian's skirt got hitched up, showing off her shapely legs to the appreciative Canadian airmen as they whizzed by.

'Hi, fellas!' she called as they blew kisses in the girls' wake.

As Freddie gave them a guided tour of the airfield, he slowed down to point out various red-brick blocks.

'Obviously that's the landing strip and the control tower is over there,' he said, pointing to the strip where Canadian planes were standing ready for take-off. 'Officers' quarters, guardhouse, hospital, theatre, operational building, supply room, latrines, chapel –'

'Bet you're not in there often,' Lillian teased.

'I'm a regular churchgoer,' Freddie quipped as he accelerated away from the domestic buildings and headed out towards the landing strip. 'Over there's the oil storage, the machine-gun range and the parachute block.'

'I'm astonished the base is up and running so fast,' said Alice.

'We Canadians don't hang about, ma'am,' Freddie answered with a wink and a smile.

After the tour was over Freddie drove the girls back over the moors to the Phoenix.

'Great to meet you,' he said as he helped them out of the jeep, holding onto Emily's hand for what seemed an extra-long time. 'Hope you'll look kindly on your friends from across the pond?' he added with another heart-stoppingly charming smile.

'We'll organize a little welcome party,' Lillian assured Freddie before he sprang back into his jeep and roared off across the moors, blowing kisses as he went.

'Well, well, well, Em, he's got the hots for you, that's for sure,' Lillian remarked as soon as they were alone.

Emily blushed but there was no doubting the extra spark in her pretty blue eyes.

'He was nice,' she said, trying to brush aside Lillian's comments.

'*Nice!*' exclaimed Lillian. 'He's bloody gorgeous – and he practically ate you up!'

'And he knows it,' said Alice. 'He's a born flirt.'

She gave her friend a knowing look.

'Don't go getting distracted by sweet-talking Canadians – remember you're engaged to Bill.'

Emily bridled at her remark.

'Of course I won't! But anyway, considering Bill's my fiancé, he's taking me a bit too much for granted. He hardly writes these days!'

Alice shook her head.

'Emily, there's a war on – thousands of letters are lost every day. Don't go blaming Bill for that.'

In a pig-headed mood, Emily pressed on, 'He never came to see me when he was at Preston barracks just after Christmas.'

Alice's eyes flashed in irritation.

'You're being ridiculous!' she cried. 'How's he supposed to breeze out of the barracks without permission?'

'Well, his mum got to see him!' Emily retorted.

'And so could you if you hadn't been working shifts,' Alice reminded her.

'Can you imagine how it feels to have your fiancé home, just down the road in Preston barracks, and he doesn't even bother to come and see you?' Emily snapped.

Alice, who knew Bill well, shook her head.

'There's got to be an explanation,' she insisted. 'You should know Bill better than to think he wouldn't bother. He's as straight as a die, loyal and faithful. He'd be gutted if you started messing about.'

Emily's cheeks flared bright red.

'Who says I'm messing about?' she asked sulkily. 'You're all getting carried away. I just enjoyed a handsome man's attention. I don't see the harm in that.'

'If I could squeeze a word in . . . ?' Lillian said with a cheeky laugh. 'What the eye doesn't see the heart doesn't grieve about.'

Ignoring Lillian's breezy attitude, Alice held her best friend's gaze.

'Please be careful, Emily,' she implored.

The girls were soon so busy and exhausted from factory work that the subject was put to one side. The one thing that kept them all going on those long shifts was the thought of the upcoming swing night at the Phoenix that Emily had taken it upon herself to organize. Lillian and Alice wasted no time in drawing Elsie and Agnes into their preparations.

With Malc's help, Lillian tracked down a local swing band, Emily and Agnes got to work organizing the refreshments, and Alice and Elsie were busy designing posters to pin up all over the factory, even in the small chapel that was regularly visited by girls who couldn't make it to the church services in Pendle.

Thankfully the days seemed to race by and the event they were all so looking forward to was suddenly upon them. Nobody was allowed time off – shifts ran as usual at the Phoenix – but Emily, Alice, Elsie, Lillian and Agnes were lucky as their shift on the Saturday of the dance was an early one so they had all afternoon to fuss about getting ready. No matter how reserved Agnes and Elsie were it was impossible not to get drawn into the excited

73

preparations going on in the old cowshed. There wasn't enough water for a bath each so it was two to a bath, with the last person having to top up what was left with boiled water from the kettle. Lillian, in her element, took charge of everybody's hair. As Joe Loss dance music blared out from the radio, the girls took it in turns to sit on an upright chair whilst she set their hair and applied make-up. Then they stood for the final finishing touch as, with an expert eye and steady hand, Lillian traced down their bare legs a black crayon line that looked, from a distance, exactly like the black seam on nylon stockings.

With the catering on her mind, Emily set off for the canteen a good few hours before her friends.

'I've got meat and potato pies to cook for two hundred!' she said cheerfully, heading for the door in her old canteen overalls. It was so nice to be preparing for such a joyful occasion when they'd had such a gruelling few months of long, exhausting shifts.

'Please tell me you won't be dancing in *that*?' Lillian gasped in dismay.

'No, Alice is bringing my glad rags over to the Phoenix later,' Emily said with a cheeky wink. 'I won't let you down, Lillian, I promise!'

At the final hour, Elsie shocked them all by having a tantrum. With her hair softly waved and her pretty heart-shaped face skilfully rouged, she looked lovely. The months of regular square meals at the Phoenix had put flesh on her bones. No longer skeletal, she now had a small bust and gently curving hips. The dress she'd borrowed from Lillian, a soft sage silk, brought out the green tones of her eyes and Alice's ballroom shoes added height to her short stature. But when she saw herself in the mirror her face changed and she refused point-blank to leave their digs.

'I can't go!' she cried, looking utterly miserable.

Her friends did a complete double-take at the sound of Elsie's angry, raised voice. This was not the little Gateshead mouse of a girl they were used to.

'Why on earth not?' Agnes gently asked.

Elsie bit her lip then burst into tears.

'I canna dance!'

'Don't cry, for God's sake!' Lillian exclaimed. 'You'll ruin your make-up!'

'I don't care!' Elsie sobbed. 'I canna go out done up like a dog's dinner and mek a fool of miself on the dance floor.'

'You don't have to dance,' Agnes assured her.

'You can just sit there looking pretty,' Alice quickly added.

Elsie looked from Agnes to Alice and back again.

'For sure . . . ?'

Her friends quickly nodded.

'Okay . . .' she said slowly. 'No dancing – and definitely no lads!'

Arm in arm the four girls skipped down the dark cobbled lane to the Phoenix canteen, which was decorated not only with balloons and banners but with large, twirling silver balls hanging from the ceiling at each corner of the room. The cold outside contrasted with the warmth inside, and the mirrored balls scattered beams of silvery moonlight onto the dance floor, transforming it into a romantic ballroom. Giggling excitedly, the four friends swung open the doors and rushed into the room, where they were met by dozens of eager Canadian airmen dressed in smart new grey and navy-blue uniforms. The girls stopped in their tracks: there were men everywhere! Handsome, young, excited men, and all curious to meet them. It was quite a shock after all the months of female-only companionship at the Phoenix, and among the smiling faces were those of black servicemen, the likes of whom Lillian, Alice and Elsie had never come across in their entire lives.

'You're not telling me that you've never seen black men before?' Agnes asked incredulously.

'We're not from London like you, Agnes,' Alice reminded her.

Lillian's dark eyes roved over a couple of stunning black guys drinking at the bar.

'WOW!' she gasped. 'I'm definitely going to make up for lost time!'

Holding her unlit cigarette aloft, she sashayed towards the bar.

'Hi, there,' she cooed. 'Anybody got a light?'

Agnes picked up two lemonades then settled blushing Elsie in a quiet corner from where she could observe the fun of the party without being overwhelmed and embarrassed.

Alice found Emily, hot and flushed, in the canteen kitchen, ready to serve up her delicious meat and potato pie.

'Let's dance our socks off later, Al,' Emily cried over the clattering noise of pots and pans.

Standing at the edge of the ballroom, looking lovely in a dusty-pink crêpe dress that clung to her waist then swirled out in a series of tiny pleats from her slender hips, Alice wondered whether to join Elsie and Agnes in the corner or Lillian, who was laughing raucously at the bar. Before she could make up her mind she felt a tap on her shoulder and turned around to face a tall, dark Canadian airman.

'Henri Laurent at your service,' he said, with a wide smile that showed off a set of perfectly even, white teeth.

Alice checked the stripes on his uniform and smiled.

'Pleased to meet you, Captain Laurent.'

'May I dance with you?' he asked formally.

Alice nodded and as they moved into the centre of the ballroom, she said, 'I hear the hint of a French accent . . . ?'

'*Français québécois,*' he replied, sliding a hand expertly around her waist and swooping her onto the dance floor as the band struck up 'Deep Purple Haze'.

Pressed against Henri, Alice abandoned herself to the music and the moment. In a mood of heightened excitement she forgot the misery of rationing, the months of hard work, the relentless worry, the fear of the unknown . . . It all faded away as she waltzed into a dream world where, for a sweet, brief time, she found romance and escapism. As the conductor waved his baton and the music changed to the Mills Brothers' 'You Always Hurt the One You Love', Alice looked shyly into Henri's face and smiled. As long as she danced, she was uplifted, drifting in a make-believe Hollywood world where nobody came home covered in yellow cordite powder.

In her quiet corner Elsie was surprised at how much she was enjoying herself.

'The Canadians look so different to our lads,' she

observed. 'They've got bonny teeth, like, all white and even,' she said with a laugh. 'And they're better dressed too.'

Agnes, ever the realist, shrugged. 'They're bound to look smarter; their uniforms are brand new whereas our lads have been wearing theirs for a good two years.'

'Oh, aye, I never thought of that,' said Elsie, then she froze as a tall, thin strip of a lad loomed up before them and nervously cleared his throat.

'Care for't dance?' he said with a broad Lancashire accent.

Thinking he was asking Agnes, Elsie shrank into the corner but a sharp kick from Agnes made her realize the question was addressed to her.

Flushed and awkward, Elsie looked up into the open, honest face of a boy not much older than her.

'Will ya?' he said with an embarrassed grin.

Agnes gaped in surprise as Elsie rose to her feet.

'Aye, go on then,' she replied.

Smiling fondly, Agnes watched them stumble about on the dance floor. They'd both got two left feet but neither of them seemed concerned; they smiled as they talked and shuffled between the more accomplished dancers.

God love them, thought Agnes as she slipped away, happy to return home alone where she had a letter to Esther to finish.

When the band was in full swing and the dance floor was packed Emily finally emerged from the kitchen. Made-up and with her long hair tumbling around her shoulders, she was wearing a floral silk dress that emphasized her full breasts and long legs. As she scanned the room for her friends, her eyes sparkled with excitement and her feet began to tap. Seeing Alice with a tall Canadian captain and Lillian in the arms of a handsome black lieutenant, Emily looked about for Elsie and Agnes. The strains of 'In the Mood' sent a shiver down her spine, which was heightened by a firm hand taking hold of hers.

'Where've you been all night, gorgeous?' Freddie whispered into her ear.

Emily smiled shyly, but before she could reply Freddie spun her round, caught her smoothly in his arms then, holding her firmly around the waist, he boogied her onto the dance floor. Breathless and laughing, Emily responded instinctively to his expert dance moves. Losing herself to the music and trusting Freddie's timing, she lost all remaining inhibition, threw back her head and laughed with joy. She might be on the dawn shift tomorrow but tonight she was going to dance till she dropped!

Chapter 10: One Little Spark

In fact, Emily did more than dance. She couldn't help being intoxicated by Freddie. Just the touch of his firm hand in the small of her back sent a charge through her like an electric shock. The smell of his skin, a heady mix of pine and limes, filled her nose, removing all reason. When they stopped briefly for a glass of beer Emily, feeling woozy even before she'd had anything to drink, passed Lillian walking onto the dance floor with Malc.

'I see you've landed on your feet,' Lillian chuckled.

'What happened to the gorgeous guy you were with earlier?' Emily whispered.

'Got to keep the boss happy!' Lillian replied with a cheeky wink

Freddie handed her a glass of beer then downed his in almost one gulp. Emily stared at him, mesmerized. He was larger than life, like no man she'd ever met before: dynamic, virile and bone-meltingly sexy. Smothering a groan of desire, she sipped thirstily at her beer.

'So tell me all about yourself,' Freddie purred in her ear.

Emily gulped as she quickly swallowed her beer.

'Me . . . ?' she said.

'Yes, you, beautiful,' he murmured as he leaned close to blow a stray strand of hair out of her face.

'Well . . . I'm a Bomb Girl,' she answered with a laugh, struggling to maintain any composure. Right now any thoughts of Bill were being pushed further and further to the back of her mind.

Bending even closer, he whispered softly in her ear, 'You've sure blown me away, babe.'

Before Emily could catch her breath he'd set down her glass and whisked her back onto the dance floor.

'I feel empty when you're not in my arms,' he said as they swung into a foxtrot.

Emily didn't think she'd ever had so much fun, and she smiled when she caught sight of Alice laughing as she danced with a tall, dark Canadian officer. She was glad Alice seemed to be having as much fun as her.

As the music changed to a dreamy waltz number, Emily closed her eyes and just swayed in sync with Freddie's every movement. Like Alice, she abandoned herself to the music, to the heady sense of romance and complete escapism that filled the improvised ballroom.

When Freddie finally moved to kiss Emily she found she couldn't hold back. Although she loved Bill it was so long since she'd seen him . . . and she didn't even know if he still felt the same way about her. But right now, in this room, a gorgeous man was making her feel a million dollars and she couldn't help but respond eagerly to his advances. As the two of them kissed and cuddled into the early hours, Emily was shocked at herself. She had never before behaved so recklessly and with so little thought to consequences. But the war had changed everything.

Long after the swing night concluded Emily and Freddie were still together, sheltered from the frosty wind and locked in each other's arms underneath the wide awning of the factory loading bay.

Eventually, as the first birds began to stir, Emily tore herself away.

'I've *got* to go,' she whispered. 'I'm on early shift.'

'Who cares?' he grinned as he pulled her back.

Melting into Freddie's body, feeling the muscles rippling beneath his uniform, Emily forgot about everything but the thrill of his soft caressing hands. The sound of the factory hooter waking the morning shift, swiftly followed by the weary trudge of boots on cobblestones, finally startled Emily into reality. Terrified she'd be discovered in broad daylight, she struggled free of Freddie, who clutched her hand.

'When are we going to meet again?' he asked urgently.

Emily couldn't help herself, again she pushed any thoughts of Bill and her guilt to one side.

'Tomorrow,' she promised, then laughed as she realized that tomorrow was already today. Blowing Freddie a kiss, she ran towards the factory doors, calling out, 'As soon as I get time off.'

Joining her friends in the changing room, Emily swapped her pretty dancing dress and high heels for white overalls and heavy work boots.

'Dirty stop out!' Lillian giggled as Emily scrunched her tumbled hair underneath her turban.

'Listen to the pot calling the kettle black!' scoffed Elsie. 'Emily wasn't the only one who didn't come home last night.'

'I was otherwise engaged,' Lillian giggled as she wriggled her shapely bottom into her overalls. 'So what did you get up to, Missie Emily?' she teased.

'Just talking,' Emily replied with a blush. 'Nothing

happened, promise,' she added as she caught sight of Alice's penetrating eyes.

'The both of you should've come home to your beds,' Elsie scolded.

'For a girl who went out saying no fellas and no dancing you did all right, Elsie,' Lillian laughed.

Agnes didn't join in the good-natured banter. She looked disapprovingly from Lillian to Emily.

'You two are in no state for work,' she snapped.

'I'll be all right after a few cups of strong tea,' Emily replied with a sleepy smile.

'And half a packet of Woodbines!' yawned Lillian.

Agnes scowled as she shook her head.

'This is stupid!' she exclaimed crossly. 'You two have been up all night. You should go back to the digs and catch up on your sleep.'

Lillian smothered a yawn as she replied, 'Give it a rest, lovie, my bloody head's banging.'

Agnes pulled out a chair and sat down beside Lillian.

'Go home, please. It's for your own good,' she pleaded.

In answer, stubborn Lillian stubbed out her cigarette then started haphazardly removing clips from her hair.

'I know what I'm doing,' she retorted. Then, pulling on her turban, she said to Emily, 'C'mon, our kid, let's hit the bomb line.'

As they walked onto the factory floor, Lillian whispered, 'So how was lover boy?'

Emily's blue eyes grew dreamy as she recalled the rapture of Freddie's long kisses.

'Oh, God . . . I just couldn't help myself. He was absolutely gorgeous.' She sighed.

Overhearing her response, Alice frowned, which made hot-headed Emily's hackles rise.

She knew Alice was right to frown but she was all over the place: besotted by Freddie, who seemed to really adore her – and still so hurt by how Bill had behaved on his last leave home.

'You don't need to look so disapproving, Al,' she snapped. 'You weren't exactly holding back last night.'

Alice's face reddened with anger.

'I'm not the one who's got a fiancé!' she snapped back.

Seeing a row about to blow, Lillian laughed as she gave a careless shrug.

'We can't all be vestal virgins!'

Emily looked shocked.

'Hey, I didn't go that far!' she exclaimed.

Lillian winked as she gave her a nudge in the ribs.

'No . . . but I bet you wanted to!'

The early shift got under way in the cold, dark, damp workshop. The rattle of the shell cases and the permanent crank and roll of the conveyor belt sent Emily into a trance-like state; all she could think of were Freddie's brooding eyes and soft caresses. As the morning wore on, Bill's smiling face and honest blue eyes drifted into her mind more and more, and the guilt nagged at her. Had she got it all wrong? Had Bill been thinking like she had been thinking, wondering why Emily didn't go and visit him? Had they got their wires crossed? Was it all down to a stupid misunderstanding?

What have I done . . . What am I doing . . . ? Guilty thoughts filled her mind as she packed one shell case after another. Al was so right. Bill would dump her if he ever found out. She bit her lip hard to fight back her tears of shame. He must *never* find out, never, ever! It would be the end of us, she thought.

Halfway through the shift, just before one of their much-needed tea breaks, Lillian raised her hand to push away a stray curl that was making her nose itch; as she did so an undetected hairpin slipped from underneath her turban.

Agnes, who'd made a point of working near Lillian because of the state she was in, saw the pin fall. Holding her breath, she watched it descend as if it was happening in slow motion: turning, it glinted a dull metallic gold as it landed on the conveyor belt then sparked as it hit the cordite powder. Mercifully, Agnes found her voice a millisecond before the flash.

'DOWN! GET DOWN!' she screamed.

Everybody scrambled to get down, but some had hardly made it to the floor before a loud bang ripped through the building followed by a huge explosion that knocked Alice flat on her back. Paralysed with fear, she lay winded and trembling, terrified there might be a second explosion. When none came she gingerly raised herself up to see what damage had been done. To her distress and horror she could see workers on Agnes's section lying unconscious, stunned or wounded. She caught sight of Agnes, who, with blood streaming down her face, was crawling from one munitions girl to another, pushing or rolling them away from the conveyor belt where shell cases continued to rattle around. A fire bell screeched out and several overseers rushed in. One immediately shut down the conveyor belt, several more hosed down the cordite line, the rest carried the wounded and unconscious to safety. Alice could hear moaning from some of the injured girls; others lay uncannily still.

'Where's Emily?' she said out loud. 'Elsie!' she called. 'Lillian!' Even as she followed instructions to evacuate the building, she frantically looked out for her friends.

'Where are they?' she murmured as hysteria rose in her throat.

Along with all the girls able to walk, Alice followed the fire-drill rules; though shaken and scared they left the factory in an orderly manner and lined up outside on the moors at a safe distance from the Phoenix, which they knew could blow sky-high if the fire wasn't controlled right away.

'What the bloody 'ell happened?' everybody was asking as they stood shivering and shaking in the howling wind.

'Nobody's sure,' an overseer told them. 'The explosion was on the cordite line.'

Huddled amongst the able munitions girls, Alice finally spotted Emily and Lillian moving through the crowd as they frantically looked for Elsie and Agnes.

Seeing Malc counting the girls on the fire-drill line-up, Lillian ran over to him.

'Have you seen Agnes and Elsie?' she asked breathlessly.

Looking bemused, Malc shook his head. 'No. There's bodies all over the factory floor, but th'ambulance men are taking them out now. Are you all right, sweetheart?' he added, seeing Lillian was as white as a sheet.

Lillian shook her head as she grabbed his arm.

'I've got to find them, Malc.' She dropped her voice to a whisper as she went on, 'I think I caused the explosion. A hairgrip slipped out from underneath my turban. I tried to catch it but –'

'Jesus Christ!' yelled Malc.

Lillian squeezed his arm hard.

'Keep your voice down,' she begged.

'You know the rules,' he whispered back. 'No metal on the factory floor. What were you thinking of, Lil?'

'I know . . . I know,' Lillian gabbled. 'I was hungover after all the booze you plied me with, not to mention staying up most of the night,' she muttered in his ear.

'Shh!' he hissed. 'If anybody gets wind of that we'll both get our marching orders.'

'Agnes begged me not to start work, she warned me, but, like the cocky cow I am, I thought I knew better. Oh, Malc, what have I done?' she wailed as she clung onto him for support.

They were pushed aside by stretcher-bearers taking the wounded to the Phoenix hospital. As they passed by, Lillian thought she caught sight of Agnes, and running along beside the stretcher she grasped Agnes's limp hand.

'I'm sorry, Agnes, I'm so sorry,' she whispered frantically. 'Please be okay,' she sobbed wildly. 'Please, Agnes . . . I don't know what I'd do without you.'

Too weak to reply, Agnes just squeezed Lillian's hand before she was whisked away for treatment.

Lillian watched her go.

This would never have happened if I hadn't clocked on for work hungover, she raged at herself.

Because of her stupid carelessness she had caused a

horrific explosion that might have killed two of the people she loved most in the world. She jumped at the touch of Malc's hand on her shoulder.

'Leave this with me, Lil,' he said. 'I'll talk directly to Mr Featherstone, see if I can't soften him up a bit.'

Lillian gaped at him in disbelief.

'I nearly took out the entire workforce – I don't want you "softening things up". I deserve what's coming to me and if that means dismissal, so be it.'

'Don't be a bloody fool, girl!' Malc replied angrily. 'You're meeting trouble head on, so let's play for time.'

Lillian looked him squarely in the eye.

'Who are you most worried about, Malc – you or me?'

The noise of the explosion alerted the people of Pendle to an accident close by but nobody quite knew what or where. Tommy Carter, his thoughts full of Elsie, heard it when he was tucking into his breakfast in his mum's two-up, two-down in the middle of a terraced block next to the mill where his parents had worked all their lives. He jumped to his feet in alarm and, grabbing his coat against the snow that had started to fall, he ran down the street towards a crowd who had gathered at the local shops.

'What is it? What's happened?' he yelled.

'Accident up at Phoenix,' a neighbour replied.

'The Phoenix!' Tommy exclaimed, and without pausing to ask another question he tore up the hill out of town.

It didn't take Tommy long to reach the moors where by now the snow was falling fast. Recognizing a local girl hurrying home, he stopped to ask her what had happened.

'Explosion on't cordite line,' she answered breathlessly. 'Lucky it didn't take out the bloody lot of us!'

With fear and panic rising in him Tommy sprinted even faster up the snowy slopes until eventually the Phoenix loomed up, cordoned off by soldiers and bomb experts.

'No entry!' a soldier called as Tommy approached.

Gasping for breath, Tommy stood wondering what to do next. He didn't know where Elsie lived; he didn't know what section she worked on; he didn't even know her last name! What he did know made him tremble with emotion: she was the sweetest, most innocent girl he'd ever met, with gentle green eyes that had captivated him all night long.

'I've *got* to find her,' he muttered under his breath.

Seeing Tommy's frantic expression, a passing overseer said, 'Can I help, lad?'

'I'm looking for a lass that works here,' Tommy replied.

'Name?'

'Elsie.'

'And which Elsie would that be?' said the overseer patiently.

Feeling foolish, Tommy shook his head. 'I dunno . . . I only met her last night.'

'The bomb squad have shut down the factory till they get the all-clear, so there's only two places she can be,' the overseer told him. 'Either in her digs or in th' hospital.'

He led the stunned Tommy into the hospital complex where he pointed to a noticeboard.

'Check the casualty list,' he said. 'You might find her there.'

Tommy's eyes quickly scanned the list; there were at

least three Elsies. He couldn't go searching the hospital wards looking for an Elsie with green eyes! Shaking his head in despair, he turned to see two girls hurrying up the hospital corridor, one small and delicate with silky blonde hair caught up in a ribbon, the other tall and slim with tumbling auburn hair flying around her anxious face.

Recognizing them as local girls, Tommy stopped them in their tracks.

'S'cuse me, do you know a little lass called Elsie?'

Emily, who'd had eyes for only one thing the previous night, didn't recognize the gawky, uncomfortable boy before her, but Alice did.

'Weren't you dancing with her last night?' she asked gently.

'Aye, I was. I've come to see if she's alreet,' he said awkwardly.

'She was injured in this morning's blast,' Alice told him gravely.

Seeing Tommy pale with shock, she grabbed his hand and pulled him along beside them.

'We're on our way to see her now – come with us.'

They found Agnes and Elsie a few beds apart. Agnes's hands were bandaged but she was wide awake and frantically beckoned them towards her when she saw them. Elsie was fast asleep.

'They're going to be fine,' the ward sister assured them. 'Both of them have burns to the face and hands, Elsie's also slightly concussed. She must have fallen and hit her head.'

As Alice and Emily hurried over to Agnes, Tommy sat down beside Elsie's bed and stared into her sleeping face. She looked so young and innocent, and the cuts on her bruised cheeks only enhanced her loveliness as far as Tommy was concerned. Peering around to make sure nobody was watching him, Tommy raised Elsie's right hand and pressed it tenderly to his lips.

'I'll be right here when you wake up,' he said softly.

A few beds away Agnes was deeply agitated. 'You know who caused the blast?' she whispered.

'Lillian,' Emily whispered back.

'She's just told us,' Alice added.

'She's not told anybody else, has she?' Agnes dropped her voice. 'You know she could be fired on the spot for gross negligence.'

'Malc thinks he can liaise between Lillian and Mr Featherstone,' Alice told her.

Emily laughed harshly.

'He's as much to blame as she is. It was him that kept her up most of the night.'

'Last time I saw Lillian, she was having fun with some handsome Canadian,' Agnes recalled.

'I think Malc made her an offer she couldn't refuse,' Alice said with a knowing smile. 'You know what a sucker she is for lace knickers and nylons!'

Agnes giggled then quickly stopped.

'Ouch! It only hurts when I laugh!'

When the ward sister saw Agnes grimacing in pain she called out sharply, 'Ladies! Can we keep our patient as calm as possible, please?'

When Elsie woke up and saw the blurred shape of a man's head and shoulders she immediately thought it was her dad come to take her back to Gateshead.

'No, Dad, no! I'm fine,' she said as she struggled to sit

up. A blazing pain shooting across her temples sent her falling back against the pillows. 'Ow!' she groaned.

'Have a sip of water,' Tommy said, and he supported her whilst she drank from a glass he was holding.

Elsie peered up as she took the proffered water. 'It's *you*!' she said softly, not quite believing her eyes.

Tommy settled her back onto her pillows and stroked hair off her damp forehead.

'Don't fret yourself, lass,' he said gently. 'You need to get some rest.'

Elsie gazed up at him, her green eyes wide with happiness.

'You came all this way to see me?'

'It's not exactly miles, is it?' he joked as he continued to stroke her forehead.

With a contented smile, Elsie closed her eyes and sank back into a deep sleep.

'You're my lass,' Tommy whispered. 'And I'm going to look after you.'

Whilst Emily and Alice were paying their hospital visit Lillian was being led by Malc into the Phoenix, which, to their surprise, had already been given the all-clear and was now back in full production.

'We were so lucky not to have more damage,' Malc said as they walked along side by side. 'I thought we might have been out of action for months.'

'I suppose that's one way of looking at it,' sighed Lillian miserably.

'What I'm trying to say before we meet Mr Featherstone,' said Malc, dropping his voice to an urgent whisper, 'is the damage was contained to your section, and there were, thank Christ, no bombs on the overhead conveyor belt otherwise we'd be talking about a wipe-out.'

'Agnes must have seen it coming otherwise she'd never have yelled a warning before the explosion,' said Lillian. 'Poor kid, she put us first as usual and got badly hurt in the process.' Lillian's shoulders slumped as she put her head in her hands. 'God! I hate myself!'

'Lillian!' cried Malc as he grabbed her hands and shook her. 'Pull yourself together!'

Lillian swallowed hard and nodded.

'Remember what I told you?'

'Don't mention the black-market booze,' she said dully.

'And don't keep yapping on about being up half the night either,' he reminded her. 'Ready?'

Lillian's stomach lurched in fear. Nodding her head, she muttered a low, 'Yes.'

'Right then.'

Straightening his tie, Malc walked ahead of Lillian and opened Mr Featherstone's office door.

'Let's face the music,' he muttered as he ushered her in.

Usually a retiring man not prone to raising his voice, Mr Featherstone was virtually incandescent.

'You know the first rule in a munitions factory: no metal anywhere about your person!' he roared when he'd heard the sorry tale.

Ignoring Malc's words of advice, Lillian stuck out her little chin and spoke firmly and clearly.

'I take total responsibility, sir.'

Malc rolled his eyes; this wasn't the way he'd planned on playing it.

Before Lillian totally shot herself in the foot, he quickly said, 'Nobody can doubt the magnitude of Lillian's mistake, it was gross negligence without a doubt, but like all the girls on the floor she's under a lot of pressure.'

'None of them have managed to cause an explosion so far!' Mr Featherstone snapped.

Malc glared at Lillian, willing her to keep quiet.

'The point is, if we withdraw Lillian from the workplace we lose an experienced Bomb Girl who right now is vital for the war effort,' Malc said calmly. 'If she can assure us that this kind of thing will *never* happen again, I believe we should put her back on the cordite line rather than suspend her or, worse still, send her to a tribunal.'

Mr Featherstone drummed his podgy fingers on his desk.

'It's the example she's set to the other girls. What if they all forgot to remove their clips? We could be blown to kingdom come!'

Lillian spoke quickly before Malc could speak for her.

'I can see that, and I will certainly apologize to my colleagues for my actions,' she said staunchly. 'I hope that what has happened has given us all a shock and we will all be doubly careful from now on.'

Seeing the strain in her face and the tears in her dark eyes, Mr Featherstone nodded slowly.

'It'd be a pity to lose an experienced Bomb Girl, that's for sure,' he conceded. 'But you'll be under close scrutiny for a very long time.'

Lillian humbly bowed her head.

'Thank you, Mr Featherstone.'

As the shifts changed hands, a crowd of munitions girls hurried through the canteen, where Alice and Emily were sitting having a cup of tea. To their surprise, they heard Lillian thumping loudly on one of the dining tables. As they stopped to stare at her, Lillian hopped onto the table in order to face her workmates.

'Many of you will be wondering what caused the explosion on the cordite line,' she said loudly. 'Well . . . it was me,' she blurted out. 'A hairgrip fell out of my hair, just one little spark . . . you know the rest. I'm so sorry. I can't believe I let that happen.' Her voice faltered but she forged on. 'I want you to know I am truly, truly sorry and it will never happen again.'

'Have you been fired?' a woman called out.

Lillian wiped away the tears welling up in her eyes.

'No, I'm back on the bomb line as from tomorrow, under close observation.' Her voice broke into a sob. 'I'm so . . . so sorry,' she mumbled, utterly shamefaced.

Seeing Lillian distraught, Alice and Emily quickly helped her step down from the table.

'You've said enough,' Alice said firmly. 'We know you're sorry. It's going to be okay,' she added kindly.

On either side of Lillian they took hold of her trembling hands.

'Come on, Elsie and Agnes are waiting to see you in the hospital,' said Emily with a wink.

The girls couldn't believe their eyes when they saw a radiant if somewhat woozy Elsie sitting up in bed, with

Tommy on a chair beside her holding her hand. Agnes smiled conspiratorially as her friends approached.

'These two love birds have got something to tell you.'

Elsie looked shyly at Tommy, who smiled and nodded.

'Go on,' he urged. 'Tell 'em.'

Looking like she would burst with happiness, Elsie said, 'We're getting wed!'

'But you've only just met!' gasped Alice.

'And you yourself said you've never been to a dance before, never even met a man before!' Agnes called from her sickbed.

Despite her bandaged head, Elsie replied with a blissful smile, 'You're right, I've never really met a lad before,' she said as she grasped Tommy's hand.

Even at such a serious moment, Lillian couldn't help but crack a joke. 'Bloody hell! Were you brought up in a convent?'

Elsie burst out laughing.

'There were lads at school but mi dad said he'd kill me if he caught me talking to 'em.'

Tommy's face flushed with anger.

'How could anybody hurt a little flower like you?'

Elsie gave a dismissive shrug.

'That's all in the past,' she said bravely. 'What I'm trying to say is that I'd never properly talked to a lad till I talked to you last night.' She blushed as she added, 'We've only just met but I know I'd be happy to spend the rest of my life talking to you.'

Overcome, Tommy wiped tears from his soft brown eyes, as did Elsie's friends, though tenacious Alice questioned the young couple further.

'You're very young,' she cautioned Tommy.

But he threw back his skinny shoulders as he replied, 'I'm twenty-four, older than Elsie. I may look like a streak of –' He stopped short of saying the swear word for fear of offending his new fiancée. 'Sorry, love.'

Elsie gave a girlie giggle.

'Don't fret, pet. I've heard a lot worse than that in mi time.'

'Before I joined the Lancashire Fusiliers I worked down't pits and when war's over I'll go back down't pits, God willing,' he said fervently. 'Who knows what'll happen to any of us? None of us are safe, whether it's here in a bomb factory or on't front line. I could take a bullet, whilst you take a bomb blast.' Still holding onto Elsie's hand, he rose to his feet to face Elsie's friends square on. 'I love this beautiful girl with all my heart and I'll take care of her and protect her all my life!' he declared.

'Oh, God!' Lillian exclaimed as she started weeping afresh. 'I'm going to be stretchered out of here if you carry on talking like that.'

Weak as she was, Elsie struggled to sit up higher.

'Tommy's right. There's a war on,' she said through a mist of tears. 'We might have a year, we might have a lifetime, but I'm going to snatch every minute of happiness whilst I can.'

It was at this point that even Alice conceded, leaning over and kissing Elsie.

'I want to hug you!' she grinned.

Elsie pointed to her wounds.

'Mebbe later,' she joked.

Lillian smiled as she mopped up her tears.

'Who'd a thowt our little Elsie would pip us all to the post!'

Chapter 11: The War Office

Emily's free afternoon came at last and she couldn't help herself; she'd thought of nothing but Freddie ever since that intoxicating night. After finishing her early morning shift she dashed back to the digs where she sneaked into the bathroom to make up her face and change into her best skirt and blouse. Hoping to avoid seeing her friends who might prick her conscience, Emily cautiously opened the bathroom door and peered out, only to find Alice leaning against the wall waiting for her.

'You're meeting him, aren't you?' Alice said accusingly.

Emily wriggled in embarrassment.

'Bill's not going to put up with you two-timing him, Em,' Alice added.

Emily threw up her arms in a mixture of frustration and guilt.

'I know!' she cried. 'It's a rotten thing to do but I can't get Freddie out of my head. Anyway, we're only going for a walk on the moors.'

Alice's gaze swept down to Emily's high-heeled shoes.

'In those!' she laughed.

Emily looked at her feet and laughed too.

'Borrow my wellingtons,' Alice urged. 'And my hat and scarf.'

'No, Alice! I was hoping to look a lot sexier than a land girl!' Emily joked.

Alice rolled her eyes.

'Okay, freeze to death,' she said.

Emily gave a loud sigh as she kicked off her court shoes.

'All right, I'll borrow your wellies, but a definite no to the hat and scarf!' she giggled.

Alice needn't have worried about Emily catching cold. The minute Freddie laid eyes on her he clasped her tightly in his arms.

'It seems like forever since we last met,' he murmured as he kissed her.

Pressed close to him, Emily smelled yet again that intoxicating mix of pines and limes. Smothering any remaining inhibitions, she laid her face against his chest where she felt the thud of his beating heart.

'What shall we do, Bomb Babe?' he whispered.

Smiling mischievously, Emily bent and quickly rolled a snowball.

'Build a snowman!' she laughed.

Catching her mood, Freddie stooped to roll a snowball too.

'Hey, just cos I'm Canadian doesn't mean to say I'm an Eskimo!' he joked.

Feeling wild and reckless, Emily whizzed her large snowball at him, he whizzed his back at her and before long they were rolling in the snow, not feeling even remotely cold as, once again, they were locked in each other's arms. Emily tasted ice and snow as Freddie hungrily kissed her, pressing her mouth open with his tongue. Startled, she pulled away from him and wiped her mouth with the back of her hand. This was all going a bit too fast.

'What's the matter? Don't you like it?' he teased.

Emily couldn't respond immediately; she was thinking of Bill's sweet young kisses. Their innocent lovemaking had been tender and experimental. He'd always been wary of offending her and they'd both agreed that she would be a virgin on their wedding day. Keeping that promise had been a struggle, especially after Bill joined up. The night before he left for active service they had both longed to make love, and if it hadn't been for Bill respecting her so much they almost certainly would have.

'I . . . I, er . . .' She stumbled over her words, but what she wanted to say to Freddie was that she'd never experienced such boldness. Frightened that he'd laugh at her naivety, she simply said, 'It was just a bit quick.'

The frosty air rang with Freddie's loud, mocking laughter.

'Jesus! What do you guys get off on up here in the wilderness? There's a war on, honey, how slow do you want me to be?'

Emily blushed as she struggled to her feet. For all of Freddie's sexy ways and charming looks, she wasn't having herself or her kind mocked.

'We manage well enough,' she said with icy haughtiness as she brushed snow from her hair. 'We certainly don't need foreigners to show us how to conduct ourselves.'

Seeing he'd gone too far, Freddie jumped to his feet.

'Babe, I'm sorry,' he murmured as he gently took her resistant hand. 'You just blow me away,' he added as he swept his palm across her flaming angry cheeks. 'Forgive me, pleeease?' he begged with a heart-stopping smile.

Feeling rather silly, Emily quickly nodded and smiled.

'Come on,' she said as she tucked her arm in his. 'Let's walk before we freeze to death.'

Freddie smiled as he moved in close.

'I promise not to move so fast, though I can't make any promises if you keep looking at me with those big blue eyes,' he said huskily.

After wading through snow drifts four feet high Freddie led Emily into an old, disused stable that still had a deep litter of straw on the floor. She was too cold to think beyond finding some shelter.

'We can warm up in here,' he said as he closed the door then pulled a small flask from his inside pocket. 'A drop of Scotch will put some fire in your veins,' he said, handing the flask to Emily, who took a sip then grimaced at the sour taste.

Freddie took a deep swig from the flask then guided Emily to an untidy heap of hay bales in a corner of the stable.

'Come on, gorgeous, I'm going to warm you up,' he said as he threw off his coat and gently laid her on it.

Lying in Freddie's strong arms, Emily was no longer able to hold back. He soon had her hot and bothered enough to cast off her coat and Alice's wellington boots.

'You are the most beautiful thing I've ever laid eyes on,' he said in a voice thick with desire.

Emily couldn't believe what she was doing but, with her head in a spin and all her senses clamouring for his touch, she was lost to everything but her overwhelming need for him.

Unbidden, an image of Bill wearing his brand-new Lancashire Fusiliers uniform popped into her head. She'd promised to wait for him, to always be there for him. As passion blazed through her, Emily thought defiantly of Bill's last disastrous visit home.

Forcing herself to stop thinking of Bill, she gripped Freddie, whose advances grew stronger as his hands went from her face and neck to her full breasts and hard nipples.

'Take your clothes off,' he whispered. 'Let me see you naked.'

Swept away by a passion she had never previously known, Emily moaned with desire as Freddie reached down to remove her underwear.

'Yes,' she murmured. 'Yes . . .'

A dog barking outside in the snow sent both of them jumping sky-high.

As if waking from a trance, Emily stared in disbelief at her open blouse.

'What am I doing?' she gasped.

'Hey, honey,' he laughed softly. 'What does it look like we're doing?' He dipped his head to kiss her again.

'*No!*' Emily cried as she pulled her blouse tightly around her. 'I-I can't! I shouldn't,' she panicked. 'I'm engaged to Bill.'

'And he's not here,' Freddie said nonchalantly.

Stunned by his dismissive tone Emily struggled to stand up.

What was she doing? Was she out of her mind to let things go this far?

'I'm sorry, Freddie, but this is wrong.'

'You weren't saying that a few minutes ago,' Freddie teased. 'Come on, don't spoil it, baby.'

Fastening the buttons on her blouse, Emily blushed as she replied, 'Please, Freddie, can we just talk?'

'*Talk!*' he scoffed as he stood up and angrily wiped straw off his uniform. 'What kind of bullshit is that? One minute you're begging for it, the next you want to talk. Gimme a break!'

Realizing the enormity of her mistake in leading him on, Emily quickly apologized.

'I'm sorry, Freddie,' she said again. 'It's as much my fault as yours.'

'Too right it is,' seethed Freddie. 'Here I am freezing my ass off on the bloody moors whilst you whinge on about your stupid fiancé. How come you didn't think about lover boy sooner?'

Colour flooded Emily's face; she was ashamed of herself for giving in to Freddie and furious with him for bad-mouthing Bill. She didn't know whether to walk away or burst into tears.

'I'm sorry . . .' was all she seemed able to say.

'To hell with sorry!' snapped Freddie as he strode out of the stable, still wiping bits of straw off his Royal Canadian Air Force uniform.

Fighting back tears, Emily pulled on her coat and hurried after him, but he was storming off through the snow without a backward glance.

'FREDDIE!' she shouted.

Still walking away, Freddie called angrily over his shoulder.

'Go and find some other schmuck to tease!'

With her head bent and her shoulders hunched, Emily walked away, oblivious of the dog that had disturbed their lovemaking now leaping joyously over the snow drifts with its owner, who squinted to get a better view of the pair.

'Ten to a penny they've been up to no good,' the dog walker chuckled to himself, then he frowned as he recognized the good-looking woman with the flaming auburn hair hurrying away.

'Bloody hell, that's Emily Yates,' he gasped in amazement. 'Wait till young Bill finds out what she's up to in his absence!'

Back at the Phoenix Alice and Lillian were visiting Agnes and Elsie in the hospital complex. Both patients, though bruised and scratched, were now on their feet.

'We'll soon be back working on the bomb line,' plucky Elsie joked.

'You're going nowhere until you're properly well,' said Tommy as he laid a protective arm around her shoulder. Elsie blushed at his touch but her face was radiant with happiness.

'Will you tell your dad?' Alice asked the happy couple.

Elsie vehemently shook her head.

'He'd kill Tommy,' she replied with a tremor in her voice.

Looking furious, Tommy swept a hand through his fine mousy hair.

'Who ses?' he said staunchly.

Elsie looked him straight in the eye.

'I'm not kidding you; he'd beat up the pair of us.'

Seeing her question had upset Elsie, Alice swiftly said,

'Not to worry. You're old enough to do what you want and your dad's far enough away not to trouble you.'

'Just let him bloody try,' Tommy muttered under his breath.

Lillian winked as Malc came wandering down the ward towards them. 'Oh-oh! Here comes trouble!'

'Hiya!' Malc said as he approached.

'Come to take the sick and the lame back to work, have you?' cheeky Lillian teased.

'At least I didn't try to blow 'em up in the first place!' Malc retorted sharply.

Seeing poor Lillian blushing underneath her perfect make-up, Agnes chided Malc.

'That was a bit near the bone.'

Malc shrugged.

'I say as I see,' he replied.

'Then try not to, it doesn't help,' Agnes replied.

Staring daggers at Malc, Lillian snapped, 'To what do we owe the pleasure of your company?'

Malc nodded towards Alice.

'Featherstone wants for't see yon brain box,' he said.

Alice looked at him in surprise. '*Me?*'

Malc nodded.

'Looks like we've got more of them bloody useless French manuals for you to translate.'

As he and Alice left the ward, Lillian rolled her eyes.

'Bastard!' she seethed. 'As if I don't know how much trouble I've caused without him rubbing it in.'

'You won't be calling him names when he comes chasing after you with silk nylons and chocolates,' Agnes reminded her.

'Won't I?' Lillian replied contemptuously. 'After the harm I've done to you and Elsie my days with Malc are well and truly over!'

Once inside Mr Featherstone's office Alice looked around for the French manuals she presumed she'd be translating.

'Sit down, Alice,' said Mr Featherstone stiffly.

Alice immediately sensed his tension.

'Is something wrong?'

Mr Featherstone shook his head.

'Far from it, young lady,' he replied as he politely pulled out a chair for her. As soon as Alice was settled, he continued, 'How do you fancy taking your French skills a step further?'

Alice looked at Mr Featherstone in disbelief. How could he, the boss of a bomb factory, help her improve her French?

'Well . . .' she said slowly. 'I'm always keen to learn more but I'm not sure how that can be achieved right now in Pendle.'

'We're not talking Pendle, Alice, we're talking London – the War Office, to be precise.' Mr Featherstone paused to let the enormity of his words sink in. 'The powers that be are recruiting fluent French speakers like you.'

'Oh, well, I'm not sure I'd call myself absolutely fluent, Mr Featherstone,' Alice protested.

'You're far too modest, Alice,' he insisted. 'Anyway I've let it be known to the powers above . . .'

What is he talking about? Alice wondered as she watched Mr Featherstone rock complacently up and down from his toes to his heels.

'I had no hesitation in telling them that we've got a regular little French speaker right here at the Phoenix, who is an excellent Bomb Girl to boot,' Mr Featherstone concluded with a proud smile.

Mystified, Alice smiled blankly at her boss, who was clearly more excited than she was.

'What do they want me to do?' she asked.

'That's for them to tell and you to find out,' he said, tapping the side of his nose as if it was a secret. 'Mark my words, you'll be hearing from the powers that be, Alice. Mark my words.'

When Alice rejoined her friends in their digs they immediately asked what Mr Featherstone had wanted.

Alice answered with absolute honesty.

'I have no idea!'

A few days later Alice was surprised to find an official, buff-coloured envelope in her pigeonhole at work. With Emily on one side of her and Lillian on the other, she tore it open to find it contained a letter from the War Office and a train ticket for travel the following Thursday to London's Euston station.

'Ooh! Going on holiday?' Lillian enquired as she eyed the train ticket.

'Well . . . ? What does it say?' Emily asked as she nodded at the letter Alice was clutching.

Alice's eyes scanned the contents of the letter.

'The War Office are interested in my French skills,' she answered quickly.

'Ha, ha! French letters!' joked Lillian.

'How come the War Office know about you?' Emily asked.

'Mr Featherstone must have recommended me after I'd translated those French manuals for him,' Alice answered.

'Lucky sod! A free trip to London and all expenses paid,' Lillian giggled. 'Maybe I should take up French too!'

Back in their digs Alice read the rest of the letter when she had a private moment in the bedroom she shared with Emily.

You are instructed to make your way to Simpson's-in-the-Strand, London, where one of our men will be waiting for you. Train tickets are enclosed and details will follow.

Alice took a deep breath as she folded the letter and shoved it to the bottom of her cardigan pocket. Today was Tuesday; she had just over a week to prepare for her mysterious meeting with the Man on the Strand.

Chapter 12: Churchill's Secret Army

The next day Alice rounded up Lillian and Emily straight after work and the three of them rushed to the hospital to see their two friends, but they were shocked to find Elsie in floods of tears.

'What's wrong? Has she had a relapse?' Alice asked Agnes, who was sat on Elsie's bed rocking the sobbing girl in her arms.

Agnes shook her head.

'Tommy's just had to leave,' she said. 'He had no idea but his unit has just been posted to Tobruk. They're literally moving out tonight,' she added quietly. 'It's been a terrible shock.'

Emily's heart skipped a beat. Like Tommy and most of the local Pendle lads, Bill was in the Lancashire Fusiliers – in a different division, which was why they had different postings – but would he be on his way to Africa too?

'I've only just met him,' poor Elsie wailed. 'I can't believe he's had to go away so suddenly. What am I going to do?' With tears coursing down her cheeks she unashamedly turned to her friends. 'If anything should happen to 'im, I'd kill myself, I really would.'

Lillian smiled as she ruffled Elsie's fine hair. She was wracking her brains trying to think of something that would cheer the poor kid up, even if that something wasn't entirely accurate.

'Listen, have you seen *Casablanca*?' she asked.

Elsie wiped away a tear and looked blank.

'Well, if you had seen it you'd know that North Africa looks like a picnic compared to any other war zone. Tommy'll be right as rain, and home before you know it,' she assured her.

Elsie didn't look convinced.

'Come on, Elsie,' Lillian urged. 'I'm sure Tommy left with a brave smile on his face?'

Elsie nodded as she recalled his last sweet gentle kiss and his determinedly upbeat tone of voice.

'Wait for me, sweetheart?' he'd whispered.

'For ever,' was her answer. Then Elsie had sat up straight. 'I'll be strong for you, Tommy,' she'd answered with a valiant smile.

As Lillian, Emily and Alice gathered around Elsie, reassuring her that Tommy would be fine, Agnes kept her mouth firmly shut. Since she'd lost her husband, who could be alive or dead, she had no words of comfort to give. This war was nothing but a long agony of waiting, praying and hoping. Poor Elsie had joined an army of women who'd been doing just that for a very long time.

The day before Alice's interview in London, Lillian washed and set her silky blonde hair.

'Chignon or bob?' she asked.

Alice considered for a few seconds.

'Er, what do you think, Em?'

She turned to Emily, who was gnawing at her nails deep in thought.

'EM!' she shouted.

Emily jumped sky-high.

'Ooh! What?' she gasped.

'Chignon or bob . . . my hair?' she said, pointing to her damp locks.

'Er . . . ?' Emily replied blankly.

Lillian quickly proceeded to brush out Alice's hair.

'Let's go for a bob. We could be here all day waiting for gormless over there!'

Alice looked worriedly at her best friend. She instinctively knew what was preoccupying her: Freddie. She'd never been the same since she'd first clapped eyes on him.

Anxious about leaving, albeit only for a few days, Alice said softly, 'What's on your mind, lovie?'

Emily turned her tear-brimmed eyes to Alice as she blurted out, 'I two-timed on Bill with Freddie!'

Ever the realist, Lillian retorted, 'Well, we all know that!'

Now that Emily had started, nothing could stop her.

'I got so carried away, I felt like I was dreaming, floating on air . . .' she said as she struggled to find words that explained the ecstasy of their kisses.

Lillian looked at her sceptically.

'Really? The earth never moved for me with young Malcolm, that's for sure!' she laughed. 'But then Malc's not exactly Mr Universe, more Mr Puniverse!'

'You don't let your emotions run away with you, Lil, you always follow the money,' Alice pointed out.

'Well, next time will be different. I'm done with making deals with second-rate fixers,' Lillian said firmly.

'Did you . . . you know?' Alice asked.

Emily shook her auburn curls.

'No,' she said quietly.

'Why not?' teased Lillian.

'First I thought of Bill, and what a bitch I was breaking promises I'd vowed to keep, then a man walking his dog on the moors disturbed us,' Emily admitted. 'Freddie was livid, I can tell you,' she added ruefully.

'I bet!' Lillian exclaimed. 'He's the kind of good-looking guy that always gets what he wants. He'll be looking elsewhere if you don't come up with the goods, Em.'

'Well, let him look!' exclaimed furious Emily. 'Just because there's a war on doesn't mean that all women are available for sex.'

'He probably thinks the Phoenix is one big knocking shop!' joked Lillian.

As she and Alice burst out laughing, Emily stayed guiltily preoccupied.

'I've never let Bill undo my blouse,' she confessed with a blush. 'He respected me, said we had to wait till we were married, but then Mr Wonderful Canadian swings by and I forget everything. Oh, what have I done?' she wailed.

Knowing Emily's fiancé as well as she did, Alice said, 'Don't go telling Bill about Freddie; he'd go berserk if he found out.' Seeing Emily's eyes brim with tears, she quickly added, 'You had the sense to stop before things really did get out of control.'

Lillian furiously waved her curling tongs in the air.

'What're we women supposed to do?' she cried. 'Incarcerate ourselves till the boys come home?'

Seeing Lillian red-faced and angry and Emily nervously gnawing her nails, Alice quickly changed the subject. Tossing her hair, she returned to the original subject as she said with a laugh, 'So come on, what style of bob are we going for, Lillian?'

'I'm thinking Lauren Bacall,' Lillian replied as she struck a sexy pose, and dropping her voice to imitate the actress's voice, she added, 'Hey, know how to whistle . . . ? Just pucker up and blow . . . phew!'

'Oh, Lil, you should be on the stage,' Alice giggled.

'Yeah . . . mopping it!' Lillian retorted.

Later, as Alice tried on her best blue suit with a cream silk blouse in their shared bedroom, Emily sensed there was something wrong.

'What's up?' she asked bluntly. 'You should be happy.'

'I am.' Alice tried to smile. 'Just nervous.'

Emily's eyes raked over Alice's pale, tense face.

'Is there more to this French malarkey than meets the eye?' she asked. 'They're not parachuting you into France on a rescue mission, are they?' she joked.

'Don't be daft,' Alice laughed.

Still baffled, Emily pressed on with her questions.

'Then why aren't you jumping up and down with joy? Here's your chance to get out of the Phoenix and study French in London with all them clever fellas at the War Office,' she teased.

'Let's not jump the gun, Em,' Alice answered. 'You never know, they might not even like me!'

Emily engulfed her friend in a big bear hug.

'They'll love you, Al,' she whispered fondly. 'We all do!'

The next day Alice left Clitheroe railway station with a lot on her mind. She was glad of the solitude of the long journey, which gave her time to think.

Did she want to leave her home, family, friends, she considered as the train rattled south.

She'd always imagined she'd go to university then return home and teach, maybe at a Manchester grammar school. She'd certainly never imagined living in London or anywhere down south. She was a born-and-bred north-erner and thrived on the culture and landscape she'd grown up with. But could she turn down an opportunity to work for the War Office and improve her French in the process? It would be madness, not to mention a bit pathetic. She was twenty-one, a grown woman who should be seeking new experiences, not worrying about leaving home!

When she arrived at Euston station and walked through the bomb-torn streets of London she felt breathless with shock. The city was crushed by relentless bombings; bar-rage balloons floated high overhead; buses rumbled round shattered office blocks, factories and churches; the air smelled of brick dust and sewers. As she walked through the city, she looked at the people she passed: carrying their gas masks, they all seemed in a hurry, as if running from the next bomb to be dropped.

Catching the nervous mood of the city, Alice felt tense as she entered Simpson's. Dressed in her best blue suit, which had looked smart the day before when she'd tried it on with her friends, Alice suddenly felt shabby and old-fashioned. Peeping out from underneath the brim of her hat, she noted the cut of the dresses worn by the glam-orous women in Simpson's. Their hems were shorter, obviously to save on material, but the skirts were cut on the bias, which gave them a lovely swing and emphasized the extra length of leg shown off by the short hemlines. The fashion was very different to Alice's tight skirt, which ended mid-calf and showed hardly any leg at all. The women's hats were different too, sharper, with a military, masculine shape. Apart from worrying about what she looked like Alice wondered how she would ever spot the man she was supposed to be having lunch with.

As her stomach gave a nervous lurch, Alice dashed into the Ladies, where she reapplied her lipstick and rouge powder then quickly combed the blonde bob that Lillian had so lovingly created. A huge wave of homesickness washed over her; she missed her friends and the warm camaraderie of their digs. She'd travelled to London twice before but on school trips, not a grown-up, nerve-wracking visits like this one. Determined not to hide in a corner and risk not being seen, Alice forced herself to stand conspicuously at the bar. She didn't order a drink, which she longed for to steady her nerves; instead she lit a cigarette with shaking hands. Men were curiously eyeing her, the only woman at the bar.

They must think I'm on the game! Alice thought.

Just when she was on the point of running away, a tall, rangy man in a smart check suit and brown hat wandered up to her.

'Darling!' he exclaimed. 'I hope I haven't kept you waiting too long?'

Alice smothered a shocked gasp as the total stranger bent to peck her on the cheek then, after ordering two Vermouths, confidently guided Alice across the room to a small table for two.

'I'm Leo, by the way,' he said as he removed her coat and settled her comfortably in a chair. 'Don't worry, I know who you are,' he said with a charming wink.

A man in tails played romantic airs like 'South of the Border' and 'You'll Never Know How Much I Miss You' on a grand piano as they were served salmon, roast beef and a delicious sherry trifle – fresh, plentiful food quite unlike anything Alice had eaten in years. Unfortunately it all tasted like sawdust in her mouth because, as soon as the introductions were over, and throughout the entire meal, Leo talked to her only in French, and clearly expected her to do the same. As she sipped from her wine glass, Alice realized this was a test. Focused on keeping her head clear and her French grammar as good as possible, she refused further wine and stuck to water.

'*Vous habitez au nord d'Angleterre depuis combien de temps?*' Leo asked.

How long have I lived in the north of England? Alice quickly translated in her head. '*Toute ma vie, j'y ai grandi,*' she said out loud.

Leo continued, '*Et votre français est parfait – vous l'avez appris comment?*'

With her heart pounding, Alice translated: Where did you learn such excellent French? She immediately answered, '*À mon école.*'

She started to visibly relax as the language came back to her. She was definitely rusty but, once she'd got over her initial nerves, she began to enjoy the challenge of answering quickly and as expansively as she could.

'And have you visited France?' he asked as he poured

more wine for himself whilst Alice covered her glass with a hand.

'No, but I would love to when the war is over.'

'And what about before the war is over?'

As Alice paused briefly to consider her reply, Leo was struck by her composure and the beauty of her stunning grey eyes.

'We live in dangerous times,' she replied.

He nodded as he offered her a cigarette and moved the conversation on to her bomb work at the Phoenix.

'We understand you have a good knowledge of explosives,' he said.

Alice's eyes grew wide. So Mr Featherstone had told the War Office about her work on the cordite section.

'The combination of your skills is very valuable to us,' Leo said. 'You might be just what we're looking for,' he concluded.

Suddenly the meeting was over.

Leo led Alice outside, then, standing on the busy Strand, he said, in English, 'Can you be at the War Office at ten thirty tomorrow morning?'

Alice nodded, at the same time wondering where she was going to stay tonight. She had expected to travel back home.

As if reading her thoughts, Leo handed her a card.

'We use this hotel; it's all taken care of.'

Later, in the dingy hotel room with the blackout blind pulled down tight, Alice threw her gas mask to the floor and flopped onto the bed, where she lay exhausted by the stresses of the day. Scenes whizzed around in her head: the long train journey down from the north; the streets of

London bombed and splintered; sandbags everywhere, heaps of rubble and twisted metal piled high on every corner; blasted gable ends of tenement flats with curtains fluttering where windows should have been; sections of houses sliced in half, open to the elements like a doll's house. She was no stranger to a bombed city, having been to Manchester often enough and seen Liverpool's catastrophic devastation. All of Britain's major cities had taken wave after wave of severe bombing, but London had shocked her rigid. Then there was the strain and pressure of her meeting on the Strand.

'Oh, God! What a day,' Alice groaned aloud as she rolled off the bed and poured herself a glass of water from a jug on the bedside table.

She was proud of her French; it hadn't failed her, but what next? Why was Leo so interested in her explosive expertise? Would tomorrow be a repeat of today?

Tired and yawning, Alice undressed and washed then climbed into bed. As she pulled the heavy, lumpy eiderdown over her head, she heard a sound she'd never heard before: a squadron of bombers on a night raid, flying overhead. Alice gave a sad sigh. It wasn't only Britain's cities that were being targeted; all of Europe was ablaze.

Before sleep finally engulfed her, Leo's words echoed in her head.

'*Vous pourriez être justement ce que nous recherchons.*'

'What exactly are they looking for and why all the cloak-and-dagger stuff?' Alice muttered as she drifted into sleep.

*

Too nervous to eat, Alice skipped the hotel breakfast and concentrated on doing her hair and make-up. If she'd had time and money she would have rushed out into Oxford Street and bought a short, fashionable skirt and a natty military-style hat, but as it was she had to put up with her old-fashioned suit and wide-brimmed felt hat. Sighing, she picked up her bag and gas mask then made her way across town, down Horse Guards Parade and on to Whitehall, where the imposing building of the War Office loomed up before her.

Hurrying along the endless stairs, Alice looked up to the glass dome where the light streamed in and felt as though she was in a church rather than in an office, but the quiet and solemn atmosphere was broken by the clatter of her high-heeled shoes as she hurried down one long corridor after another. She was ushered into a room where she expected to see Leo, but instead there were three men sat behind a long desk.

'Do sit down, Miss Massey,' said the secretary as she drew up a chair so that Alice was facing the imposing line of men.

As the secretary hurried to her desk to take notes, the man in the middle cleared his throat and barked, 'Colonel Miller. Mind if we run through a few questions?'

Before Alice could reply, Miller continued, 'Married?'

'No,' Alice replied.

'Engaged?'

'No.'

'Any relationships?'

'No.'

'Any obligations?'

'No.'

'Family?'

'I have a mother, and I'm an only child.'

Miller nodded curtly as he turned to his neighbour, who introduced himself as Carmichael then took up the questioning.

'Leo tells us your French is good but we have to work on removing any trace of your English accent.' He glanced down at the papers lying on the desk before him. 'You have experience of bomb work,' he remarked. 'That too will need refining for what we have in mind.'

Blushing, Alice seized the moment to butt in and ask, 'May I enquire as to what exactly you do have in mind?'

Carmichael turned to Miller, who answered her question. 'Churchill's Secret Army.'

Alice felt as if somebody had thumped her hard in the chest.

'What me? Working with spies?' she gasped.

Carmichael nodded.

'We prefer the term Special Operations Agent, Miss Massey. We'll train you in communications, decoding and surveillance, we'll test your French and we'll ascertain your suitability for this kind of work. All this, of course, is top secret and not to be repeated.'

He grasped Alice's small hand and shook it so hard she thought she'd cry out.

'That'll be all for now, we'll be in touch.'

Chapter 13: Preparations

Alice was mobbed by her friends on her return from London. They were keen to hear how the interview went, then they all fired a range of questions at her: in Elsie's case they were about what she had eaten at Simpson's and where she'd stayed; Emily and Lillian wanted to know what the high fashion points were; and for Agnes it was all about London itself.

'The food was wonderful,' Alice said. 'Salmon, beef and sherry trifle, and wine too, but I didn't drink as the interview was conducted in French.'

Elsie's eyes nearly rolled out of her head.

'You had to speak French and eat at the same time!' she gasped. 'How did you do that?'

'By concentrating and sticking to water,' Alice replied. 'It was really hard because my French was rusty at first, but it kicked in after a while and I started to enjoy myself.'

'Did you see much war damage in the city?' Agnes asked.

Alice nodded.

'Sandbags everywhere and barrage balloons floating in the sky. Even walking down Whitehall I had to avoid piles of rubble and gaping holes. Complete blackout too and you daren't go anywhere without a gas mask,' Alice replied. 'It was spooky hearing squadrons of bombers flying over in the dark.'

Agnes shuddered.

'The Germans have been hitting major cities hard,' she said. 'Thank God I left when I did.'

'There're strange conflicting atmospheres in the city,' Alice continued. 'A mixture of tension and misery combined with bursts of cheerfulness. There were troops on open-topped motor buses waving and singing "Tipperary" and blowing kisses. At Euston station there were loads of jolly volunteers helping little kids with numbers pinned on their coats onto packed trains.'

Agnes nodded grimly.

'I've been there,' she said quietly. 'I know it has to be done but it doesn't make doing it any easier.'

'There were rumours flying everywhere,' Alice told her friends

'Like what?' Emily asked.

'That Hitler's gone mad!'

'That's not news, that's a fact!' scoffed Lillian. 'The bloody man's stark-raving bonkers!'

'He's so insane that Goering has taken over as Commander,' Alice added.

'God!' gasped Emily. 'It's bad enough being at war but being at war with a maniac is terrifying!'

To lighten the heavy atmosphere, Alice told them about the clothes she'd seen in London.

'The skirts are shorter, above the knee, with a really nice swing, and the hats are sharper, more masculine.'

'I'm not wearing an 'at that looks like a fella's!' Elsie laughed.

'And the shoes are flatter – brogues with a tie. The

women in the city look busy and confident, like they've a serious job to do.'

'We've a serious job to do but we don't wear posh clothes,' Lillian chuckled.

Agnes nodded in agreement with Lillian. 'If I'm honest I'd much rather be here in Pendle in my work overalls than in London – and I am speaking from experience!' she said with a knowing smile.

'Oh, me too,' sighed Elsie. 'It'd break mi heart to leave this town.'

'I wouldn't mind being on one of the open-topped buses with all them cheerful fellas,' Lillian mused.

'I'd love to have a snoop round Simpson's canteen,' sighed Emily. 'Imagine roasting beef and boiling salmon, not to mention making trifle with real fresh eggs.'

'Oh, shut up!' wailed Elsie. 'You're making me hungry just talking about it.'

Alice laughed as she said fondly, 'I bet the pies at Simpson's don't even begin to compare with Em's meat and potato pies.'

Lillian nodded in agreement with Alice.

'They're bloody legend!'

As the weeks passed, Alice began winding down her job at the Phoenix and making preparations for her move to London. There was no alternative but to be sparing with the truth. She'd told her friends in all honesty that she'd been accepted by the War Office as a trainee translator; however the Special Ops business she kept entirely to herself. In fact she hardly dared think about it, never mind articulate it. It was a terrifying prospect that filled her with a mixture of utter dread and wild excitement.

Her mind reeled.

Get a grip, Alice, she firmly told herself.

At the War Office Carmichael had been clear about her training. She'd be working in communications and learning to decode Morse; her French would be tested and at some point she'd be assessed. They had expressed interest in her bomb experience but that didn't mean she was going to be dropped into enemy territory in France and work undercover for the resistance movement, did it? That was the sort of drama she usually watched in films like *The 39 Steps* or *Man Hunt* at the Phoenix picture house, sitting back in her seat whilst eating a choc ice. Spy work wasn't what people like *her*, Alice Massey from Pendle, did. She wasn't a hero; she was terrified of mice and the dark!

Conflicting with these thoughts was her strong sense of patriotism. She wanted to do more than fill shell cases; she wanted to save lives and pass on information that could change the course of the war. Though frightened, the knowledge that she could play a vital, important role made her skin tingle and her pulse race. But it was top secret and even her mum didn't know what she was up to. Thank God, thought Alice. Mrs Massey would drop dead on the spot if she thought her only daughter was leaving Pendle to train as a Special Ops agent!

There was also the problem of Emily, who could read Alice like a book. If she so much as guessed what Alice was planning to do she would lock her up in the digs and throw away the key! The less her friends knew about her plans the better but Alice knew there'd be awkward questions. They'd all asked for her forwarding address, which even she didn't know. She'd received instructions to report to the War Office on a certain date after which she'd be dispatched to a training centre, whereabouts unknown.

Luckily, the plans for Elsie's wedding to Tommy, due to take place in the summer when he'd be home on leave from North Africa, were claiming everybody's attention. Because Elsie in effect had no family, Emily, Agnes, Alice and Lillian saw themselves as her next of kin and were therefore determined to put on the best wedding they could for her. Along with Tommy's mother, they had pooled their clothes and food coupons and begged, borrowed or traded anything they could.

Elsie found a picture of a wedding dress in a magazine.

'This is my dream dress,' she said shyly, as she showed it to her friends.

They all scrutinized the cut and style; it was modest and delicate, just like Elsie.

'Right,' said Lillian, and grabbing a tape measure she expertly spun Elsie around. 'Thirty-three ... twenty-two ... thirty-four,' she measured.

Elsie looked baffled.

'How are you going to make a wedding dress without a pattern to work from?' she asked.

'Watch!' said Lillian with a confident smile.

With Elsie's measurements as a guide, Lillian sketched out the pattern on sheets of newspaper then fitted and pinned it around Elsie's slender frame.

'All we need now is a bit of silk and lace,' she said with great confidence.

'Silk and lace!' Agnes scoffed. 'There's a war on!'

'We're not having our little Elsie getting wed in sack-cloth and ashes,' Lillian said firmly. 'This will be "fashion on the ration",' she said, quoting one of the familiar slogans of the day.

When they had an hour to spare Emily and Alice went into Pendle to scrounge anything they could from friends and family. Alice's mum didn't want to part with her wedding dress, which she was keeping for Alice, but she had her sister's old one stored in the attic. It was faded and moth-eaten in parts but the old-fashioned style was a bit like the wedding dress worn by Elizabeth Bowes-Lyon, now Queen of England, and it had plenty of good cream lace. In a pawn shop they found a length of satin that just needed a proper wash, and Mrs Carter donated her wreath and wedding veil.

'I've kept them wrapped up on the top shelf of the wardrobe for twenty-five years,' she said. 'It's about time they were put to good use.'

'All sorted!' said Lillian gleefully.

Using a hand-driven Singer sewing machine with a heavy treadle, Agnes and Lillian took it in turns to stitch the dress whilst Elsie watched them in rapt delight.

'It's beautiful,' she sighed. 'So, so beautiful.'

Elsie had grown up darning socks and mending thread-bare clothes but she'd never done delicate needle work and she took to it with great enthusiasm once Agnes showed her how to sew a fine seam.

Meanwhile Emily was in her element planning the wedding breakfast and the cake. Sitting at a canteen table during one of her breaks, she drank strong sweet tea as she wrote down a long list of ingredients. Agnes and Alice settled down beside her with wedges of toast, marg and rhubarb jam.

'Where are you going to get all that sugar and dried fruit?' Agnes asked.

'If we pool together all our food coupons –' Emily started.

'Nowhere near enough!' Alice pointed out.

Emily slumped back in her chair.

'I know . . .' she groaned.

'You could make a cardboard cake and use fake icing . . . ?' Agnes tentatively suggested. Seeing Emily's blue eyes grow big with disapproval, she quickly went on, 'Betty in packing did that. She said it looked nice . . .'

'But tasted of nothing!' Emily laughed. 'Actually,' she said with a secret smile. 'I was thinking of Malc . . . ?'

Agnes and Alice shook their heads in unison.

'No chance,' Alice replied.

'He and Lillian avoid each other like the plague since the explosion,' Agnes reminded Emily.

'It wasn't Lillian I had in mind. I was thinking maybe Elsie could sweet-talk him?' Emily explained.

Agnes smiled.

'It's worth a go.'

Surprisingly, timid Elsie agreed to talk to Malc.

'He might bite your bloody head off!' Lillian warned.

'As long as he doesn't knock mi bloody 'ead off, I don't mind,' Elsie said cheerfully.

The next day Malc, ignoring Lillian, who glared at him from across the conveyor belt, walked up to Elsie on the cordite section.

'All sorted,' he said quietly in her ear. 'You'll have 'em by Friday.'

Elsie turned and smiled gratefully at Malc.

'Consider it a little wedding gift from me to you and Tommy,' he added awkwardly.

Then he quickly walked away before Elsie could say a word.

'What the 'ell 'ave you got that I haven't?' teased Lillian.

'I didn't do anything cheeky, like,' Elsie blurted out. 'Just said we was getting married.'

'It was always NORWICH when I asked him for any favours,' Lillian laughed.

'What's NORWICH got to do with anything?' innocent Elsie enquired.

Stressing each word, Lillian answered, 'Knickers . . . off . . . ready . . . when . . . I . . . come . . . home.'

Watched by her grinning friends, mystified Elsie slowly repeated her words.

'Knickers off ready . . .'

When the penny dropped, Elsie blushed to the edges of her turban.

'Ooh, Lillian!' she gasped in embarrassment.

As the conveyor belt rattled and rolled along and every girl on the line began to laugh, Elsie laughed so much tears rolled down her face.

Before things got out of control, Agnes called out to her section.

'Ladies! Can we forget about Norwich and get back to the business of bomb-making right here in Pendle!'

As Emily became inventive and creative with donated

food coupons and limited rations, Lillian, Elsie, Alice and Agnes sewed well into the night every night. Not only was there Elsie's wedding dress to make, there were their own bridesmaids' dresses too and a sweet little blue silk dress for Esther, who was going to be a flower girl. All the girls were determined they would manage to get her there.

Alice's imminent departure to London was the only thing that spoiled the happy, excited wedding planning.

'I'll be back for the wedding! It's not like I'm going forever,' Alice pointed out to Elsie, who got upset every time Alice talked about leaving.

'Promise you'll come back,' the anxious bride asked.

'Cross my heart and hope to die,' Alice said as she hugged Elsie, who immediately thought of something else to worry about.

'How're we going to finish your frock if you're in London?'

'I've cut out the pattern for her dress and I'll sew it whilst she's away,' Lillian assured Elsie.

'But what if she loses weight down in London?' Elsie persisted.

'Then we'll have to fatten her up as soon as she gets back!' Lillian joked.

Before Alice left for the War Office, she and her mother went on a shopping trip to Manchester. In the Cooperative department store Alice bought her heart's desire: a bright lilac tweed skirt, cut short and swirly, with a matching jacket and a natty navy-blue, military-style felt hat that framed her face and emphasized her dreamy silver-grey eyes.

Mrs Massey, who was torn between pride and sadness at her daughter's promotion, insisted that her daughter should have a number of new clothes. 'We can't have them southerners thinking we go about in clogs and rags in the north,' she joked.

Alice chose a mushroom-coloured crêpe dress trimmed with orange velvet ribbon plus a short grey summer coat and a pair of soft, navy-blue leather brogues.

'Sensible working shoes,' her mother said as the shop assistant parcelled up their purchases.

Back in the digs, as Alice showed off her new wardrobe, Emily returned from picking up post from their pigeonholes in the Phoenix. Without saying a word, she rushed into the room she shared with Alice and slammed the door.

'Oh-oh! Trouble,' Lillian whispered.

'I'll go,' Alice said.

She found Emily flat out on her bed, weeping bitterly into her pillow.

'He's finished with me,' she sobbed. 'Bill's dumped me!'

Alice picked up the letter that Emily had dropped on the bedroom floor.

A family friend saw you and a man on Pendle moors. I can't believe you could do this to me, Emily. I've loved you all my life, nobody else but you, yet whilst I'm away on active service you're running around with a fella in a Royal Canadian Air Force uniform.

You've broken my heart, Em.

You can keep the ring I bought for you but our engagement is over. Please don't get in touch with me again.

Bill

There was nothing Alice or any of the other girls could do to ease Emily's heartache. Lillian did whisper mutinously in the kitchen that she'd like to shoot the man who'd blabbed Emily's wicked secret to Bill.

'He should've kept his big nose out of other people's business,' she seethed.

'It's a small town,' Agnes reminded her. 'News gets around.'

As they comforted her with a hot-water bottle, a nip of brandy and a mug of cocoa, Emily continued to weep.

'What Bill doesn't know is that I stopped!' she cried. 'I knew what I was doing with Freddie was wrong and I stopped,' she repeated.

'Well, I'm not sure that would redeem you in Bill's eyes,' Lillian pointed out.

Removing her modest engagement ring, a tiny diamond set in marcasite, Emily returned it to the velvet box Bill had given her.

'I've hardly worn it since I got here,' she murmured. 'And now I'll never wear it again.'

Sobbing, she stuffed the box under her jumpers in the bottom drawer of the wardrobe. Then she climbed into bed, where she rolled into a ball and lay weeping in the foetal position till dawn.

The morning that Alice left the Phoenix she handed Emily an envelope.

'Will you take it to Henri at the airbase?' she asked.

White-faced Emily, who had dark bags under her eyes from days of crying and sleeping badly, looked puzzled, then remembered the man Alice had danced with at the swing night and nodded.

'It's just to tell him I'm going to London and won't be able to see him again,' Alice explained as she snapped the lock on her suitcase.

Emily looked at her curiously.

'Why not? It's not like you're never coming back here, is it?' she asked.

Alice shrugged as she lifted her case off the bed.

'There's no point in stringing him along,' she answered.

She was grateful that there was nobody in the digs but her and Emily, who had been given twenty minutes off by Agnes so she could accompany Alice to the nearest bus stop. Her farewells to Lillian, Agnes and heartbroken Elsie the night before had reduced Alice to streaming tears. Standing at the open door and looking back into the sitting room where they'd spent so many happy hours, laughing and chatting, sharing each other's secrets, Alice choked up again.

'What will I do without you all?' she whispered.

'We'll keep in touch and you'll be back for the wedding,' Emily said as she firmly guided Alice out of the digs and down the cobbled lane to the bus stop outside the Phoenix.

When the bus loomed up the girls embraced each other. Holding back tears, they smiled bravely then Alice hopped aboard.

'*À bientôt!*' she said with forced jollity.

'See you, cock!' Emily answered, using the old local endearment familiar to them both.

As the bus pulled away, she blew a kiss and waved.

'Take care, Al. Love you!' she called.

It was odd in the digs and on the cordite section without Alice. Her happy, smiling face and insightfulness were missed by all the girls, but it was Emily who suffered her going the most. Unhappy and nursing a broken heart, Emily preferred to be outside rather than inside after her shifts; walking the moors brought back happy childhood memories of Alice, which lifted her low spirits.

The afternoon that Emily set off to take Alice's letter to Henri at the Canadian airbase she wondered what she'd do if she bumped into Freddie.

It's not like I'm an engaged woman any more, she thought bitterly as she struck out over the hills with skylarks singing all around her. Forcing herself to stop thinking of Bill and the love she'd so carelessly destroyed, she quickened her step.

There's no point in beating yourself up about the past, she told herself. You've got to move on whether you like it or not.

As she neared the airbase, where she could see dozens of airmen busy about their daily routine, Emily's heart gave an involuntary lurch. It was impossible to hold back the images that surged into her head: Freddie's heart-stopping smile, his intense blue eyes, his husky Canadian accent and the unforgettable smell of pines and limes that she always associated with him. He'd turned on her last time they'd been together but perhaps she'd asked for it after pulling back. Maybe he deserved a second chance?

Emily muttered sternly to herself as she approached the main gates of the base, where the Canadian flag flapped briskly in the stiff north wind.

'Don't make a fool of yourself again, Emily Yates!'

When she enquired after Captain Laurent she was told that he was off base.

Taking a deep breath, she nervously asked, 'Is Lieutenant Bilodeau on base?'

The guard on duty checked the roster and shook his head.

'Sorry, ma'am, he's not available either.'

Feeling deflated, Emily left Alice's letter with the guard then walked back over the moors, where she was suddenly overcome with curiosity to see the old stable where things had gone so wrong with Freddie. Without a deep covering of snow the stable exterior looked dirty and decrepit, but just as she was turning away she heard loud girlish laughter coming from inside the building. Ducking down behind a boulder, she peeped out and saw Freddie walking out of the stable with a pretty young girl from the Phoenix on his arm. He stopped to gently remove straw from the girl's cardigan then his hand lingered there to caress her well-formed breasts.

'God, honey, you're gorgeous,' he said as he kissed her full on the mouth.

Wriggling and giggling with pleasure, the girl kissed him back then turned to go.

'Same time tomorrow?' he called after her.

'Same time,' she answered with a happy smile.

Emily slid down the boulder and crouched in the

heather where, blinking back tears of anger and shame, she raged at her own stupidity.

Of *course* there'd be a string of other girls, she thought. Like Lillian said, Freddie wouldn't nurse a broken heart when he could get what he wanted elsewhere.

When both Freddie and the girl had disappeared Emily stood up and, looking one last time at the dilapidated stable, she took a deep breath and set off across the moors for home. She lifted her face to the falling rain and let it mingle with her tears. What a price she'd paid for a kiss and a cuddle. A few mad, infatuated hours had cost her the best man she'd ever known, and all for a player like Freddie. Stumbling and sobbing, Emily headed back to the digs and the comfort of her waiting friends.

Chapter 14: Helford House

Wearing her new lilac tweed suit and navy-blue hat, Alice felt a lot more confident when she walked into the War Office than on the previous occasion.

At least I look fashionable, she thought to herself.

Thinking she would be given a briefing, Alice was surprised when a prim, middle-aged secretary simply handed her a letter then returned to tapping away on her Remington typewriter. As the machine dinged back and forth in the background, Alice opened the envelope and took out a railway ticket and a letter which instructed her to take the twelve forty-five from Paddington to Helston in Cornwall where she would be met on arrival. Baffled, Alice folded up the letter, pocketed the ticket and picked up her case before doing exactly as she was told.

Paddington was packed with servicemen, mostly sailors blocking the way as they lounged on the ground, leaning against their bulging duffle bags and smoking. Amidst a chorus of wolf whistles and appreciative winks from admiring young men happy to see a beautiful girl, Alice made her way to the train on platform ten. Luckily her seat had been pre-booked. After stowing her case in the overhead netted luggage rack, Alice settled in a corner and watched bomb-torn, ravaged London drift by. She stared in horror at the ruins of suburban Acton, Ealing Broadway, Wormwood Scrubs, where MI5 were housed,

Southall and Slough. The barrage balloons receded as the train gathered speed and cast plumes of thick smoke in its shadow as they rumbled through Slough and Reading, both devastated by air strikes. Once past Swindon the English countryside opened up before her, vernal green and breathtaking in the sunshine. Desperate for air, Alice pulled on the leather strap to open the window and release the dense cloud of cigarette smoke that had built up since their departure from Paddington.

The train slowly emptied out at Bristol and at Exeter, and by the time they left Plymouth there wasn't a sailor in sight. Starving hungry and very thirsty, Alice had enough time to pop out of the train at Bodmin station to buy a cup of tea and a stale bun. As the train continued on its journey, the sun slowly set over the sea. Alice sighed as she watched it slide over the horizon in a blaze of red and gold. When confronted by such perfect beauty it was impossible to believe that, just across the English Channel, a mad German was hell-bent on a world war that was destroying the happiness of millions.

Lulled by the rattle of the wheels on the track, Alice fell asleep, then woke with a start when the train pulled into Truro. Standing on the dark platform with a cold wind gusting around her, she shivered as she waited for the train to Helston. Tired, hungry and cold, she wondered when this long journey from the north-west would ever end. A slow, local train puffed up to the platform and, after it had stopped at numerous empty stations to pick up the night mail, Alice finally disembarked at Helston at nearly midnight. She waited for the train to clank away in a plume of smoke then, blinking in the dark, she looked around for her lift. There was nobody on the platform but a car parked behind a picket fence flashed its lights and Alice approached.

'Are you the lady from the War Office?' the driver enquired.

Alice nodded.

'Hop in!'

The journey through the night over rutted moorland tracks seemed endless but eventually, after what seemed like hours, the car stopped and Alice walked towards a darkened entrance hall where a tired housekeeper in a dressing gown stood waiting for her.

'Breakfast's at eight,' she said as she showed Alice to an overnight guest room.

Yawning, Alice slipped out of her clothes and into her warm winceyette nightdress. She managed to stay awake long enough to clean her teeth then fell asleep to the sound of water lapping outside her bedroom window.

Alice would have slept the morning through if she hadn't been awakened by the sound of clattering feet hurrying down the corridor just outside her room.

'Aargh! Ten to eight,' she cried as she checked her watch and leaped out of bed.

Flinging back the curtains, she gasped at the sight of a sweeping garden running down to the banks of a wide, rushing river. With no time to admire the view, Alice put on clean underwear, a fresh blouse and her new suit. She threw water on her face and pulled a brush through her glistening hair then hurried along the winding corridor wondering what her first day would bring.

After a hearty breakfast of boiled eggs, toast and fresh

coffee the trainees were taken into an oak-panelled drawing room that overlooked the gardens and river. Alice was surprised at the mix of thirty people, roughly one-third women and two-thirds men, who, on first encounter, appeared to be from all walks of life and occupations. As she chatted to Gwynne from Aberystwyth, she noticed a good-looking man across the room peering at her as he lit up his pipe. Blushing, Alice caught his smile then quickly turned away as the introductory meeting got underway.

Brigadier Russell Kingsley welcomed the newcomers in English but told them that from now on they would be speaking only in French.

'Welcome to Helford House,' he said.

Alice smiled to herself. At last I know where I am, she thought.

'*Alors, nous continuons en français*. We have prepared a programme of work that will help you out in the field and in some cases might save your lives. So pay attention. An eye for detail is vital at all times,' he said. 'The first thing we need to do is iron out any trace of accent or any incorrect grammar. The wrong noun or the wrong accent could get you shot,' he added gravely. 'You'll be taught the art of surveillance and counter-surveillance, how to receive, decode and transmit encrypted wireless messages, how to assemble a bomb, load a revolver and kill the enemy. Listen well, learn quickly.'

Continuing to speak in French, he explained that the new recruits would start with exercises to teach them techniques on arranging clandestine meetings and establishing communications. '*Bonne chance!*' he concluded.

As they split up into teams, the pipe-smoking man introduced himself to Alice.

'How do you do? I'm Robin Fairfax.'

'Pleased to meet you,' Alice replied formally. 'I'm Alice Massey.'

'*En français, s'il vous plaît!*' the Brigadier barked.

'*Pardon, monsieur,*' Robin said with a wink at Alice.

For their first lesson, led by a middle-aged French-woman called Monique, the agents had to give a concise description of a person in another team and set up a contact point where they would meet.

'Each team must use its own initiative as to how they'll make contact and rendezvous with the link man or woman, using pre-arranged passwords,' Monique instructed. '*Alors, on y va!*'

Laughing awkwardly to start with, the groups quickly got into the exercise, agreeing passwords then adding clues that would help the go-between make contact. In no time at all Alice quickly realized that though the exercises might initially seem a bit silly, acted out in a sun-drenched, oak-panelled drawing room in a lovely part of England, they were in fact an effective way of building up group rapport and improving their French vocabulary. When Alice, in a flurry of nerves, said she was standing on the ceiling instead of walking across the floor everybody burst out laughing. Shortly afterwards a sweet-looking girl called Gladys completely messed up her sentence; she said she was singing in the hills instead of sitting in the park.

Monique smiled bleakly then said, '*Attention! Pas d'erreurs, s'il vous plaît!*'

The smile fell off Alice's face. Monique was right: it was vital to pay attention because a silly mistake would definitely cost lives.

After each exercise the trainees were tested by interrogators on their cover story. Alice was terrified of them breathing down her neck, barking commands at her in French and demanding immediate, precise answers. It was an adrenalin-driven ordeal that went on every day, sometimes two or three times a day, and it was exacting, nerve-wracking and utterly exhausting.

It was impossible not to bond with everybody. They were Special Ops in training, Churchill's Secret Army, who might one day be called upon to put their life on the line for one of their team.

In the four-berth female dorm Alice discovered a similar camaraderie to the one she'd enjoyed in her Phoenix digs. She, Gladys from Coventry, Gwynne from Aberystwyth and Iris from Bristol were good friends by the end of the first week of training. But here, unlike at the Phoenix, they had to chat in French. The French-speaking rule was upheld at all times, even in the dorm and the bathroom; Alice even began dreaming in French!

At the end of a long day, lying stretched out on the sunny lawn, with the lovely Helford River gurgling by, the girls teased each other about the numerous handsome men they were training with.

'Robin can't take his eyes off Alice,' Gladys said as she gave her a dig in the ribs.

'*En français!*' Alice scolded.

'Oh, bugger that!' laughed Gladys as she yawned and rubbed her tired eyes.

'He's an interesting man,' Iris said. 'A writer at the BBC.'

'He's also gorgeous,' teased Gwynne. 'Come on, Al, admit it, you fancy him!'

'I do like him!' Alice laughed. 'But I'm not sure how much he likes me.'

Gladys winked.

'I don't think it'll take long to find out!' she chuckled.

The next day, in one of their surveillance and counter-surveillance exercises, mischievous Alice laid a convoluted trail for Robin that led him into the Ladies, which was their designated contact point. Sitting on the toilet seat, she bit her lip in order to stop herself from giggling. When Robin knocked three times on the toilet door Alice gave the pre-arranged response.

'*Enchantée, monsieur,*' she said.

'*Vous avez* Le Monde?' he asked.

Alice opened the door and gaped at Robin; how could she have forgotten to bring with her to the contact point the clue that was vital to her identity? Casting about, she improvised; grabbing a toilet roll, she handed it over to an astonished Robin with a confident flourish.

'*Voilà*, Le Monde!' she said as she burst into peals of laughter.

Every night after supper the trainees would gather at the bar for a drink and chat through the events of the day. Sometimes Alice, too brain dead to speak another word of French, preferred to walk in the grounds and soak up the peaceful tranquillity of the lovely Helford River. As she sat in the twilight one night, listening to the distant hoot of an owl, she felt a touch on her shoulder.

'*Ça va, mon amie?*'

'Too tired to speak French,' Alice replied, grinning.

'Shall we risk a ticking-off and break the first rule of the house?' Robin chuckled as he hunkered down beside her.

Surprised that he had tracked her down, Alice said, 'I never imagined it would be so demanding.'

Settling comfortably beside her, Robin lit his pipe and puffed fragrant cherry-smelling tobacco smoke into the air.

'May I ask what made you sign up?'

'At first it was the excitement of going further with my French but I soon realized it was more than that,' Alice replied.

'I gather you were previously building bombs in a munitions factory,' he said.

Alice smiled; she was pleased to hear he'd been making enquiries about her.

'There are thousands of women all over England doing their bit for the war.' She paused before she added, 'I suppose I want to do more than fill shell cases.'

Turning to face him, Alice admired Robin's handsome profile etched sharply in the moonlight.

'What about you, Robin? What brought you here?'

'I was recruited from the BBC where I was writing news reports and doing some continuity,' he replied. His voice suddenly rang with a fierce intensity. 'I want to write about the real war, Alice, I want to see it, feel it – report it.'

Struck by his passion, Alice asked, 'When do you find the time to write?'

'At night,' he replied.

'*En français?*' she teased.

'*Bien sûr! Toujours en français!*'

Method actors were brought in to teach the new recruits simple ideas on disguise.

'We'll show you how small props can change your normal behaviour,' the lead actor explained. 'Really small things, like parting your hair the wrong way, walking with a limp, wearing a scarf or glasses, can immediately take you outside your normal self.'

Though the class began with riotous laughter as people limped around wearing glasses and fake moustaches, the amusement factor quickly faded as the trainees saw how effective the small props were and how they could transform their personality in a blink. After their exercises with the method actors Monique stressed how important it was to match their clothes to whatever role they were playing.

'Play the part one hundred per cent,' Monique told them. 'Take meticulous care with clothing and accessories; they *must* be exact replicas of items manufactured in France. Check buttons, seams, collars, ties, even cigarettes and matches, anything that suggests "British" could cost you your life.'

Monique went on to tell them about an experienced agent in Paris who went into a café and ordered a black coffee.

'Coffee is always black in France, and only a foreigner would use that expression. The agent was immediately arrested, interrogated and shot,' she ended bleakly.

Sombre moments like these, which brought the room to silence, reinforced the point that it was a dangerous world they were entering, a world where they needed permits and papers, properly stamped and water-marked, to fit their cover story and credentials. Alice and her friends were given crisp French franc notes which they were asked to soften in their bras!

'Need a hand getting them in there?' one of the men teased.

'I think we can manage!' Gwynne giggled.

The days were exciting, terrifying, exhausting, but for Alice the evenings, which she longed for throughout the day, were bliss. As their training progressed, Alice and Robin developed their own playful spin on spying, turning what they'd learned during the day into a bit of fun in their time off. One evening she entered the packed bar, where she found Robin with a crowd of colleagues; their eyes met and she winked twice; he swivelled his eyes towards the window overlooking the garden. Without another word or gesture, Alice turned and left the bar, but not before dropping the evening paper on the table next to the door.

Out in the beautiful garden under a huge copper beech tree, Alice rocked with laughter as Robin approached bearing two large gin and tonics.

'That was the worst bit of clandestine behaviour I've ever seen!' she giggled as she took her proffered drink. 'I must have looked like I had a tic in my eye!'

'You always look breathtaking,' Robin said as he slipped an arm around her slender waist and led her along the garden path to the river.

'What must the others think we're up to?' Alice mused as they sat down on the riverbank.

'What do you think they think?' he asked softly.

Alice held his intent gaze.

'I don't care!' she replied.

Sensing she'd said too much, she blushed and turned away.

But Robin gently took hold of her chin in order to turn her face back to him.

'You little northern madam,' he teased as he pulled her close and kissed her.

The touch of his warm lips roused Alice, who up until now had little experience of men. She folded her arms around his neck and kissed him back with equal passion.

Pulling away from her, Robin chuckled softly.

'My word! For a girl who looks like an angel you kiss with a punch!'

Alice's eyes sparkled in the moonlight.

'What were you expecting from a secret agent?' she teased.

As nightingales sang in the warm night air, neither of them wasted time with words. Under the shadow of a copper beech, wrapped in each other's arms, they kissed until dawn.

Alice was flabbergasted when she and the other female spies were issued with sexy black underwear.

'Just in case,' Brigadier Kingsley said with a cryptic smile.

'Just in case *what*?' asked Iris as they tried on the new black lingerie in their dorm.

'Just in case we have to remove our knickers to take the Gestapo's mind off slitting our throats,' Gwynne replied without a hint of humour in her voice.

'But I'm a virgin,' Iris protested.

'That might make it all the more interesting for the enemy!' Gladys joked.

'Oh, God!' groaned Alice. 'We've got cyanide pills sewn into our hems for a quick exit and lace knickers to distract the Führer – what next?'

Chapter 15: Wedding Bells

Back on the Lancashire moors wedding preparations were in full swing. The day and time had been fixed around Tommy's leave but everybody was on tenterhooks, most of all Elsie. What if his leave was postponed? It wasn't an uncommon event; nothing stopped for the war, and everybody knew that.

'I could be left standing at the altar holding a bunch of flowers, like,' Elsie fretted.

'Come on, Elsie, think positive and trust in the Lancashire Fusiliers,' said Agnes briskly.

Just hearing the name of the regiment made Emily's heart lurch. She had found out just this week, after bumping into Bill's mum, that there had indeed – as Alice had suggested – been a perfectly innocent explanation for the fact that he hadn't managed to see her on his last visit home. He'd been given brief leave only once during his stay at the barracks and had immediately headed to the Phoenix; but he'd been denied entry till the end of her shift. *Why* had she been so pig-headed? If only she'd seen Bill she would never have thrown herself at Freddie Bilodeau.

'Penny for your thoughts?' Elsie teased when she saw Emily's brooding face.

Emily gave a quick smile.

'Oh, just working on the wedding menu. You know me, always thinking about food!' she joked.

Thanks to Lillian and Agnes the wedding dress and the bridesmaids' dresses were finished, and Lillian just needed to hem Esther's blue silk flower-girl dress when the little girl arrived in Pendle. The veil was washed and starched and Elsie's wreath was to be embellished with fresh wild flowers on the morning of her wedding.

Malc, who'd become the girls' go-between with Mr Featherstone, wangled compassionate leave so that in between her shifts Agnes could travel to Keswick to pick up Esther, then, after Elsie's wedding, return the little girl to Keswick hospital. It would be a rush but if it meant that Esther would walk down the aisle as Elsie's flower girl it was certainly worth it.

Elsie helped Emily print out the menus, one to be placed on each table in St Columba's church hall, where the wedding breakfast was to be served after the nuptial mass.

'First course,' Emily proudly read, 'Pendle boiled ham cooked in sage and thyme, fresh new potatoes, selection of salads, pickled beetroot and red cabbage.'

'Good we have the locals helping us out,' Elsie said gratefully. 'It would have been a veggie affair without Mrs Carter's neighbour donating half a side of bacon.'

'Good we have a thriving black market in Pendle,' Emily added. 'Where else would we have got a barrel of beer and sherry too? Second course,' she continued, 'rhubarb and ginger tart with ice cream.'

'I'll never know how you managed to find enough cream for the ice cream,' Elsie said incredulously.

'I didn't – some of it's not actually cream!' Emily confessed.

Elsie's eyes grew huge.

'Ooh, Em, you've not done anything dangerous like add chemicals?' she gasped.

'As if I'd ruin your wedding day by giving your guests the trots!' Emily laughed. 'I mixed dried milk and water in with the cream. How else could I spin it out among forty people?'

'Will it be all right in the canteen cold store?' Elsie asked.

'It's packed around with ice cubes and is solid as a rock,' Emily assured her anxious friend.

Elsie hugged Emily excitedly.

'You've all been so kind to me,' she said as tears sprang to her eyes. 'You're like the sisters I never had.'

'No time for tears,' Emily said as she hugged Elsie back. 'I've got to finish icing the wedding cake. Thank God every girl on the cordite line contributed their sugar rations otherwise it'd be a cardboard mock-up.'

Grabbing Elsie's hand, she pulled her towards the door.

'Come on, we've got to get it done before Alice arrives tomorrow,' she said happily.

Alice arrived at the Phoenix having spent a day and a night travelling from one end of England to the other. Glowing with happiness, she rushed into the digs, where she dropped her case and immediately threw her arms around her best friend.

Emily looked into Alice's radiant face and said knowingly, 'You've met someone.'

Alice nodded.

'I'm sooo in love, Em!' she cried. 'He's called Robin

Fairfax and he's brave and clever and very good-looking. I can't wait for you all to meet him.'

Rushing forwards, she embraced Elsie and Lillian too.

'Is he loaded?' Lillian teased.

Alice's eyes sparkled. 'Yes, he's that too!'

Lillian, Elsie and Emily had finished their shift for the day so they were free to spend all night chatting and laughing with Alice, who they'd missed dearly.

'So why did they move you to Cornwall?' Lillian asked.

Before she left Helford, Alice and Robin had carefully prepared answers to difficult questions.

'It's important you don't put your friends in an awkward position; make it simple,' he'd said on their last evening sitting by the river. 'Say you were sent here to attend a crash course in advanced French.'

'That's a good idea,' Alice had said, running kisses down his neck and under his shirt. 'Shall I tell them that my favourite place for lovemaking is right here on the banks of the river?'

Robin had buried his face in her fine, silky, blonde hair.

'I'll miss you, darling.'

'I'll miss you too, my love.'

'So why waste time talking about it?' Robin had laughed softly as he pulled Alice down beside him.

'At least I won't have to talk French all the time in Pendle,' Alice had joked.

'I'm there for an advanced crash course in French,' Alice said, repeating Robin word for word.

'And then what? Where next?' Emily asked.

Alice shrugged.

'I have no idea,' she answered in all honesty.

Long after midnight, tucked up and cuddling hot-water bottles in the bedroom that they used to share together, Alice dared to broach the subject she knew Emily was avoiding. In the darkness, with a soft rain spattering against their window, she said, 'Have you heard from him?'

Emily didn't need to ask who.

'Not a word since he sent me the letter,' she replied. 'Mum says he's been home on leave but he's not been up here to see me.'

'It'll take time, Em,' Alice said gently. 'He's a proud lad, always has been.'

'And I'm an idiot, always have been,' Emily groaned.

'You lost your head; I know what that feels like since I met Robin. I'm crazy about him.'

'Like I was crazy about Bill till I met sweet-talking Freddie, who couldn't wait to get my knickers off.'

Alice let a few minutes pass before she said, 'Have you seen Freddie?'

'I tried to see him when I delivered your letter to Henri,' she admitted. 'He wasn't on the airbase but I did see him when I was walking over the moors.'

'Did you talk?'

Emily gave a bitter, hard laugh.

'It was hardly the right moment, Al. He was with another woman; they were leaving the old stable where he took me.'

'Oh . . .' Alice's voice trailed away.

Wretched Emily burst into tears.

'Lillian got it right. He was never interested in me! He's a player and he'll go where he can get it.'

Alice jumped out of bed and gathered Emily into her

arms, then sitting beside her she rocked her friend slowly back and forth until her sobs had subsided.

'You and Bill are meant for each other,' she soothed.

'And we would be with each other if it wasn't for stupid me!' Emily wailed.

Alice remained silent; it wasn't the best moment to agree with Emily when she said that Freddie had been the biggest mistake of her life.

When Agnes arrived with her daughter she was beaming with pride. Their reunion in the Keswick hospital had been a joy, their train journey south full of laughter and excitement, and now here she was, standing holding her daughter's hand, about to share her for the first time with the four women in the world she loved the best.

'I'd like you to meet Esther,' she said with a choke in her voice.

Emily, Lillian and Elsie had rushed back to the digs after they'd finished their shift, keen to meet the little girl they'd heard so much about, but Esther, overwhelmed by shyness at the sight of them, hid behind her mother's skirts.

'It's all right, cherub,' said Agnes as she guided Esther to stand next to her. 'Emily, Lillian and Elsie are my best friends.'

Esther peeped out and solemnly eyed the girls, who were enchanted by her long, dark curly hair, huge brown eyes and skin as pale as alabaster.

Typically it was Elsie who knew instinctively how to approach the shy, serious little girl.

'Would you like a sweetie, pet?' she said as she offered Esther a toffee.

The little girl's eyes grew even bigger at the sight of the treat, and limping on her calliper she slowly approached Elsie, who hunkered down to be on the same level as Esther.

'Thank you for coming all this way to be mi bridesmaid,' Elsie said as she gently kissed the little girl on the cheek.

'Are you the beautiful bride?' Esther asked shyly.

'Well, I'm hoping to be tomorrow, pet!' Elsie joked.

Lillian swept Esther up into her arms.

'Come on; let's try on your bridesmaid's dress!'

After visiting her mum in town Alice joined the girls later and they had a happy, giggly, girlie night drinking nips of sherry, although Elsie and Esther stuck to lemonade, whilst they all tried on their dresses.

'I'm a princess!' cried Esther as she limped round and round in a circle, swirling the skirt of her blue dress around her.

'You're the most beautiful princess I've ever seen!' Lillian said with tears in her eyes.

The tears soon flowed unchecked as Esther threw herself into Lillian's arms and hugged her tightly.

'Thank you, William,' she said, sweetly mispronouncing her name. 'Thank you for making me beautiful!'

'The pleasure's all mine, darling . . . and you can call me William anytime you want!' Lillian added as she burst out laughing.

Agnes, Emily, Elsie and Lillian hadn't been allowed time off work just because Esther was in town. They'd had difficulty enough getting a day off work for the wedding, though Elsie had been granted a weekend's leave for her brief honeymoon. So for a few days Esther had been obliged to fall into the factory's routine. She'd been dispatched to the Phoenix nursery, which she tolerated because as soon as their shift was over the girls collected her and took her back to the digs, where she slept in the same single bed as her mum. During Esther's brief visit the digs rang with the delightful sound of her excited laughter.

When Emily took Esther out on to the moors to pick thyme and sage for the wedding-breakfast ham she was astounded by the child's determination to walk unaided. Half skipping and half limping, Esther made her way to the top of a small tufty mound where she picked sprigs of thyme.

'Mmmm, it smells nice and sweet,' she said. 'Can I eat it?'

'Yes, but not too much; we don't want you dashing to the toilet during the wedding,' Emily teased.

Esther burst into a fit of giggles.

'I might spoil my bridesmaid's dress,' she said as she hiccupped with laughter.

Emily gazed at Esther and smiled; she was the most adorable child she'd ever met. Behind her solemn curiosity was a mischievous, happy spirit with a bravery the likes of which Emily had never before seen in a child. As Emily stroked the little girl's long dark curls, she saw a lanky man in army uniform striding up the hill to the digs.

'TOMMY!' she gasped.

Grabbing Esther with one hand and holding the basket of herbs in the other, she ran as quickly as she could towards Tommy, who grinned shyly, showing the gap between his two front teeth.

'Hiya, cock!' he said.

Forgetting formalities, Emily laid a hand on his shoulders.

'Where are you going?' she panted, breathless after her sprint down the hill.

With his eyes alive with anticipation, Tommy replied with a bit of a swagger, 'To see mi fiancée!'

'You can't!' Emily cried as she gave him a gentle backwards nudge.

'Why not?' he asked as he resisted her nudge. 'I've just come home from Africa and I've not seen Elsie for months!'

'It's bad luck!' Emily retorted.

'Bad luck to be back home and alive and wanting to see the woman I love!'

Emily took a deep breath as she steered him away from the digs.

'What I mean is it's bad luck to go in there – you might see Elsie's dress and spoil the surprise,' she explained.

Hearing the word 'dress', wide-eyed Esther tumbled to what was going on.

'You're the handsome prince!' she cried.

Liking the romantic description, Tommy ran a hand through his short, mousy-brown hair and threw back his skinny shoulders.

'You could say that, lovie!' he replied. 'I've come 'ere seeking mi princess!' he added proudly.

'I'll go and get her,' Esther replied excitedly. 'I'm her flower girl. I'm sure it's all right for you to see her for a few minutes, though Lillian might be painting her toes red at the moment!'

Emily gave her a playful shove and sent her on her way. 'Hurry up, Tommy's not got all day,' she chuckled.

Thrilled as she was to see Tommy, she couldn't help but watch Esther scamper away. Nobody would ever think she was sick, thought Emily, as the little girl hopped and skipped down the cobbled path to their digs.

Before Elsie arrived, Emily quickly turned to Tommy.

'How are things out there?' she asked anxiously.

The happy smile fell from Tommy's face as he blurted out, 'Bloody awful! It's better now Montgomery's in charge. He's a bloody legend. Him and his Desert Rats are pushing further and further north.'

Emily's heart dropped like a brick. Was Bill part of that battalion leading the big push?

'I don't suppose you've seen Bill?'

Tommy avoided her penetrating blue eyes as he answered non-committally, 'He's all right.'

Then he quickly changed the subject, saying, 'Bloody scorching hot out there, well into th'undreds, day after sodding day –'

He stopped short as a high-pitched scream pierced the air.

'TOMMEEEE!'

Radiant with happiness, Elsie, with her arms flung wide, was hurtling up the lane towards them.

'Tommy . . . Tommy . . . Tommy!' she cried over and over again before she landed in his arms and burst into tears of joy.

'Oh, my love,' she sobbed before Tommy stopped her mouth with his kisses.

On Elsie's wedding morning the girls washed, dressed

and made themselves up in a flurry of excitement, but not before Elsie walked out on the moors with Esther very early in the morning to pick wild flowers for her bridal wreath and bouquet. As the skylarks wheeled over them and the first swallows swooped by, they laughed as they gathered ox-eye daisies, cow parsley and wild anemones. Elsie held back, encouraging Esther to go ahead and discover the flowers herself. Carrying an overflowing basket, they returned to the digs to find Lillian in her knickers and bra standing over Agnes with hot curling tongs.

'You won't recognize yourself by the time I've done with you, Agnes,' Lillian promised.

Agnes looked at the hot curling tongs in dismay.

'What have you got in mind?' she asked anxiously.

Lillian winked.

'Put it this way: move over, Rita Heyworth!'

Sitting having her hair done on the morning of Elsie's wedding, holding her daughter in her arms and watching her friends wriggle into their salmon-pink silk dresses, Agnes smiled as she realized she hadn't felt so happy in years.

At 11 a.m., Malc, who Elsie had asked to give her away, swooped up in his big old Austin to collect the bridal party.

'Hop in, Canary Girl,' he said as he and Lillian exchanged a forgiving smile.

Tommy and Elsie were married in the local Catholic church. The aged Irish priest made the Latin nuptial mass interminably long, but nobody cared. It was a simple joy to be brought together as a community to bless the wedding of two young people so much in love. Elsie, in her 'fashion on the ration', simple home-made gown glowed with radiant happiness whilst Tommy, dashing in his Lancashire Fusiliers uniform, couldn't stop smiling. Elsie wept as she gripped Tommy's hand in hers and made her vows in a voice that, for a girl so shy, was loud and assertive, as if she was announcing to the world that the drudgery of the past was over and a new wonderful life with the man she loved was beginning.

After the constant round of hardship, hunger and the drab greyness of their everyday working lives it was a pleasure to sit in a church drenched in rich colours reflected down from the stained-glass windows and to inhale the sweet smell of home-grown roses. It was also a pleasure to see people dressed in their Sunday best instead of uniforms and overalls, the costumes of war.

Emily's wedding breakfast, laid out on rows of trestle tables in the church hall, was a sight for sore eyes. For almost a minute before everybody sat down, there was a hushed silence as the guests' eyes feasted on fresh ham, home-made pies and ice cream.

'Bloody 'ell, lass,' said one appreciative guest after another to Emily, 'you should open a shop or write a recipe book, at least!'

Emily smiled happily as she sliced up the rhubarb and ginger tarts, topping each slice with a blob of vanilla ice cream.

'I couldn't have put this meal together without the Phoenix girls donating their food coupons for Elsie's wedding,' she replied.

'She's worth it!' laughed Tommy as he raised his pint of bitter in a toast to his new wife.

As Emily helped Mrs Carter and her friends wash dishes in the small kitchen attached to the church hall, she considered the suggestions that had just been thrown at her.

Nice ideas, but I've not got the money to open a shop and certainly not the time to write a book, she thought to herself.

She was interrupted by an excited Esther, who came skipping up and grabbed her soapy hands.

'Come on, Em!' she cried. 'The prince and princess are dancing!'

Emily and Esther ran into the hall, where Tommy and Elsie led the dancing to the sound of their favourite song by the Andrews Sisters, 'Don't Sit Under the Apple Tree'.

The bride and groom left the party at four o'clock to catch a train to Blackpool, where they planned to spend two nights together before Tommy returned to active service in North Africa.

Back in the digs after the wedding party there was a distinct air of deflation. Whilst Alice packed her case for a dawn start the following day, Agnes, afraid of upsetting Esther, tried to pack her daughter's case behind her back. Sensing mounting tension, Emily and Lillian took Esther, still in her bridesmaid's dress, for a walk on the moors.

'Why can't I stay and live with you for ever?' Esther asked the girls on either side of her.

Lillian and Emily exchanged a knowing look.

'One day, you and your mummy will live together for ever,' Emily assured Esther.

'And Daddy too?' Esther persisted.

Tears stung Lillian's eyes.

'God! How do we answer that?' she muttered under her breath.

Determined to stay upbeat, Emily replied firmly, 'And Daddy too, of course!'

And so the following day, whilst Lillian and Emily returned to the cordite line, Alice went south, back to Helford, and Agnes, with a heavy heart, went with little Esther north to Keswick.

As the conveyor belt rolled out shell cases ready to be filled with explosive and detonators, Emily grew pensive. When would she see Alice again and why hadn't she asked her a lot more questions about her future?

Chapter 16: Lillian's Yank

As victories were won in North Africa, the news boosted morale at home, for surely defeat would have an impact on the Germans and increase Britain's chances of winning the war and bringing the boys back from the front.

At the Phoenix morale was further enhanced by the sudden influx of American servicemen in the area. Not only had a squadron of US airmen moved onto an airbase nearby, but charismatic Yanks were now arriving at the factory every week, to deliver consignments of amatol and collect loaded bombs and rockets.

'God! I feel like I've died and gone to heaven,' said one of the munitions girls as she eyed up a handsome Yank in the canteen.

Lillian gave an appreciative wink, but since the explosion caused by her on the cordite line, for all her talk about 'fellas', she had seriously backed off. Malcolm's relationship with Emily, Elsie and Agnes was relatively easy and he had seriously helped all of them when needed: Elsie's wedding, Agnes's compassionate leave, Emily's frequent taking over of the canteen kitchen, to which he turned a blind eye. But his relationship with Lillian was cool, and it went both ways. Neither of them wanted to overstep the line again, and although Malc's eyes lingered over Lillian's hourglass figure at times, both were keen to move on. On top of this, Lillian had undergone a profound change when it came to men. Formerly she'd gone for rich, influential boyfriends who could make her life easier, help her through the irritating hardships of the war, but since the blast she had kept herself to herself.

'What's come over you?' Elsie teased.

'I'm saving myself for Mr Wonderful!' Lillian laughingly replied.

Then one day, as the strains of 'When They Begin the Beguine' drifted out from the factory wireless, Mr Wonderful did indeed walk into the Phoenix and into Lillian's life, in the form of Gary.

'The minute we caught sight of each other the world stood still,' Lillian later told her incredulous friends.

Lillian was instantly drawn to the sheer physical presence of the tall, blond, well-built, tanned American who moved through the room with ease and confidence. His smile was relaxed and friendly, his east-coast accent totally sexy, but for Lillian it was *him*, the man himself, who mesmerized her. It felt like a magnet had been planted inside her chest and she was being drawn inexorably towards him. Nothing on earth could have stopped Lillian from sitting down at the table where Gary sat smoking a Lucky Strike.

When Gary saw the swing of her long dark hair, the twinkle in her big dark eyes and the smile that parted her full pouting mouth to reveal small white teeth, his heart skipped a beat. With trembling hands he offered her a cigarette.

'Good morning to you. I'm Gary.'

'Hi! I'm Lillian,' she squeaked, hardly able to speak.

'I'm from Ohio,' he added with a grin.

'I'm from Bradford,' she replied, then said with a contagious giggle, 'We should have plenty in common!'

During that first unforgettable meeting, with the strains of 'When They Begin the Beguine' weaving its way through their conversation, Lillian learned that Gary, who she later described as 'the spit of Frank Sinatra – but taller and blond', had never been posted so far north since his arrival in England.

'I'll give you a tour of the area when you've time,' she instantly volunteered.

'That would be an honour, ma'am,' he replied with a slow smile.

'When he smiled I swear to God the earth moved,' Lillian told her pals later.

Hearing his superior officer shouting to him, Gary shot to his feet and, standing before Lillian, he gave her a quick-smart salute that made her heart lurch.

'May I see you again, ma'am?' he said with the utmost civility.

Lillian just about managed to squeeze out a reply, though she could hardly breathe.

'Any time, Gary from Ohio!'

And with that he gave her a final grin and was off. Back at the digs Lillian went into overdrive.

'He is gorrrrgeous,' she told Emily, Elsie and Agnes. 'Gorgeous Gary from Ohio!'

It was hard for her friends to take Lillian's new crush seriously.

'I've never felt like this before,' she insisted. 'I've never met a man more perfect.'

Agnes smiled ruefully.

'I bet he's perfect,' she said. 'The Yanks, unlike us Brits who've been on food rationing since 1939, aren't starved of milk and meat and eggs, so no wonder they all look so fit and their teeth are shiny white. We're short of protein and calcium and undernourished by comparison.'

Lillian shrugged as she snatched Elsie up and started dancing her around the room, all the while singing 'When They Begin the Beguine'.

'This is our song,' she said dreamily.

Still raw from her affair with sweet-talking Freddie and its heartbreaking repercussions, Emily shook her head at Lillian blissfully waltzing around the sitting room.

'I can't believe you, of all people, getting carried away by a Yank,' she said over Lillian's loud singing. 'You know what they say: over here, overpaid and oversexed!'

Unruffled by Emily's harsh words, Lillian replied without breaking the tempo of her steps.

'Gorgeous Gary from Ohio's not like that, just you wait and see!'

Gary searched Lillian out, and every time he came to the Phoenix they found time to be together, first for a cigarette and a chat, then, as he extended his stay, for long walks on the moors, where they lay kissing in the deep heather.

Their love bloomed and the force of it blew Lillian away; she had never known such emotion in her life. A worldly woman who thought she could handle any situation, she was weak at the sight of Gorgeous Gary from Ohio, as she always called him with a smile on her lips.

One afternoon, alone in the digs with the blackout blinds rolled down, Lillian received her first gift from

Gary: a bottle of American scent. Called Mary Chess White Lilac, it was exotically different from Lavender Water, the only perfume commonly available in Britain during the war years.

Lillian opened the bottle and inhaled the heady perfume then, smiling, she leaned back on the sofa.

'Put some perfume on me,' she said in a low, husky voice.

Gary's deep blue eyes grew wide with desire.

'Sure, honey?'

Lillian ran her hands through his wonderfully thick blond hair.

'Never surer,' she murmured.

Gary sat back and looked into Lillian's brown eyes, which were blazing with desire.

'Honey, I don't want to hurt you,' he said softly. 'I don't know how long I'll be posted here in the north, or where I'll go next. Our squadron could go anywhere, and we're only biding time here till we get orders to move on.'

'Gary . . .' she whispered. 'I really don't care.'

Gary grasped her hands and slowly kissed each of her small fingers.

'But I do,' he said firmly. 'I love you too much to play around.'

Lillian looked him straight in the eye as she laid one of his hands on her right breast.

'I love you too,' she said simply. 'I want to be with you for ever, and I don't think either of us is playing around.'

With his hand on Lillian's full, firm breast, Gary was having trouble sticking to his argument. Taking a deep breath, he said, 'What happens if I'm posted to an unknown destination tomorrow?'

'Then I'll wait.'

'What happens if I don't come back?'

'Then I'll have known love for the first time in my life and I won't regret a thing,' she said as she reached for the bottle of White Lilac. 'Now, are you going to do as I ask or do I have to do it for myself?'

Struggling to keep control of the passion raging inside him, Gary said, 'I –'

But Lillian stopped his mouth with her hand.

'I love you, Gary from Ohio, come what may.'

Gary started with a tiny dab behind her ears then ran his finger down the line of her neck and into her cleavage, where he slid his hand underneath her bra, slipping it off without any protest from Lillian. She reached up and pulled his face down onto her breasts, which he kissed; then, sweeping his palm over her slender ribcage, he kissed her navel and flat stomach.

'Stop!' Lillian said.

She rose to her feet and led Gary down the corridor to her bedroom.

'What about your housemates?' he asked as she pushed him onto her bed. 'Aren't they due home soon?'

Lillian smiled as she removed her underwear.

'I gave them sixpence each to go to the chip shop in Pendle.'

Smiling in anticipation, she climbed on top of Gary and whispered in his ear, 'Darling, they won't be home for hours!'

*

As Lillian and Gary's romance bloomed, and even though he and Lillian were no longer an item, Malc became both irritated and humiliated by their public shows of affection. Because he had no right to pick on Lillian in particular, he picked on the whole cordite line instead.

'Late this morning, ladies,' he'd say peevishly when they weren't.

Or, 'Taking an early break?' as the girls rushed out, eager for their first cuppa of the shift.

'He's picking on the lot of us because of Lillian taking up with Gary,' Emily pointed out.

'It's none of his bloody business who I see,' Lillian seethed.

'You're rubbing his nose in it,' Agnes said. 'Rushing across the canteen floor and throwing your arms around Gary every time he walks into the Phoenix.'

Lillian bridled at Agnes's criticism.

'Haven't you ever been in love, Agnes?' she snapped.

Agnes's face grew pale with anger but she kept her composure.

'Yes, with my husband, since you ask,' she replied with icy calm.

Lillian blushed to the roots of her long dark hair.

'Agnes, I'm sorry!' she blurted out as she grabbed her friend's hand. 'I wasn't thinking.'

'That's the point, Lil. You're not thinking about anything or anybody but Gary,' Agnes replied.

Elsie, who hated any kind of trouble, looked at Lillian imploringly.

'At least hold back on your canoodling when Malc's around,' she begged. 'He still carries a flame for you, pet.'

Lillian rolled her eyes.

'Malc's long gone; it's time he got over it.'

'He's quite capable of turning nasty, Lil,' Emily pointed out.

'He could get you into trouble with the boss, pet,' Elsie fretted.

Lillian looked at her friends and smiled.

'It's about time Malc took a long walk off a short pier!' she said with a loud laugh.

Emily was right; Malc did turn nasty. There wasn't a day went by when he didn't walk slowly down the cordite line checking the girls' every movement.

'Is that shell packed tight?'

'How many cases have you filled this morning?'

'Speed it up, ladies, we're not on our holidays,' he'd say sarcastically.

Luckily, under Agnes's experienced eye, her team didn't put a foot wrong.

'Ignore him, concentrate on the job, hum along to the music, think of something else if he starts,' Agnes advised her section.

Surprisingly it was Emily who broke the stalemate. Increasingly depressed and missing Alice more than she could ever have imagined, Emily couldn't stand Malc prowling up and down, watching them pack cordite into the shell cases.

'As you would say, Lillian, he's really getting on my tits!' Emily giggled.

'He got on my tits long ago!' Lillian laughed.

The situation blew one morning as the girls sang along to George Formby's 'When I'm Cleaning Windows' on the factory radio. Malc was peering over their shoulders and making comments that caused the hairs on the back of Emily's neck to stand on end as he approached.

'Whilst you're fooling around singing along to bloody George Formby, our boys are dying on the front line for lack of bombs and ammo. Get your fingers out!' he almost shouted.

It was poor little Elsie who broke under the pressure of his words, and it was ironic that it should have been her as she was without doubt his favourite little lass. Bursting into tears, she sobbed.

'Don't talk like that, Malc. My husband's one of them boys on the front line and I would rather die than not do my job for King and country!'

Gathering herself together, she turned to Agnes and said, 'Excuse me.' Then, without another word, she fled across the factory floor.

Before Agnes could say a word to Malc, who was visibly shaken by gentle Elsie's reaction, Emily totally lost it.

'How could you say such a thing when Elsie's out of her mind with worry about Tommy?' she raged.

'She's not heard from him since they got married,' Agnes icily pointed out.

Malc looked uncomfortable but he pretended to shrug it off.

'It's not my job to keep track of everybody's relationship.'

Emily stormed towards Malc.

'Emily, don't!' Lillian warned as she tried to grab her by the arm, but Emily was well past cautioning.

'You've been breathing down our necks for weeks, picking and criticizing everything we do. If you've got a gripe, be a man and spit it out instead of intimidating the workers.'

Malc's dark bushy eyebrows shot up.

'Are you accusing me of intimidation in the workplace, Miss Yates?'

'Yes!' Emily replied without a moment's hesitation.

Behind her back, Agnes groaned.

'Oh, no, now she's done it.'

Furious Malc eyeballed equally furious Emily for a few seconds before he snarled, 'I think you need to air your grievances with Mr Featherstone, young lady.'

'I think I do!' Emily retorted.

After her long meeting with Malc and Mr Featherstone Emily returned to the digs to find her friends anxiously awaiting her.

'What happened?' Lillian, Elsie and Agnes cried in unison as Emily walked through the door.

'Case to be considered,' said Emily as she sank into a chair. 'Suspended until the case has been decided,' she added grimly.

'Well, I suppose that's one way of getting off work,' Lillian joked.

'Oh, Em, you should never have gone and defended me,' said Elsie, on the brink of tears.

Emily smiled at her sweet, anguished face.

'It wasn't just you, lovie,' she answered softly. 'He's been looking for a fight since Lil took up with Gary.'

'Why couldn't you just have ignored the narky sod?' Lillian asked.

Emily slumped further back into the chair.

'I dunno. He just pushed me too far.'

'What're you going to do now?' Agnes asked.

'I can't stay here,' Emily replied. 'I've got to leave the Phoenix.'

Elsie smiled as she tried to look on the bright side.

'It'll be nice to spend some time at home, pet,' she said.

Emily shook her head.

'I'm not letting on to Mum and Dad about this,' she said. 'I'm going to see Alice . . . She'll talk some sense into me!'

'But we don't know where she is,' Agnes pointed out.

'She said if we sent mail to the War Office it would be forwarded to her. I'll write today,' Emily replied.

Sweet, generous Elsie looked wide-eyed at Emily.

'Do you need any money for the train fare to visit her?' she asked.

'I'm all right, lovie. I've got a bit saved up,' Emily replied with a hint of her old smile. 'It's not like there's much to spend your money on in Pendle!'

Emily's letter went off and the War Office must have forwarded it immediately because very soon Emily received a telegram from Alice saying she had been granted a short leave. Emily's blue eyes sparkled with excitement as she scanned the telegram.

'I'm going to see Alice in London!' she told her friends.

'I hope you'll come back happier,' Lillian teased. 'I've had enough of your mopey moods!'

The day Emily left was unusually mild for the time of year, and Lillian and Gary took advantage of their free time to walk on the moor.

'Tell me about how you grew up,' Lillian said as they lay in a bed of warm heather near Witch Crag.

'Why?' he teased as he tickled her cheeks with a prickly fern leaf.

'Because I want to imagine what it'll be like when we bring up our children in America,' she replied honestly.

'And who said a cheeky little Brit like you is going to the US of A?' he asked with a smile.

'Wherever you go, I go!'

He bent to gather her up in his arms.

'That's true, honey,' he said as he pressed his lips to hers and felt the line of her little white teeth, which he parted so he could kiss her more deeply. 'But . . .' he added on a more serious note.

'But what?' she asked sharply. 'You're already wed?'

Gary threw back his handsome blond head and hooted at the idea.

'No way, babe. I've been waiting all my life for you.'

'So what's the *but* . . . ?'

The smile fell from his face to be replaced by a still, thoughtful expression. 'There's a war on, sweetheart.'

'That must be why I'm doing a seventy-hour week packing bomb cases!' she joked.

'No kidding, Lil,' he retorted. 'We don't know when this damn war will end, and I could be called away like that,' he said, snapping his fingers with a hard click. 'I told you, babe – my squadron is only posted up here whilst we wait for orders from the top. We're a bomb squadron, so when the action kicks off we'll be kept busy. And it won't be on this side of the Channel,' he ended bleakly.

'But you'll always come back to me, won't you?' she said, suddenly scared of what he might say next.

He took hold of both her hands and stared deeply into her troubled brown eyes.

'Listen very, very carefully to me, Lillian. I will *always* come back to you. Even if it takes me a lifetime, I will *always* come back.'

Tears rolled unchecked down Lillian's face. She could hardly speak for the emotion she felt, but she did manage to say the words that would live with her through the long years ahead: 'And I will always wait.'

They clung onto each other as if they would never let go, then Gary said, as he kissed each of her eyelids, 'Still wanna hear about Ohio?'

'Yes!' she laughed as she took his hankie and wiped away her tears.

'It was a pretty perfect childhood,' he said with a happy smile. 'Our home was in the country, in a small town called Darcy, set in a valley surrounded by a mountain range and pine forests. Dad had a farm where we grew fruit, mostly apples and pears, and acre upon acre of potatoes.'

Lillian closed her eyes as she lay back in his arms and imagined a place half the world away where her beloved grew up.

'Were you a naughty boy?' she asked with a cheeky smile.

'A little sod, as you would say,' he laughed. 'There are five of us, three boys, two girls, and we all helped out on the farm. I loved it. Climbing trees, playing in the big barn, horse-riding, skiing –'

Lillian sat bolt upright.

'Skiing on snow?' she gasped.

'Sure, you great doodle,' he teased. 'There's plenty of snow in the mountains of Ohio. I always wanted to join the air force and travel,' he continued. 'When the war started in Europe I couldn't wait to get over here and get in the thick of the fighting.'

Lillian gazed dreamily up into the vast blue sky where a goshawk hovered, quivering overhead.

'The US Air Force brought you to me and the US Air Force will take you away from me too,' she said prophetically.

She was right. Suddenly and without a word of warning, just as Gary had predicted, the US servicemen were withdrawn from the temporary delivery work they'd been doing at the Phoenix. At first Lillian assumed they'd just changed shift patterns, but when British soldiers drove up with the amatol consignment and drove away with the explosives, Lillian questioned them.

'Yanks have been withdrawn from service,' she was told.

'I can see that!' Lillian snapped when they stated the obvious. 'Do you know where they've been posted?' she asked, on the verge of tears.

'No idea, love,' a spotty lad in uniform replied.

Nevertheless, during her break times, heartsick Lillian paced the delivery area where Gary and his crew had previously drawn up.

'They've been hanging around waiting for orders from the top,' Agnes pointed out. 'The orders must have finally come through.'

Elsie nodded eagerly in agreement with Agnes.

'That's right. It's not like it's just Gary that's disappeared; it's all the other Yanks too,' she said, earnestly hoping her words would comfort Lillian, which they didn't.

Lillian sadly shook her head.

'He'd write and let me know. He'd never just dump me,' she said with utter conviction.

'Who says he's free to write?' Agnes asked. 'If his squadron are on high alert they'll be holed up in the middle of nowhere with no communication with the outside world.'

Very quickly Lillian lost all pride and stooped to begging Malc for information. Looking at her gaunt grey face minus the usual glitzy make-up, he just shrugged.

'Bloody Yanks have been posted elsewhere, that's all I know,' he said as he turned to walk away from her.

Desperate, Lillian grabbed him by the arm.

'Where? Do you know where, Malc?'

Malc shook her hand off.

'Do I 'ell,' he snapped. 'Bloody good riddance to the bastards!'

Chapter 17: London Weekend

All the trainees were due a short break at the end of the week. They'd worked hard and many were looking exhausted.

'Back 1200 hours, Monday,' barked the Brigadier.

Robin, Alice and several other Special Ops had started making plans to go to London when Emily's letter arrived. Alice, thrilled at the thought of seeing her best friend so soon, immediately sent her a telegram with instructions on where to meet.

The girls, overjoyed to see each other, booked into a cheap B&B just off Charing Cross Road then made their way to a nearby Lyons café, where Alice ordered tea and carrot buns whilst Emily picked up the menu and scoured it with a critical eye.

'Lord Woolton Pie: leeks, swedes, turnips, parsnip and carrots – ugh! Murkey: mock turkey with sausage meat – no, thanks. Rabbit stew could be interesting. Kidneys fried with onions? That might be tasty . . .'

After waiting patiently for well over a minute Alice gave her absorbed friend a nudge.

'When you've finished rearranging Lyons' menu I want to know why you were suspended.'

Emily smiled an impish smile.

'Lip!'

'Oh, Em, that temper of yours will be the undoing of you,' Alice cried.

'I would have bottled it if you'd been around,' Emily replied as she crumbled cake on her plate. 'I miss you, Al. You've always had a steadying influence on me.'

'Who did you fly at?' Alice asked.

'Malc.'

Alice rolled her eyes.

'God! You really pick 'em,' she chuckled.

'He was winding us up on purpose because he's jealous of Lillian's American boyfriend,' Emily explained, then smiled as she continued, 'She calls him Gorgeous Gary from Ohio!'

A tired-looking waitress delivered their tea, which Alice poured as Emily inspected their carrot buns.

'Erm, would have been sweeter and moister with a sprinkle of coconut,' she said.

She took the cup of tea Alice offered.

'So when am I going to meet Gorgeous Robin from the BBC?' she teased.

'Tonight,' Alice said excitedly over their second cup of tea. 'He's meeting us later on. He's bringing an old school friend so you won't feel like a gooseberry,' she added with a smile.

Putting on a posh voice, Emily asked, 'Eton or Harrow?'

'Harrow, actually,' Alice laughed.

Emily rolled her blue eyes.

'Well, he's not going to like me with my northern accent and cheap clothes,' she answered.

'He'll like you well enough . . . as long as you don't lose your temper,' Alice giggled. 'Talking of your foul temper, tell me what happened with Malc.'

'He just kept on picking and picking, breathing down

our necks, then he started talking about us not producing enough bombs for our boys on the front line.'

'That sounds nasty,' Alice said hotly.

'It was!' Emily retorted. 'And the person he hurt most was sweet little Elsie, who's not heard from Tommy since their honeymoon. She ran out of the factory sobbing her heart out and I . . . I just lost it.'

'Sounds like Malc was being a pig,' Alice said.

'And to Elsie of all people. You know how fond he is of her,' Emily added. 'From the look on his face when she ran out, he knew he'd gone too far.'

'Then what?'

'I was marched off to Featherstone's office and given a bollocking for insubordination then suspended until my case has been considered,' Emily concluded.

'Then we'd better make the most of it,' Alice said with a smile.

Emily looked Alice straight in the eye.

'I'm keen to meet this Robin fella; I want to see if he's up to scratch.'

'He's more than up to scratch,' Alice enthused. 'He's wonderful!'

'Good, so at least one of us won't finish up on the scrap heap,' Emily joked.

Alice gazed into her friend's lovely face, which was dominated by her big blue eyes and framed by a mass of tumbling auburn curls.

'I think the scrap heap is the last place you belong, Em!'

As they walked back to their cheap digs, Emily nodded at the barrage balloons, which were like huge silver worms blocking out the sky.

'Why are they everywhere?' she asked.

'They're supposed to confuse the enemy,' Alice replied. 'Come on,' she said as she tugged at Emily's arm. 'Don't dawdle or a warden will have us down an air-raid shelter for the night.'

The thought of being stuck in a bomb shelter for the night made Emily sprint down the pavement.

'We've got better things to do than sit in the dark, singing "Roll Out the Barrel"!' she giggled as they raced along the street together.

Back in the dingy B&B, with the blackout blinds pulled firmly down, the girls dumped their gas masks on the bed and for a few hours forgot about war-weary London right outside their window.

They shared a tepid bath then tried on each other's clothes in preparation for going out that evening. Emily, inches taller than Alice and curvier too, couldn't fit into her friend's tweed suit but she swanned around in her new military hat.

'You're so stylish, Alice,' she said, with a hint of envy in her voice.

'Mum kitted me out before I left Pendle,' Alice explained. 'Otherwise I'd still be wearing my old blue suit and cream blouse.'

'As soon as I get back home I'm going to take up the hems on all my skirts,' Emily said.

'We could make a paper pattern then Lillian could kit out all the Canary Girls with short skirts,' Alice laughed.

After doing each other's hair and borrowing each other's make-up they set off, threading their way along bombed streets, past unoccupied houses with gaping windows and blasted gable ends. Unable to believe the level of devastation, Emily lingered to stare at the mountains of rubble and row upon row of bomb-shattered terraced houses.

'People lived here,' she said sadly. 'It makes me realize how lucky we are in Pendle,' she said as she hurried after Alice. 'Manchester and Liverpool get it bad but we've had an easy time of it. Thank God!' she added earnestly.

They went to the Astor Ballroom, which was dark and smoky. Gilt chairs and tables were grouped around a dance floor, and on a raised stage the Tommy Dorsey Big Band were playing 'Chattanooga Choo Choo'. Keen to dance to the fabulous swing music, Emily and Alice left their coats in the cloakroom, where the attendant was a girl wearing a very short dress and a very low top.

'It's like being on another planet,' Emily giggled as they clinked their fluted glasses of pink gin.

'Here's to the Bomb Girls!' Alice replied.

Emily took a long, luxurious drink.

'You know, we've been building bombs for so long we've forgotten what it's like to be young.'

Alice nodded as she too sipped her gin.

'Remember when we used to go dancing every Friday night at the local palais?'

Filled with the happiness of the moment, Emily pushed back her chair and grabbed Alice's hand.

'Come on, Al, let's dance!'

Laughing with the sheer joy of being alive, Emily and Alice clasped hands and almost ran onto the ballroom floor.

'It's like being young again,' Alice laughed as they jived

under the spinning silver balls to 'It Don't Mean a Thing if it Ain't Got That Thing!' followed by one of their all-time favourite tunes, 'Woodchopper's Ball'.

'Oh, Al,' Emily shouted over the orchestra. 'Were we ever young?'

'It's not that long ago,' Alice replied as she spun under Emily's arm. 'Only three years since the war started.'

Three years, Emily thought. So much had happened in so short a time, including her break-up with Bill.

Alice boogied around her.

'Em, if you don't lighten up I'm going to have to find another partner,' she teased.

The girls danced themselves into a fantasy world of pleasure and escapism where hardship, hunger, grief and rationing were briefly replaced with laughter, excitement and *fun*!

Breathless and giggling after dancing non-stop for well over half an hour, Emily and Alice returned to their table to find Robin and a very smart man with short, thick brown hair and a neat little moustache were waiting for them.

'Darling!' cried Alice as she rushed to kiss her boyfriend. 'You should have told us you were here.'

Robin smiled adoringly at Alice.

'And interrupt the two most stunning dancers on the floor? I don't think so,' he laughed.

Robin's friend drew out a chair for Emily and, as she settled into it, Robin introduced him.

'This is my old school friend Rodney, or, to be more precise, Flight Lieutenant Rodney Harston-Binge.'

'Pronounced Bing, not Binge as in excess!' guffawed

rather goofy Rodney as he kissed an astonished Emily on both cheeks. 'I've been told that northern girls are beauties but you, my dear, are the living proof!'

In the dim candlelight, sipping champagne as Tommy Dorsey's band played one great big-band hit after another, the four of them laughed and chatted about the girls' life and work in the north.

'It sounds frightfully exciting,' Rodney said as he leaned over to speak exclusively to Emily, who giggled at the idea of the Phoenix being 'exciting'.

'Believe me, it isn't. It's mucky work,' she said bluntly.

Rodney smiled at her strong Lancashire accent.

'I love the way you say that,' he murmured as his eyes roved over her face then lingered on her full smiling lips.

Unused to excessive flattery, Emily couldn't help but giggle again.

'Nobody's ever said anything like that to me before,' she replied.

'That's because you're a rare northern bloom that's never travelled further south than Sheffield,' he teased.

'You're right there,' Emily retorted. 'Down south's another country!'

Pushing back his chair, Rodney rose and bowed to Emily before taking her hand.

'May I?'

As they took to the floor, Emily saw in the rotating light of the silver balls hanging from the ceiling that Rodney was tall and well built; he was confident too, holding Emily close to his chest, with his left hand hovering dangerously near her bottom. He swept her into an expert foxtrot followed by a tango then a jive, a dance she excelled in and he didn't. To the syncopated beat of drums and brass Emily was in her element. Spinning, smiling and flirting in the middle of the Astor Ballroom, she felt like she was a star in a Hollywood musical.

'You have a passion for life,' Rodney observed.

'I'm enjoying myself,' Emily replied giddily. 'I've never drunk champagne in a London nightclub before.'

'You mean you're not swept off your feet every night?' he teased.

Emily threw back her head and laughed out loud.

'Not exactly. Believe me, there's little time for dancing, apart from in the canteen when we're listening to *Music While You Work*!'

Rodney gripped her close as they spun into another foxtrot.

'Alice failed to tell me how enchanting you are.'

Emily wriggled away.

'We're all beautiful at the Phoenix factory,' she joked.

'Then maybe I should come and visit you in your Pennine hideaway?' he said.

By now a little tipsy, Emily was taken aback but didn't want to be rude.

'Of course. Any time, Rodders!'

Back at their table, Emily tried to learn more about what Robin and Alice did at their training school in Cornwall.

'Are you a French expert too?' she asked Robin.

'Yes,' he replied with a sweet smile. 'Though my French is not up to Alice's high academic standard. I'm more BBC Home Service.'

Alice leaned over to kiss his cheek.

'Don't believe a word he says, Emily; he's way too modest,' she said adoringly.

Emily pushed on with her questions.

'Do you know where you'll go next, Robin? Alice says she's no idea.'

Robin and Alice exchanged a quick look, then Robin replied, 'Afraid we're both in the same boat on that subject. We'll be assessed at the end of our training then, depending on the level of our expertise, we'll be allocated a post, probably somewhere abroad. That's all we know.'

'It's all very mysterious,' said Emily suspiciously. 'And it's not clear what you're training for. What if you're split up?' she teased. 'How will Alice live without you?'

'I'll survive,' said Alice as she pulled Robin to his feet. 'Come on, darling, let's dance.'

As they waltzed off, Rodney slid an arm around Emily's shoulders.

'Shall we dance again?' he murmured thickly in her ear.

Rather fed up with his smarmy advances, Emily rose from her chair and shook her head.

'Not right now. I must pop to the Ladies.'

It was difficult to get away from Mr Harston-Binge, and the drunker he got the more determined he was to get Emily into bed. Finally, at about two in the morning, Robin carted him off in a taxi, but not before putting Emily and Alice in their own separate taxi.

'Night, darling,' he said as kissed Alice goodbye. 'It's been a great pleasure meeting you, Emily.' Doffing his soft brown trilby, he said, 'I do hope we meet again soon.'

Emily leaned forward to kiss him on the cheek.

'Promise you'll look after Alice,' she said as the cab dimmed its lights and drove away in the blackout.

'Promise!' Robin called after her.

Once back in their B&B Emily, now rather drunk, was not taking no for an answer.

'After seeing you with Robin tonight I think you're not telling me the truth about what you're training for,' she said as Alice sat before the dressing-table mirror removing her make-up with blobs of Pond's cold cream.

'Oh . . . and what's that?' Alice asked as she studied Emily in the mirror's reflection.

'Well . . .' Emily said slowly as she worked it out for herself. 'Whatever it is, it's very specialized – all this intense training in a place where visitors aren't welcome.'

'I never said that!' Alice retorted.

'No, but you did say it would be difficult to see you in Cornwall because of the security checks,' Emily reminded Alice, who nodded her head but said nothing.

'Then there's the French, translating documents and stuff from English to French, French to English.' Emily sat on the edge of the dressing table so she could eyeball her best friend. 'Put all that lot together and it's clear you're not training to be a teacher.'

Alice flushed under Emily's penetrating gaze.

'You're working for the government on something top secret that involves translation. Come on, Al, it's obvious . . .' She hesitated before she asked the question she dreaded the answer to: 'Are you a spy?'

Alice went white. She jumped up and hurried to open the door; she looked into the hallway from left to right, then quietly came back into the room and locked and bolted the door.

'Well . . . ?' Emily persisted.

'Something like that,' Alice told her as she sat down on the double bed.

'I knew it!'

'Emily, you must keep your voice down,' said Alice as she patted the bed, indicating that Emily should sit down beside her. Dropping her voice to a whisper she said, 'I'm swearing you to secrecy, Em.'

Goggle-eyed, Emily quickly nodded.

'It's Special Ops training,' Alice explained. 'Breaking codes, translating and surveillance. It's not quite spying but it's top-secret war work, hence all the cloak-and-dagger stuff.'

'Why didn't you tell me?' Emily whispered back.

'Because I'm not allowed to. It really is as simple as that.'

A shiver of fear slipped down Emily's back like a shard of ice.

'Oh, Al, it sounds dangerous,' she said softly.

Alice took hold of her hand and squeezed it hard.

'I chose this, Em. Nobody pushed me or persuaded me. I could have said no, but I didn't want to. I actively wanted to train in Special Ops. I want to dedicate myself to fighting the enemy undercover.'

'Special Ops . . .' Emily repeated under her breath. 'Oh, my God!' she said as she remembered numerous war films she'd watched at the Phoenix. 'Will they send you to work with Resistance fighters?'

Alice put a finger to her mouth.

'Will you please keep your voice down, Em?' She took a deep breath then continued in half a whisper. 'We're being trained to work in enemy territory, intercepting and breaking encrypted coded messages. It's nothing as dramatic as you think,' she said modestly.

'You must be bloody joking!' Emily hissed as she tried to suppress the shock in her voice. 'You're so small and gentle, Alice! You should be settling down, marrying Robin, living in London, teaching young ladies in a posh private school.'

'I might be small but I'm tough, Em. You should know that better than anybody.'

Emily smiled as she recalled the numerous fights they'd had as little girls, hard fights in the back streets, where little Alice with the face of an angel could pack a punch, not to mention a kick and a smack.

'You were always a tough little sod,' Emily conceded.

Alice continued on a more serious note.

'As I said, my training is mostly about decoding, translating and intercepting. At my interview the War Office asked about my experience with explosives but nobody's mentioned it since.'

Emily's blue eyes grew huge with alarm.

'Jesus!' she cried, then quickly muffled her mouth with a hand. 'That's a relief.' She paused then asked nervously, 'Do they train you how to look after yourself . . . you know, if you're threatened by the enemy?' Emily shuddered with fear as she said the word.

'Actually we are trained to shoot and kill with an A.45 pistol,' Alice replied calmly.

By this time Emily was beginning to feel a bit faint.

'Don't suppose we can open the window?' she asked.

'Only if we sit in the dark.'

'Let's do that; let's get into bed.'

Quickly removing their clothes, they slipped into their winceyette nighties and cuddled up to each other in the dark, under the lumpy satin eiderdown that slid from one side of the bed to the other before finally sliding onto the floor.

'Oh, Al, when will I see you again?' Emily whispered.

'As soon as I get leave I'll come home and see Mum, who, by the way, you mustn't mention a word of this to.'

'As if I would!' Emily exclaimed indignantly. 'The shock would kill her.'

'Poor thing, she's not the faintest idea what I'm doing,' Alice said sadly.

'I think you're the bravest woman I've ever known,' Emily blurted out. 'You've answered a call from the War Office and you've taken on training that sounds terrifying to me. Aren't you ever scared?'

'I get worried when I can't break an encrypted message that, in a real-life situation, might cost someone's life,' Alice admitted. 'After our intense training my French is good but I worry about liaising with a French person who only speaks in local dialect; that would be very tricky.'

'Sounds like me trying to make conversation with Rodders!' Emily joked.

Alice gave her friend a cheeky dig in the ribs.

'Buck up, kid, this is beginning to sound like a soppy war film,' she giggled.

Emily sighed as she snuggled up to Alice.

'Sounds more heroic than soppy,' she whispered.

Alice deftly changed the subject.

'Rodney said he was planning to visit you in Pendle.'

'He's so posh!' Emily laughed. 'Hopefully, he'll forget all about me.'

'Don't you believe it!' Alice replied. 'He'll come knocking on your door sooner than you think!'

As the first birds began to sing in the dawn light, the girls, holding tightly to one another, finally fell asleep.

On their last day together Emily and Alice took a flask of tea and some corned-beef sandwiches to Regent's Park, where they sat in the sunshine trying to ignore the bleak backdrop of bombed mansions and shattered church spires.

'Tell me about the girls,' Alice said eagerly.

'Lillian's seriously in love, and Elsie's still devouring chip butties like they're going out of fashion. As for Agnes, nothing's changed; no news of the husband and Esther's still miles away.'

'And you, Em?' Alice asked as she poured tea from the flask.

Emily lay back on the warm grass and with her arms behind her head, gazing dreamily at the large cumulus clouds drifting by, she answered pensively,

'Me . . . ? Well, you were right: I totally screwed up over Bill. I still miss him with all my heart.'

Tears welled up in Emily's eyes and Alice reached out to squeeze her hand.

'Don't give up on him, Em. It might just take time.'

Emily smiled bravely before adding, 'On a more positive note, I enjoy doing my bit for the war effort, I love my girl friends and our digs, although we miss you and nothing's been the same since you left.'

As they packed up their meagre picnic, Alice said, 'Don't give the girls any reason to worry about me. Promise, Em?'

Emily stared into Alice's lovely face framed in a halo of shining silver-blonde hair.

'I promise,' she replied as tears welled up in her eyes again.

It was an agony saying goodbye to Alice the next morning but fortunately, with early trains to catch, they parted swiftly, Alice for Paddington, Emily for Euston. Their final hug reduced them both to sobs.

'Go, please, go,' Alice cried.

Giving her friend one last kiss, Emily turned and walked away, and when she looked back Alice had gone.

Chapter 18: Thingummybob

Emily got off the train at Clitheroe station, where she stood clutching her suitcase and wondering what to do. She didn't know if she should return to the Phoenix because she didn't know whether she was welcome; the only way of knowing was to see if there was a letter for her at home from Mr Featherstone, but she couldn't just stroll into her mum's house holding a suitcase! Mrs Yates would immediately suspect something and question her until she got to the truth.

Stuffing the suitcase behind a neighbour's hedge, Emily went round the back of her house and let herself in.

'Hello, lovie,' her mum said warmly as she proceeded to do exactly what she did every time anybody walked through her door: she put the kettle on.

Emily sat and drank tea with her mum, talking about work and her friends, asking if any news of Bill had been gleaned from his mother, who lived just round the corner. All the time she was sitting in the back kitchen, she was itching to say, 'Have any letters arrived for me?' but she avoided the question, hoping her mum would volunteer some information.

Just as Emily was leaving, spurred on by the fact that her suitcase had been sitting under next-door's hedge for over an hour, her mum said, 'Ooh, I nearly forgot, there's a letter for you.'

Emily took the letter, kissed her mum, then waited for her to shut the front door before she yanked her case from its hiding place and hurried around the corner to open the envelope. She let out a long sigh of relief as she read the letter; she was recalled to work on condition there would be no more insubordination.

'I'll try to keep my trap shut, Mr Featherstone,' Emily said aloud, smiling as she folded the letter and stuffed it in her pocket. 'I really will try!'

When Emily returned to the digs Lillian was fast asleep on the sofa after a long night shift. She was struck by the shocking change in Lillian, who, in Emily's short absence, had become even thinner and – wearing no make-up – looked years older.

'What's wrong with her?' she asked Elsie, who was anxiously tucking a blanket around Lillian.

'She keeps being sick,' she replied, both relieved and delighted to see Emily back. 'Agnes is at the Phoenix trying to get something from the chemist to make her feel better.'

'She looks terrible!' Emily said.

Lillian stirred when she heard Emily's voice.

'Hiya, lovie. Nice to have you back,' she said weakly.

Emily quickly put down her case and sat on the sofa beside Lillian.

'How long have you been feeling poorly, sweetheart?' she asked as she stroked one of Lillian's limp hands.

'I've not felt myself for a while but this sickness is new,' Lillian replied.

Emily paused to look into her friend's tired brown eyes.

'Is there something you're not telling us?'

Lillian burst into floods of tears.

'I might be pregnant!' she sobbed.

Elsie slapped a hand over her mouth to smother a gasp of shock whilst Emily gathered weeping Lillian into her arms.

'Why didn't you say something sooner?' she asked as she patted Lillian's back.

'I wasn't thinking straight,' Lillian replied. 'What with all the trouble we had with Malc then the shock of Gary disappearing overnight ... Honestly, Em, I never even thought about it till I started feeling sick.'

'Did you not take precautions?' Emily asked.

'Obviously not,' Lillian replied bluntly.

'Well, why not, for heaven's sake?'

'Because I didn't care!' She looked at her friends' anxious faces. 'I'm not ashamed,' she insisted. 'Gary and I plan to spend the rest of our lives together, raise a big family in Ohio ...' Her voice broke as she talked about their plans. 'I was having such a wonderful time with Gary I hardly noticed I'd missed a period, but then when my breasts started to feel tender I thought I might be pregnant.'

As fresh tears rolled down Lillian's thin cheeks, Elsie sat on the floor at her feet.

'Do you want the baby?' she gently asked.

Lillian vigorously nodded her head.

'It's Gary's baby, and it's all I've got of him. Of course I want it!'

Elsie blinked back tears as she said, 'I would feel exactly the same, pet. I would want my Tommy's bairn whether he was here or not.'

Lillian took the hankie that Elsie offered and wiped away her tears.

'But who'll look after us,' she murmured, 'me and the baby?'

Without a moment's hesitation, Emily said, 'We'll look after you.'

'Emily's right, pet,' Elsie agreed. 'We're like family; we'll all take care of you.'

Lillian looked incredulously from one friend to the other.

'But where will I go? Where will I have it?' she asked.

'You can have your baby in the Phoenix hospital, then you can move in with my mum until Gary comes to find you,' Emily said with great assurance.

A slow smile illuminated Lillian's face. *'Really?'*

'Other mothers give birth in the Phoenix, so why not you?' Elsie exclaimed.

'I won't be married . . .' Lillian retorted. 'The baby will be a bastard.'

Emily and Elsie exchanged a quick look. Even though the war was changing many long-held views, the stigma of having a child out of wedlock was hard to bear for both mother and baby; but now certainly wasn't the time to talk about it.

'Gary could turn up tomorrow and you could be married in a month,' Emily said with a confidence she didn't entirely feel.

Elsie smiled as she rose to her feet.

'Everybody loves a bairn,' she said. 'Now come on, let's have a brew. We certainly need it.'

As she headed towards the small kitchen, the front

door was flung wide open and Agnes stood before them, white-faced and trembling.

'Any luck with the –' Elsie never finished the sentence, but stared at Agnes as she swayed in the gaping doorway.

'You won't believe it. My Stan's alive!' she gasped.

Elsie and Emily dashed to grab her before she fell in a faint on the floor.

'Sit down,' said Emily as she steered her to the sofa where Lillian was now sitting bolt upright. 'Get her some water, Elsie.'

In shock, Agnes stared in total disbelief at her friends.

'I just heard. Apparently he managed to escape from the concentration camp . . . Oh, God! He's alive!' She took a deep shuddering breath. 'After three years of hoping and praying, my husband is alive.'

'Oh, Agnes!' cried Elsie as she proffered a glass of water to her friend. 'That's wonderful news. Who did you hear it from?'

Agnes took a sip of water, though her hands were shaking so much the water sloshed all over the sofa.

'Mr Featherstone. He saw me on my way to the chemist and called me into his office; he said he'd received a letter from the War Office asking if I was working at the Phoenix . . .'

Her voice trailed away as if she simply couldn't take the news in.

'They asked him to inform me that my husband is alive!' Her voice dropped as she added, 'Stan's in a bad way, though . . .'

'But he's *alive*!' said Elsie joyously, squeezing her friend's hand.

'Where is he now?' Emily asked. 'Will you be able to see him soon?'

Tears welled up in Agnes's dark eyes.

'He's in a specialist POW convalescent unit in Cambridge,' she replied in a stunned voice. 'I've got a pass to visit him. I'm leaving tomorrow; it's all sorted!'

Emily winked at her friend.

'You're going nowhere, Agnes, till we've celebrated this glorious day with a proper dinner!' she announced.

That night the four of them sat down to one of Emily's creations: pumpkin soup, corned-beef fritters with rosemary and lemon, Emily's speciality chips, and pear crumble. As she laid the table, Agnes, Lillian and Elsie gasped in disbelief.

'Where did it all come from?' Lillian asked.

Emily smiled proudly.

'Pumpkin – locally grown; pears – off a tree overhanging the Phoenix car park; corned beef – a ration tin; herbs – free on the moors; the rest – *me*!'

It was a joy to see Lillian tuck in, and the colour returned to her thin wasted cheeks as she enjoyed Emily's delicious food. Agnes didn't eat that much but Elsie made up for her lack of appetite and ate for two.

Raising her glass of tap water, Agnes said with a choke in her voice, 'Here's to tomorrow – wish me luck!'

Before Agnes left at dawn the next morning Emily managed to have a word alone with her.

'Lillian's pregnant,' she whispered.

'Why didn't I see that?' Agnes scolded herself. 'She's not been well and she's not been eating – apart from last night, and that was a sight to see,' she added fondly.

'Best not to appear too anxious,' Emily said. 'She's edgy enough as it is. If only Gary would make contact,' she added wistfully

'A letter from him would make all the difference,' Agnes said with a sad smile. 'I should know – that's what I've been praying for, for three years.'

It was strange not having Agnes in the digs and even stranger not having her as their section manager. Working under their temporary supervisor, the girls realized how much they'd come to depend on Agnes's maturity and experience. Without either Agnes or Alice they felt incomplete and lonely.

As war news varied, it brought a conflicting mixture of elation, fear, depression and utter weariness. When the Bomb Girls heard that the Germans were failing against the force of the Russian army their hearts rose, then they fell again as disquieting news leaked out of Jews fleeing Germany and seeking asylum elsewhere in Europe. Nobody could fail to be elated when news came through of Montgomery's troops in North Africa forcing Rommel and his German army into a retreat.

'We'll soon have them German buggers running for their miserable lives,' said Lillian with undisguised relish as they worked through their shift.

'Oh, Lillian,' said Emily. 'Remember that even Germans have mothers, wives and children.'

Without taking her eyes off the rolling conveyor belt, Lillian answered with brutal sarcasm, 'Sometimes I quite forget they're not all monsters.'

Elsie kept silent; any talk of North Africa sent her

spiralling into a silent depression. Only two letters had made their way through to her from Tommy, even though he said in one of the letters that he wrote to her at least twice a week, action permitting. He also said that he'd only received half a dozen of her letters, and she wrote to him nearly every day so clearly a lot of mail went missing in North Africa.

She blinked hard as she bit back tears. How she yearned for Tommy. Having never loved or known a man in her life, Elsie couldn't believe the well of emotion he'd untapped in her. He was the shyest, tenderest lover; as Lillian said, 'The pair of you are so innocent you'd spoil another couple!'

It wasn't just what went on in bed, though Elsie was surprised at how much she liked that; it was the sweetness of Tommy, his utter conviction that he would come home to her and they would spend the rest of their lives in Pendle, where they would live happily ever after. She knew from the Pathé News reels that her husband was understating the suffering and despair out there in Africa, and that was the way Tommy was; he put a brave face on everything and always tried to see the funny side of life. She tried to follow his selfless example, but it grew increasingly hard to keep cheerful, keep hope burning, keep praying.

Lillian's rallying cry when spirits were low was, 'Keep calm and carry on, Bomb Girls!'

'There seems no end in sight,' Emily said as they sat exhausted, halfway through their night shift, drinking pints of tea in the canteen that now seemed like their second home.

'You could see the fires and explosions as Liverpool burned last night,' Elsie said sadly.

'Poor sods,' sighed Lillian, who, as a result of her pregnancy, had stopped smoking but taken to sucking mints instead.

'It's not just Liverpool that's getting it,' Emily added. 'It's all the major cities outside of London – Coventry, Birmingham, Cardiff, Swansea, Sheffield. What will be left of our lovely country?'

Lillian popped another mint into her mouth as she retorted angrily, 'If the bloody Luftwaffe have their way they'll wipe us off the map!'

'We could do with a bit of cheering up,' Elsie said bleakly.

'That'd take a couple of miracles!' Emily replied grimly.

After nearly eighteen months of grinding work, morale in the Phoenix workshops was unquestionably at its lowest ebb; music still blared out as usual from the factory loudspeaker, but most of the workers hadn't the heart or the energy to sing along as they had done in the early days of the war. And the government updates designed to boost morale didn't have quite the same effect as they used to have.

'We're all getting bitter and twisted,' said one woman from the cordite line.

'More like worn out and weary,' Lillian grumbled.

'I wish the government would stop treating us like kids,' Emily said, sipping her strong scalding tea. 'We don't need to be told we're doing well because we know we're not.'

'That's not true,' Elsie answered staunchly. 'Since the

Americans have come in, we've got Hitler on the run and –' She stopped short when she saw Lillian's face fall at the mention of the Americans. 'Sorry . . .' she stammered. 'I didn't mean to upset you, pet. Talking about the Americans, like . . .'

Lillian smiled bleakly.

'Forget it, Elsie.'

A yawning canteen worker cleared and wiped down their table.

'Heard the good news?' she asked.

'Hitler's dead?' Emily said hopefully.

'No, nearly as good,' the canteen girl replied. 'ENSA are coming to the Phoenix.'

'ENSA?' Elsie stumbled over the initials.

'Entertainments National Service Association,' Emily explained. 'Singers, dancers, comedians, whatever, they travel around the country entertaining the factory workers. It's supposed to be a morale booster.'

'That's nice,' said Elsie sweetly.

'It's hit and miss,' said Lillian, sucking hard on a sweet. 'Some folks say ENSA stands for "Every Night Something Awful"!'

'You never know,' said a pretty, though tired-looking girl at the next table. 'It might be Frank Sinatra or Gracie Fields.'

'We should be so lucky!' snorted Lillian.

Frank Sinatra wasn't available, but the Phoenix girls were thrilled when they heard the news that one of the nation's sweethearts was coming to the Phoenix to entertain them.

'GRACIE BLOODY FIELDS!' Lillian yelled. 'She's

a local lass too,' she babbled on excitedly. 'Lives just down the road in Rochdale.'

'She'll cheer us all up,' said Emily brightly. 'She's a real bonny fighter!'

'Just so long as she doesn't sing too many sad songs,' Lillian said on a lower note. '"Count Your Blessings" or "When I Grow Too Old to Dream" would just about break me apart at the moment.'

'And Arthur Askey's coming too,' said Elsie with a smile, referring to the cheeky little comedian. 'He makes me laugh, even if he is a bit naughty at times.'

Lillian playfully threw a box of matches at Elsie.

'Anything would shock you, little Geordie girl!'

Elsie threw the box back.

'I'll have you know I'm a married woman!' she replied archly.

The anticipation of having a star coming to visit the Phoenix lifted the munitions girls briefly out of their drab, uneventful lives, and Gracie didn't let them down.

She turned up in a big open-topped car wearing an evening dress, diamonds, a fur stole and make-up, even though it was only two o'clock in the afternoon. The Bomb Girls, who'd been given a few hours off, greeted her with loud cheers, whistles and clapping. Beside her, Arthur Askey waved and smiled whilst exuberant Gracie blew kisses with both hands. The girls followed the star into the canteen, where, on a makeshift stage, her songs and laughter took away their woes and worries for a while.

'Thank you for having me, ladies!'

A roar of appreciation went up.

'We'll have you any time, Gracie!' a woman in the audience shouted.

'There's not much difference between us,' Gracie continued. 'I might look posh with all mi flash diamonds,' she laughed. 'But I come from Rochdale, just down't road.'

Another roar of appreciation went up.

'Like you Lancashire lasses, I'm not for giving up. We'll keep on going until we've won this war and trounced Hitler!' Gracie declared.

The cheers and clapping from the ecstatic workers nearly shattered the window panes.

'Yeah, we'll show 'em, Gracie!'

'Lancashire folk are fighters and we don't let folk down, do we?'

'NO! NEVER!' cheered the munitions girls.

And with that Gracie launched into 'Sally, Pride of Our Alley', followed by many of her popular songs: 'Roses of Picardy', 'When I Grow Too Old to Dream', which did indeed make Lillian sob, 'Sing as We Go', and more.

Then, to everybody's joy, she said with a wink and a laugh, 'And now I've got a song especially for all you lasses working round the clock making weapons for our lads at the front.'

Raising her voice to the rafters, Gracie sang the 'Thingummybob' song, which brought the house down. Giggling, Elsie grabbed Emily's hands and skipped up and down like an excited child.

'Em, we're the girls who drill the hole that holds the ring!' she cried.

Emily laughed as she sang her own version of the song.

'Bomb Girls work the Thingummybob!'

As Gracie curtsied and blew kisses the two-hundred-strong audience begged for more.

'Join in, girls!' she yelled.

Laughing and clapping, the workers sang along with Gracie who, after the song finished to a rousing cheer, was replaced by Arthur Askey.

'Hello there, playmates!' he cried as he bounced onto the stage where he reduced the girls to hysterical laughter with his saucy jokes and slightly smutty anecdotes. Gracie reappeared for the finale, and there wasn't a dry eye in the house when she sang 'There's a Boy Coming Home to Me'. Then she finished with a rousing recital of 'Land of Hope and Glory'.

A few hours of laughter, camaraderie and singing energized the workforce. Filled with renewed hope and energy, they waved Gracie off and returned to work with smiles on their faces.

'I'm proper proud to be one of the girls that drives the rod that turns the knob!' Elsie joked.

'Come on,' laughed Lillian for the first time in weeks. 'Let's go and work that Thingummybob and bring the bloody war to an end!'

It was shortly after their excited return to work that Lillian, hurrying to the toilet in the middle of her shift, slipped and fell on the damp factory floor. It was a nasty fall and she lay sprawled face down on the grimy floor, groaning as she tried to get up. Horrified, Emily and Elsie, who'd seen their friend fall but couldn't leave the line for fear of unfilled bomb shells rattling down to the packing department, called for help at the tops of their voices:

'HELP! SOMEBODY DO SOMETHING!'

Ironically it was Malc of all people who went to Lillian and helped the white and trembling girl to her feet.

'Come on, cock, come and sit down,' he said gently.

Lillian smiled gratefully as he put an arm around her waist and led her into the canteen where he went to get her a mug of hot, sweet tea.

'That was quite a fall. How're you feeling?' he asked as he set the tea down in front of her.

'I don't feel quite right,' she admitted as she rubbed her belly.

'Take it easy, get your breath back,' he urged.

But when she'd finished the tea Lillian insisted she was fine. She rejoined the cordite line and dutifully finished her shift, looking very pale.

It was only when she, Elsie and Emily returned to the digs in the dark that Lillian discovered she was bleeding. For all of Elsie's and Emily's efforts to keep Lillian calm, to keep her lying down with her legs up, Lillian lost her longed-for baby. There was no comforting the devastated girl; all words were lost on her as she sobbed and sobbed.

'It was all I had of Gary. It was our baby!' she cried hysterically. 'Now I've got nothing left to live for,' she wailed.

Her sad loss sent her spiralling into a deep depression. Nothing Elsie or Emily said helped or comforted Lillian, who looked and behaved like she'd given up on life.

'We've got to get her to a doctor,' Emily insisted. 'She needs professional help.'

Elsie simply nodded. What she didn't say was that she needed to see a doctor too. It wasn't unusual to miss a period – long shifts and a poor diet often caused erratic menstrual cycles – but missing two periods meant only one thing. Elsie was sure she was pregnant, but now wasn't the time to share her joyful news with anybody.

Chapter 19: Cambridge

As Agnes travelled nearly two hundred miles from Pendle to Cambridge, she had plenty of time for thought. Her initial reactions of shock and total disbelief were slowly being replaced by joy and a rising excitement.

'My Stan's alive!' she said to herself incredulously. 'My husband's alive.'

The further the train rattled south and the closer she got to him, the more Agnes's elation was tempered with anxiety. What was he like now? What horrors had he been through, what privations, what abuse and pain had been inflicted on him?

She closed her eyes as she tried to recall Stan before he was captured: handsome, tall and lean with thoughtful brown eyes and a shock of dark curls, just like Esther. He had been a gentle, thoughtful lover, a wonderful, adoring father, a man who always put his family first. She smiled fondly as she allowed herself, over the long journey, to remember the first time she'd seen him – well, heard him, actually.

They'd met in the dark at the Rex picture house in Walthamstow, east London. Agnes had arranged to go with a girl friend to see *The Wizard of Oz*, but the friend had backed out at the last minute so Agnes, mad about Judy Garland, went to the Rex on her own. Self-conscious that she was sitting alone, she studiously avoided eye contact with anybody in the packed picture house, fiddling awkwardly with her ticket till the lights went down. Half an hour into the film, just as Dorothy and Toto were embarking on their journey along the yellow brick road, a nudge on her arm made Agnes jump in fright.

''Scuse me,' said a tall man nodding towards the empty seat on the other side of Agnes. 'May I?'

Agnes stood up to let him pass then breathed in so that no part of her touched the arm of the chair on which his elbow was resting. During the interval she got to her feet and dashed to the Ladies, and only returned to her seat when she heard the music playing as the film recommenced. Sitting down, she completely ignored her neighbour and stared intently at the screen.

'I bought you an ice cream,' he whispered as he handed over a rather sloppy choc ice to Agnes, who blushed.

'Sorry,' he said with a low chuckle. 'It might have melted a bit.'

At the end of the film, when Dorothy is finally back home, reunited with Aunty Em, Agnes surreptitiously wiped away a tear.

'Real tear-jerker, eh?' said her neighbour as he offered her his neatly ironed white handkerchief.

'Goodness,' Agnes laughed as she accepted the hankie. 'You're a man that thinks of everything.'

At that time Agnes was a typist in a London insurance office and Stan was a bus driver. They met several times afterwards, always at the Rex in Walthamstow, then they started courting properly. With the war looming, Stan didn't waste time with an engagement; he asked Agnes to marry him and shortly after their registry-office wedding

Agnes fell pregnant with Esther, who was the light of their lives. On his first leave home, even though the Blitz was at its height, with constant aerial bombing taking out more than a million homes and forty thousand lives, they'd had a rapturous time together. The sight of Stan waltzing round the kitchen with baby Esther held in his arms and singing Gracie Fields' 'The Biggest Aspidistra in the World' had reduced Agnes to tears of laughter and giggling Esther to hiccups. It was an image of family that lonely Agnes would treasure in the hard months to come.

All too soon those happy days ended when Stan was reported as missing in action.

Strange to think that Stan never knew his child had developed polio, the debilitating disease that had taken her away from home to be nursed by strangers. Agnes shuddered as she thought of all they had been through as a family, then she straightened her shoulders as she came to a firm decision. She was determined that Stan would know nothing of Esther's illness until she knew for certain that he could cope with such a terrible shock. The poor man had been through enough, and more bad news could wait.

It grew bitterly cold as the train emptied out and night fell. At Ely station Agnes couldn't believe the landscape, with the black fen peeling away towards the horizon, which was streaked orange and crimson from the huge golden sun setting over unending flat fields.

By the time she got into Cambridge she was frozen to the bone and weary with travelling. With the college gates locked for the night the streets were empty, and she hurried along, following the instructions she'd been sent to get to Addenbrookes Hospital, where Stan was being treated in a specialist POW convalescence unit. It was far too late to visit her husband so Agnes checked into a nearby B&B, where the landlady offered her a hot-water bottle, a mug of cocoa and a Spam sandwich. Exhausted physically and emotionally, Agnes collapsed into bed, but sleep didn't come. She lay awake till dawn, listening to the college clocks all over the city chiming out the hours, wondering with fear in her heart what tomorrow would bring.

It was far worse than Agnes could ever have imagined. When she walked up to her husband, who was sitting in a metal upright chair staring blankly out of the window, Agnes barely recognized him. Skeletally thin, with livid scars on the parts of his body that were exposed, his hands, face, forearms and neck, he sat with deep lines etched in his once-happy and smiling face.

'Stan . . . darling,' she whispered as she approached.

As he continued to stare out of the window, Agnes thought he hadn't heard her. Crouching before him, her face on a level with his, she waited for him to drag his gaze from the falling autumn leaves littering the hospital garden. When he did turn he looked straight through her, as if she simply wasn't there.

With her heart breaking, Agnes swallowed hard and repeated herself.

'Stan . . . darling,' she said as she gently laid a hand on his bare arm.

At her tender touch, Stan went hysterical.

'NO, SIR! I did nothing. As God's my judge I never touched your food.' Struggling with demons, he was thrashing the air as if trying to free himself from an unseen grip. 'No, no, please no, not again,' he cried as he flung himself out of the chair and lay grovelling on the floor where he inched forward to kiss her feet in abject supplication. 'Please, I beg you, not again.'

With tears streaming down her face, Agnes tried to lift her husband, to stop him begging, to stop his pain, but she was powerless. In his frenzied fear Stan's strength seemed double her own, and no matter how she tried she couldn't release the grip of his hands around her ankles.

A nurse, hearing Stan's sobs, came to the rescue.

'Not to worry, Stan. Just a bad memory,' she soothed as she calmly helped him to his feet.

Looking wild-eyed, Stan stared at her healthy pink face and kindly blue eyes. He trustingly took her hand and dumbly allowed her to guide him back to bed.

'Just a bad memory,' she repeated. 'Let's get you back to bed for a nice little sleep.'

Left alone and quite devastated, Agnes went in search of the doctor, who said bleakly, 'It will take time.'

'How much time?' Agnes asked.

The doctor shrugged; he clearly had no more idea than she had.

'Years, sometimes less. It depends on how quickly his memory returns. The more time he can put between his experiences in the POW camp and the present, the better.'

From inside the doctor's glass-fronted office, which gave a view onto the ward, Agnes could see Stan lying wide-eyed on his narrow hospital bed.

'And what if his memory doesn't return?' she asked.

The doctor shuffled the files on his desk before replying.

'In some cases we've found electric-shock treatment effective.' As Agnes's eyes flew wide open in alarm, he hastily added, 'It's our last resort. Of course we're trying to rehabilitate Stan with drugs and therapy, but so far neither has had much effect. We're hoping that spending time with you may bring back memories of happier times before the war, before his capture.'

'What's the best thing I can do for Stan?' Agnes eagerly asked.

'Take him out, talk about your life together, your family, anything that's not related to his war experience.'

'Can he walk far?' she asked.

The doctor nodded.

'Yes, but you'll have to guide him as he gets quite shaky – and be warned, he doesn't like crowds.'

'When can I start?'

'No time like the present,' the doctor said with a hopeful smile.

In the beautiful autumn sunshine, with gold and russet leaves falling around them, Agnes, arm in arm with Stan, walked along King's Parade, where students in flapping black gowns hurried in and out of King's College, but Stan hardly seemed to notice. Thinking he might prefer to be off the busy high street, she led Stan down winding medieval lanes, across a looping bridge over the river and onto the Backs. Here she sat Stan down on a bench, and from a flask she'd brought along with her she poured him a cup of tea. Stan took the tea and held it in his trembling hands, but he didn't drink it.

'Listen to the birds,' Agnes urged as blackbirds, thrushes and robins warbled in the treetops overhead. 'And look at the cows!' she exclaimed as she pointed to a cluster of cows grazing on King's Meadow.

Seeing Stan's bewildered expression made Agnes realize that the whole excursion meant nothing to him; he might have been sitting in the sunshine on a bench in a bucolic part of England but he wasn't registering any of it. A punt drifted by, full of laughing students who waved as they passed.

'Look, Stan!'

With Stan remaining totally impassive, Agnes abandoned all attempts at trying to distract him; instead she tried to jog his memory by talking of their happy courtship.

'Remember when we first met at the Rex? We went to see *The Wizard of Oz*.' She laughed as she recalled the moment, then began to sing their favourite song from the film, 'We're Off to See the Wizard'.

Dropping the tea, Stan suddenly jumped to his feet. Thinking the song had jogged his memory, Agnes jumped up too.

'We used to sing it together walking home from the picture house,' she reminded Stan, who began hurrying away along the river path past Queens' College. 'Stan, wait!' she called as she grabbed the flask and dashed after him.

To her horror, he walked straight out onto the busy main road.

'STAN!' she screamed as a car, mercifully going slowly, screeched to a halt and missed hitting Stan by inches.

The furious driver leaped out and started yelling at both of them.

'What the bloody hell do you think you're doing?' he bellowed.

At the sound of his angry voice Stan buckled at the knees and fell to the ground where he covered his head with his hands as he curled into a foetal position.

'I'm so sorry,' Agnes gasped. 'My husband's not well.'

'I can see that,' said the shocked driver. 'It's a wonder he's not dead!'

Once he'd driven away Agnes bent down and tried to lift Stan to his feet.

'It's all right, love, he's gone. You're safe,' she said as she smoothed his black hair, now heavily streaked with bands of grey.

Tears streamed down Stan's haggard face.

'Take me back to my cell. Please, get me out of here!' he begged.

Back on the ward an agitated Stan was put to bed and injected with a tranquillizing drug that sent him into an immediate deep sleep. Agnes sat by his bed, holding his hand as he ranted in his sleep.

'No . . . no . . . don't hit me,' he whimpered as he tossed and turned. 'I don't know, no, not again . . .'

Stroking his hair, Agnes tried to calm her husband, who, twitching and shivering, finally slipped into a ragged, restless doze.

'It's all right, my love, you're safe now. You're home, and we'll look after you. Nothing to worry about, just rest . . . shh . . .' she soothed as the light faded and night set in.

Depressed beyond words, feeling like she'd done more harm than good, Agnes braced herself for her final visit to Addenbrooke's Hospital before she had no choice but to return, for the time being, to her war work. She wished she could stay, but would try to get back for another visit as soon as she was allowed leave. With her heart in her mouth and her stomach churning, she walked down the long ward to say goodbye to Stan. She found him sitting in the same old metal chair, staring out of the same window at the falling gold and ochre leaves.

I leave him just as I found him, she thought hopelessly.

'Stan . . .' she whispered.

She didn't make the same mistake of touching him; she just hunkered down so she was on the same level as him.

'I've got to go.'

Stan remained impassive. Holding back the tears that threatened to engulf her, Agnes waited patiently, until she got cramps in her legs from crouching so long.

'What the hell am I waiting for?' she muttered angrily to herself. 'A miracle like you see in the pictures? Stan rising and taking me in his arms and us walking off into the sunset! Snap out of it, Agnes, and leave the poor man alone. You've done no good here.'

She rose, swiped away her tears of pain and despair and then, with one last lingering look, she left the hospital and headed home to the only people in the world she could talk to.

Weary and heartbroken, she returned to the digs where her friends were eagerly awaiting her return.

'How was he?' Elsie asked as she removed Agnes's

damp coat, although she knew from the sight of her friend's face that she didn't really need to ask.

Weak and depressed as she was, Lillian's heart went out to Agnes, who looked like she'd aged twenty years since she'd left them.

'Sit down and get warm, then have some tea,' she urged as she settled Agnes on the sofa.

'Tell us your news?' Emily begged.

Clutching a mug of steaming-hot tea, Agnes gazed into the loving faces of her devoted friends. Tears welled in her eyes and the heartbreak she'd bottled up all day on the train bubbled out of her.

'Stan might be alive . . .' she sobbed. 'But he's a living corpse – he didn't even recognize me!'

Chapter 20: Payback Time

As a hard winter set in and the year turned, families in Pendle heard that their lads in the Lancashire Fusiliers were battling it out against Rommel's German army in Tripoli. Elsie, who'd hardly ever attended school in Gateshead, had no idea where Africa was, never mind Tripoli. During one of their tea breaks, Emily, who'd been avidly following news of the Lancashire Fusiliers, took it upon herself to teach Elsie some geography on the back of a copy of the *Daily Herald*. She drew the bulky shape of Africa and put a star where Tripoli was, then she drew a sketchy map of occupied Europe.

'We're here,' she said as she put a big circle around England. 'And Tommy is, fingers crossed, there,' she added as she pointed at the star that represented Tripoli.

'Oh . . .' Elsie's voice trailed away. 'He's a long way away.'

'Hopefully, he'll soon be heading this way,' said Emily as she drew an arrow up to the heel of Italy. 'Across the Med and into Italy.'

As Elsie's geography lesson continued, a woman the girls knew from the loading bay yelled over the high notes of the all-women Ivy Benson Band blasting out from the radio, 'Lillian Liptrott, Lillian Liptrott!'

Lillian, who was humming along to the music, didn't even hear the call.

Agnes waved a hand in the air.

'Over here.'

In a hurry, the woman dropped a letter on top of Emily's sketch of North Africa.

'Just found this in my pigeonhole, cock,' she said with a cheery laugh. 'Must've got there by mistake.'

As if in a slow-motion dream, Lillian looked at the grubby, crumpled, airmail envelope with writing on the front so smudged she could barely decipher her name. The back of the envelope was half open, which indicated it had been read for censorship purposes.

Struggling for breath, she gasped, '*Gary!* I think it's from Gary.'

Then, turning as white as a sheet, Lillian swayed in her chair.

'Catch her before she faints!' cried Agnes.

On either side of her, Emily and Elsie grabbed Lillian by the arms and steadied her.

'Deep breaths, sweetheart, deep breaths,' Agnes said as she wiped Lillian's clammy brow.

Grasping the letter in her trembling hands, Lillian croaked, 'Read it.'

Agnes read aloud.

'My darling girl, can you ever forgive me? I've kept you in the dark because my squadron were totally in the dark too! We were transferred from our Lancashire base overnight, no chance of saying goodbye to you, my love. We were driven to an unknown destination then our training began for a top-security mission . . .'

What followed had been crossed out by the censor.

'Trust me, sweetheart, I was going crazy thinking about you. I asked if I could write to you, phone you? The answer was always a definite no. None of us could have any communication with the outside world till our mission to . . .'

'The censors have crossed out wherever they were going to,' Agnes said as she scanned down the letter.

'*He* was going out of his mind? How about *me*?' laughed Lillian as colour returned to her cheeks.

Agnes continued reading.

'We flew out at dawn, a bunch of us in B-17s, on a mission to strategically bomb enemy bases. I tell you, Lillian, we had no idea we were part of an offensive air operation against Germany – a massive all-American air attack in Europe! Believe me, it was damn scary, but we got the Hun on the run! Hell, when we found out what we'd achieved, we were proud, man, we were so proud!

Since then we've been detailed in some God-awful place in Wales, awaiting further orders.

Darling, when I think of you I just ache with love . . .'

Agnes smiled as she folded the letter and handed it back to Lillian.

'The rest is a bit personal,' she laughed.

'Check the envelope,' Emily suggested. 'See where it was posted?'

Lillian squinted at the small print.

'Nothing but the date,' she said, then she gasped in disbelief. 'Can you believe it?' she cried. 'It's taken all these months to get here! All the time I was thinking Gary might be dead ... and losing the baby ...' Her voice choked with emotion. 'All that time he was in Wales!'

'Well, he couldn't have done anything even if he'd wanted to,' Emily pointed out. 'Not if he was banged up on a top-security mission.'

Lillian nodded and smiled; already the sparkle was back in her big brown eyes.

'As long as he's alive and he loves me, I can wait for ever,' she said dreamily.

Seeing Lillian radiant and happy for the first time in a long time gave Elsie the confidence to reveal her secret.

'I'm got something to tell you,' she said shyly.

Her friends turned expectantly towards her.

'You're not going on a bombing raid too?' Lillian joked.

Elsie shook her head and blushed bright scarlet as she replied, 'I'm pretty sure I'm pregnant, like!'

Agnes, Lillian and Emily leaped to their feet and threw themselves on Elsie, squeezing and hugging her until she could hardly breathe.

'Give us a bit of air,' she cried.

'Why didn't you tell us sooner?' Emily asked.

'It didn't seem right, what with Lillian being so sad and poorly,' Elsie answered quietly.

'That's all in the past,' said Lillian staunchly. 'Now it's time to think about *you*, Elsie.'

'Does Tommy know?' Agnes asked.

'I wrote to him straight away but ...' Her voice trailed away.

Her friends knew what the 'but' meant. Her letter, like thousands of others, could have got lost or, worse, Tommy could be dead, imprisoned, lying injured by a roadside somewhere between Tripoli and Tunisia, never knowing he was a father-to-be.

'This bloody rotten war,' Lillian seethed under her breath.

'Don't fret, lass,' said Emily, her voice upbeat, her tone defiant. 'We're your Phoenix family and we'll take care of you till Tommy gets home.'

The following day, as the girls clocked off their shift, Agnes was taken aside by the personnel officer, who told her that the empty bed vacated by Alice would soon be taken by a new munitions girl from London. When Agnes broke the news back at the digs a loud groan went up from Elsie, Lillian and Emily.

'Oh, no!' said Emily. 'And I'm the one who has to share with the new lass.'

'I suppose it couldn't last for ever,' said Elsie. 'Though I was secretly planning to put my wee bairn in the spare bed when it was born,' she added with a giggle.

'What if this London woman's posh?' Lillian said.

'That's all we need,' Emily laughed. 'Somebody with airs and graces living alongside us in a cowshed!'

Towards the end of the week Elsie, tired and with an aching back brought on by constantly bending over the conveyor belt, took herself off to the digs for a stretch-out on her bed.

'We'll join you soon,' Agnes said as she lingered behind in the canteen, drinking tea with Emily and Lillian.

Yawning and rubbing the small of her back, Elsie opened the door of the digs and walked in, only to get the shock of her life. There in front of her was a man she'd hoped she'd never see again: her tyrant of a father. He was waiting for her in the sitting room.

In a single split-second the camaraderie she'd just been

enjoying with her friends was banished from her mind as she was whizzed back to her former existence in Gateshead: the fear, poverty, pain and constant abuse. How had her monster of a father tracked her down? What did he want?

Terrified, Elsie looked wildly around.

'You shouldn't be here. It's not your house,' she cried.

'I've come for your wages,' her dad snarled.

'I haven't got any money,' she lied.

With an arm raised, her dad took a step towards her.

'Don't give me that shit!' he yelled as he laid into her, hitting her hard around the head and face. 'Everybody knows munitions girls earn a packet and I've come for what's owed to me.'

Elsie, who did have savings hidden under a loose floor-board not six feet away from where her father was standing, would have preferred to lose a limb rather than part with the money she'd saved up for her baby.

'I've got no money!' she repeated and before he could hit her again she bolted for the door.

'BITCH! Get back here,' her dad bellowed as Elsie shot like a terrified rabbit out of the house.

Though pregnant, Elsie could run faster than her father, who, unused to moorland tracks, stumbled as he gave chase.

'Wait till I get hold of you,' he gasped as he tried to keep up with her.

Coming back from the canteen, Emily and Lillian were surprised to find the digs empty and the front door standing wide open. Hearing cries coming from the moors, they ran to see what was going on. Nothing could have prepared them for the sight of Elsie being pursued by a man.

'Quick!' Lillian yelled as she set off running. 'Elsie's in trouble.'

Emily followed, but not before picking up the bread knife from the kitchen table.

Out of breath and gasping for air, Elsie was forced to stop as a sharp pain shot across her side. Scared that she might have damaged her baby, she fell onto the soft ground.

When her father found her hugging her small rounded belly his anger doubled.

'Filthy bitch!' he yelled at her again. 'You've got your-self knocked up too!'

Seeing her father coming at her, Elsie curled into a tight ball.

'Dad! No, please, no!' she screamed.

'I'll beat the bastard out of you,' he raged, and without a doubt he would have done if Emily and Lillian hadn't thrown themselves on his back and dragged him away from his sobbing daughter.

He put up a good fight, punching out in all directions, but finally Emily drew the bread knife on him.

'Come one step nearer and I'll cut you,' she said. The blazing light in her blue eyes gave Elsie's dad no cause to doubt her words.

With a busted lip and scratches all over his face, he stepped away.

'I'll be back, whore,' he snarled at Elsie, who was crouched hiding behind her friends. 'I want my money.'

Still pointing the blade at him, Emily replied, 'Don't even try it, mister.'

Threatening all kinds of revenge, Elsie's dad slunk

back across the moors, leaving his daughter half fainting with relief.

'Oh, God, has he gone?' she whispered.

'He's gone,' said Lillian as she reached down to help Elsie to her feet. 'Come on, lovie, let's get you home.'

Trembling, Elsie was too frightened to move.

'What if he follows us? He knows where I live.'

Emily shook her head.

'He won't come back, not now anyway. Like all cowards, he knows when he's outnumbered.'

Standing on either side of Elsie, they got her to her feet and half carried her back across the moors, which were now dark in the fast-fading light. Once in the digs they patched up her wounds and settled her into bed, where they kept her warm with hot-water bottles. All night long Agnes, Lillian and Emily took it in turns to sit with Elsie, who slept fitfully due to the cuts and bruises on her face and the agitated state she was in.

'I'm scared stiff she's going to lose the baby,' Lillian fretted.

'As long as we keep her calm and quiet, she'll be all right,' Agnes assured her friends.

Eventually all the girls fell into an exhausted sleep. A hand shaking her shoulder and a soft voice in her ear roused Lillian early the next morning.

'Cuppa tea?'

Lillian started awake and stared into the face of Elsie, who was bending over her with a steaming mug of tea.

'Get back into bed!' she cried as she removed the mug from Elsie's hand and ushered her back into her empty bed.

'I'm dressed and ready for work,' Elsie pointed out to her bleary-eyed friend.

Hearing voices, Agnes and Emily came rushing into the bedroom.

'What're you doing up?' Agnes cried.

'Will you all stop your fussing?' Elsie replied.

Nothing would convince Elsie to stay at home and rest. In the end she confessed that she was scared of being alone just in case her dad came back. Seeing her so nervous and vulnerable, her friends agreed she'd be safer in numbers and they all clocked on for their morning shift with Elsie sporting two black eyes.

During their first tea break, with *Workers' Playtime* jangling out over the loudspeaker system, Elsie begged her friends not to tell Tommy of the previous day's events.

'It's not like he's here to tell,' Lillian pointed out with a laugh.

'You mustn't say a word to him when he gets home,' Elsie replied in all earnestness. 'The less he knows, the better.'

'Putting Tommy on one side for the moment,' Agnes said grimly, 'we need to establish a plan, should that bullying father of yours turn up again.'

Elsie went pale and started to tremble.

'He said he'd come back,' she whispered. 'Next time he might kill my baby.'

'Not if we've got anything to do with it!' Emily said fiercely.

'We've got to make sure he can't get into the house again,' Agnes said.

'We could padlock the door and windows,' said Emily.

'And keep a constant eye on you, buggerlugs!' Lillian fondly added as she laid a protective arm around Elsie's skinny shoulders.

Elsie smiled trustingly at her devoted friends.

'What would I do without you all?'

'I don't know, sweetheart,' joked Lillian. 'I really don't know!'

'Seriously,' said Agnes, 'for the time being, let's not let Elsie out of our sight.'

Exhausted by the previous night's vigil, all four girls were ready for a nap at the end of their shift.

'Who's on hot-water bottle duty?' Lillian asked as they clattered up the cobbled lane that led to their digs.

Suddenly Elsie froze in her tracks.

'The light's on!' she gasped.

As Lillian, Emily and Agnes stared from one to the other, Elsie started to cry.

'Oh, God! He's back,' she wailed.

Convinced it was Elsie's crazy dad come back to kill her, a furious Emily strode forwards and flung open the door so hard it smashed against the wall.

'Get out or I'll kill you!' she cried.

Emily's eyes grew wide as a slim, elegant woman smoking a cigarette in a long cigarette holder walked towards her

'Hello,' said a voice that could have cut crystal. 'I'm Daphne.'

Lillian, Agnes, Elsie and Emily gaped in wonder at the apparition in their sitting room.

'God!' exclaimed Daphne as she tossed her fox fur onto the sofa. 'Isn't this place absolutely ghaaastly?'

Chapter 21: Cracking

Winter at Helford House was a perfect white wonderland outside, but inside it was ten degrees below zero with only two fires in the entire establishment. A huge log fire in the drawing room and a wood burner in the dining room, both of which were kept going day and night, were the only sources of heat, but luckily Alice and Robin had their love to keep them warm.

As Christmas approached, Alice wondered if they'd get Christmas leave. She so wanted to take Robin to Pendle to meet her family and friends, but theirs was no ordinary war work. Their demanding schedule rolled on regardless of bank holidays, and although she never voiced it, Alice was secretly glad because while she might not be with her family and friends, at least she'd be with Robin. And, she thought to herself, who knew how many Christmases they could look forward to together?

They were no longer referred to as the 'new recruits' since fresh trainees had arrived and the senior team mysteriously disappeared over the space of a few days.

'Dropped', the word went round.

It gave Alice food for sombre thought. Thirty recruits at a time underwent thorough training for dangerous, intensive action – then they disappeared like they had never existed. One chilling question she and her friends had discussed in their freezing dorm, smoking cigarettes to keep warm, was what was the average life expectancy of a Special Op. Gwynne said six weeks if they were captured; Gladys said much longer if they could operate effectively behind enemy lines; Iris starkly said, 'But then there's torture.'

Whatever the answer, Alice now knew that Special Ops were a breed apart; they were all motivated by the certainty that right was on their side and that victory was a prerequisite for any kind of decent future. Equipped with false identities, they would be expected to play a deadly cat-and-mouse game with the Gestapo while doing their best to wreak havoc deep inside enemy ranks. To this end Alice and her colleagues had had to acquire a range of new skills, spending their time on shooting practice and parachute training, wireless operating and Morse decoding, which was drummed into them daily, month after month.

They started with learning the Morse alphabet by rote, which was slow, tedious and boring.

'I'll need bi-focals by the time I've got this lot under my belt,' joked Gwynne as she squinted at the arrangements of dots and dashes that formed letters.

For days on end they practised writing five words a minute, and after a few weeks of this exacting process the whole Morse alphabet was familiar to the Ops.

In her sleep Alice dreamed Morse and in her dreams she recognized the series of metallic tips and taps that spelled out a random assortment of words like weather, horse, car and train.

'Been dreaming in Morse code again,' Alice told her dorm friends as she dressed one morning. 'I wish it would stop. Not only am I decoding all day, it's all night too!' she grumbled.

Alice's training in the munitions factory made her instinctively good at bomb assembly, plus she was given additional training in explosives, which set her apart from the others. In the isolated snowy countryside she was taught how to set a bomb in order to sink a boat, blow up a bridge or bomb a railway engine. She was also taught how to derail an express train with an overcoat if there wasn't a bomb handy!

Robin, who'd been selected as a Special Op because of his previous wireless experience, was streets ahead of his contemporaries; luckily for Alice, he spent a lot of his spare time helping her acquire the expertise he had a natural flair for.

'One of the terrifying problems in the field is atmospheric conditions. It's a bloody nightmare,' he said as they practised late one night. 'Dampness causes weak transmissions and lightning interferes with electricity in the atmosphere – that's when you get hisses as transmitting cuts out.'

'So what do you do if that happens?' Alice asked.

'Try to find a dry place to transmit, preferably indoors – and avoid lightning,' he said with a cheeky wink.

One of their most fascinating lectures was their tutor's introduction to poem codes.

'From a poem you select five words, you give each letter of those words a number and from those numbers you transpose the message,' their communications tutor explained. 'You repeat the process for security purposes – this is called a double transposition – and then, just to be on the safe side, you do it a third time. It's tedious but it works.'

He paused to look round at his class eagerly taking notes.

'Never choose an obvious poem or something predictable like "God Save the King". If the enemy were to intercept it they could probably break the code because the poem is so well known. Go for something more obscure, so that even if the enemy managed to break one message they wouldn't automatically break the rest.'

On top of learning so many facts, there were the vital physical details to take on board too.

'In order to transmit you need an earth cable, an antenna wire and, of course, your radio set. Take care of the valves that power your set; they're fragile and if they break in transmission, you'll have a problem. And remember that once you're hooked up, the valves take a long time to warm up; they don't just ping into life.'

Alice's stomach churned. How would she ever be calm enough or have time enough to set everything up? How could she avoid making mistakes that might cost her her life?

As if reading her thoughts, the tutor continued, 'Agents in the field, surrounded by the enemy, petrified, might sometimes panic and make mistakes when coding. There might be no electric light; the Germans might be in the next room. If you make a mistake whilst transmitting and London can't read it, London might ask you to re-encode that message, but in that time you could end up getting caught.'

Next to her, Robin surreptitiously took her hand and

squeezed it as the tutor pressed on with the worst-case scenario.

'If an agent's captured it's essential that he should be able to tell us so that we can take the necessary steps to rescue him.'

Alice let out a low sigh.

'That's the best news I've heard all morning,' she murmured under her breath.

'For example some agents use an agreed security check; they have a system of making a deliberate spelling mistake every third or fifth or tenth word. If they fail to make repeated spelling mistakes, it sends out an alert that they've been caught.

'What if you're on the run and working in the dark? You're bound to make a mistake,' Robin pointed out. 'Won't London assume, because of all the mistakes, that you've been captured?'

'Hopefully, the mistakes you're talking about will be a lot more random than a conscious mistake every third or fifth word,' the tutor replied. 'These are the fine details that we, at this end, must sieve through in order to protect our Ops out in the field.'

In another lesson the tutor tapped out a message on the Morse code machine.

'Listen to how loud these metal keys sound.'

Everybody held their breath to listen.

'Unfortunately these machines are noisy enough to give your location away. There's nothing we can do about that, apart from muffle the keys, which would be pointless. The quicker you transmit your message, the safer you'll be. Do the job, then get the hell out!'

Over coffee in the common room the nervous Ops swapped notes.

'Why doesn't somebody invent silent keys made of plastic?' Gwynne said as she blew out a cloud of tobacco smoke.

'The chap's right about getting the job done fast,' Robin said as he puffed on his pipe. 'The Huns are better than us at quickly detecting where the enemy signal's coming from; they can trace the agent's location on the map in no time.'

'It's all well and good him telling us the quicker the better, but what if we've smashed the valves in the radio set or there's a bloody lightning strike and the atmospheric conditions are abysmal?' Gladys asked gloomily.

A long silence followed as they fiddled about lighting up cigarettes and stirring their coffee while they all avoided voicing the answer to Gladys's grim question. Alice secretly wondered whether, if she was cornered by the enemy, she would rip open her shirt cuff and swallow the cyanide pill hidden there.

Advanced parachute training followed their wireless and decoding classes. After a daily, heavy-duty workout, followed by a cross-country run in freezing conditions, they practised various jumping routines. Leaping through apertures that were cut in the bottom of the fuselages of obsolete aircraft, they dropped about twelve feet onto coconut matting, which helped to break the impact of the fall. The daily practice helped Alice, who was terrified of heights. She slowly built up her confidence by repeatedly jumping out of the fuselage, familiarizing herself with the drop, then rolling neatly into a ball after landing. The instructor constantly varied the techniques of the exercise, asking the trainees to fall into forward or backward rolls as they dropped. Agile as a cat after months of hard training, Alice and her team learned the importance of keeping their knees and feet together during the drop.

'Don't part your legs,' the instructor bellowed if their thighs, knees and feet weren't clamped tight. 'You're not in bed with a tart!'

Even though they were taught thoroughly, nothing prepared Alice for her first drop from a Whitley aircraft. When they were flying at an altitude of a thousand feet the navigator gave the red light for the first parachutist to stand by the door, ready for the green light that gave the signal to 'Go'. With the aircraft travelling at around a hundred miles an hour, even a slight miscalculation by the navigator could mean missing the drop zone by a considerable distance and might result in death in real life.

When the green 'GO' sign came up for Alice she closed her eyes, held her breath and dropped out of the Whitley. In a matter of seconds she was plummeting to the ground whilst experiencing a tight, gripping sensation in the pit of her stomach that made her feel slightly sick. As air rushed through her mouth and nostrils, she dropped like a stone at a hundred and twenty-five miles an hour. Overwhelmed by sheer terror, Alice was opening her mouth to scream when what felt like a giant hand swept her up by the shoulders. A great flood of relief rushed over Alice as the silk canopy of the parachute billowed open above her like a huge mushroom. Floating gently earthwards,

Alice laughed out loud with a wonderful sense of exhilaration.

'I'VE DONE IT!' she yelled into the arching blue sky.

By manipulating her harness straps she could control and guide her parachute into snowy fields down below rather than land in a densely wooded area or, worse still, ditch in the freezing waters of the Channel.

Once on the ground Alice struggled out of her parachute then, remembering her instructor's words, she proceeded to bury it. Robin, who'd landed minutes before her, muttered angrily as he too buried his parachute.

'Bloody waste of precious time,' he said. 'It takes half an hour! By which time you could have been caught by the enemy.'

'What else are you supposed to do with the wretched thing?' Alice laughed.

'The professionals on the ground say just chuck the parachute into the nearest bushes and get away from the drop point as quickly as possible,' he replied.

A shiver ran through Alice as she thought of how soon their turn would come to make their first real drop into dangerous enemy territory.

Meanwhile, back at Helford House, they embarked on a more sophisticated form of surveillance training that was termed 'cracking'.

'Cracking is something we expect the women on the course to excel at,' the commanding officer said with a knowing smile. 'Which is why we prefer our female agents to be clever, pretty *and* seductive.'

'That would explain the naughty black lingerie,' Gwynne giggled.

'Learning to outwit, outmanoeuvre, second-guess and deceive are tools special to a spy,' their commanding officer said.

One wintry afternoon Alice was put to the test; she was sent undercover to link up with a new recruit, who she was instructed to 'crack'.

'We've got to find out if he's trustworthy,' her commanding officer told her. 'No point in going to the trouble of training the lad if he's all blab and no action. See if you can crack him with your pretty face and innocent eyes; see if you can squeeze the poor bastard,' he ended with a chuckle.

Choosing her best mushroom-coloured crêpe dress and a fur coat borrowed from Iris, Alice waited in a hotel overlooking the Helford River for her recruit to arrive.

Wearing a thick tweed suit and a flashy cravat, he bounced into the hotel lobby and vigorously shook Alice by the hand as he introduced himself.

'Clive Rees,' he said with a wide smile.

Alice chose a quiet corner by a roaring fire, and they ordered gin and tonics and cheese and pickle sandwiches. As the light faded over the wide river, Alice, looking pretty and deceptively delicate, made apparent small talk with Clive, who was already on his second gin.

'Are you going to be here for long?' she asked casually.

'Well, no, actually, I'm leaving next week,' Clive replied with a fake self-conscious smile.

Alice's mind reeled at his indiscretion. Was he just trying to impress her or had he already forgotten the basic rules of his training? *Never* reveal anything.

Feigning surprise, she batted her eyelids as she pressed on with her questions.

'How thrilling!' she gushed. 'Where are you going?'

With a swagger, the raw recruit moved closer to Alice, so close she could smell the gin on his breath.

'I'm organizing resistance groups so that when the invasion comes there are people ready to stand up and rebel against the Germans,' he blabbed. Lowering his voice to a melodramatic whisper, he added, 'I'm being parachuted into enemy-occupied territory.'

You've totally blown it, Alice thought, but her expression remained sweetly impressed.

After half an hour of even more careless talk from Clive she rose and said she had to go. By now rather tipsy, Clive lurched towards her and tried to plant a kiss on her cheek. Alice skilfully evaded his advances by pretending to look for her gloves.

'Can I see you again before . . . you know, I disappear into the ether?' Clive said *sotto voce*.

Alice agreed to meet him early the following week, a date she had no intention of keeping, but at least it got him out of her hair.

The next day the commanding officer called Alice and Clive into his office.

'Do you know this woman?' the Brigadier asked.

Realizing he'd been busted, the raw recruit flushed in embarrassment then shouted at Alice, 'You bitch! You set me up!'

Later Alice guiltily told Robin what had happened.

'I did a terrible thing,' she confessed. 'The poor chap was dismissed on the spot.'

Robin gave her a hug.

'Don't be silly, darling,' he said. 'If the man can't resist showing off to a pretty face he's going to be useless in the field, when it won't only be his life that's in jeopardy but many others too.'

As 1943 dawned the Ops at Helford House threw a party. Food was procured from the surrounding countryside: a side of smoked ham was bought from a neighbouring farmer with their combined food coupons, and eaten with allotment-grown potatoes, cabbage and leeks. And there was no shortage of booze, thanks to their local black-market contacts.

'After all, we *are* spies!' joked Robin. 'If we can't track down contraband goods, who can?'

Helford House was bright with bunting and flickering candles, and the Christmas tree in the drawing room was so tall it almost touched the ceiling. After the meal the recruits took to the floor, dancing all night to the strains of Cole Porter, Anne Shelton, Glenn Miller and Joe Loss.

It was a wonderfully romantic evening, which Alice and her friends had carefully prepared for. Iris already had an evening dress but Alice, Gladys and Gwynne hadn't. They tracked down lengths of cloth in junk shops and stayed up late into the night stitching their gowns with frozen fingers. Alice's silver-grey velvet dress had a deep V neckline and long sleeves, and it fitted tightly around her slender frame, emphasizing her pale skin and stunning silver-blonde hair.

She gasped when she saw Robin, elegant in an evening suit, waiting for her on the stairs.

'You look so handsome,' she sighed as she stroked the lapels of his fine suit.

'And you look like a dream!' he said as he bent to kiss her full pink lips. 'That dress is so lovely I want to take it off!'

As they dipped and spun to a lovely Vera Lynn waltz number, Alice closed her eyes and lost herself in the moment. With Robin's arms around her and the music playing out, she promised herself that she would treasure this golden candlelit moment, keep it for ever and remember it when times weren't quite as wonderful.

'Do you love me, darling?' Robin whispered in her ear.

Standing on tiptoes, Alice pressed her lips to his neck, which she kissed.

'I love you very much.'

'When the war's over will you marry me?' he asked.

Alice stared up into his sweet, smiling face.

'Marry you?'

'Be my wife?'

Throwing her arms around his neck, Alice cried, 'Oh, yes! Of course! Yes!'

As she continued to dance, pressed against Robin's warm, strong body, his words rang through her head.

'When the war's over . . .'

Alice closed her eyes and prayed.

'Please, God, let that be soon.'

Chapter 22: Surprise, Surprise

The year began well, with news of further successful Allied bombing raids over Germany.

'I bet my Gary's one of them brave lads,' said Lillian proudly.

A few weeks later there was even more good news for a nation exhausted by war.

'The Germans have surrendered in Stalingrad,' the BBC news reporter announced on the Phoenix radio.

Everybody in the entire factory thumped the air in triumph as they cheered at the tops of their voices.

The German drive on Stalingrad, which had begun in the summer of 1942, resulted not in a great triumph for Hitler, but quite the opposite, in fact: the Germans' retreat from Stalingrad was their first major defeat in Europe.

'There'll be no stopping them Soviets now,' Malc predicted as he walked down the bomb line with a grin on his face. 'They're tough sods, them Soviets, fighting all winter in freezing temperatures and no food in their bellies. Bloody superhuman, if you ask me.'

'It seems like this ghastly war's finally turning,' said Daphne.

Elsie's green eyes widened as she asked hopefully, 'Are you serious, like, about the war ending?'

'Put it this way, darling, it's the Huns that are

running instead of us, for a change!' Daphne smiled. 'I admire those plucky Soviets. Malc's quite right: they're heroic.'

'So are the Yanks!' Lillian said staunchly.

Later, in the canteen, Emily laughed as Daphne fixed a cigarette into her long silver holder then elegantly puffed clouds of smoke into the air.

'You're not in the movies, Daf!'

'Darling, I'm not prepared to let my principles drop just because I've been forced to work in the arctic north,' Daphne joked.

After the shock of finding Daphne in their digs the girls had quickly grown to like her. She was great company and told hilariously funny stories of her pre-munitions days when she was a secretary in Kensington.

'I did as little as possible,' she said candidly. 'So boring, banging away all day on a Remington typewriter. It ruined my nails, darlings! I spent most of my working days having long lunches with chinless wonders,' she added with a languid smile.

The girls laughed at her posh accent, but equally she howled at their Lancashire accent and quaint idioms.

'Pleeease don't tell me you seriously call your friends "cock"?' she cried in horror.

'It's an affectionate name,' Emily explained.

'You'd certainly have to be on close terms with somebody you addressed by the name of the male genitalia,' Daphne replied.

'What's genitalia?' innocent Elsie enquired.

Daphne covered her face with her hands.

'Elsie, dearest, didn't you ever go to school?'

'No, mi dad wouldn't let me, like,' Elsie replied honestly and in all innocence.

Daphne, who had a tender heart, for all her airs and graces, patted Elsie gently on the top of her head.

'Dear child, you're intuitively cleverer than most women who've had an education.'

Elsie blushed and smiled at the compliment although, if the truth were known, she didn't quite understand it. All she knew was that Daphne was her friend and, like Emily, Lillian, Agnes and Alice, she loved her very much.

Lillian and Daphne were a scream together, doing imitations of film stars and singers, some of whom Daphne had met and could perfectly mimic. Together they'd do renditions of the Andrews Sisters till late into the night; harmonizing and improvising they'd click their fingers, stamp their feet, bang pan lids, even tap dance.

'Do "Tuxedo Junction",' Emily begged.

'It's gone midnight,' Agnes pointed out. 'We really should be in bed.'

'In a minute,' Elsie pleaded. 'After "Boogie Woogie Bugle Boy".'

Agnes wagged a finger at heavily pregnant Elsie.

'You, young lady, should be in bed,' she scolded, but Agnes loved their sing-song evenings just as much as her friends did.

For all of her wild ways, posh tastes, funny stories and string of boyfriends, there was a serious side to Daphne. Deeply patriotic, she pitched into gruelling munitions work with zeal and determination. On wet winter mornings, as they slithered and slipped on the muddy cobbled path that led to the Phoenix, Daphne would skip over the puddles.

'No slacking, girls! This is no worse than hockey at prep school!' she'd call.

The national euphoria brought on by the success of the Soviet offensive and the increase in Allied bombing of Germany plummeted in the spring, when news began to creep through about the continuing and relentless Battle of the Atlantic. During one particularly bleak week in March twenty-seven merchant ships were sunk by German U-boats.

The mood was sombre in the canteen, and some women, wives and sweethearts of sailors aboard the fated ships hadn't even clocked on for work but had taken themselves into Pendle to be with their families as more news filtered through.

It was around this gloomy time that Agnes received a letter from Cambridge, which she told her friends about during one of their tea breaks. She'd been finding it unbearably hard not being with Stan, but factory work, sometimes with back-to-back shifts, had distracted her a little.

'The doctors say there's no improvement in Stan's condition and therefore they have no alternative but to administer electric-shock treatment,' she said miserably.

'Oh, God! Isn't that a bit experimental?' Daphne asked.

Looking careworn, Agnes continued, 'They mentioned it when I was in Cambridge; they said it was something they would only do as a last resort . . . when nothing else worked.'

A heavy silence hung over the table.

'I've got to go to Cambridge to sign the consent papers,'

she said as she folded the letter and slipped it into her overall pocket. 'Poor Stan,' she whispered as tears rolled down her face. 'I never thought it would come to this. They'll have to give me compassionate leave.'

Elsie handed her a hankie, which Agnes gratefully accepted.

'I wish Esther could see him before he has the treatment,' she said as she mopped up her tears. 'Who knows what state he'll be in afterwards . . . ?'

Unknown to Agnes, Emily and Lillian began devising a secret plan.

'There's nothing to stop us from going to pick up the little girl ourselves,' Emily said excitedly. 'If we can sort our shifts to get Esther here, Agnes could take her to Cambridge.'

'You can't kidnap a child!' Daphne cried in shock.

'It's not kidnap,' Lillian pointed out. 'She knows us.'

'Well, why don't we run the idea past Agnes?' Elsie asked.

'Because she'll refuse,' Emily said pragmatically. 'You know how principled she is; she'll think we have to go through all the formal channels, but that would waste precious time.'

Lillian quickly added, 'The less she knows, the better.'

'You sure you can get to Keswick and back in between shifts?' Elsie asked.

'I reckon we can. It's only up the road,' Lillian replied.

'Hardly, darling,' Daphne laughed as she gave an elegant little shudder then said, 'I'm told it's damp and misty and surrounded by mountains.'

'Stop being dramatic, Daf,' Lillian said. 'Em's right: time-wise it's do-able.'

Emily grinned.

'So let's do it!'

Daphne rolled her eyes.

'Oh, my God! What have Emily Yates and Winston Churchill got in common?'

'Dunno. Tell me,' Emily asked.

'True grit!' Daphne replied.

A few days later Lillian and Emily finished their morning shift and by three o'clock they were on a slow train to Preston, changing at Lancaster and Kendal and finally getting into Keswick around six o'clock. They went straight to the place where Esther was housed – Lillian had found the address in Agnes's bag – but Mr and Mrs Sugden were more than wary about letting the little girl leave with total strangers.

'But we're not strangers,' Emily explained as she showed them a photograph of Esther with them at Elsie's wedding.

'We're Esther's friends,' Lillian said as she cuddled the little girl, who'd climbed onto her lap and was tugging her earrings.

Emily decided the only way forward was the stark truth.

'Agnes really wants Esther to see her dad before he has electric-shock treatment, because after that, well . . .' She paused then added bleakly, 'He could be a vegetable for the rest of his life.'

The old couple finally conceded and then it was a mad

rush to get the last train. Taking it in turns to carry the giggling, excited Esther, they ran through the dark streets of Keswick and hopped on a train just as the guard blew his whistle. The return journey involved only one change, at Preston, where some American GIs fed Esther chocolate and chewing gum. By the time they stepped out of the taxi at the Phoenix it was gone two in the morning and all was quiet in their digs.

Taking Esther to Agnes's room they quietly opened the door.

'Go and give Mummy a kiss,' Emily said as she gave the little girl a gentle pat on the bottom.

Esther limped over to the bed and, on tiptoes, she stretched up to kiss her mother.

Agnes woke with a start. Looking into the face of her daughter, she genuinely thought she was dreaming.

'Hello, Mummy.'

Gathering Esther into her arms, Agnes wept with joy.

'Tomorrow we're going to see Daddy,' she said.

Though Agnes was overwhelmed by her friends' generous and daring plan to bring Esther to the Phoenix, there was hardly time to thank them as Malc was waiting early the next morning to take mother and daughter to Clitheroe railway station.

'I'll never forget what you've done for me and Esther,' Agnes said as she clung emotionally to Emily and Lillian.

As usual Lillian down-played her important role, fobbing it off with a joke.

'We needed the fresh air!' she laughed.

The long journey across England would have seemed

interminable but Agnes and Esther had months of catching up to do. Esther gloried in the excitement of the train journey; she loved exploring the corridors, stepping over sleeping soldiers or playing games with those that were awake. 'I Spy' was her favourite as the train rattled through the spring countryside. Agnes couldn't believe how unencumbered she was by her disability. As she hopped over bulging kitbags to get to the toilets, she played a game called 'Bouncing Bunnies', which involved all the young soldiers copying her actions.

'I never thought I'd be playing "Follow My Leader" on the way back to barracks,' one smiling young soldier said as Esther made him stand on one leg and wobble just like she did.

When Esther got sleepy Agnes cuddled her and stroked her long dark hair as she told her stories of when they lived together in London and Daddy drove a big red bus. Then, while Esther slept, Agnes stared at her daughter's tranquil face. Would Stan recognize her? Would Esther even remember who he was?

As before, it was late when the train pulled into Cambridge. Agnes hailed a taxi and drove to the B&B she'd previously stayed in, then, curling up in a single bed with Esther, she fell asleep.

The following morning, with her stomach churning in fear, a nervous Agnes led Esther into the hospital ward. Assuming that Esther might be overcome by the sight of doctors in white coats and rows and rows of beds, Agnes started to say, 'Darling, it might seem a bit strange to begin with –'

But Esther took her mother totally by surprise. Well

used to hospitals, she was unperturbed by what she saw, and dropping her mother's hand she limped the length of the ward looking for her father. Remembering the photograph of Stan that Agnes kept by her bedside table, Esther miraculously managed to pick out her emaciated father sitting in a high-backed chair and staring blankly out of the window.

'Daddy! Daddy!' she cried as she hurled herself into his arms.

Time stood still.

Agnes saw Stan look at their daughter, and as she watched she prayed desperately for some sign of recognition. But a tremor went through her husband as if he'd been shot.

'Oh, my God! He looks like he's going to have a stroke!' she gasped as she dashed forwards.

The doctor put a restraining hand on her arm.

'Leave them,' he said as he gave his full attention to the interaction between father and daughter.

The shock of seeing his little daughter smiling up at him with tears in her big dark eyes seemed to shift something long locked in Stan's brain.

'Remember me, Daddy?' she said.

Seconds ran into minutes as he searched his memory for the name of his daughter. Agnes hardly dared breathe.

'Esther . . . ?' he said hesitantly.

The little girl nodded and smiled encouragingly. Agnes looked hopefully at the doctor, who kept his eyes on his patient.

'I'm Esther and you're my daddy.'

Taking him by the hand, she pulled him up out of his

chair. He never took his eyes from hers as she led him through the open French window into the sunshine.

'Let's go and pick some flowers,' she said sweetly.

With tears streaming down her face, Agnes watched her husband and daughter walk hand in hand across the lawn. Esther was limping but chatting and laughing as she picked flowers to make a daisy chain for her dad.

'Your daughter seems to be doing a better job than we are!' the doctor remarked, clearly overcome.

When father and daughter returned Esther confidently took hold of her mother's hand and placed it in her father's.

'We're a family. Mummy, Daddy and Esther,' she said happily.

Stan looked at Agnes as if seeing her for the first time. After a moment he raised his hand and started to stroke her radiant face, as sweet memories started to flow back of the life he'd lived before the nightmare began . ... Esther being born . . . bathing her in a tin bath in front of a warm, crackling fire . . . signing up with the Sappers . . . saying goodbye on a misty autumn morning.

'Family,' he said as he clung to his wife and child.

The three of them spent a wondrous day walking by the river, feeding the ducks then sitting under an old weeping willow tree. They shared a simple picnic as students drifted by in punts. Smiling happily, Agnes turned to her husband, who suddenly looked hollowed-out with exhaustion.

'You've done enough,' she said softly.

Stan nodded.

'It's been quite a day.'

Holding hands, they walked slowly back to Addenbrooke's, where Esther made no complaint about leaving her new-found Daddy. For all of them, like Stan said, it had been quite a day.

Agnes and Esther had to leave the next morning, but because of Stan's vastly improved condition, brought about by Esther's loving nature, they separated with smiles on their faces and hope in their hearts.

The journey back to Pendle was endless, with umpteen changes and long delays in cold draughty stations. It was at Sheffield, in the smoky waiting room, that Esther started to feel ill, and by the time they reached the Phoenix it was gone midnight and Esther was running a high temperature. Agnes kept her as cool as she could through the long night, then early the following morning she carried her to the Phoenix hospital. There, after examining the feverish little girl, the doctor grimly announced that Esther had got measles.

Chapter 23: A Warning

The only advantage of having her sick child in the Phoenix hospital was that Agnes didn't have to send her back to Keswick, and she could see Esther at least three times a day. One night, when Esther's fever was sky-high, Agnes asked the terrifying ward sister if she could stay with her.

'Parents are not allowed on the hospital wards outside of visiting hours,' she snapped.

Tears filled Agnes's dark eyes.

'But she might need me in the night,' she pleaded. 'She's so small and sick.'

The granite-faced sister's expression melted slightly.

'You can sleep in the waiting room,' she said curtly. 'I'll make sure the nurse on night duty knows you're there; she'll call you if necessary.'

Grateful for small mercies, Agnes tried to sleep on two chairs pushed together. She was shaken awake just before dawn by a pretty young nurse.

'The fever's passed and Esther's asking for you. Follow me.'

Sitting up against her pillows, with damp hair and flushed pink cheeks, Esther held out her arms as she cried, 'Mummy! Mummy!'

'Shh, darling, we mustn't wake anybody up,' Agnes whispered as she gathered her daughter into her arms.

'Where's Daddy?' asked Esther sleepily.

'He's in hospital too and, like you, he's getting better,' Agnes assured her.

The little girl smiled contentedly as she snuggled up to her mother.

'Can I live with you and your friends in the digs when I'm well?' she asked.

Agnes skirted the question.

'We'll sort something out, sweetheart,' she promised. 'But first you've got to get properly better.'

'I don't want to leave you again, Mummy,' Esther whispered.

Agnes gave her a squeeze as she cautiously replied, 'Don't worry, lovie, Mummy will work something out.'

When the baby was kicking strongly inside her Elsie received news that Tommy was not only safe but heading home on leave after the battalion's victories in North Africa.

'Months of waiting and now this!' cried ecstatic Elsie as she waltzed around the canteen clutching Tommy's letter close to her pounding heart.

'You're not the shy, wilting violet that walked in here a few years ago,' Lillian teased.

'You'll give birth in the canteen if you don't stop jumping about,' Agnes said with a smile.

Elsie proudly rubbed the big, round, baby bump.

'To think Tommy might not even know he's going to be a dad,' she said with a dreamy expression on her face.

'He's in for the shock of his life. I'd faint clean away if somebody presented me with a baby,' Daphne said as she pulled down the corners of her mouth in disgust.

'Wouldn't you like bairns, Daphne?' Elsie asked.

Daphne shuddered at the thought.

'Certainly not!' she exclaimed in her snootiest voice. 'Though . . .' she dropped her voice to a sexy whisper, 'I do like the way they're made!'

'Me too!' laughed Lillian as Elsie blushed bright crimson.

'We're surrounded by sex maniacs!' Agnes joked.

Emily smiled feebly. If Tommy was coming home would Bill be coming home too? She'd heard from her mum, who'd heard from Bill's mum, that Bill's division were waging war on the Tunis line. It seemed unlikely that the entire battalion would be granted leave at such a crucial time of fighting.

As they prepared for bed back at the digs, Elsie, who was calmer than earlier in the day, returned to the subject that worried her more than anything: her dad.

'Remember not to mention a word to Tommy of mi dad coming here and knocking me about,' she reminded her friends.

'We won't do anything that will upset your time together,' Emily assured her.

'What will I do about seeing Tommy?' Elsie asked. 'I mean . . .' She hesitated shyly.

'You mean where will you sleep with him?' Lillian finished the sentence for her.

'You can have my room,' Agnes volunteered.

'Darling!' Daphne gasped. 'You can't possibly be thinking of having sex in your condition!'

The look on Elsie's face was a comical mixture of shock and horror.

'I wasn't thinking of that, like . . .' she stammered. 'It was more where could we be a bit private, you know . . . ?'

Before poor Elsie fainted clean away in embarrassment, Emily came to her aid.

'In your condition you could get a few days' leave,' she said. 'Then you can stay at Tommy's mum's house, you'll have much more privacy than here.'

'Yeah, this place gets more and more like Bradford market on a busy Saturday afternoon!' joked Lillian.

Daphne rolled her eyes as she teased Elsie further.

'I just hope you survive your night of orgy, Elsie darling!'

Emily picked up a cushion and whizzed it across the room at Daphne.

'Leave the poor kid alone!' she laughed.

Elsie had no problem getting a few days off.

'You're one of the hardest-working girls at the Phoenix,' Malc told her. 'I'll have a quiet word with Mr Featherstone, so don't worry your pretty little head.'

'I'll be back at work as soon as possible,' Elsie said earnestly.

Malc smiled as he looked at her burgeoning bump poking through her overalls.

'Not too soon, lovie. We don't want a babby on the bomb line, do we?'

The same day that a smiling Elsie walked down the hill to meet her husband at Clitheroe station, Esther was discharged from hospital and brought back to the digs, where she was fussed and petted. Daphne had ordered a beautiful china doll with blinking blue eyes and a golden wig, from Hamleys toyshop in London; Emily had baked a mock-chocolate cake using all their sugar rations;

Lillian had made her a new blouse. With her usual ingenuity for 'fashion on the ration', Lillian had made the blouse out of an old green silk blouse of her own. She'd added a Peter Pan collar made of lace she'd picked off an old pillow case and some tiny pearl buttons rescued from a moth-eaten cardigan in a second-hand shop.

'It cost nowt!' Lillian announced as she showed off the pretty new blouse to her friends.

'Darling, you really should go into business,' said Daphne, who was distinctly impressed by her friend's nimble fingers.

'Darling, I couldn't possibly!' Lillian fondly mocked. 'I'm far too busy on the bleedin' bomb line!'

During Esther's convalescence in the Phoenix hospital, Agnes had had plenty of time to develop a plan that would keep Esther close to her side. She visited the day nursery, where she asked the nursery nurse in charge if Esther could join the children of other factory workers. Agnes explained that Esther wouldn't be strong enough to travel back to Keswick when she was discharged from the ward; plus, she and Esther needed time together after their traumatic trip to Cambridge.

'Esther worked a little miracle when she visited her dad in hospital,' Agnes explained to the nursery nurse. 'But she'll need time to understand that Stan won't be joining us right away.'

The nursery nurse agreed that they could care temporarily for Esther while Agnes was working. So when Mr Featherstone made enquiries about Agnes's domestic arrangements she told him with a smile, 'It's only temporary, until she's well.'

But in her mind, Agnes was already formulating a more permanent plan for Esther, one which she prayed would mean they'd never have to part again.

Elsie took the bus to Clitheroe station, where she stood on the platform with her heart pounding, waiting for the London train to chug into view. Tommy was only minutes away! Her husband, who she hadn't seen since their honeymoon, her wonderful loving husband, was coming home! She spotted Tommy before he saw her: tall and lanky with a mop of mousy brown hair that, even with an army crop, still fell over his eyes. He dropped his duffel bag when he caught sight of Elsie and ran the length of the platform to scoop her into his arms and kiss her full on the mouth.

'Tommy!' she said, torn between modesty and a lustful longing that shot through her body like fire.

Tommy didn't answer. His eyes were locked on her belly, gently swelling from underneath her duffel coat.

'I'm pregnant,' she said, stating the obvious.

'A baby!' he cried as he crushed her in his arms.

'Not too hard!' breathless Elsie gasped.

'Why didn't you tell me?' he asked.

'I did!' she cried. 'I wrote loads of letters to your battalion in North Africa.'

'Probably got blown up or scorched by the heat,' he answered with a laugh. 'Christ, it was as hot as hell out there. Worth it, though. Montgomery reckons we'll break through the Tunisian line soon then we'll move on Italy.'

Elsie wrapped her arms around her husband and kissed him long and hard.

'Let's not talk about the war,' she pleaded. 'All I want is you safely home with me and the baby.'

He smiled as he again gazed incredulously at her bulging tummy.

'I still can't believe it,' he said.

She laughed as the baby started to kick.

'You'd better! This one's a real bonny fighter!'

The terrifying meeting with her dad, which Elsie was desperate to keep secret from her husband, was accidentally revealed to Tommy when he came across a letter in her handbag, written by Elsie's grasping stepmother.

You should be helping your family at a time like this. If you don't hand over your wages as a dutiful daughter should then your father will pay you another visit and this time you won't get away with it.

'What's all this about?' Tommy asked when Elsie walked into his mother's kitchen and found him reading the letter.

Elsie went as white as a sheet then swayed as if she might faint. Tommy grabbed her and led her to a chair.

After giving her a glass of water, he said in a softer voice, 'You never mentioned your dad paying you a visit, sweetheart?'

Tears welled up in Elsie's eyes.

'He turned up out of nowhere,' she blurted out. 'He wanted mi wages.'

'The bastard!' Tommy seethed.

As she anxiously watched Tommy pace the room, Elsie attempted a half-hearted smile.

'I lied,' she said. 'I told him I had no money, but all mi savings were in a tin under the floorboards he was standing on.'

Tommy didn't seem to hear what she was saying; shocked and angry, he continued to pace around the room.

'He threatened you – in your condition?'

'Nothing stops him when he gets a mood on,' she replied.

'I'll KILL him!' Tommy said through gritted teeth.

'He won't bother me again,' Elsie said with a pretend laugh. 'Emily put the fear of God in him.'

Seeing she was getting agitated, Tommy appeared to drop the subject. But later, whilst Elsie was taking a nap, Tommy, wearing his regimental uniform, stood on the main road north, where, with all the army transport on the move, he had no difficulty hitching a lift to Newcastle. Feeling guilty that he was leaving his beloved Elsie, Tommy reasoned he had plenty of leave left to spend with her. He didn't relish the thought of a single moment out of her sight, but this was one thing he really had to do.

With Elsie's letter folded in his pocket, Tommy arrived in Newcastle grimly determined. He soon tracked down her family home in Gateshead, and, straightening his rather thin shoulders, he rapped on the door.

It was opened to him by a woman with a face like a greedy hawk.

'Aye?' she asked.

'Can I speak to Mr Hogan?'

'Who is it?' a man's voice yelled from inside the house.

'A man ... for you,' the woman yelled back. She

grudgingly opened the door for Tommy to pass. 'He's in the back,' she said.

Tommy walked into the grubby kitchen, where Elsie's dad sat smoking at the table with Elsie's two stepsisters on either side of him. They all eyed Tommy with dislike and suspicion.

'I'm Elsie's husband,' he announced.

'And who the bloody hell gave you permission to marry my daughter?' Mr Hogan snarled.

'She didn't need your permission; she's over twenty-one, and a woman in her own right,' Tommy replied.

Mr Hogan sprang up from the table and glared at Tommy, who was roughly the same height but half the size.

'Was it you that knocked her up or some other bastard soldier home on leave?' Mr Hogan demanded.

Struggling to keep his temper and stick to the reason why he'd travelled a hundred miles to confront Elsie's half-crazed father, Tommy retorted, 'If you threaten my wife again I'll have the police on you.'

It was as if somebody had lit a blue fuse paper under Mr Hogan; he went up like an erupting volcano. Blind anger replaced words as he picked up a chair and threw it into Tommy's face. As Tommy ducked to avoid getting his head smashed, Mr Hogan grabbed him by the hair and started to drag him around the kitchen.

'I'll bloody kill you,' he snarled.

As the three women stood in a corner screaming, Tommy lunged at his attacker and butted him in the chest with all the strength he could muster. Losing his balance, Mr Hogan fell over backwards and banged his head hard against the kitchen sink. To Tommy's amazement, he slithered down the edge of the sink, leaving a trail of blood from a wound on the back of his skull.

Elsie's stepmother ran to him, trying to rouse him.

With a mounting sense of unease, Tommy watched, hoping to see the wretched man stir. But his eyes were blank and his colour terrible.

And then, after what felt like the longest wait, Mrs Hogan let go of her husband's hand and looked at Tommy with venom.

'You've killed him!' she snarled. 'MURDERER!'

Tommy stood gaping in horror at Mr Hogan, who was lying spreadeagled on the floor with an ever-growing pool of blood seeping under his head. Reaching down, he shook him, but Mr Hogan's head lolled over sideways like that of a hideous broken doll.

Hysterical now, the stepsisters ran out of the front door screaming, 'HELP! MURDER!'

Tommy stared down at the dead body of Elsie's father, while her stepmother eyed him malevolently.

'You'll hang for this, soldier boy. I'll see you swing!'

Tommy froze. This was never meant to happen. He'd travelled north to sort things out once and for all with Elsie's bastard of a father, and now he was lying dead on the floor. What on earth had he done?

Hours and hours later, the Gateshead constabulary tracked down Elsie's whereabouts, listed officially as the Phoenix Munitions Factory. It was Agnes who took the phone call from the police in Mr Featherstone's office.

'It sounds urgent,' said Marjorie, his nosy secretary as she handed the phone to Agnes, who'd been called off her line by Malc minutes earlier.

'Hello, Agnes Sharpe speaking.'

'Are you a supervisor at the Phoenix Munitions Factory, Pendle, Lancashire?'

Agnes's pounding heart slipped at least three beats: had Stan escaped from the hospital ward? She swayed as a more hideous thought assailed her. Could he have committed suicide? Thrown himself in front of a train or overdosed in order to escape his demons?

'I am,' she answered calmly even though her palms were clammy with sweat.

'Is there a young woman in your charge by the name of Elsie Carter?' the police constable continued.

By this time Agnes was so tense she felt like throwing the phone at the wall.

'Yes!' she almost snapped. 'What is it?'

'Her husband, a Mr Thomas Carter, has been arrested and is being held in custody, charged with the murder of Mr Hogan.'

A picture of young Tommy, tall and lanky with a shy smile, floated into Agnes's head.

'You can't be serious!' she exclaimed.

The constable ignored her outburst.

'You are requested to inform Mrs Elsie Carter, née Hogan, of her husband's situation right away.'

Feeling sick, Agnes placed the phone back in its cradle.

Marjorie was inquisitive.

'Bad news?'

Agnes nodded vacantly, then, walking almost in a trance, she returned to her friends on the cordite line.

'Is Stan all right?' Emily immediately asked.

'He's all right,' Agnes answered weakly.

'So what's up?' said Lillian.

'Tommy's only gone and murdered Elsie's dad,' Agnes said bluntly. 'He's in custody.'

Given the gravity of the situation, Malc allowed the four women a few hours off. After changing out of their work overalls they walked down the hill into town to Mrs Carter's house. Crazy with worry, Elsie rushed towards them as they crowded into the room.

'Have you seen Tommy?' she cried. 'We've not heard or seen him since this morning.'

'Sit down, sweetheart,' Emily said as she guided Elsie towards the nearest chair.

Clutching her tummy, weary Elsie slumped into the chair.

'Is he hurt . . . is he in trouble?' she whispered.

Agnes took a deep breath.

'Look, there's no easy way to tell you this . . .' She paused, then added. 'Tommy went to see your dad, lovie. And something awful's happened. I don't know quite what, but your Tommy's with the police now, charged with murder.'

Elsie went white. She knew in her heart that Tommy, like the honest man he was, would think that he could straighten things out with her dad. What Tommy had never understood was that Elsie's dad was like no other man; he was a monster. Feeling sick, she hardly dared ask the question.

'Was it my dad he killed?'

Emily slowly nodded.

'Yes, it's your dad,' she replied.

'NO! NO!' Elsie gasped.

She looked desperately up at her friends. How could everything have gone so wrong when just hours earlier she had been rejoicing in Tommy's homecoming?

'I've got to get to Tommy. I've got to tell the police what my dad's like. Tommy wouldn't have stood a chance with him – it must have been self-defence,' she said in a panic. She got up and started looking for her bag and coat.

'Quick, one of you please take me to the –'

But before she could say another word, she stood stock-still as a dribble and then a rush of liquid gushed out from between her legs. Daphne gagged at the sight and almost fainted.

'Oh, God!' she cried. 'The poor girl's in labour!'

Chapter 24: Lancaster Assizes

The nearest hospital to Mrs Carter's house was the Phoenix.

'She'll need somebody with her,' said the ambulance driver who came roaring down the hill to fetch her. 'But I can only take one of you lasses.'

'Agnes!' Emily, Lillian and Daphne said in chorus.

As the ambulance drove away, the remaining three girls ran up the hill to the hospital, where they sat tense and anxious in the waiting room for some time. They jumped to their feet when Agnes finally joined them.

'She's having a hard time of it,' Agnes told her friends. 'She was so frantic about Tommy that the midwife gave her morphine to calm her down. Now she's rambling so much she doesn't know where she is and can't handle the contractions.'

'Can you stay with her till the baby's born?' Emily asked.

Agnes nodded.

'This midwife doesn't seem to mind me being with Elsie, given the circumstances, but she's not sure that the next one will be so accommodating.'

'Thanks for the update, now for God's sake go back and calm the poor girl down,' Daphne urged.

As she turned to go, Agnes said, 'Can you pick up Esther from the nursery? I could be here all night.'

The girls made tea for Esther, who'd settled into the digs like it was her second home.

'Where's my mummy?' she asked as she tucked into toast and dripping.

'She's helping Elsie have her baby,' Emily explained.

Her big dark eyes widened with excitement.

'Ooh! Can I help too?' she cried. 'I know all about doctors and nurses in hospital,' she added proudly.

Emily smiled as she kissed the little girl on the cheek.

'You can help as much as you want once the baby's home,' she promised.

They took it in turns all through the evening to pop into the hospital for an update.

'She's calmer now the morphine's worn off. And she's well dilated and breathing with the contractions rather than fighting them like she was earlier,' Agnes told Daphne, who went green at the thought.

'Too much information, darling,' she said with a grimace.

'Well, you did ask!' Agnes laughed.

When Emily visited an hour later Agnes couldn't leave Elsie for more than five minutes.

'She's started bearing down, so it could be any minute now,' she said as she hurried back to Elsie.

Emily was sitting on a chair in the corridor when she heard Elsie's baby give its first cry. She was so happy for her friend – but her happiness was tinged with worry over what on earth was going to happen with Tommy. Pacing up and down, she waited for Agnes to appear, and when she did she was carrying a tiny bundle in her arms.

'Elsie's son,' she told Emily, who burst into tears at the sight of the little boy.

'He's so beautiful,' she said as she stared into his peaceful, sleeping face. 'How's Elsie?'

'Exhausted, losing a lot of blood and worried sick,' Agnes replied. 'If she carries on fretting her milk might not come through and the baby needs feeding,' she said as the little boy stirred in her arms.

'It's one problem after another,' groaned Emily. 'Does Tommy's mum know the baby's born?'

'The ambulance driver said he'd call in and tell her on his way home. Poor woman, she must be worried sick too,' Agnes answered.

'I'll go and tell the others,' Emily said. 'None of us could settle until we knew Elsie was okay.'

The next forty-eight hours were a nightmare, despite the happy new arrival. The girls visited Elsie as often as they could, dashing to the hospital whenever they had a spare moment, but there was no consoling feverish, frantic Elsie, who – probably due to stress and weakness – suffered a haemorrhage and had to be removed to a private room, where visitors were banned until her condition stabilized. The girls watched in helpless misery as the poor little baby was taken to the hospital nursery.

Tommy's mum, in floods of tears, visited her grandson, but mercifully she wasn't allowed near her daughter-in-law.

'You have to leave,' the ward sister told the anxious visitor. 'Mother and baby need peace and quiet.'

'Poor Mrs Carter. She's so upset she'll just make things a thousand times worse,' said Emily.

*

When Elsie's son, who she named Jonty, was five days old Agnes was allowed to see her.

'I've got to see Tommy, I must see him!' a fretful Elsie told Agnes, who didn't argue with her for fear of making her ill again.

'We'll sort something out as soon as you're well enough to leave here,' she promised. 'Right now, you've got to focus on getting your strength back and trying to feed your son.'

'He's not taking to the breast,' Elsie said anxiously.

'He won't whilst you're so upset; there won't be enough milk to satisfy the poor little thing. The calmer you are, the more contented he'll be,' she assured Elsie.

The thought of seeing Tommy did calm Elsie, who improved slowly but steadily, though Jonty's hungry cries kept her awake night and day.

'How on earth am I going to keep my promise once she's out of hospital?' Agnes asked her friends. 'I more or less promised I'd get her and the baby to Preston Prison and back.'

'God!' Daphne exclaimed. 'That's a big ask.'

Lillian shocked them all by saying quite calmly, 'Malc's already agreed to drive Elsie there as soon as she's on her feet.'

'You asked him?' Agnes gasped.

'Course I did,' Lillian laughed. 'He's the only man I know with a car!'

'Lillian, you didn't . . . ?' Emily started, but Lillian finished the sentence for her.

'No, I didn't go behind the bike sheds in return for a favour,' she replied. 'Those days are well and truly over.'

Daphne let out a peal of laughter.

'The quaint things you do on these heathen moors!' she teased.

'Malc may not be my lover but he's not my enemy any more,' Lillian pointed out. 'He'd do anything for Elsie; we've seen that in the past. I don't know why you're all so surprised – or suspicious,' she added with a smile.

So as soon as she was well enough, Malc drove Elsie and her baby, Tommy's mum and Agnes to Preston Prison. His new Austin 10 just about accommodated all the passengers. They were quiet as they drove over Belmont Moors, which were bright green with fronds of new ferns and loud with the sound of spiralling skylarks.

'You wouldn't believe that anything bad could happen on a day like this,' said Elsie, who hadn't been outside the Phoenix hospital since her baby was born.

They found Tommy in the visitors' room, waiting for them with a haunted expression on his face. Always a long, lanky boy, he now looked painfully thin, with sunken cheeks and a neck so skinny his Adam's apple protruded like a stone caught in his throat. Tommy took one look at his son cradled in Elsie's arms and he started to sob.

'My boy, my little boy,' he said as he pulled Elsie and his son into his arms.

'Take him, hold him,' said Elsie.

'I might drop him,' Tommy replied nervously.

'You won't,' said Elsie as she handed over the baby.

Shaking with emotion, Tommy took Jonty, who stirred and made a sound like a kitten.

'I've made him cry!' he said in alarm.

'He's only dreaming,' Elsie assured him.

Rocking the baby in his arms, Tommy told them what had happened on his fateful visit to Gateshead.

'I couldn't risk your dad troubling you again, Elsie,' he explained. 'I went up to ask him not to visit you, nothing more than that. You have to believe I had no intention of killing him!'

Elsie vehemently nodded her head.

'Of course I don't think you killed him on purpose!' she cried. 'But you can't . . .' She quickly corrected her grammar to the past tense. 'You could never talk to mi dad like he was normal; he was mad, always had been. For sure he'd try to kill you – that's the only language he spoke.'

'He *would* have killed me if I hadn't pushed him away. Admittedly it was a hard shove, but I didn't expect him to go down like a tree. He smashed his head on the sink on the way down and cracked his skull; that's what the police said when they charged me with his murder.'

'Murder!' cried his mother as she started to wail, causing the baby to wake up and scream too.

'At worst, it's a case of manslaughter,' Agnes yelled over the din.

'That's what my solicitor says,' Tommy replied. 'But Elsie's stepmother's saying that I went there with the intention of killing him, and both her daughters agree with her. So it's their word against mine,' he added miserably.

'So she's got two witnesses?' Agnes said grimly.

'Two scheming, bloody little liars!' Elsie raged.

'Whatever they are, Elsie, love, they're witnesses and

I've got nobody to speak in my defence,' Tommy told her gloomily.

With both his mother and baby bawling their eyes out, nobody could hear themselves speak.

'We'll go outside for a few minutes,' Elsie said, taking Jonty from Tommy and dragging her mother-in-law with her.

Once alone with Agnes, Tommy crumpled into the nearest chair and sat with his head in his hands.

'I'm trying to keep a brave face for Elsie's sake,' he blurted out. 'Poor kid, she's suffered enough. She looks so thin and drawn, and the last thing I want to do is worry her even more.'

Agnes nodded in agreement.

'She's been through a lot. But she's tough, Tommy, a lot tougher than she looks,' she added.

He smiled as tears filled his eyes.

'Thanks for looking after her so well. I don't know what she'd do without you girls,' he said with a sob in his voice.

'We're family, Tommy; we look after each other all the time,' Agnes answered.

With a face as white as stone, Tommy murmured, 'If I'm found guilty of murder at Lancaster Assizes I'll hang.'

Agnes's blood ran cold but she smiled hopefully as she reassured him.

'If your solicitor presents a good case you'll get manslaughter. Don't give up hope, Tommy.'

Tommy nodded glumly.

'And the charge for that stands at ten years.'

*

Later that evening at Mrs Carter's house, Elsie's friends came down to see her after her stressful prison visit, and they were shocked. She was deathly white and still, staring blankly at the wall.

Without any preamble, she suddenly spoke in a flat, calm voice.

'I'm going up to Gateshead.'

Her friends gazed at her, open-mouthed.

'You're bloody mad!' Lillian exploded.

'What on earth can you possibly hope to achieve?' Daphne asked.

'I'm going there to bribe my lying stepsisters,' Elsie announced

'Bribe them? How?' Agnes asked.

'I've got savings,' Elsie replied. 'We're well-paid munitions girls, remember?' she said with a shadow of her old sweet smile. 'I've had no cause to spend much,' she said with a self-deprecating grin.

'No, you've never been one to lash out on fags and gin!' Lillian joked.

'I'll use mi savings to twist their rotten little arms,' Elsie said with steely determination.

'Isn't that somewhat illegal?' Daphne asked.

'No more illegal than what I know they've done,' Elsie retorted.

'You're confident you can do it, just like that?' Agnes said as she snapped her fingers.

'I know exactly what makes those scheming little bitches tick,' Elsie answered with confidence. 'Will one of you come with me?'

Agnes had had too many days off work and was

desperately missing Esther, and she hesitated, but Emily immediately volunteered.

'I will.'

It wasn't a problem leaving Jonty with Tommy's mum. After struggling to breastfeed her baby Elsie had finally given up and switched to Cow & Gate powdered baby milk, which Jonty took to in a blink. Before she left, Elsie prepared several bottles then left Tommy's mum written instructions so she could make up fresh feeds in her absence.

Elsie and Emily took the train to Elsie's family home in Gateshead where, hiding behind a bush, they waited in the rain for Elsie's stepmother to leave the house. Holding her breath, Elsie watched her stomp up the road with a shopping basket over her arm. The minute she was out of sight, Elsie bolted towards her old home with Emily in her wake.

'Stay outside and keep an eye out for my stepmother coming back,' Elsie told her.

'Will you be okay on your own?' Emily nervously asked.

Little Elsie threw back her slight shoulders and nodded.

'I'm not frightened of them!' she declared.

'When you see her, come round the back and knock on the door,' Elsie said as she slipped down a side alley then into a back yard.

Knowing the back door was always left unlocked, Elsie stepped straight into the kitchen, where her stepsisters were washing up.

'What're you doing here, bitch?' Ivy snarled.

'Gettout!' snapped the younger sister, Edie.

Elsie didn't bat an eyelid but got straight down to business.

'I'm here to save you from joining my husband in Preston Prison,' she said, cold as ice.

'What've we done wrong?' Ivy demanded.

'Perjury for a start. That carries at least a ten-year sentence,' Elsie replied.

Clearly, neither girl had a clue what perjury was, but they weren't prepared to admit that.

'What the hell are you on about?' Ivy shouted.

'Lying in court,' Elsie answered calmly. 'Telling the judge that Tommy killed Dad on purpose is a black lie, and you know it.'

'Who ses? You weren't even bloody here!' Edie yelled.

'I know how mad mi dad was,' Elsie answered emphatically.

The sisters exchanged a conspiratorial look.

'Your bloody husband killed him; he pushed him,' Ivy insisted, but Elsie detected a wobble in her voice.

'Totally unprovoked?' Seeing her sister's blank expression, Elsie simplified her question. 'Did mi dad start the fight?'

She left the question hanging in mid-air. Neither girl replied but Elsie could tell they were hiding the truth.

'Here's the deal,' she said as she cut to the chase. 'I'll give you a hundred pounds each, every penny of mi savings, if you'll give me written evidence of what really did happen when Tommy met Dad.'

The girls' eyes almost bugged out of the heads.

'*A hundred pounds!*' they said in unison.

'*Each?*' gasped Ivy.

'Each!' Elsie said as she opened her bag and took out a thick wad of banknotes, which her stepsisters ogled incredulously. 'On condition I have a written statement of exactly what happened between Dad and Tommy.'

Ivy dragged out a chair in order to sit at the table.

'Give us a pencil and some paper,' she said with a greedy glint in her eyes.

Elsie had everything ready for them. Taking paper and pencils from her bag, she laid them on the table too.

'Mi mam'll be back any minute,' Edie said in a panic.

Though her heart was pounding in her ribcage, Elsie kept her calm.

'I've posted a look-out in the street; she'll let us know when your mother's on her way back. Don't rush, and write down everything that happened in the order you remember.'

'Your dad lost his temper and threw a chair at your husband's head,' Ivy said.

'Write it down,' Elsie urged.

'He ducked and it smashed against the wall,' Edie added as she copied her sister and quickly wrote down her evidence.

'Then your dad grabbed hold of your husband's hair and dragged him round the kitchen, punching him around the head and face. Your husband butted your dad in the chest and he fell over backwards. That's when he hit his head against the sink,' Ivy added.

'He flopped onto the floor and then he bled a lot; it were a big pool of blood all over't floor,' Edie said out loud as she scribbled the words onto the paper in front of her.

'Mother said he was dead . . . She said we was to tell the police your husband murdered him. She said she'd kill us if we didn't.'

'Write it down,' Elsie said.

A sharp rap at the kitchen door made all of them jump sky-high.

'She's on her way back!' Emily called from the yard.

With a sweat breaking out on her brow, Elsie cried, 'Sign your names! Don't forget the date. Quickly, quickly,' she begged.

'She'll kill us,' gasped Edie as the kitchen door opened.

Ivy grabbed the banknotes off the table.

'Not if we've got this, she won't!'

As they grasped their money, Elsie folded the precious sheets of written evidence and carefully put them into her bag. Before all hell could break loose, she sidestepped her bewildered stepmother and, with a victorious smile on her face, she joined Emily waiting for her outside.

'I've not a penny in the world,' she said. 'But I've got enough evidence to save my Tommy from swinging!'

Tommy's trial took place a few days after Elsie's dad's funeral, a ceremony that Elsie had no intention of attending. From across the courtroom she watched her stepsisters cower under the beady eyes of her stepmother. When they were questioned by Tommy's lawyer, who had read their written evidence, they didn't falter from what they had written, which left their mother in a more than awkward position.

'So why, madam, did you accuse an innocent man of

murder?' the lawyer said as he turned on the dead man's widow.

Feigning grief and shock, Mrs Hogan said she was in no state at the time of the accident to know exactly what was going on. The lawyer sternly warned her that if her daughters had not volunteered the truth, they might all have gone down for ten years on a charge of perjury.

The court decided Tommy's actions were carried out in self-defence and he was allowed to leave the courtroom a free man.

As Tommy walked out, clutching a tearful Elsie in his arms, Mrs Hogan tapped her stepdaughter on the shoulder.

'Don't you ever darken my door again,' she said with hatred in her voice.

Elsie gave her and her miserable, cowering daughters a radiant smile.

'With the greatest of pleasure,' she said as she turned her back on them for ever.

Chapter 25: Flight Lieutenant Rodney Harston-Binge

Tommy was granted a few weeks' compassionate leave with his wife and new baby, and when he did finally return to his battalion it was to wonderful news: after the surrender of the Germans and Italians in North Africa, the Lancashire Fusiliers, under Montgomery, were already advancing in mainland Italy.

Though their farewell was tearful, both Elsie and Tommy knew it could have been a lot worse – at least he wasn't in prison with a death sentence hanging over him. And Elsie, after some happy and relaxed time with her husband and son, was a picture of health again.

'Sweetheart, are you really well enough to go back to work at the Phoenix?' Tommy fretted.

'I'm a lot better than I was!' she laughed. 'Anyway, if you're doing your bit, fighting the Eyeties, I can do mine by filling shells to end the war,' she answered robustly.

'And what about our little lad?' said Tommy as he cradled Jonty in his arms.

'He'll be fine. He's got a place at the Phoenix day nursery, so he'll be close to me, and there's your mum too – best of all worlds!' Elsie answered with a happy smile. 'Little Esther was pushing him around yesterday and I heard her telling everybody he was her little brother!'

For all their brave words and determination, Elsie and

Tommy clung onto each other at Clitheroe station on the morning of Tommy's return to his battalion.

'I love you so much, Elsie,' he whispered.

'And I love you,' she replied. 'Come back soon, my love, come back safe,' she cried as the train pulled out of the station.

Normal life began to resume. Lillian heard from Gary from time to time, but communications were frustratingly sporadic as he was stationed in some secret location and regularly on bombing raids over Germany. Agnes heard from Stan, who was fully off his medication and had just started working on a fruit farm in the Cambridgeshire countryside.

'I'm planning on coming up to Pendle to see you and Esther as soon as I'm discharged,' he wrote.

'It's good to be back to normal,' said Elsie as she resumed her work filling shell cases on the cordite line. 'Though I wish Tommy could have stayed, of course.'

'Don't tell me you're not missing the drama of the last few months?' Daphne teased.

'Oh, yeah, I'm sure she's missing the fact that nobody's being murdered or sent to prison,' Lillian joked.

'I'm just glad it's all over,' Elsie said with a happy smile.

One Friday evening at the end of a long hard week, Elsie, Emily, Lillian, Daphne and Agnes, arm in arm, swung up the cobbled lane singing Vera Lynn's heart-wrenching song, 'Yours' at the tops of their voices.

Emily, who always associated that song with Bill and the early carefree days of their courtship, started to choke up. Seeing Emily's sad face, Daphne called out.

'Change the record, girls, something more cheerful, please.'

Lillian immediately burst into a rendition of 'Somewhere Over the Rainbow' and everybody joined in.

Standing on the moorland just outside their digs, with the wind lifting her hair and the warm sun beating down, Emily suggested they all went for a walk.

'Darling, you have got to be joking!' Daphne exclaimed. 'I've just finished a gruelling twelve-hour shift and I am on my knees, stained with cordite and, more importantly, desperate for a gin!'

'It's a wonderful time of the year for wandering the moors,' Emily said as she recalled the happy times she'd spent rambling with Alice.

Agnes and Elsie, who'd left their children with Tommy's mum for the evening, were looking forward to a relaxing time with their friends, not a route march across the wild Pennine moors.

'I thought we were having a girlie night-in,' Elsie said enthusiastically. 'Hot bath, hair wash and a sing-song before bed.'

Agnes came up with a compromise that pleased Emily.

'We could go walking on the moors tomorrow with the children?' she suggested.

Emily nodded.

'We'll go winberry picking and I'll make a big fruit pie and custard when we get back,' she said with a happy smile.

Baths were shared out, then, sitting in their winceyette nighties with rollers in their hair, the girls took it in turns to paint each other's nails ruby red.

'Just like Elizabeth Taylor,' Lillian laughed.

They were all startled by a loud bang as a car pulled up outside their house.

'Who could that be?' asked Agnes as she peeped under the blackout blind.

Curious, Lillian joined her by the window.

'My God!' she gasped. 'It's an RAF officer in a flash sports car.'

All further speculation was stopped by a sharp rap at the door. Agnes went to cautiously open it and there, filling the doorway and wearing a huge RAF navy-blue overcoat, stood none other than Rodney Harston-Binge.

'Hello, ladies! Rodney Harston-Binge – pronounced Bing not Binge as in pissed – signing in for duty!'

Nobody but Emily had a clue who the booming man was and Emily, in a nightie with rollers in her hair, felt very much at a disadvantage.

'Bloody hell, look what the wind blew in,' Lillian giggled. 'Mr Bing not Binge! Any relation to Bing Crosby?' she asked cheekily.

As Rodney stared at her in humourless confusion, Emily stood in front of her irrepressible friend just in case she blurted out any more rude comments.

'Oh! Er, please come in,' Emily mumbled as she tried to surreptitiously yank rollers from her hair.

Oblivious to the commotion, not to mention amazement he'd caused, Rodney strode in and surveyed their digs as if assessing a residence for war requisition.

'Whiffs a bit,' he said with a bit of a goofy grin.

Wishing the floor would open and swallow her up, Emily was at a loss for words, but Daphne, who'd had time to remove her rollers and change into a sexy purple satin dressing gown, rescued her awkward friend.

'Welcome to our humble abode,' she said in her snootiest voice. 'Do, please, sit down,' she added, waving towards the sofa as if they were at the Ritz.

'Just got to pop orff for a few bits and pieces I left in the car,' Rodney said as he exited.

The second the door closed behind him, Lillian snorted with laughter.

'Pop orfff! What planet is he from?'

'Shh! He'll hear you,' Emily hissed at her outrageous friend.

'Where did you dig him up?' Elsie giggled.

'I met him in London when I went to visit Alice. He asked if he could see me again, and I was drunk and said yes, but I never thought he'd turn up!' she babbled.

'Well, he has, darling, and he's got the hots for you, so get those rollers out and for God's sake change out of that wretched nightie!' cried Daphne as she began to push her out of the room.

'What're we going to do with him?' Agnes whispered. 'He can't stay here.'

'He absolutely definitely can't stay here,' cried Emily as she dashed to change in her bedroom.

Rodney returned with a hamper containing Martini, gin and a silver shaker in which he flamboyantly made cocktails. Then he handed out dry biscuits and caviar, which promptly made Elsie, unused to rich and exotic food, feel quite sick. How on earth had Rodney got his hands on all this, the girls wondered.

'Not used to the high life, eh?' Rodney said as he hooted with laughter.

Little Elsie blushed.

'I'm not used to fancy food, like,' she said apologetically. 'I prefer simple food, like chip butties and meat pies. They suits me far better than fish eggs,' she said, turning green at the thought of the salty caviar she'd just thrown up.

One by one the girls drifted to bed, leaving only Emily and Daphne.

'Don't leave me alone with *him*!' desperate Emily whispered to Daphne when Rodney popped outside to relieve himself.

'He's rather sweet,' said Daphne, who'd imbibed too many gin cocktails.

'He should have written to tell me he was coming and not just turned up out of the blue!' Emily muttered angrily under her breath.

'Darling, don't you know officers in the RAF think they're God's gift to women?' Daphne replied tipsily. 'He'll be expecting to have your knickers down soon, believe me!' she added with a loud hiccup.

Emily clung to Daphne like an Elastoplast, listening for what seemed like hours to Rodney's tedious stories and cringing as he cracked dreadful jokes that made him guffaw with laughter but left her totally unamused.

They finally offloaded Rodney at three in the morning, sending him to the Station Hotel in Pendle.

'Thank God he's gone,' sighed Emily as he roared away into the night.

'Prepare yourself, darling, he'll be back!' Daphne laughed.

Daphne was spot on: Rodney was back the next day. He stood on the threshold with yet another hamper, this time packed with a picnic for him and Emily.

'Picked it up from Fortnum & Mason's on my way up here,' he said with a rather conceited smile. 'Mother has an account there. Makes all the difference.'

'I bet it bloody does, Little Lord Fauntleroy!' Lillian scoffed behind his back.

In high spirits, Rodney swung into the digs quoting a poem in a silly high voice.

'"Oh, to be in England now that April's there!"'

'Oh, God!' giggled Elsie.

Standing in the middle of the sitting room, Rodney struck a dramatic pose as he boomed:

'That's the wise thrush;
He sings each song twice over,
Lest you should think he never could recapture
The first, fine careless rapture.'

Consumed by a fit of giggles, Elsie hid her face in a pillow, and Agnes covered her smile with her hand whilst Lillian rolled her eyes to the ceiling.

'Un-bloody-believable!'

Daphne took his unappreciated poetry rendition in her stride.

'Robert Browning, "Home Thoughts, from Abroad",' she said as she clapped Rodney politely. 'Always popular at prizegiving.'

'A poem I cherish in my heart as I fly out over the Channel on a bombing raid,' Rodney bragged.

'Take him onto the moors, lock him up in a troll cave and throw away the key!' Lillian said sotto voce to Emily.

Seeing Agnes and Elsie hysterical with laughter, Emily pushed Rodney out of the door before Lillian could dream up further withering comments.

'Toodle-oo, chaps,' Rodney said hurriedly.

Perfectly mimicking his posh voice, Lillian waved the open-topped MG off.

'Toodle-oo, Rodders, old boy! For God's sake don't come back!' she called, reducing Elsie, Agnes and even Daphne to howls of naughty laughter.

Out on the sunny moors loud with the calls of curlews and skylarks, Emily should have been happy showing Rodney the countryside she loved and knew so well. Unfortunately all she could concentrate on was Rodney's hand, which he planted firmly on her knee the minute he got in the car. As he drove, his hand crept further and further up her thigh until she had to shake it off and twist in her seat so he couldn't clutch her any more.

Emily purposefully didn't choose a private spot for their picnic: if Rodney was all over her in the car, what would he be like surrounded by heather and rolling moorland? She suggested they stopped quite near the road; it seemed safe and relatively public. But after knocking back half a bottle of Chablis and even more caviar, Rodney decided to throw himself at Emily and started kissing her passionately. Horrified, Emily squirmed as he stuck his tongue into her mouth. Apart from the fact that she found Rodney repulsive, she'd made up her mind long ago that she'd never be easy prey again.

Wriggling free of Rodney's groping hands, she stood up and said briskly, 'Shall we walk?'

Rearranging himself down below, Rodney scowled.

'I had something entirely different in mind from a damn walk,' he said as he grumpily stumbled to his feet. 'Look, Emily, let's not beat about the bush – we're both grown-ups. I came up here expressly because I fancy the pants off you. You're a rare northern beauty and I'd like to get to know you a lot more,' he said, leaning forward to plant yet another wet kiss on her lips.

Ignoring his advances, Emily strode along the path that wound its way up the hillside onto the tops, where the wind caught her thick auburn hair and whipped it around her face. Hearing Rodney puffing and blowing behind her, she desperately tried to change the subject.

'Have you seen Robin?' she asked. 'I've not heard a word from Alice for months.'

Annoyed at not getting his own way, Rodney grunted behind her.

'Haven't seen either of them since the night I met you,' he growled.

As Alice's best friend, Emily constantly worried about her, but Rodney seemed not to care about his old school-boy chum, Robin.

'Aren't you concerned?' she asked.

Rodney shrugged.

'It's perfectly clear they're training to be Joes in some remote location,' he replied curtly.

'Joes?'

'Spies, Special Ops.'

Emily didn't say she already knew that.

Fed up with stomping over the moors, Rodney about-turned.

'I've had enough of this bloody nonsense!' he swore as he headed back down the hill, tripping and stumbling over tufts of ragged heather.

Driving back in his MG, with the hood down and the wind whistling around them, it was, mercifully, impossible to make any conversation. Rodney screeched to an abrupt halt at the digs then he leaped out and unceremoniously threw open the door for Emily.

'It's perfectly clear you've had enough of me,' he said peevishly. 'I'll go back to my hotel.'

Edging out of the car, Emily struggled for something to say.

'Is the Station Hotel comfortable?' she asked.

He scowled like a spoiled little boy as he barked a reply.

'Absolutely not up to scratch!'

Emily fell through the door of the digs and collapsed on the sofa.

'What a disaster!' she cried as her friends gathered round and questioned her. 'He tried it on with me on the moors,' she said as she burst out laughing.

'You must've led him on when you went gallivanting in London,' Lillian said knowingly.

'I told you, I was tipsy on champagne but I never said I fancied him!' Emily replied honestly. 'And I definitely didn't!' she added with a grin.

'You'd have to be drunk to pick up a plonker like Rodders,' Lillian scoffed.

Emily groaned as she buried her head under a cushion.

'What am I going to do with him tomorrow?' she wailed.

Daphne popped a cigarette into her long holder and languidly lit up.

'I'll take him off your hands, darling,' she said.

Emily gaped at her.

'Are you serious, Daf?'

Daphne nodded as she took a long drag on her cigarette.

'Not a problem. I'm used to his sort!'

The next morning Rodney roared up to the digs. His half-hearted smile widened to a big beam when he saw both Daphne and Emily waiting for him.

'My word, this is my lucky day,' he gushed. 'Two gorgeous women to entertain!'

Daphne, glamorous in a fitted silk tea dress with a scooped neckline and high heels that showed off her long, slender legs, pressed herself close to boggle-eyed Rodney as she slipped into the convertible.

'Darling, none of us can resist a handsome RAF officer,' she cooed.

As Emily was about to slide in beside Daphne, a breathless Elsie came running up the lane. Waving her hands, she flagged down the car just as Rodney started the engine.

'STOP! WAIT!' she hollered.

Daphne gave Emily a secretive nudge in the ribs.

'What is it, Elsie, what's the matter?' Emily cried.

Elsie, who'd been rehearsing her lines all morning, put a hand over her mouth to hide the laughter that threatened to bubble out of her.

'You can't go, Emily,' she said woodenly. 'You're urgently needed back at the Phoenix.'

In a blink, Emily hopped out.

'Just me?' she said, winking at Elsie.

Elsie nodded as she clunkily repeated her practised lines.

'Only you,' she replied.

'Tough luck!' Rodney boomed as he hit the accelerator and roared off over the moors with smiling Daphne by his side.

Chapter 26: Fancy Pants Bilodeau

Everybody was surprised by Daphne's interest in 'Rodders', as the girls, even Esther, called Flight Lieutenant Rodney Harston-Binge.

'He's great marriage material,' said Daphne as she soaked in the bath surrounded by her friends. 'We share the same background, have friends in common; plus, he's stinking rich . . . and I quite like his MG too!'

'Money isn't everything,' Elsie said wisely.

'But it helps, darling,' Daphne said as she lathered soap on her long, slender legs.

'Can you bear the way he kisses?' Emily asked with a grimace.

'Really, you northern girls are so naive,' Daphne replied.

'Count me out of the northern bit. I'm a Londoner born and bred,' Agnes reminded her.

'I control the kissing and we do it my way or we don't do it at all,' Daphne said, at which point Agnes ushered wide-eyed Esther out of the bathroom.

'Don't want to give her any ideas,' she said.

'You can never start too young!' Lillian teased.

'Did you, you know, do it with him?' Elsie asked.

'Absolutely not!' Daphne cried. 'He suggested we rolled about like heathens in the heather but I have my standards.'

'Good, cos Rodders definitely hasn't,' laughed Emily.

As summer came round and optimism heightened across the nation after the Allies landed in Sicily, Emily organized a jitterbug night at the Phoenix. Elsie, Agnes, Lillian and Daphne threw themselves into the preparations.

'We'll order in a couple of barrels of beer from Malc's pal who makes his own home-brew,' Emily said as she got onto her favourite subject: food.

'Witch piss, more like,' Lillian added.

On a roll, Emily ignored her.

'I'll beg, borrow or steal anybody's ration coupons to buy extra meat for a meat and potato pie with mushy peas and pickled red cabbage.'

'At least Churchill's not rationed pickled cabbage and peas!' Elsie laughed.

'Really, darling!' Daphne said as she wrinkled her small nose in distaste. 'It sounds awfully like peasant fodder!'

'Well, what were you expecting?' Emily exclaimed.

'Something a little more luxurious,' Daphne said wistfully. 'Salmon canapés, Martini cocktails, foie gras, lamb cutlets with mint sauce . . .'

'Remember rationing, Daphne?' Lillian asked. 'Or has that completely passed you by?'

'There are ways and means,' Daphne insisted. 'You just have to use your imagination.'

'I *am* using my imagination,' Emily pointed out. 'I'm imagining what I can make with the few food coupons I can cadge'

'But, really, peas and pies and pickles?' Daphne scoffed. 'How are we supposed to handle platefuls of steaming food in the middle of a boogie night?'

'Stick around, kid, and find out,' Emily said with a knowing smile.

Lillian organized a popular swing band from Bradford to play for the evening.

'We'll pay them out of the takings,' she said confidently.

Agnes, Elsie and Esther helped decorate the canteen with bunting and Union Jacks, whilst Daphne and Lillian stacked away all the metal tables and chairs so there was a large enough space for dancing.

Emily was in her element in the kitchen, where Esther soon joined her, eager to help with rolling out the pastry. Emily gently simmered minced meat in a pan, stirred in Oxo cubes and onions, then bulked out the mixture with carrots and potatoes, adding a bit of gravy browning to give it depth, and a generous sprinkle of wild herbs freshly picked from the moors that morning.

'Mmm, it smells good!' Esther said as she sniffed the bubbling pan.

'Come on, sweetheart, let's roll the pastry whilst the meat cools down,' said Emily.

The pastry was made with brown flour, white lard and as much shin-beef dripping as Emily could scrounge from the canteen cook, and to add moisture she added mashed potato and milk; then she rolled it carefully on a well-floured board. She and Esther made over a dozen huge savoury mince and onion pies, which Emily intended to cook during the dancing so that she could serve the food fresh and piping hot.

Excitement increased as preparations heightened. Esther was thrilled when the Bradford Swing Band arrived early to set up and rehearse. As they struck up 'Chattanooga

Choo Choo', she danced all through the number, regardless of her calliper, and received a standing ovation from the band.

'I'm going to be a dancer when I grow up,' she announced.

'Move over, Ginger Rogers, is all I've got to say,' said Lillian as she picked the little girl up and swung her round the floor to 'In the Mood'.

Only one thing dampened Emily's anticipation of the dance night and that was Freddie Bilodeau. He would inevitably be there along with all the other Canadian servicemen, now well established in the nearby airfield.

'I wish we could stop Freddie from coming,' she said as they hung bunting in the canteen.

Lillian, balanced on a ladder, said, 'We can't ban him on the grounds that he's a bastard!'

'I know,' Emily answered. 'I just wish he'd drop off the edge of the universe so that I never have to see him again.'

'No chance. Where there're women there'll be Freddie Bilodeau,' said Lillian knowingly.

'Who is this wretched Casanova character?' Daphne asked.

'The man I cheated on Bill with,' Emily said miserably.

'Only to discover he's a womanizer,' Elsie added.

'Believe me, he's been through half the workforce,' said Agnes.

Emily cringed as she covered her ears.

'STOP!' she cried. 'I made such a fool of myself.'

'Darling, we've all been fools for love,' Daphne said as she passed yards of bunting up to Lillian.

'But this fella's not worth the heartache,' Elsie said indignantly. 'He behaves like he's cock of the roost.'

'My dear, you say the quaintest things,' Daphne laughed.

'You know what I mean,' Elsie replied. 'He's only out for what he can get.'

Daphne and Lillian exchanged a mischievous look.

'Mmm,' Daphne said. 'Maybe it's about time Mr Fancy Pants Bilodeau was taught a lesson.'

Agnes and Elsie declined invitations to the dance, preferring to spend the evening in the digs with their children, but it didn't stop them helping their friends get ready.

Agnes ironed their rather dated dance dresses.

'What wouldn't I give for a new frock?' Lillian sighed as she repaired a rip in the sleeve of her dress.

'You could've knocked one up in no time,' Elsie laughed.

'Oh, yeah! Done an Olivia de Havilland and made a new ball gown out of the curtains,' Lillian mocked.

Elsie polished their shoes until they shone, Daphne did their make-up and Lillian washed and set everybody's hair, including Esther's, which she brushed into an elegant chignon.

'You all look lovely!' Esther cried as Lillian, Emily and Daphne paraded up and down the sitting room in their party attire.

'I just hope I don't get mushy peas down the front of my best dress,' Emily joked.

Freddie did arrive, with a large crowd of airmen who made a beeline for the bar then headed eagerly onto the dance floor. He saw Emily straight away – who could miss the blue-eyed beauty with the flaming hair? – but he chose to blank her, for which she was deeply grateful. Taking the hand of a small pretty girl who Emily recognized from the packing department, he swung onto the dance floor, showing off his great body as he moved in sync with the music.

Sighing, Emily made her way into the kitchen. In fact she was happy to spend most of the night preparing food for the revellers who she knew would be starving come nine o'clock. Hopefully, Freddie would leave early with his girlfriend; he'd probably take her back to his love shack, the stable where he would seduce her, as he had so many before.

Through the serving hatch, Emily saw Lillian wink at Daphne then nod in the direction of Freddie, who had returned to the crowded bar. Waving her cigarette holder, Daphne sashayed up to the bar, where she asked for a gin and lime. As she turned her back and walked away, Freddie's eyes widened at the sight of her swaying, shapely bottom in her tightly-fitted red dance dress. Leaving his drink on the bar, Freddie quickly followed Daphne to the edge of the dance floor.

'Hey, are you new round here?' he asked.

Daphne turned her exquisitely made-up face to him and smiled languidly.

'Not exactly. I've just been incarcerated in the munitions factory for months,' she replied with a seductive smile.

'What a waste!' he said with a twinkle in his charming eyes. 'With a body like yours you should be in the movies.'

Daphne batted her false eyelashes.

'How kind,' she drawled.

Ignoring his waiting partner, Freddie held out his hand to Daphne.

'Care to dance, honey?'

Through the serving hatch Emily watched Daphne and Freddie take to the dance floor.

'What is she up to?' she hissed to Lillian, who popped her head through the hatch and laughed at Emily's astonished expression.

'Teaching lover boy a lesson,' Lillian replied.

Knowing how anarchic Lillian could be, Emily eyed her nervously.

'What are you up to?'

Lillian smiled and winked.

'Wait and see . . .'

Clearly enchanted by Daphne and oblivious of the now rather upset pretty girl he'd started the evening with, Freddie danced the foxtrot, the waltz and the square tango with his new partner, then excelled at the jitterbug.

'Is there nothing you can't do?' Daphne gushed.

'With a gorgeous girl like you in my arms I could fly!' Freddie announced as the band struck up another jive number.

Before she could protest, Freddie swung flabbergasted Daphne over his shoulder, then with a deft flick he brought her back down and spun her around before sliding her between his legs.

'Oh, my God!' gasped Daphne.

In the kitchen Emily and Lillian were rocking with laughter.

'I think I just saw our Daphne's camiknickers!' Emily gasped.

'I think I just saw what she had for breakfast!' Lillian giggled.

To the Andrews Sisters' 'Beat Me Daddy, Eight to the Bar', Freddie continued to spin, throw and catch Daphne, who, with dishevelled hair and crumpled dress, was beginning to look more like a scarecrow than a glamour girl.

'Poor kid!' howled Lillian. 'She hadn't reckoned on being thrown about like a rag doll.'

'From the look in her eyes, she's ready to kill Freddie,' said Emily.

'Well, that'd make two of you, wouldn't it?' said Lillian.

Finally the dance number finished.

'Grub's up, so we'll take a break!' said the hungry band leader. 'Best meat and potato pie this side of the Pennines.'

As Emily and Lillian dished up supper, they spotted Freddie leading Daphne out of the canteen.

'Where are they off to?' Emily asked.

Behind the steaming meat pies, Lillian winked.

'Can't you guess?'

'Gorgeous grub, love,' said appreciative airmen as they tucked into Emily's delicious home-made food.

'You should open a shop, honey,' one of them said.

Emily smiled.

'Maybe I will one day,' she replied.

Meanwhile, out on the dark moors, Freddie was keen to get Daphne into the stables he so favoured for his lovemaking but she persuaded him into walking to Witch Crag.

'It was used by the Pendle Witches,' she said alluringly. 'It has magic powers,' she added, holding his hand as she led him along the narrow moorland track.

With only one thing on his mind, Freddie followed like a lamb to the slaughter.

'It's kinda isolated,' he said as he breathed heavily in her wake.

'Just us and the stars,' she replied beguilingly.

'Sounds good to me, honey,' he replied.

Once on the rather blustery crag, which Daphne had explored only the day before with Lillian, there was no holding Freddie back.

'God, you're driving me crazy,' he gasped as they lay down together. 'I gotta have you, babe,' he said as he threw off his jacket.

Daphne responded convincingly to his kisses, letting him reach up her skirt, and as he fiddled with her suspenders she huskily suggested that he removed his trousers.

'We're not going to have much fun if you're wearing those, are we?' she teased.

Freddie's trousers quickly joined his shirt and jacket on the heather. Daphne had no problem in whipping off his underpants, by which time Freddie was begging for it.

'C'mon, get your clothes off,' he cried impatiently.

Daphne stood up and, whilst pretending to loosen her bra, she cast her eyes around the dark moor.

'Speed it up, babe,' Freddie implored.

As he reached to pull her down on top of him, a light

flashed from a gravel track that ran alongside Witch Crag. Freddie was too far gone to notice but Daphne certainly saw it. In a blink, she grabbed Freddie's clothes then ran across the moors as if the devil were on her heels.

'*Oi!*' bellowed Freddie as he sprang to his feet and gave chase.

Daphne, clothed and shod, made better progress along the twisting narrow path than naked Freddie, who tripped over spindly heather roots, cutting his feet and legs.

'*Bitch!* Come back!' he shrieked.

Waiting on the gravel track was a grinning Malc, who'd kept his promise to pick up Daphne on his mate's motorbike and sidecar.

'Hop on before lover boy catches you!' he chuckled.

Sitting in the sidecar, breathless Daphne reached into her bag and pulled out a Kodak Brownie. It was far too dark to line up the shot but she aimed the camera in the direction of Freddie's furious roars then hit the flash. As the livid jilted lover bore down on her, Daphne threw his clothes into the heather whilst Malc, revving at full throttle, burned down the track. Freddie was left scrambling for his trousers and muttering foul curses that would have made his mother weep.

A few days later, as soon as the photograph was printed, a smiling Daphne returned to the digs and, in front of all the girls, presented it to Emily with the negative.

'Payback time!' she said with a laugh.

Emily gasped in shock then burst out laughing.

'How on earth?' she cried.

'Lillian and I hatched a little plan,' Daphne told her.

Emily turned to Lillian in amazement.

'So that's what you were up to! I knew there was something going on.'

'Actually, we all knew about it,' Agnes said with a smile. 'Even Esther – not *all* the gory details, obviously,' she quickly added.

'He had it coming,' said Elsie. 'Mebbe he'll mend his dirty ways after this.'

'Want to see a photograph of Fancy Pants Freddie Bilodeau stark bollock naked?' Daphne teased.

Elsie blushed as she covered her eyes.

'*No!*' she shrieked. 'Tommy would never forgive me.'

'I'm not shy,' said Lillian as she grabbed the photograph and scanned it appraisingly. 'He's certainly got all the tackle!'

'Will you shurrup before I die of embarrassment!' Elsie pleaded, though in truth she was laughing so much that tears were pouring down her face.

Emily looked at the photograph, not quite as appreciatively as Lillian, and shook her head in disbelief.

'How did you get him to take his clothes off?' she asked.

Daphne rolled her eyes.

'Darling, do credit me with some sex appeal! He started to strip the minute we reached Witch Crag.'

'You must have been egging him on a bit,' Agnes said with a wide smile.

'Of course I was!' Daphne exclaimed. 'But I was worried sick that Malc wouldn't show up – otherwise I'd certainly have been rogered right there and then on the spot!'

'Malc's turned out to be our knight in shining armour,' Elsie said fondly. 'He's always there when you need him.'

'You know, now you've seriously hurt Freddie's pride he might come back for vengeance,' Agnes pointed out.

Lillian snorted with laughter.

'We've hurt more than his pride! With this photograph we could blackmail him till he flies back to where he came from.'

Emily smiled at her naughty, scheming friends.

'One thing's for sure – I wouldn't want to get on the wrong side of you two!' she joked.

For all their laughing and joking, there was a sadness in Emily's pale blue eyes.

'Out with it, darling,' Daphne said as she gave her friend a quick poke in the ribs.

'It's so humiliating to think I fell so easily for a sex maniac like Freddie,' Emily confessed. 'I hate myself for it.'

'We all make mistakes,' Lillian said as she handed her a cigarette. 'For God's sake, look at me!'

'Yes, but you didn't ditch a good man for a waste of space,' Emily said as she lit up a Woodbine and deeply inhaled.

'Come along now,' Daphne said briskly. 'This exercise wasn't carried out in order to make you miserable.'

'Sorry,' said Emily. 'I am grateful to you for setting Freddie up. Like Elsie said, he had it coming.'

'So . . .' said Daphne. 'Would you like to do something for me, in exchange for risking my all on Witch Crag?'

'Of course,' Emily answered, then, seeing the mischievous gleam in Daphne's eyes, she hesitated.

'. . . As long as it doesn't involve me running around Pendle moors stark naked?'

Daphne paused and smiled as she looked Emily in the eye.

'Darling, will you be my chief bridesmaid when I marry Rodders? He's asked me, you know!'

Chapter 27: Claridge's

Daphne's courtship with Rodders was unquestionably a whirlwind affair. After his flamboyant visit to the Phoenix Rodney didn't seem to mind being dumped by one woman only to be picked up by another. In his ever-egotistical mind, the entire visit blurred into a beautiful romantic scenario. He'd had a wonderful time with Daphne on their first date on the moors; at least she'd responded to his kisses and not suggested they went for a walk! Daphne had managed a few visits south, where he'd introduced her to his parents in their country house in Wiltshire. Over port and cigars, his father had announced his opinion of Daphne.

'Right out of the top drawer!'

So that same evening, Rodney had taken her into the fragrant garden. There, by the tinkling fountain adorned with sea nymphs and naked mermaids, he had, in his own words, 'popped the question' and Daphne, like the good girl she was, had accepted. Of course, the 'Aged Ps', as Rodney called his parents, had to be introduced to Daphne's parents, who were certainly a little more risqué in their tastes and dress than the county set; but altogether it was a most acceptable arrangement.

Back in the digs, Daphne was planning a very grand affair.

'You're being granted more compassionate leave than

Montgomery!' Lillian joked as Daphne packed her bag for an 'urgent trip' to London.

'Darling, I've got an appointment with Hartnell that I can't refuse,' Daphne answered breezily.

Everybody but sweet little Elsie knew exactly who Hartnell was, and as the others all looked stunned at the mention of his name, she turned to them with her usual characteristic innocence.

'Who's he when he's at home?'

'Only the best designer in England,' Lillian replied.

'He's not designing our frocks too?' Elsie gasped.

'Depends how indulgent Daddy's feeling,' Daphne said as she snapped her crocodile-skin suitcase shut. 'I can usually wrap him round my little finger, but since he got remarried to the daughter of Satan, I have to be very devious.'

'Eeh, and there was I thinking I had the stepmother from hell,' laughed Elsie.

'Oh, you do, Elsie. You really, really do!' Emily affirmed.

'Well, this one's a money-grabber and she loathes me,' Daphne said. 'But she fancies Rodney, so he can sweet-talk her whilst I twist every penny I can out of Pops,' she said cheerfully.

'When will you be back?' Agnes asked.

Daphne clicked her heels and gave a Gestapo hand salute.

'Just as soon as I can, boss!'

There was a sense of disbelief across the nation as the war finally began to turn. With Mussolini arrested and the Fascist Italian government in pieces, Britain was no longer the underdog. But after four years of rationing, striving, fighting, hoping and grieving, the population were almost too tired to celebrate.

In the Phoenix factory, as the shells rattled by and *Workers' Playtime* belted out the top favourites – 'Pennsylvania 6-5000', 'South of the Border', 'I Only Have Eyes for You' and 'This is the Army, Mr Jones' – Elsie tried to cheer everybody up.

'Where would you like to go on holiday?'

At first nobody could be bothered; it was early in the morning, the din from the conveyor belt was relentless and a cold wind whistled in from the moors.

'Mars!' said Lillian grumpily.

'Come on, be serious,' urged Elsie. 'I'll go first,' she yelled over the clatter of the overhead conveyor belt carrying filled bomb cases across the factory into the packing department. 'Blackpool!'

Smiling at the sweet simplicity of Elsie's answer, Agnes went second.

'Walthamstow Rex, with Stan, watching *The Wizard of Oz* for a whole week with beer, fish and chips and choc ices thrown in,' she laughed.

Without any pause in her work, Emily filled the shells rolling by as she thought for a moment or two.

'I'm not going to think about a holiday with Bill, though we did plan a honeymoon in Rhyl,' she said sadly.

'Come on,' urged Elsie cheerily. 'Keep it upbeat, Em.'

'Okay, I'd love a holiday with Alice, camping in the Lake District, talking and walking and laughing just like we always did. That'd be my choice.'

'Your turn, Lil,' said Elsie, but when she turned to

Lillian, instead of getting a cheeky reply, like 'South of France with nowt on', she saw Lillian was crying.

Still keeping an eye on the conveyor belt that rolled interminably on whether its attendants laughed, cried or fainted, Elsie moved up closer to Lillian so she could lay an arm over her.

'Lil, love, I'm sorry,' she said.

'It's not your fault, Elsie,' Lillian said as tears rolled down her pretty face. 'I'm so sick and tired of hardly hearing from Gary. I'd give anything just to be near him; even sitting beside him in a plane on its way to bomb the bloody Germans would be a treat!' she sobbed.

Agnes nodded at the twenty-five-pound bombs swinging overhead.

'Blow one of them a kiss; they're all on their way to Gerry!'

The girls cheered up when Daphne breezed back into the digs with her suitcase bulging with fabric samples, dress designs, gin, chocolates and toys for Jonty and Esther.

'Daddy's agreed to everything!' she announced as she picked up a bottle of Bollinger's. 'Wedding at St James's, Piccadilly, reception at Claridge's, honeymoon shooting grouse in Scotland!'

'It's a miracle what you can get on the black market if you're loaded,' Agnes remarked.

Without a moment's guilt, Daphne beamed at her.

'I know, darling, isn't it marvellous?'

As the cork whizzed across the room and the champagne fizzed, Daphne poured everybody a cupful then raised hers for a toast.

'Here's to the eighth of September, my wedding day!'

'Heck! You've moved fast,' Agnes remarked.

'There's a war on, darling, we can't hang about!' Daphne giggled as she raised her glass. 'To me!'

'Yeah! Cheers! Good luck!' her friends replied.

They all drank, all but Elsie, who, after taking a cautious sip, shuddered.

'Ugh! It tastes like Eno's Liver Salts!'

Daphne rolled her eyes.

'Elsie, darling, you are truly a philistine.'

Elsie copied Daphne and rolled her eyes too as she replied.

'Lucky I canne understand posh words!'

This time there was no stitching and sewing, begging and borrowing like there had been at Elsie's wedding. Measurements were taken by Lillian and recorded by Daphne, and colours were finally agreed, after many hours of anguished indecision.

'Green,' said Elsie.

'Blue,' said Emily.

'Red,' laughed Lillian.

'Pink!' said Esther.

Daphne looked at the samples.

'I'm in cream silk with a strapless lace top, bouffant skirt and Brussels lace veil, and you, my gorgeous bridesmaids, must blend in around the bride.'

'This isn't exactly fashion on the ration!' Agnes said as she quoted one of the familiar slogans of the day.

Lillian swept a professional eye over the silk samples on the table.

'Not green, not red . . . blue,' she finally said.

'And me?' asked Esther.

'Pale pink,' Lillian replied as she planted a kiss on the little girl's dark curls.

The samples and the girls' measurements were sent off to the dressmaker.

'Sorry, not Hartnell,' Daphne apologized. 'He's just for *moi* – the virgin bride!' she joked.

Lillian snorted with laughter.

'Try telling that to the vicar!'

Daphne left ahead of the girls for her final dress fitting with Mr Hartnell.

Emily, Agnes, Elsie and Lillian followed later, travelling overnight with Esther, who asked Elsie why baby Jonty couldn't be a bridesmaid too.

'Well, he's a lad for a start, and he's too little to travel all the way to London so he's staying with his nan in Pendle,' Elsie explained.

Daphne, generous to a fault, had booked her bridesmaids into Claridge's, where a taxi dropped them off.

'Mummy! Mummy!' shrieked Esther as they walked into the hotel glittering with gilt and shimmering mirrors. 'Is this Buckingham Palace?'

Agnes smiled in delight as she took in the opulent surroundings.

'No, it's even nicer!' she exclaimed.

Words completely failed Agnes a few minutes later when she walked into the grand reception area and found Stan waiting for her. Faint with delight, Agnes swayed and grabbed hold of Emily.

'You never said,' she murmured incredulously as she gazed up at her smiling husband.

'Daphne arranged it all,' he said as he gathered his wife and daughter into his arms.

'*How?*' gasped Agnes.

Stan shrugged as if he wasn't quite sure how.

'Via the hospital, she sent me a wedding invitation and money to cover my train fare to London. She's quite a girl,' he added, impressed.

'She's a miracle worker,' sighed Agnes as she pressed her face against Stan's warm chest.

'Darling girl,' he chuckled into her hair. 'We're going to have ourselves a hell of a weekend!'

Esther, impatiently squeezing Stan's hand, looked up adoringly at him.

'We missed you, Daddy.'

Stan bent to pick his daughter up in his arms.

'And I missed you, my princess,' he said as he gave her a big kiss on both cheeks.

Having only heard about Stan and the horrors he'd gone through, Emily, Lillian and Elsie were surprised to see a tall man, admittedly on the thin side, with a strong face, thick black hair streaked with grey and dark, intense eyes that, right now, burned with love and happiness.

'Nice to meet you, ladies,' he said as he shook each of them warmly by the hand. 'Thank you for looking after my wife and daughter!'

Esther insisted that her daddy took her to the nearest park to feed the ducks, leaving the bridesmaids alone with the bride, who was eagerly waiting for Lillian to set her long blonde hair in an elegant chignon.

The girls bathed in turns in a sumptuous bathroom,

revelling in an endless supply of hot water, bath salts and bubbles.

'I feel like Marlene Dietrich!' laughed Agnes as she waved one soapy foot in the air.

'Say that when you're cuddling up to Stan in bed tonight!' giggled Elsie.

'Save some bubbles for me!' Lillian called from the bedroom, where she was attaching Daphne's long, flowing veil to her family's diamond heirloom tiara.

Once everybody's hair was done, including her own and little Esther's, Lillian sank into a fragrant bath, where she groaned in luxurious delight.

'Ooh,' she sighed. 'I've never had so much fun without laughing.'

The taxi arrived for the bridesmaids and they squeezed in, in a froth of blue silk and tulle, holding their carnation bouquets high so they wouldn't get damaged. With Esther the flower girl squashed between her mum and Elsie on the back seat, they drove through the September sunshine to Piccadilly.

'Heard the news?' asked the taxi driver as they wound their way through bomb-torn London streets where silver barrage balloons floated overhead. 'The Eyeties have surrendered to the Allies.'

The girls in the back stared at each other in disbelief, then whooped with joy.

'My Tommy might be there right now, celebrating in Rome,' said Elsie wistfully.

'We really are winning,' the taxi driver said as he swung to a halt in front of St James's church. 'About bloody time too!'

After the ceremony the bride and groom hosted a lavish meal for their hundred guests back at Claridge's: wild salmon, fillet of beef and chocolate soufflé washed down with Chablis, Châteauneuf-du-Pape and Dom Pérignon champagne carefully selected from Daphne's father's wine cellar. And then the party danced till dawn. Esther, who spent most of her time riding up and down in the glittering gilt lift lined with mirrors and equipped with a sofa on which she lay like Sleeping Beauty, was finally put to bed, blissfully happy and exhausted, leaving her mum and dad time to take to the dance floor.

'You look so beautiful, Agnes,' Stan said as they swayed to the music of the Joe Loss Orchestra, hired exclusively for the night by Daphne's wealthy father.

'Oh, Stan,' she sighed as she laid her head on his shoulder. 'I don't think I've ever been happier. I've got you back, strong and healthy, Esther sleeping upstairs and the best friends in the world.'

'They're wonderful girls, every one of them,' Stan agreed.

'They'd do anything for me and I would definitely do anything for them,' Agnes said with tears in her eyes. 'And they couldn't be more different,' she said with a fond smile. 'Little Elsie, so poor and frightened at the beginning, has now blossomed into a wonderful mum and loving wife. Emily's a star, loyal and strong no matter what gets thrown at her, and Lillian . . .' She laughed as she said the name. 'She could cheer anybody up but she carries her own burden. God knows when she'll see her Yank again.'

'And Daphne?' he asked.

'Daf's like a golden star that landed in our orbit. She's brilliant and exciting but I think we're going to lose her. I suspect Rodders will want her by his side in London, and whatever Flight Lieutenant Rodney Harston-Binge wants Flight Lieutenant Rodney Harston-Binge gets!' she concluded with a knowing smile.

Across the crowded ballroom, Flight Lieutenant Rodney Harston-Binge was rather drunkenly dancing the foxtrot with Emily, who looked radiant in her blue silk gown and pretty floral headdress.

'I really should apologize for behaving like a cad and a bounder,' he said as he held her close and swirled her around the room.

'Don't be daft!' laughed Emily. 'It's more my fault for leading you on when we met in London.'

'Well, you were pretty irresistible,' he said a little too intimately. 'What's a red-blooded man to do but jump in the car and chase after the prey!' He laughed his over-loud snorting laugh. 'But there you go. And if it wasn't for chasing after your skirt I would never have met my wonderful wife. All's well that ends well, as Shakespeare would say,' he said with another snort.

As the next Joe Loss number swung into a waltz, Emily, clasped ever tighter in Rodney's arms, dared to enquire about Alice and Robin.

'Last time I asked you said they were in training,' she reminded him. 'Do you know where they might be now?'

With his tongue well loosened by alcohol, Rodney bent to whisper thickly in her ear.

'It's all supposed to be hush-hush but for those in the know,' he winked meaningfully as if he was privy to top-secret information. 'It wouldn't surprise me if they were behind enemy lines as we speak.'

Emily, overcome at the very idea of this, bolted out of the room and into the Ladies, where she burst into tears.

'Oh, Alice, Alice,' she sobbed into her tiny lace handkerchief.

She jumped when the door opened, then smiled with relief when she saw Elsie standing in the doorway.

'I saw you rush off,' she said with her characteristic bluntness. 'What's wrong, like?'

Though Emily longed to pour her heart out to Elsie, who she trusted implicitly, she knew it wouldn't be fair to Alice and Robin.

'Nothing,' she said.

'Dun't look much like nothing to me,' Elsie said knowingly.

'It's just this wedding . . . It makes me miss Bill,' Emily lied.

'Aye, well, that makes sense, pet,' said Elsie as she laid an arm around Emily's shoulders. 'Now come on, let's have another dance to Mr Joe Loss then get ourselves to bed. We've a long journey back tomorrow.'

Just after dawn the next morning, Stan had no choice but to kiss his wife and daughter goodbye.

'Come with us, Daddy,' Esther begged.

His heart melted. How he wished he could. 'I'll join you just as soon as the doctor allows me to leave Cambridge,' Stan replied as he gave his daughter a big kiss.

The journey home was long but the girls were all so tired they slept most of the way. When the train stopped at Clitheroe station Elsie skipped out and smiled at the moors surrounding the town.

'Eeh, but it's grand to be home, like,' she exclaimed joyfully.

Back at the Phoenix, Agnes found a letter in her pigeonhole. It was from the Keswick hospital, recalling Esther for treatment. Agnes had known all along that this day would come; how could it ever have been otherwise? Her daughter was sick, and it was an undisputed fact that she needed hospital attention, but somehow, with all the recent events and the buzz and excitement of Daphne's glitzy wedding, Agnes had managed to blank out the prospect of Esther leaving her again. She'd drifted into a make-believe world in which Esther would grow up with baby Jonty in a happy environment where she could see her at least once, if not twice, a day.

The bubble's popped, thought Agnes as she bit back tears and screwed the letter into a hard ball.

Her daughter's happy, carefree days in Pendle were drawing to a close.

Chapter 28: Parachute Drop

Autumn in Cornwall was soft and golden, like a final caress of a summer that seemed reluctant to leave. As the Italians surrendered to the Allies and the Soviets valiantly recaptured Kiev in the Ukraine, the Special Ops were sent on an overnight recce into unknown territory where, in a raging storm, they were instructed to transmit at all costs.

'I don't think I've ever been as sodding wet in my whole life,' Gwynne said as they arrived back at Helford House at dawn, drenched to the skin.

'That tutor was dead right about stormy atmospheric conditions,' Iris said as she stripped off her wet clothes. 'I got nothing but a series of bloody hisses all night long.'

After removing her clothes, Gladys snuggled up under her eiderdown in an attempt to get warm.

'I had a disaster with the aerial. I tied it to an overhead branch, which snapped and landed on top of my radio set – bang went three valves and any chance of me getting top marks for code-breaking,' she said with a rueful laugh.

'Come on,' urged Alice, who was the first to change her clothes and was heading out of the door, hungry for her breakfast. 'Back to work!'

When they worked together Alice's and Robin's combined skills made them an effective team, so much so that the commanding officer called them into his study for a word.

'It's been pointed out that you two work well together in the field,' he said to the young couple standing before him. 'Miss Massey's French is practically flawless and her handling of explosives is first rate. Your wireless and messaging skills, sir, are highly commendable,' he said to Robin. 'Therefore it's been decided that when the time comes for active service you two will remain together.'

'Thank you, sir,' said Robin as he gave a smart salute.

'You'll be dropped behind enemy lines in France in the very near future. That will be all. Thank you.'

As Alice turned to walk out of the room, her face lit up with happiness; from now on, whatever happened, she'd always be with the man she loved.

Soon afterwards, on one of their precious short leaves, Alice and Robin pooled their precious petrol coupons and drove around Cornwall in Robin's old Austin. As they rattled and bounced over narrow, unmanaged roads, Robin lit two cigarettes, one of which he handed to Alice.

'So you think our training's coming to an end?' he asked.

'The Brigadier's dropped enough hints,' she replied. 'Plus, we can't stay here for ever, much as I'd love to,' she sighed as she gazed across the wild moors and out to sea.

Robin took a thoughtful deep drag on his cigarette.

'So far we've been taught how to parachute, drive a locomotive, use a pistol, receive and transmit Morse, decode messages, make invisible ink and how to kill ourselves,' he laughed bleakly. 'Think we're probably ready.'

'But are we really?' Alice asked quietly. 'Are *you*?'

'Yes!' Robin answered robustly. 'I want this, Alice. I've never wanted all that ghastly military rigmarole; I've always preferred independence and the freedom to fight a personal war at close quarters. It might sound unpatriotic but I want to be master of my own destiny rather than a pawn in somebody else's grand battle plan.'

'I think your principles are far finer than mine,' Alice answered.

'Alice, my darling, whatever your motives you're without question the best bomb-assembler on the course and you're a mean shot with an A.45 pistol.'

'Oh, Robin,' Alice said as she leaned her head on his shoulder. 'Don't you ever feel scared?'

'Of course! It's sensible to be scared, like an actor getting stage fright just before the curtain goes up. It's good to keep the adrenalin high; it keeps one focused.'

'Oh, I love you!' she laughed as he answered with his usual characteristic honesty and fervour. 'Let's not think about the war tonight, let's just think about us.'

Changing gear, Robin put a hand over hers.

'No cracking tonight, young lady!' he chuckled.

The road led them to Lamorna, a tiny hamlet near Mousehole fishing harbour, where they were forced to stop because of the sea mist rolling in and totally obscuring the narrow road. Luckily they found accommodation in an ancient inn, in a room with a crackling fire and an old four-poster bed. When the mist lifted towards the end of the day they walked hand in hand along the cliff tops and looked out over the wide English Channel towards France. With the wind whipping their cheeks and sea birds wheeling around them, it was impossible to imagine anything other than being in love in a beautiful part of England. They climbed steep iron steps down to the tiny cove, pleased to find they had it all to themselves. Sheltered by large slabs of rock, they watched the autumn sun sink over the metal-grey sea, which churned relentlessly against the pebble shore. All too soon the sun dipped quickly over the horizon, and the sea, briefly coloured a shimmering lavender, faded, in a blink, to grey.

'I don't want this moment to end,' Alice said as she snuggled her hands underneath Robin's great coat and felt his flesh, soft and warm, beneath.

Robin ran a line of kisses down her delicate neck and into her soft cleavage.

'Sorry, darling, but I need supper and then I need to get you into that warm four-poster bed!'

Supper was a real treat: local lamb roasted with potatoes, plus delicious sprouts and leeks grown by the landlady on her own allotment. They washed it down with cider, then made their way to bed, where Alice had no guilt or inhibitions about making love to Robin.

The pressures of war and their dangerous work only added to their determination to share and give as much as they could to each other. Their lovemaking not only strengthened them but it focused them on their mission too; both of them were committed to their work as Special Ops and both of them knew full well that they might die fighting to keep the Britain they loved a free country. Those few golden days driving around Cornwall on petrol coupons were memories they would cherish and take to the grave.

*

Back at the training centre, the Brigadier told the senior Special Ops that their next assignment was a night-time training exercise.

'Choose suitable clothes for an evening sortie, black up and return here at 2000 hours with your revolvers.'

Returning to their dorm, Gwynne sprawled out on her bunk.

'Well, that gives us the day off,' she yawned. 'I think I might sleep till 2000 hours.'

'You must be joking!' Alice laughed as she rummaged through her clothes trying to find something to wear for their assignment.

'Hey, don't forget a hat and gloves,' said Gladys as she stood in the middle of the dorm wearing her bra and knickers, a black beret and a pair of woolly gloves.

'Oh, dear, it's good that we can laugh,' sighed Iris. 'I have to admit I'm pretty terrified of wandering about in the dark waiting to feel a gun in my back.'

'It'll be fine,' said Alice confidently. 'Better we learn these things on our own patch than behind enemy lines.'

Eventually, after sharing out their clothes, they all went to supper suitably clothed, then blacked up their faces in readiness for the sortie.

'We've chosen tonight because there's a full moon,' the Brigadier told the team. 'It's easier to hide in the shadows when the moon's bright. We've set up targets; shoot fast and straight when you see them.'

They were driven to a forest where they were told to walk on, with revolvers at the ready.

'Don't bunch up. Split up and go in search of your

targets,' instructed the Brigadier, who was leading the exercise.

With her heart hammering against her ribcage, Alice scanned the trees. Every breath of wind in the treetops brought her out in a sweat; it was as if all her senses were on high alert. Metal targets attached to the trees on hinges suddenly popped out, causing Alice to jump in alarm, but she kept her cool and shot fast and straight. If a target dropped she knew it was a clean hit; if it remained upright she knew that in real life she'd be dead by now. As she crept deeper into the forest, she heard footsteps behind her. With the hairs on the back of her neck standing on end, Alice turned and held her revolver at arm's length, ready to shoot. A soft laugh startled her, then a friendly voice spoke to her in French.

'*Une boisson, ma belle?*'

Alice could hardly believe her ears; why would somebody ask her if she wanted a drink on a night raid in the middle of a dark forest?

'*Non!*' she snapped, whilst keeping the revolver trained on the head of the approaching man.

'I have brandy and it's a cold night,' he added in French.

And then the penny dropped. Of course! This was just another form of cracking: somebody was playing out the part of a friendly French Resistance worker who might or might not be a German spy. When she heard the metallic sound of a bottle being unscrewed she spoke sharply.

'Identify yourself!'

'Okay, you've passed the test,' said the man, who, as he neared Alice, she recognized as one of the sergeants in the Intelligence Corps at Helford House. 'I'll go and see if I can dupe some other poor bugger,' he said as he slunk off into the forest, leaving Alice feeling quite shaky.

She leaned against a tree until her breath had steadied, panicking that if she was like this on a training exercise on home ground, how would she cope when it was for real?

They got back to Helford House at four in the morning and were up as usual at eight, ready for what turned out to be their final exercise.

'Thank God it's daylight,' said Iris as they piled into trucks and were driven to the nearby demolition pit for an explosives training session.

'Let's see how you cope with booby traps,' the commanding officer hollered.

Half a mile down a track, Alice saw a branch of a tree blocking the path. Not taking any chances, she sidestepped it but Gladys gave it a hefty kick and 'BOOM!' an explosive went off that sent Gladys flying into the undergrowth.

The track ended by a roadside, where the commanding officer told a dozen of the Ops to guard the area.

'Three men will cross this road twenty yards up,' he said. 'I guarantee you won't even see them.'

Looking at the empty road with no obstructions in sight, the trainees shook their heads. It was impossible not to see anybody; they had a clear view for miles. As they stood watching and waiting, a big explosion went off behind them, the force of which sent them all flying to the ground. When the smoke cleared and they were back on their feet the commanding officer smiled.

'Remember the three men?'

He paused as he waited for their response. 'Well, they all crossed the road whilst you were flat on your bellies, and they're well away by now.'

The Special Ops groaned at their own stupidity.

'Such a bloody obvious trick,' said Gwynne.

'We fell for that, hook, line and sinker,' chuckled Gladys.

'It's instinctive to fall flat if a bomb goes off but in doing so you might miss vital action up ahead; train yourselves to look around, even as you fall.'

'Easier said than done,' said Robin as he sidled up to Alice for a surreptitious cuddle.

At the end of a very intense week they were given an operational box that contained a tommy gun, a Smith & Wesson automatic, sharp knives and knuckledusters. They also had their own thirty-four-pound radio set, which was the size of a large suitcase.

'They'll parachute drop the radio in two halves,' Robin told her.

'And the other stuff – aerials, earth wires, head sets, spare valves?' she asked.

'They'll be dropped too,' Robin replied.

One by one, sometimes in couples, they were called into the Brigadier's office, where they received instructions on their first drop. When it came to their turn Alice and Robin were surprised to find themselves in the presence of another couple.

'You four will be dropped on Friday night,' the Brigadier told them all. 'You will separate on landing, one couple going west, the other going south. Your aim is to link up with the French Resistance who will take you to separate places of hiding. From there you will infiltrate the community.'

The Brigadier gave them a smart, swift salute. 'Good luck and God speed.'

Outside in the corridor, Alice and Robin stared at each other.

'Scared?' he asked softly.

Alice shook her head as she took hold of his hand.

'Not when I'm with you,' she replied.

After the intense training and all the endless waiting, wondering and worrying, it was almost a relief to be doing something, to be focused.

When Iris entered the dorm and saw Alice packing she knew not to ask questions; she just nodded, gave her the thumbs-up and left the room.

'Will I ever see her again?' Alice whispered to herself as Iris closed the door behind her.

The two couples were driven to a small airfield where, in a Nissen hut, the final checks were made for every imaginable detail: suits, skirts, blouses, shoes – all had to have a French label; teeth were checked for French fillings; wristwatches had to be French or Swiss; loose change, notes, cigarettes, handbags, hairslides, headscarves – all had to be recognizably French. The last sombre check was for cyanide pills sewn into their hems and cuffs and trouser turn-ups.

Bearing the heavy packs containing their parachutes, the two couples left the hut and walked to a Whitley bomber, which was completely stripped out and had a large hole in the floor. They huddled together, and Alice shivered as they took off and roared across the English Channel.

'Action at last, sweetheart!' Robin whispered.

After what seemed a surprisingly short time they heard the pilot's voice announcing that they were approaching the drop zone. Alice's heart almost stopped beating. Tensing herself, she waited for instructions that would send her tumbling to earth on a thousand-foot drop. As she took deep breaths and psyched herself up for the command to jump, she heard the pilot speaking sharply.

'We've got to go round again.' He swung out in a wide arc then added, 'Our people on the ground are supposed to signal two letters in Morse, so far we haven't received anything.'

Totally wired up, the agents slumped as their adrenalin levels dropped, but after two or three rotations the pilot finally received the correct signal.

'Okay, chaps, it's safe to go,' he said. 'Wait for the all-clear, red to green then jump.'

This is it! Alice thought to herself as she waited for her signal. Then an image popped into her mind: a memory of running over the moors with Emily, who was holding her hand and calling out excitedly, 'Fly, Alice, *fly*!'

'Now!' said Robin.

In pairs, they dropped through the large hole cut into the Whitley bomber, and even after months of training, Alice gasped in amazement as she left the plane. She seemed to float for a few seconds on an air current, then her chute opened, blooming like a flower overhead as she gently fell to earth. By the silver light of the moon she could see vast stretches of French countryside, the fields, tracks and trees way down below. Then came the landing. As the ground rushed towards her, Alice was dragged for yards by a brisk ground wind before she managed to hit the quick-release box that enabled her to drop out of the heavy parachute harness. She frantically looked around for Robin, who had landed in the lower boughs of a nearby tree. Without either of them saying a word, she helped him struggle out of the tree, then they stuffed their parachutes into the nearest bushes and cast about for their radio sets, which were dropped along with them.

'God,' Alice prayed as she frantically crawled around in the dark, 'please let them be close.'

'Found them!' hissed Robin.

Before Alice could join him, and from their separate positions, they each heard footsteps. They instinctively pulled out their revolvers.

'*C'est qui?*' Robin whispered.

Fortunately, it was only the couple who had parachuted in with them.

'Keep down and wait for the contact,' Robin said.

Crouching in a bush, Alice held her breath. Surely everybody in the area must have heard the Whitley circling over the drop area? When she heard hurrying footsteps approaching she almost fainted with terror.

'*C'est qui?*' hissed Robin again.

'The fox at midnight,' a low voice said in French.

'Howls at the moon,' Robin completed the pre-arranged password in French.

'*Allons! Rapidement,*' came back the urgent whisper of their contact.

The four of them were taken to an abandoned

farmhouse and told to lie low. Alice's worst fears were confirmed when their contact spoke again.

'The plane made so much noise before the drop, everyone in the area knows something has happened. The police are already out looking for you,'

'Should we separate?' Robin asked.

The contact shook his head.

'No, stay here until I return with more information.'

As he hurried away, swallowed up by the darkness, the four spies stared at each other.

'Better get some kip,' said Robin. 'God only knows what tomorrow will bring.'

Chapter 29: A Royal Visit

Agnes wondered how she could best prepare Esther for her return to Keswick and the difficult parting that would necessarily ensue. She desperately wanted to talk to Stan but couldn't get through to him on the phone; the Cambridge fruit farm where he worked didn't run to such a luxury. When she phoned Addenbrooke's Hospital Agnes was told by the doctor that Stan only came in once a week for a check-up. So she gave the doctor a message to pass on, just in case he saw her husband before Stan received the letter she'd posted to him.

When the day came to leave Pendle little Esther screamed the place down. Everybody cried, but most of all Agnes, who had wracked her brains trying to think of an alternative to Esther living in Keswick. Eventually, she'd had to bite the bullet. This wasn't just about care and accommodation; this was about hospital treatment for polio. Sentiment had to be put aside if she ever wanted her daughter to walk normally again.

Clutching the pretty china doll that Daphne had bought her from Hamleys toy shop months ago, Esther sat on the train and sobbed. When they arrived in Keswick Agnes asked Mr and Mrs Sugden, who were to take care of Esther again, if she could spend at least one night there, just to soften the blow before Esther went back into hospital. The old couple kindly agreed, but counting down the hours to her departure the next day was a torture for Agnes, and Esther, of course, picked up on her mood. In between being moody and emotional, she clung to her mother like a limpet, and Agnes seriously wondered if she'd let her go the next day.

As Agnes led a very reluctant Esther along Keswick High Street the following day, she pointed out Catbells, which was bright and sharp in the morning sun.

'Look, darling,' she cried. 'That's where Mrs Tiggy-winkle lives, right up there. That's where she hangs out her washing to dry on sunny days.'

Esther, who loved the story of Mrs Tiggywinkle, didn't respond. She just limped along beside her mother, her calliper dragging heavily on the ground.

Agnes stopped and bent down to talk to her sad little daughter.

'Esther, this is for your own good,' she said, with a briskness she didn't feel. 'If your leg goes untreated it will never get better.'

Esther nodded. She'd been in hospitals long enough to understand her mother's words.

'I don't want to leave you, Mummy,' she said as tears slid down her ashen-grey cheeks.

'Oh, sweetheart, I don't want to leave you either!' cried Agnes, stifling a sob.

They walked down the old familiar ward, where the staff greeted Esther with genuine pleasure.

'This is your bed,' said the ward sister as she whipped back the cubicle curtain.

'Hello, sweetheart,' came a voice.

A beautifully familiar voice. Agnes looked up, scarcely

able to believe what she had just heard. It couldn't possibly be . . . But, yes, it was Stan!

He stepped out from behind the curtain and, laughing with happiness, he lifted his astonished daughter into his arms.

'Daddy! Daddy!' she cried as she hugged and kissed him.

'You came and helped me get better so I thought I'd come and help you,' he told her.

'Daddy, pleeease stay for ever,' Esther implored as she clung onto him.

'Do you know what? I will!' said Stan simply. 'I've sorted it. I'm going to stay right here with you.' Over the top of his daughter's head he winked at Agnes, who was so flabbergasted she could hardly speak. 'Mummy has to go back to work but we'll stay together in Keswick till you're better,' he promised.

Agnes wasn't sure she'd ever felt such relief. She looked at the two most precious people in her life and felt utter joy.

As the staff nurse took care of Esther, Agnes and Stan slipped into the canteen where, over a cup of tea, he explained what had happened.

'Why didn't you tell me?' gasped Agnes.

'There wasn't time.' He smiled as he recalled the conversation he'd had with the doctor in Cambridge. 'They were more than happy to discharge me. They said I had more important things to attend to up here.'

'Are you well enough, Stan?' Agnes asked anxiously. 'I mean really well, not just putting on a brave face?'

'I'm fine, love. Hard, outdoor work's done me a world of good. I still have terrible nightmares, mind, but they're nothing like as bad as they were; and sometimes the old wounds flare up. But, God's honest truth,' he said with a happy grin, 'I'm not the walking dead man I was a year ago.'

The farewell she'd been dreading turned out to be much easier, although, of course, she wished she could stay with them both too. A smiling Esther, with her father holding her hand, waved her mother goodbye and blew kisses till the train disappeared from sight. As she journeyed back to the Phoenix, Agnes knew she couldn't leave her daughter in more caring hands than Stan's.

Nevertheless it was a hard winter and a cold one too. The fact that after a long shift they could come home and light the wood burner with wood they'd gathered on the moors made an enormous difference. They didn't have to sit hugging blankets like other women in draughty accommodation; they could light a fire that crackled and blazed as they set about making their shared tea. When the dark descended early and they pulled down the blackout blinds the girls felt like they were shutting out the world.

'We're a lot warmer than the poor Ukrainians on the front,' Lillian said as they sat in their cosy sitting room, warming their hands around mugs of hot tea. 'How cold must those poor buggers be?'

'They're giving the Germans a good run for their money,' said Emily.

'So are the Lancashire Fusiliers,' said Elsie proudly. 'Tommy's in Naples now, you know.'

'It's good his letters are coming through,' Agnes said.

'He writes whenever he can and never fails to ask how little Jonty is,' Elsie said with a proud smile.

'And you write whenever you can, Elsie,' Emily reminded her.

'Yes, with a bit of help from my friends,' Elsie laughed. 'I am a bit of a dumb bugger!' she added.

'You're not dumb,' Emily insisted. 'How could you learn to read and write if your dad never let you go to school?'

'I'm learning now,' Elsie said happily. 'You've all been doing your bit, teaching me where Italy is – I can find Rome on the map now,' she winked in Emily's direction. 'Agnes lent me some of Esther's little reading books and they helped a lot. I didn't have time for learning when I was growing up but I do now.'

'I tell you what, next time you write to Tommy ask him to send us some of that gorgeous Neapolitan sunshine back in a bottle,' joked Lillian.

Elsie winked over her steaming mug of tea.

'I will if you can tell me how to spell Neapolitan!' she laughed.

After the heaviest British air raid on Berlin, patriotism was high and the desire to help the brave lads on the front line was so intense that all the munitions girls at the Phoenix volunteered to do unpaid overtime.

'It's the least we can do when you think about it,' said Agnes as they put in a fifteen-hour day, starting work in the dark and finishing in the dark too.

'Good job Daphne left when she did!' laughed Elsie.

'We should have known that Flight Lieutenant Rodney Harston-Binge would keep her close to home.'

They all missed Daphne: her wit, beauty, searing

honesty, languid smile, long cigarette holder and her devilish sense of mischief. When her letters arrived, and she wrote a lot, in a flamboyant, elegant script on thick, embossed paper, they always read them together, sitting round the wood-burning stove in the digs.

I miss you all so much, my darlings.
It's just that Rodders likes me at home, close to the home fires, so he can have his way with me whenever he's on leave.

'Still the same naughty Daphne,' Elsie remarked.

Don't run away with the idea that I'm doing nothing for the war effort. Rodders found me a nice little job in the War Office where I'm surrounded by handsome officers from dawn till dusk! I have long lunches with them, which so improves their morale! I miss you, though, dearest friends, and, believe it or not, I miss the ghaaastly digs where I spent some of the happiest days of my life.

On top of missing Alice and Daphne, they missed little Esther too, but Stan wrote often to say she was improving in leaps and bounds. At least they had baby Jonty to kiss and cuddle whenever Elsie or Tommy's mum brought him to the digs for a visit.

As Christmas approached and the days were cold and dark, life seemed to be one long drudgery.

'It's nowt but sleep, work, sleep then work again,' groaned Lillian.

'We mustn't grumble; we're a lot better off than others,' said Agnes as they dragged themselves out of bed one freezing-cold morning and broke ice in the sink to wash themselves.

When they arrived at the Phoenix there was a buzz going around the canteen. As they queued for their tea and toast, a woman in the line turned to them.

'Have you heard about the King and Queen coming here?'

Lillian burst out laughing.

'Pull the other one, it's got bells on!' she joked.

'It's God's honest truth!' the woman declared. 'Featherstone announced it t'morning shift and they've just towd us.'

When Lillian passed on the news to her friends Emily shook her head.

'Why are they coming here?' she asked incredulously.

'What's so bad about coming here, like?' Elsie retorted. 'Us Bomb Girls deserve a bit of attention.'

A few days later the Phoenix got more attention and publicity than it had ever received in its time as a munitions factory. Not only did the King and Queen arrive, bumping over the cobbled lane to the factory in a smart black car, but along came the press, photographers, local councillors, even the mayor in his fine flowing gown and gold chain. Children, who were given the day off school in honour of the visit, waved flags and cheered as they ran alongside the royal car.

'God save our King!'

Elsie, Lillian, Emily and Agnes clapped and waved along with the entire workforce as Mr Featherstone greeted the royal couple.

'I love her hat!' Lillian exclaimed at the sight of the Queen's silk hat, its wide brim decorated with a spray of bright feathers.

'And her silver fox fur,' said Emily.

'And look at that crocodile-skin bag!' gasped Elsie.

Cheeky Lillian started to giggle as her boss bowed low to his sovereign.

'Mr Featherstone looks fit to pop with pride,' she giggled.

'I'd die if they spoke to me,' said Elsie.

'Don't worry about that, Elsie,' Agnes assured her. 'Mr Featherstone will be keeping them well away from the toxic cordite line!'

But an hour later the Queen of England breezed into the damp and draughty workshop.

'God help her if she slips and falls on the bloody wet floor!' Lillian muttered under her breath.

'Shh!' hissed Agnes as she eyeballed Lillian and the rest of the giggling girls on her bomb line.

Of all the girls to stop and chat to, Queen Elizabeth chose Elsie, who was so hard at work packing cordite into shell cases she didn't even look up when the royal visitor asked with a charming smile what she was doing.

With a shell case in one hand and a lump of cordite powder in the other, Elsie could no more have explained what she was doing than orbit the outer stratosphere.

'I'm ... I'm ...' she gulped as she stared into the Queen's kind periwinkle-blue eyes. 'I'm making bombs for my Tommy on't front line, like!' she blurted out.

The Queen blinked and smiled as she politely asked how Tommy was.

Elsie's lovely green eyes widened as she smiled back; Tommy was a subject she could speak about with great confidence.

'He's a lot better now he's in Italy, Your Majesty,' she replied. 'It's not as 'ot as Africa where they were nearly boiled alive in't desert!'

Before Elsie launched off into a long list of Tommy's war experiences, Agnes quickly interrupted.

'This is the cordite line, Your Majesty. We pack an explosive called cordite, this yellow stuff,' Agnes said as she pointed to it. 'We pack it into shell cases then slide in a detonator like so,' she said as she demonstrated. 'The bombs are then carried across the factory floor,' she nodded to the bomb cases hooked onto the conveyor belt rattling overhead, 'and sent to the packing department where they're picked up and taken to RAF centres for immediate shipment.'

Seeing the Queen peering closely at the yellow stuff, Agnes couldn't stop herself from giving a warning.

'Best not to go too near it, ma'am, it's a toxic chemical and it can turn your skin and hair yellow. That's why our nickname's the Canary Girls – we're always covered in the yellow stuff ... it gets everywhere,' Agnes finished in a rush, self-consciously aware that she'd said too much.

A photographer appeared and after asking the Queen if he could take a photograph of her with the Bomb Girls, he arranged Elsie, Lillian, Agnes and Emily on either side of her, with the bomb cases clearly in shot too.

Before the Queen moved away she spoke again to Agnes's team.

'It's been a great pleasure to meet you all,' she said graciously. 'I think you're doing a sterling job for King and country and I wish you every success, ladies.'

When she'd gone the girls looked at each other in amazement.

'Who would have thowt any of us would be talking to the Queen of England about cordite?' Emily burst out.

Lillian winked.

'And our Elsie chatting like they were best friends about how hot it gets in Tobruk!'

Elsie blushed, not with embarrassment but with pride.

'Wait till I write and tell Tommy I mentioned him to Her Majesty!' she said with a giggle.

The following afternoon, as they queued for tea and chip butties, the girls were delighted to see pictures of themselves in the national daily papers.

'Look at us with the Queen!' Elsie gasped. 'I'm going to cut it out and frame it,' she added proudly.

'I only hope Her Majesty didn't have to soak that beautiful fox fur in milk after half an hour on the cordite line!' Lillian laughed.

The girls had more visitors that Christmas. Stan and Esther arrived in a flurry of snow on Christmas Eve, and Elsie brought little Jonty, who was now crawling everywhere, to the digs to see Esther. The little girl scooped him into her arms and kissed him.

'I've missed you, baby,' she said as she sat on the sofa with Jonty on her lap.

Emily's eyes widened as she saw Esther's legs dangling over the edge of the sofa.

'She's not wearing her calliper!' she gasped in surprise.

Stan nodded as he grinned.

'The physio's been doing a great job with Esther,' he said. 'They work her hard but she's tough and determined.'

He turned to his wife, sitting beside him and holding his hand. 'No idea who she gets that from!' he joked.

Happy and relaxed, they sat around the boiling-hot, wood-burning stove drinking beer and eating chips and apple fritters that Emily cooked in deep fat she'd been saving for weeks. Before the children went to bed they sang their favourite carols, 'Silent Night' and 'Away in a Manger', as snow fell on the Pennine moors. After a rousing chorus of 'Rudolph the Red-nosed Reindeer', the excited children were put to bed then Agnes and Stan slipped away too.

'You won't need a hot-water bottle now you've got Stan to keep you warm,' irrepressible Lillian teased.

Whilst Stan was brushing his teeth in the freezing-cold bathroom Agnes confided in her friends.

'It's the first time we'll have slept together since he went off to fight,' she whispered.

'Really?' asked Emily.

Agnes nodded.

'He's been in no fit state since he got back,' she said. 'And when he was better he went to Keswick and I came here.'

'Like unlucky ships passing in the night,' Lillian remarked. 'Well, at least you've seen your fella and you're going to get your hands on him in bed tonight,' she added with a giggle. 'I don't know when I'll ever have my arms around Gary again,' she added wistfully.

Emily hid the tears brimming into her eyes. Whilst she was visiting her parents just the day before she'd seen Bill crossing the street. He hadn't seen her but she'd had a very clear view of him in his soldier's uniform: tall and muscular, thinner but still with the mop of thick dark hair, the same fine, chiselled features and lovely laughing mouth.

My Bill, she'd thought as her heart contracted with love.

Before he saw her staring at him she turned a corner and hurried into her mother's house where, putting on a brave face, she put presents for the family underneath the Christmas tree. She wondered sadly what joys and sorrows 1944 held for her.

Chapter 30: Marseilles

After they'd been holed up in the dilapidated farmhouse for nearly a week the French contact decided it was safe for the bored and very hungry agents to move on.

'You will go separately,' he said on his final visit. 'For your own safety the less you know about each other's destination the better.'

The agents, who'd lived and trained together for many months in Helford House, briefly shook hands, said goodbye and went off in their pairs, never thinking they'd ever see each other again. Robin and Alice were driven – they weren't sure where as there were no signposts along the way – to a clean, airy barn with a hayloft for a bedroom.

'Stay here until we come back for you,' said their contact before he drove away. 'Don't leave the building until we know you are not being watched.'

As the roar of his departing car receded into the distance, Robin and Alice looked at each other and smiled.

'Well, it's not exactly the Ritz!' Robin laughed.

'But it's clean and with a great view,' said Alice as she looked out on to the vast sweeps of fertile French farmland.

Robin swept a hand under Alice's long silver-blonde hair and let it trickle through his fingers.

'We're stuck in the middle of nowhere, we've been instructed not to leave the premises ... what on earth shall we do to pass the time?'

Alice's eyes lit on the sunny hayloft overhead.

'That looks like a very comfortable bedroom!' she giggled.

Five or six days spent waiting for the all-clear might have been a nightmare for any other agents, but for Robin and Alice, who treasured every moment they snatched together, it was an unexpected bonus. They weren't short of food, wine or water; plentiful supplies appeared every day, brought by the farmer's wife, who made her own bread, cheese, smoked ham and pâté. She brought local fresh vegetables too, and tiny tomatoes bottled in oil and garlic; she also provided rugs to keep them warm at night and towels so they could wash in the bubbling stream that ran close by. Early one morning, along with warm bread and coffee, the farmer's wife brought news, which they'd been starved of for days.

She spoke in a thick French dialect, which, for all their training, Robin and Alice had difficulty understanding.

'We have just heard on the news that the British dropped three thousand tons of bombs on Hamburg last night.'

'Three thousand tons!' Alice's thoughts flew to the Phoenix factory. How many thousands of those bombs had been made by her munitions sisters working round the clock there, she wondered.

'They must have just about razed the city to the ground,' Robin muttered.

'It is time the Germans had a taste of their own stinking medicine,' said the farmer's wife with relish, then with a curt '*Au revoir*' she went on her way.

One day Alice found Robin attaching his radio aerial to one of the stout wooden rafters.

'What are you doing?' she gasped in alarm.

'We need to know what's going on,' he answered tersely.

'No, Robin!' she cried as she grabbed his hand to stop him. 'We were told to lie low – the enemy are still looking for us.'

'If I could get one quick message out I'd feel easier,' he replied.

'And if it's not a "quick message" we could be traced. It's not worth taking the risk. Please, darling, we have to wait. We're sure to get news soon,' she implored.

Robin sighed then set about taking down the aerial.

'You're right,' he said with a rueful smile. 'I've never been good at doing what I'm told!'

That evening as they lay side by side watching the stars come out, Robin ran his hands along her silky, slim thighs and mused.

'You have the most wonderful bottom!'

Rolling onto him, Alice stared down into his deep blue eyes.

'And you are the best lover in the world!' she exclaimed.

'And how many have you had?' he teased.

'Oh, hundreds!' she replied with a laugh. 'They were queuing round the block at the Phoenix munitions factory.'

'I bet they were,' he replied as he rolled her over and kissed her passionately on the mouth.

After several minutes of kissing Alice came up for air.

'Actually,' she said as she pulled a warm rug around her naked body, 'I was so lost in books and reading I hardly ever thought about men.'

'I bet they thought about you!' Robin murmured.

'They may have but I never noticed.'

'Bookworm!' he joked as he tickled her cheek with a prickly hay stalk.

'Emily and Bill were courting by the time they were fifteen. They met at school ... Childhood sweethearts,' she added. 'Pity it didn't stay that way.'

They both wanted a cigarette but they obviously couldn't smoke in the hayloft. Wrapped in blankets, they crept outside where they sat smoking Gauloises on a stone bench outside the barn.

A new moon the size of a baby's fingernail appeared in the evening sky.

'Make a wish,' Alice said dreamily.

'I wish –' he started.

'Shh! Don't tell me, it's bad luck,' she said.

'I wish . . . mumble . . . mumble . . . mumble . . .' he said as he covered his mouth so she couldn't hear what he was saying. 'Then when that wish has come true I hope we have three little girls who all look like you!'

'No! Three boys, just like you.'

'Okay, six in all,' he agreed as he put out his cigarette. 'Back to bed, my love,' he said softly.

Taking his hand, Alice followed him into the barn now bathed in silver moonlight.

'Not to sleep, I hope!' she whispered with a giggle.

After five days they were roused at dawn by their contact.

'Time to go,' he said urgently.

He waited in his old Citroën whilst they packed their equipment into French suitcases. As she straightened her beret and removed hay from her hair, Alice's eyes swept round the barn.

'Will we ever be this happy again, Robin?' she murmured as tears filled her silver-grey eyes.

'Darling, we'll always be happy just as long as we've got each other!' he cried as he hurried her out of the barn and onto the next leg of their journey.

The contact dropped them off at the local railway station where he handed them both a copy of *Le Figaro* before telling them to take a train to Marseilles.

'Some interesting reading for your journey south,' he said and then he was gone.

Holding the newspapers under their arms and carrying their suitcases, Robin and Alice strolled down the long platform and boarded a train for Marseilles. As they settled in a crowded compartment, they unfolded their newspapers. Buried inside, they found their next addresses written on scraps of paper. Pretending to read a news column, Alice memorized the address before shredding the scrap of paper between her thumb and fingers. Neither she nor Robin exchanged a word or a glance about what they'd found but Alice's heart was sinking fast. For the first time she'd be separated from Robin; she'd be on her own, without his love and support. Straightening her shoulders, Alice stared blankly out of the window. She hadn't become an agent to become soft and sentimental, she told herself firmly; she'd joined up to fight for her country. Falling in love with Robin had been a bonus but not the purpose of the exercise. Now she was about to do the task she'd been trained for and she vowed to herself to do it well.

They only had one opportunity to talk throughout the whole journey and that was when their compartment briefly emptied out.

Making the most of the time before anybody else joined them, Alice quickly said, 'We'll split at the station, yes?'

He nodded but he looked pale and anxious.

'You'll be all right?'

'Of course,' she said with a bravery she didn't feel.

'We're going to safe houses,' he added. 'So we should be able to meet.'

Alice didn't dare reply for fear of bursting out crying.

'And we can send messages,' he said.

'How?' she asked.

He stopped short as the door of the compartment was yanked open and an old woman with a basket of squawking chickens struggled in.

'*Merde!*' she grumbled as she slammed the basket down on the floor. 'It's bloody hot for this time of the year!'

As the train rattled on its way, Alice gazed out at the rolling landscape and thought of the Lancashire moors where she had run wild with Emily. Holding hands and laughing, they had often stood on the windy tops with their hair flapping around their faces.

'I'm Emily Brontë,' Alice had said once. 'And you're Charlotte.'

Emily had grimaced.

'Don't they both die?' she laughed.

'Yes, but it's very romantic,' Alice had insisted.

Smiling at her happy memories, she dropped off to sleep as the train rolled inexorably on its way south.

Alice's training kicked in almost immediately she got out of the train at Marseilles station. She could have easily picked up a road map of the city from one of the railway kiosks but that would have flagged up the fact she was a stranger in town. Without giving Robin a backward glance, she walked away from the station without a clue where she was going. Well away from the bustling main streets, she stopped and asked local vendors for directions.

Alice's safe house turned out to be a rather small but tidy flat in the suburbs not far from the waterfront. The key to the flat was in one of the post boxes in the dark hallway. Alice removed it and made her way up a sweeping staircase to the flat where, once safely inside, she locked the door then hid her radio equipment and explosives in a wooden chest that contained kindling for the fire.

'Now what?' she said to herself.

Once again Alice recalled her training and the words of her tutor.

'Don't just sit there waiting for instructions; make the place looked lived in.'

Taking cups, plates and cutlery she placed them around the kitchen and half laid the table as if she'd just finished a meal. There were several books on a shelf, so she took one and put it by her rickety bedside table; some she left opened and lying around in the sitting room as if she was in the middle of reading them. And then she waited.

Scared to go out in case she missed her contact, Alice paced the room. Then, as night fell, she prepared for bed. But sleep did not come. Only the night before she had been in Robin's arms, pressed up to his naked body, half asleep, listening to owls hooting in the treetops that surrounded their hayloft hideaway.

'I love you, my darling,' she whispered into her pillow.

She awoke starving hungry and thirsty; she had no

choice but to go out in search of bread, coffee and milk. On her way back from the local shops she looked into the post box, where she found an envelope with no name on it. Stuffing it inside her coat pocket she hurried up the staircase to her flat where, over a bowl of *café au lait*, she read the letter left by her contact.

'Oh, my God!' she gasped.

Her instructions were not exactly what she'd been expecting. Her brief was to blow up a stretch of railway line, part of the network of routes that kept the German army supplied with food and ammunition. They would contact her again with further instructions and a date.

'Why am I on an explosives mission?' she wondered out loud. 'I thought we were here to gather information and break encrypted code and transmit messages. Nobody mentioned bombing a bloody railway line!'

In a panic she dashed to the firewood box to check she had enough plastic explosive and pencil detonators to take out a major railway line. Now she knew what her mission was, Alice had to endure a further wait for the exact details: date, time and location – and, most important of all, who she would be working with. Or would she be sent on a solo mission?

After too many long, fretful days, Alice decided she'd pass the time by reading every book in the flat. At least it would prevent her French from going rusty.

Towards the end of an interminable, lonely week, just as she was embarking on another novel by Zola, there was a sharp knock on the door. Hardly daring to breathe, Alice slowly opened the door to two French policemen holding revolvers.

'We've come to search your flat,' they snapped. *'Bougez-vous!* MOVE!'

When Alice strongly protested the gendarmes pushed her aside.

'Silence!' they barked.

Alice stood silently in the middle of the room watching the gendarmes turn the place upside down. They emptied every cupboard, cleared the shelves with a swipe, threw the bed against the wall to look underneath it; they even levered up loose floorboards. And then one of them approached the kindling box. With her heart almost bursting with terror, Alice feigned disinterest as she pretended to be absorbed by something outside the window. Out of the corner of her eye she watched the gendarme rustle about in the box. He lifted piles of newspaper and kindling, then dropped the lid.

'Nothing,' he said. 'Let's go.'

With a shrug and a grunt, they headed for the door. When they'd gone, Alice, sweating and shaking from head to toe, collapsed in the nearest chair.

'Oh, my God!'

Another rap at the door sent her pulse racing. Jumping to her feet, she crept towards the door, which this time she didn't open.

'Who is it?' she whispered.

There was a pause followed by a gentle tap.

'Robin.'

Sobbing with relief, Alice threw open the door and flung herself into his arms.

'Quickly, back in the room,' he said.

He stepped inside and locked the door behind him.

'I've been waiting outside,' he gasped as he swept her into his arms and kissed her soft mouth. 'When I saw the gendarmes I thought they'd come to arrest you. Oh, my love,' he murmured frenziedly as he kissed her eyes, her nose and her forehead. 'I was going out of my mind!'

Even though her pulse was racing at the sight of her beloved, Alice's first thought was of their safety.

'Did anybody see you come in?'

'I don't know. I had to take the risk – it's no longer safe to send messages from my house.'

Tugging at Robin's sleeve, wide-eyed Alice whispered her news.

'I've been instructed to blow up a section of railway.'

'I know,' he mouthed back.

He pointed to the battered old suitcase he was carrying.

'I need to set up the wireless to get further instructions.'

Robin quickly laid the case on the dining-room table. After undoing the metal clips he hooked up the wireless aerial then laid the earth connection as close to the window as it would reach.

'Please, God, let it work first time,' Alice prayed. 'Please, God, don't let the Nazis pick up the signal. Please, please, God.'

Robin winked and gave the thumbs-up as he listened intently through his headset.

'It's okay,' he said.

Hardly daring to breathe, they listened to the sequence of tips and taps which they were both able to decode. The hairs on the back of Alice's neck rose as they were instructed to blow up a section of rail track heading east out of Marseilles at 23.00 hours that night. As Robin disconnected the aerial and turned off the wireless, Alice rolled up the earth wire and replaced it in the battered suitcase.

'I thought we were on a communications and interception mission,' she said quietly. 'I didn't think they'd hit us with explosives the minute we were in the field.'

'Neither did I,' he admitted. 'Somebody must have bought it, otherwise they wouldn't have asked us to step up to the plate.'

He looked her square in the eye.

'Are you okay with this, Alice? If you're not now really is the time to say so.'

She looked him steadily in the eye as she answered calmly.

'I'm a Bomb Girl, Robin. Give me five minutes to get ready.'

Alice quickly removed her block of plastic explosive and her pencil detonators from the chest then laid them on the table alongside a baguette. Robin looked baffled.

'You're not thinking of making sandwiches, are you, sweetheart?' he teased.

'Watch,' said Alice with a cheeky smile.

Tearing off the top of the crusty baguette, she scraped out a quantity of bread, and into the empty space she pushed the explosive and the slim detonators, both carefully protected by plastic wrapping. Alice laughed as she popped the baguette, now containing enough explosive to take out the main line between Marseilles and Paris, into a shopping bag containing a string of onions.

'Let's do it, *mein Herr*!'

Chapter 31: Factory Explosion

As the Allies advanced on Germany and Italy in the spring of 1944, more and more bombs were needed by the British forces to win the war.

'I feel like I've been filling bloody shell cases all my life,' groaned Lillian as the tired workforce continued to do unpaid overtime.

'Making bombs and living off chips, tea and toast,' grumbled Emily.

'I quite like chips, tea and toast,' giggled ever-upbeat Elsie.

'When I think back to my days at the mill canteen, when I used to dream of running the place, it seems like I was another girl,' Emily said nostalgically. 'I was so young and naive, I thought I'd only got to bat my eyelashes and I'd get what I wanted.'

'Welcome to the real world, lovie,' said Agnes.

Lillian snorted as she recalled her own selfish naivety.

'We were just kids,' she said as she shook her head. 'I thought I could dodge conscription and carry on doing exactly what I wanted. Stupid or pig-headed or both?'

'I wouldn't change a single thing,' said Elsie. 'I've loved every single moment here with you. They've been the best days of my life.'

'Oh, Elsie, you are the sweetest, kindest girl,' said Lillian as she hugged little Elsie till she went pink in the face.

'Can you remember food before rationing?' Emily said with a sigh.

'Was there life before rationing?' Lillian joked.

'We used to think nothing of going down to the shops for cheese, sausages and bacon,' Agnes said.

'Eggs, chocolate, butter, cream, white bread, pork chops . . .' Emily said longingly.

'I wouldn't mind if I never saw another tin of Spam again,' Lillian laughed.

'By fair means or foul, I've got to lay my hands on some fresh meat soon,' said Emily. 'We deserve a good square meal after all the extra unpaid overtime we've put in.'

Luckily for Emily, the local allotment pig, fattened up on slops from the neighbours, had just been butchered and Mrs Yates had kept back some pork for her daughter.

'Here,' she said as she wrapped the fresh meat in brown paper. 'Treat yourself and them lasses in yon digs to a good meal.'

Emily hungrily eyed the small piece of fresh pink pork.

'Oh, Mum, the things I could do with that!' she cried.

Her thoughts raced through delicious recipes: roast pork and crackling with apple sauce, softly stewed pork with prunes, pork baked with sage and thyme.

Emily jumped as her mother spoke and snapped her out of her reverie.

'Just eat it!' her mother laughed. 'You all look like you need fattening up.'

Emily rushed back to the digs wondering how she could spin out the meat to make a meal for four. She decided to mince the pork, to which she added salt, pepper, fresh sage, an egg and some flour, then she rolled the mixture into little patties.

'Mmm, the smell's driving me mad!' cried Elsie as she watched Emily fry the patties in sizzling hot fat.

'I don't remember when I last had fresh meat,' Lillian said.

'And mashed potatoes with cabbage and leeks,' Agnes added as she laid the table for supper. 'Fresh locally grown veg instead of dried peas and butter beans. Mmm, just thinking of it makes my mouth water.'

'I always feel sorry for the poor pig,' said Emily as she drained the fat off the patties and popped them onto a warm plate. 'He thinks everybody loves him until somebody comes along one morning and slits his throat.'

'Life's never fair,' said Elsie as she hurried after Emily bearing the plate of steaming, aromatic meat to the table.

'Especially if you're a pig!' laughed Lillian.

It was a nice change to sit down to a really good meal in their own home without the relentless din of the clattering conveyor belt and the constant blare of *Workers' Playtime*. After they'd eaten every bit of the delicious pork they sat full and contented around the crackling wood-burning stove smoking Woodbines and drinking tea.

'I think I might have "When the War's Over" tattooed on my forehead,' chuckled Lillian. 'I say it so often I don't know what I'll say when life gets back to normal.'

'Whatever normal is any more,' said Agnes thoughtfully. 'I can't ever imagine living in London again.'

Emily, Lillian and Elsie looked at her in surprise.

'Really?' asked Emily.

Agnes nodded.

'I've grown to love the north and the people round here,' she said as she smiled fondly at her friends.

'One thing's for sure – I am *never, ever, ever* going back to Gateshead,' said Elsie emphatically.

'Don't blame you,' laughed Lillian. 'Not whilst the stepmother from hell is alive!'

'My life's here in Pendle, with Jonty and Tommy . . . when he comes home,' Elsie added wistfully.

'Come on, no moping!' Lillian said briskly. 'You've seen Tommy a lot more than I've seen or heard from my Gary this last couple of years. Sometimes I think I dreamed him,' she said with a sigh.

'He was real all right. He was larger than life and heart-stoppingly good-looking,' Agnes reminded her. 'He'll come back to you just as soon as he's finished bombing Germany.'

'I hope every bomb he drops has Hitler's name on it,' said Lillian vengefully.

'And Goering's and Goebbels's, Rommel's and Himmler's,' Agnes added gleefully.

Elsie topped up their mugs with fresh tea.

'I wonder where Alice is now?' she said thoughtfully.

Lillian shook her head.

'No idea. It seems ages since she lived with us. Don't you hear from her, Em?'

Emily shook her head.

'Not a word since I saw her in London.'

'I've often wondered what keeps her down south so long,' Elsie said in all innocence. 'I mean, I know she speaks French, like, but what does she really do down there?'

Emily was surprised to catch a knowing look in Agnes's eyes.

She's guessed Alice's secret, Emily thought.

She hadn't breathed a word to anybody but Agnes wasn't stupid; she was an intuitively clever woman and had obviously worked out for herself exactly what Alice was up to.

Without giving anything away and avoiding Emily's eyes, Agnes turned to Elsie.

'I think Alice is probably locked up in an office for hours on end translating French war memos for a lot of stuffy old soldiers.'

'I bet Daf's doing no such thing,' laughed Lillian.

'Knowing Daf, she'll be out on the town dancing at the Ritz every night,' said Elsie, who, though often shocked by Daphne, was also immensely entertained by her.

'I bet she's got a string of fellas to keep her happy when Rodders is away,' chuckled Lillian.

'Come on, ladies, bed,' said Agnes as she got to her feet and started to clear away. 'We've got an early start tomorrow morning.'

The bright light of a lovely spring morning, combined with riotous birdsong, woke the girls just after dawn.

'God, I wish I was as chirpy as a bird,' Lillian groaned as, half asleep, she staggered into the bathroom.

'Be quick in there,' Elsie called after her. 'Let's clock on early then we can get some tea and toast before we start work.'

'I've never known anybody eat so much and stay so thin,' said Emily as she brushed her long, unruly hair.

'It's cos I was half-starved as a kid,' Elsie replied

cheerfully. 'Everything tastes so good here – and it's free!' she added with a laugh.

The usual morning routine kicked in: women greeted each other familiarly as they dispersed to their workplaces, *Music While You Work* struck up loud and chirpy and the conveyor belt rolled the empty bomb cases down the line.

'Now come on, girls, let's bash out a couple of thousand bombs for our boys to drop on Berlin,' joked Lillian as she got into the swing of the music.

'What about our lads in Italy?' Elsie called over the sound of the rattling machinery.

'Them buggers too!' Lillian replied.

'We could write notes and stick them in this batch,' Emily suggested.

'Saying what?' Elsie asked.

'"Give 'em some welly, lads"!' Lillian suggested.

'"This one's for Hitler"!'

'"Come home soon",' Elsie murmured softly.

As Frank Sinatra sang 'Mack the Knife', the girls tapped their rubber boots on the damp concrete floor and sang along. Lillian, who knew every word and action, wiggled her shapely bottom as she sang the loudest.

Singing along with Lillian, Elsie suddenly caught sight of an overfilled shell case. Her eyes widened in horror as loose cordite spilled out of the case onto the rattling metal conveyor belt. She froze as she took in the leaking yellow powder, knowing without a doubt that it would ignite. Without a moment's hesitation, she pushed Lillian and Emily, who were either side of her, as far away as she could and then slammed her hand over the sparking cordite. In the split second that Lillian and Emily, startled by Elsie's aggressive action, turned towards her, a white flash and a deafening roar sent all the girls falling to the ground. As metal components exploded around them, the girls covered their heads, and when they dared, one by one, to look up they saw flames spreading over the factory floor. Seeing the loaded bombs swinging from the overhead conveyor belt, the prostrate girls instinctively knew that if those went off they'd all die.

As the alarm siren shrieked out, a girl not twenty feet away panicked, leaping to her feet and running through the flames.

'RUN FOR YOUR LIVES!' she yelled.

A blazing beam fell from the ceiling and landed on the girl, setting her overalls on fire. As she screamed and writhed in agony, Emily's instinct was to run to her and help. But somebody was dragging Emily the other way.

'NO! Let me go!' she heard herself scream too.

Smoke blinded her eyes and filled her throat, but as she gagged for breath she made out Malc's face and realized it was he who was dragging her outside to safety.

'Malc! Malc!' she cried. 'Where's Lillian? Where's Elsie?'

Knowing there were enough bombs in the place to blow them all to kingdom come, Malc was half-crazed with fear. He swore loudly.

'Just get a bloody move on.'

With a grip of steel, he literally shoved Emily out of the building and onto the edge of the moors opposite the blazing factory. Nearly two hundred terrified women were huddled together there watching parts of the

Phoenix blow clean away, its walls and windows collapsing as flickering orange flames leaped high into the sky.

'GET BACK!' hollered Malc as he pushed the women away from the blaze. 'Get away from the sodding building before the whole bleeding lot goes!'

With acrid black smoke swirling around them, Emily and the other survivors coughed and choked as they watched stream after stream of fire engines, police cars and ambulances roar up to the burning factory.

In despair, Emily searched the crowd for her friends, who were nowhere to be seen.

'Oh, my God!' she said out loud. 'Please don't let them still be inside.'

As she made a move to bolt forwards, she was dragged back by the women around her.

'Emily! No!'

'Don't be a bloody fool!' they cried.

'I've got to save my friends!' Emily screamed hysterically.

She was stopped in her tracks by the sight of Malc staggering out of the factory wreckage bearing an unconscious Elsie in his arms. Horrified, Emily rushed towards them.

'Will she be all right?' she gasped.

'We're got to get her to the hospital!' Malc said grimly.

In the chaos and confusion that followed, everyone was looking for somebody whilst at the same time being told to get as far away from the factory as possible. The desperate need of the women to stay and search for loved ones was at odds with the needs of the police, who were removing or arresting anybody who refused to leave the Phoenix.

'The site's got to be cleared,' the officer in charge bellowed.

As Emily watched the flames licking the factory roof, she prayed they wouldn't spread to the packing area where there were enough loaded shell cases to blow the entire site halfway to Yorkshire.

'Get in the car,' somebody called out.

Emily turned round to see Malc, covered in smut and dirt, at the wheel of his Austin. Still in a daze, she shook her head.

'I'm not leaving till I find my friends,' she told him.

'Don't bother,' Malc retorted. 'Whoever's not here is either dead or in hospital.'

All the injured munitions girls had been taken to Manchester Royal Infirmary where Emily discovered from a frantic nurse with a clipboard that Elsie, Agnes and Lillian had each been admitted. As she sat in the hospital corridor waiting for news, one loaded stretcher after another passed her by. If she approached any hospital official she was virtually pushed aside. Outside, ambulances screeched into A&E delivering an endless stream of injured workers. At one point it seemed like the whole of the Phoenix factory was in the infirmary, either being treated for injuries or waiting to find out if a loved one was alive or dead.

Emily didn't remember falling asleep but she woke up with a jump when Malc shook her by the arm.

'There's nowt we can do here,' he said wearily. 'You'd best go home.'

Thinking Malc was talking about her going back to the Phoenix digs, bleary-eyed Emily nodded as she got to her feet.

'I mean home, Emily,' Malc said. 'Not the digs.'

'Why?' she asked blankly.

'The Phoenix won't be open for some time,' Malc replied as he bundled her into the car and drove her home to Pendle.

The next morning the papers were full of the tragedy.

FIFTEEN DEAD SO FAR

The papers reported that nobody knew how the explosion had happened, but as Emily woke up from a very disturbed sleep she had a vivid memory of Elsie turning wild-eyed towards her then holding out her hand as a white flash went off and the thunder of exploding bombs filled her ears.

'How did I survive that?' Emily asked herself as she struggled out of bed.

The overalls she'd come home in lay on the floor, burnt and filthy. Emily quickly washed and changed into clean clothes, then, after grabbing a cup of tea, she caught the bus into Manchester where she returned to her hospital vigil.

'This time I'm *not* moving until I find my friends,' Emily muttered as she walked the length of a long, tiled corridor where the echo of her hurrying feet bounced off the walls.

After several hours she learned that Lillian had a bad head injury and Agnes was half-blinded in one eye, but it was sweet little Elsie who had sustained the most serious injury: she had lost her right hand. But they were alive.

There was no way Emily could see her friends so she just sat in the cold corridor because that was the nearest place to the ones she loved. Sitting alone, Emily went over and over the explosion in her mind. As she replayed it, almost literally blow by blow, she realized with blinding clarity what Elsie had done: she had put her right hand over the cordite and sacrificed a part of her body in order to put herself between the explosion and her friends.

'She would have died for us,' sobbed Emily as tears flowed uncontrolled down her cheeks.

A passing ward sister took pity on the weeping girl in the corridor.

'Can I help?' she asked.

'I've got to see my friend – she saved my life,' Emily replied as she dabbed her wet cheeks with a hankie. 'I can't leave here till I've seen her.'

'What's your friend's name?'

'Elsie Hogan.' Emily quickly corrected herself: 'Elsie Carter's her married name.'

'Come with me,' the sister said kindly.

She led her to a women's ward where Emily found Elsie lying in a bed with her right hand heavily bandaged.

'Only a few minutes,' the sister instructed 'She's lost a lot of blood.'

Emily knelt beside the bed so she could kiss Elsie's sleeping face.

'Thank you for saving my life.'

Suddenly Elsie's eyes opened; weak though she was, she smiled her own sweet smile.

'You would've done the same for me,' she whispered.

Unable to find words that could express her love and gratitude, Emily smiled back but in her heart she wondered if she would have been quite so heroically selfless as dear, faithful Elsie.

Chapter 32: Aftermath

Emily visited her friends every day, sometimes with Tommy's mum or Malc, and once with Mr Featherstone, who was overseeing the extensive repair work at the Phoenix, which remained closed indefinitely.

'Maybe we won't be needing so many bombs now that the Germans are running scared,' Lillian joked from her sick bed. Repeating the often-used wartime expression, she added with a gleeful smile, 'Yeah! We've got the Hun on the run!'

'Don't count your chickens,' said Agnes wisely. 'We need to keep churning out bombs until Hitler's dead and all the heads of Europe have signed a peace treaty.'

Lillian snorted.

'I could be claiming my bloody pension if we have to wait for the heads of Europe to agree on anything!'

'What'll happen to the Phoenix if peace is declared?' Elsie asked as she lay propped up on her pillows.

'It'll be converted into a knocking shop!' Lillian joked.

'Stop making me laugh, Lil,' pleaded Agnes, giggling as she pressed a hand to her wounded brow. 'It pulls my stitches apart.'

'Will the Phoenix *really* close?' Elsie persisted.

'It was closed for years,' Emily said. 'Then it was re-opened in 1941 for war work.'

'Three years ago . . .' sighed Agnes. 'I feel more northern than southern these days.'

'That'll be our influence,' Lillian quipped.

'And all them chip butties,' Elsie added.

'One thing's for sure – the Phoenix won't be churning out any bombs for a while,' Emily told her friends, who, lying in their hospital beds, had no idea of the extent of the bomb damage done to the factory. 'There's a lot of rebuilding to be done before it opens its doors again.'

As the days rolled by, the deep gash on Lillian's temple, caused by flying shrapnel, healed well, and the sight in Agnes's damaged eye started to come back. But poor Elsie, who'd suffered the biggest loss, had the most pain.

'It's not so bad, like,' she said with a weak smile.

Elsie had had an emergency operation to remove metal debris and clean the wound before it was stitched and then wrapped in layers of bandages that made her hand look like a big white club.

'When it's mended good and proper the doctor said they could fit me with a false hand,' Elsie said bravely.

'They'd better make it big enough to hold two chip butties!' Lillian teased.

Though Elsie smiled and tried to remain upbeat, it was obvious she was in great pain, and when Jonty was brought to see her for the first time she completely broke down.

'I can't even cuddle mi little lad,' she wailed.

Emily, who had taken Jonty to the hospital, popped the solemn little boy at the bottom of Elsie's bed where he sat sucking his thumb.

'You will be able to hold him soon when your hand doesn't hurt so much,' she said soothingly.

But now that Elsie had started crying the tears wouldn't stop.

'What will Tommy say when he sees me deformed like this?' she sobbed.

'Tommy would love you if you had webbed feet and no teeth!' Emily said with a smile. 'He adores you, Elsie; you know that better than anybody.'

Elsie smiled at that.

'C'mon, help me cuddle Jonty before you take him home,' she said determinedly.

By propping pillows around Elsie, they settled Jonty comfortably in the crook of her good arm, where he sat chewing toffees and burbling happily until the bell rang to announce the end of visiting time.

'See, you managed that all right,' Emily said.

Elsie was restored to her usual chirpiness after cuddling her little boy.

'It'll get better before it gets worse,' she quipped, with a wink.

During the second week of her stay in hospital Lillian turned twenty-five. On the eve of her birthday she sighed with frustration.

'It should be a laugh a minute having a birthday on Ward D2 with a granite-faced sister and a gash on my head that's ruined my good looks for ever.'

Emily, who was visiting, laughed along with Elsie and Agnes.

'Nothing will ever spoil your looks, Lillian!' Agnes said fondly.

'Seeing as I can't go back to my former flawless beauty I've decided to build on my wounds,' Lillian announced.

As her friends gazed at her blankly, she continued.

'As soon as I'm on my feet I'm going to restyle my hair and cut myself a fringe, just like Lauren Bacall.'

'Why?' asked Elsie.

'To cover my scar, of course!' Lillian replied.

'Oh, Lillian,' giggled Emily. 'Only you could turn a war wound into a fashion statement.'

Before Emily left she bent over her friends' beds and gave them all a kiss.

'Please get well soon,' she said.

When she bent to kiss Lillian she saw a tell-tale tear in her eye.

'What's up, sweetheart,' she whispered softly.

Lillian, who liked to come over as tough and savvy rather than wet and soppy, wiped the tear from her eye.

'I'm bloody missing Gary, that's what's up,' she growled like a grumpy bear. 'It's bad enough lying here in pain day after sodding day,' she said as she swiped away another tear. 'I'm finding it hard to hold it together, Em!' she blurted out as the tears flowed fast and furious. 'When will I ever see him again?'

Avoiding her head wound, Emily rocked the weeping Lillian in her arms.

'You've been a brave kid for so long,' she commiserated. 'It's because you're in pain that your resolve has crumbled. You just want loving – and why not?' Emily said, on the point of tears too. 'Isn't that what we all want?'

Elsie and Agnes hurried from their beds and joined Emily and Lillian.

'We're going to get such a bollocking from the sister,' Lillian giggled.

'I could get into bed with you and pretend to be a patient too!' Emily joked.

'I only welcome handsome Yanks into my bed!' Lillian retorted.

'Seriously, Lil, you have written and told Gary about the accident, haven't you?' Agnes asked.

Lillian nodded.

'I couldn't write but Emily sent a note to say I'd been in an explosion and was in hospital,' Lillian replied. 'Whether he'll ever get it, God only knows!'

Elsie gently stroked Lillian's arm with her good hand.

'It's this bugger of a war that keeps us from our loved ones!' she said with a sad sigh.

The next day Emily picked up the cards and a parcel that had been left at Pendle post office for Lillian.

'They can't be delivered to the Phoenix as it's closed,' she told Lillian as she dropped the cards on the bed. 'Happy Birthday, beautiful!' she added as she handed over the parcel.

Lillian looked at the writing on the label and sat bolt upright.

'It's from Gary!' she gasped.

With trembling fingers she unwrapped the parcel, which contained a small black-leather jewellery box. Lillian flipped the lid then gazed in wonder at the twinkling diamond ring.

'It's so beautiful!' she cried, overwhelmed.

Gathered around Lillian's bed, her friends urged her to read the card that came with the jewellery box.

'What does it say?' Elsie asked impatiently.

Smiling radiantly, Lillian read Gary's words on the card.

Marry me, Bomb Girl!
Your loving Yank,
Gary XXX

It wasn't just Lillian who burst into tears of joy – her friends all joined her.

'Oh, for this – it's been worth the wait!' cried an ecstatic Lillian as she popped the diamond ring on her wedding finger.

Their cries of laughter soon brought the sister hurrying into the ward; her starched white apron seemed to bristle with her disapproval of noisy, laughing visitors.

'Ladies, what on earth are you up to?' she snapped.

Lillian waved her new engagement ring in the air.

'Look, Sister!' she exclaimed. 'I'm engaged to be married.'

The sister scowled.

'Don't let it go to your head. If your temperature rises there'll be no visitors for the rest of the week,' she retorted.

Lillian's temperature did go up later in the day when smiling, elegant Daphne swanned into the ward in a pink silk summer dress and a wide-brimmed straw hat.

'Darlings! I just had to come when I heard the ghaaastly news!' she exclaimed as she bore down on her afflicted friends with her usual flamboyance.

They all cringed in pain as Daphne, with her arms full, kissed them passionately one by one.

'Aargh, watch my head!'

'Ouch! My eye!'

'Ooh! Don't touch mi arm!'

Daphne dropped her gifts of fruit, chocolates and cigarettes onto Agnes's bed then, after popping open a bottle, she poured fizzing champagne into plastic tooth mugs.

'*Ugh!* Not that stuff,' Elsie laughed as she wrinkled her nose at the fizzing wine.

'Don't let the hatchet-faced sister see us drinking!' Lillian giggled as she took a brimming mug from Daphne.

'I'll just tell her it's Eno's Liver Salts,' laughed Elsie.

Daphne raised her mug.

'Here's to you all, my brave and wonderful Bomb Sisters!'

As the girls thumped their mugs together, Emily solemnly added a second toast.

'And here's to our little Elsie, the girl who saved all our lives!'

Elsie blushed.

'Don't be daft!'

She grimaced as she forced herself to swallow a drop of Daphne's champagne, then gave a little burp.

It was lovely to go back to the digs with Daphne.

'I've been so lonely here,' Emily admitted as they settled down in front of the crackling wood-burning stove that Emily had lit on their return. 'Tell me,' she urged, 'how's married life suiting you?'

Daphne took her time placing a cigarette in her long silver holder then lighting it with a silver-filigreed cigarette lighter.

'Not at all,' she said as she exhaled a cloud of smoke.

Emily's big blue eyes widened in disbelief.

'You're not serious?'

Daphne nodded.

'It's rather a bore,' she said without a hint of emotion.

Emily was so stunned she couldn't think of a word to say.

'Rodders is all right but he's either on a bombing raid, or holed up in a Nissen hut waiting for a bombing raid, or he's home talking about the bally bombing raid!'

Emily burst out laughing.

'There's got to be more to it than that!' she exclaimed.

'Well, there're the cocktail parties in the officers' mess and the dinner parties, but to be honest I've had more fun sitting in this room with my hair in rollers and drinking beer whilst laughing with my dearest girl friends.'

'We've had some happy times together,' Emily agreed. After a thoughtful pause she said, 'So what will you do?'

'Oh, put up with it, of course,' Daphne replied cheerfully. 'See if things improve when the war's over. Hope for the best!' she finished with a shrug. 'Anyway, what about you? Still the vestal virgin of the Pennine Way?' she teased.

'I haven't been chasing around after Freddie,' Emily replied. 'Not that I've seen him,' she added with a cheeky giggle. 'If he sees me he runs a mile.'

'Wouldn't you in the circs?' Daphne tittered. 'Knowing you've got a photo of him stark bollock naked on a moonlit moor might curb his randy ways till peace is declared.' Daphne paused as she gave Emily a long critical stare. 'Believe me, darling, there are plenty of fish in the sea for a gorgeous young woman like you.'

Emily shrugged.

'I've lost interest in men, apart from one, and he's definitely lost interest in me,' she replied.

'Time to move on, darling.'

A few days after Daphne had left for London, little Esther suddenly appeared at the open window beside Agnes's bed.

'Hello, Mummy,' she said as she thrust a bunch of spring flowers through the window. 'Daddy and I have come to visit you!'

Agnes stared at her daughter in joy and disbelief.

'How did you get here?' she gasped.

'Daddy brought me,' Esther replied. 'But children aren't allowed inside so I've got to stay out here!'

Emily rushed outside to see Esther whilst Stan hurried into the hospital to kiss his wounded wife.

'You never told me you were coming!' Agnes cried.

'I wanted to come as soon as I heard about the explosion,' Stan said as he sat with his arm around his wife's shoulders. 'But Esther fell ill with a hospital tummy bug – constant sickness and diarrhoea – and I couldn't risk passing that on to you, sweetheart, not in your fragile condition.' He gently stroked her bandaged brow. 'I tried phoning . . . Did nobody pass on my messages?'

Agnes shook her head.

'It's been chaos in here since the accident,' she said. 'Never mind, you're both here now,' she said as she smiled tenderly. 'Seeing the two people I love most in the world is the best medicine I could possibly have.'

Suddenly Stan was deadly serious.

'There's something I need to tell you, Agnes, something that's going to affect all of us.'

Agnes's heart sank. Was it going to be bad news about him returning to Cambridge for further treatment? Or was it about Esther's hospitalization?

'Esther's making great progress; she's well on the way to recovery. So I've decided that as soon as she's discharged from the hospital in Keswick I'm going to look for work round here. We're going to come and be with you.'

'Stan!' Agnes spluttered as tears stung her eyes.

'We're all going to be together from now on,' he concluded.

'But . . .' she said hesitantly, 'if you're discharged won't you get called up again?'

Stan's dark eyes clouded.

'No,' he answered firmly. 'I've looked into it, and my mental history exempts me from further combat.'

Unable to throw herself into her husband's arms, Agnes laid her head against his warm chest and wept.

'Thank God,' she whispered.

Wiping tears from his own eyes, Stan said, 'Come on, let's go and see Esther.'

Leaning on her husband's arm, Agnes blinked in the bright spring sunshine as Esther approached her, then tears filled her eyes as she realized that her little girl was walking confidently towards her.

'Look, Mummy, I'm getting better,' Esther cried as she fell into her mother's open arms.

'Oh, my darling! My darling!' Agnes sobbed with joy.

Stan brought a chair, which he set under an apple tree heavy with pink blossom. Esther clambered onto her mother's lap, where she made a daisy chain, similar to the one she'd made for her father in the hospital garden in Cambridge. Esther draped the flowers around her mother's neck and laid a pretty crown of blossom on her head.

'Queen of the May, the prettiest mummy in the world!'

After a few days Stan and Esther went back to Keswick to finalize the details of their move and Agnes had an eye operation.

Lillian had her stitches taken out and she returned to the digs, the first to be discharged from the hospital. Then she stuck to her word and immediately cut herself a Lauren Bacall fringe, which hid her scar and made her look even more sexy.

'Wait till Gary sees my new look!' she laughed excitedly.

As Agnes's damaged eye slowly healed, Emily worried about Elsie.

'What will you do when you're discharged?' she asked when they were alone during her hospital visit.

'Stop fretting, it's all arranged,' Elsie replied. 'I'm going to live with Tommy's mother and look after mi son.'

Emily looked down at the damaged arm that wasn't swathed in bandages any more but neatly plastered into a tight stump.

'But . . . ?'

Elsie answered the question before Emily could ask it.

'Mi left hand's all right and when this has properly healed,' she waved the stump in the air, 'I'll get a fake hand fitted.'

Emily bit her lip hard to fight back the tears; if Elsie was holding it together she damn well could.

'I'll miss working at the Phoenix and I'll really miss living with you all in the digs, but I've missed my little boy,' Elsie confessed. 'I'll be happy to spend more time with him.'

'We'll miss you,' Emily said softly.

'Eh! Don't run away with the idea that you won't see

me regular, like,' Elsie laughed. 'Them Phoenix chip butties have a right big pull on me!'

The Phoenix reopened a month after the explosion. The factory area that housed the bomb line had been blown clean away, leaving nothing but a shell, and the entire section had had to be rebuilt: walls, roof and a new concrete floor. Luckily the flames never reached as far as the loading sheds so the bombs stored there, so urgently needed on the front line, had been transported to airbases for immediate dispatch.

When the Phoenix doors opened again Mr Featherstone welcomed the Bomb Girls back.

'I know you've heard it before, girls,' he said as they gathered in the rebuilt canteen. 'But Hitler and his armies *really are* on the run and we need more bombs than ever – in our case especially so, since the forced closure of the factory after the blast reduced our productivity to zero!'

'Don't worry, Mr Featherstone, us Bomb Girls'll make up for lost time,' said a stout woman in the crowd.

'I don't doubt it, ladies – there's none finer than you,' their boss answered with undisguised pride.

'Back to work!' called Malc.

Determined to destroy the enemy once and for all, the indefatigable munitions girls returned to work, little knowing that in just a few days' time their bombs and many thousands more would be needed for the D-Day landings on the coast of northern France.

Chapter 33: Capture

It was a lonely and frightening existence for Alice and Robin after they successfully destroyed the vital railway link out of Marseilles.

'We have to lie low till the heat's off,' Robin had said as they went their separate ways in the dark.

'I wish we didn't have to live separately,' Alice grumbled one night as they dodged the night curfew in order to snatch five precious minutes together.

Robin nodded as he nuzzled her soft warm cheek.

'It's tough, darling,' he agreed. 'But if my safe house gets busted at least the Gestapo will only find me and not you; it's simply minimizing the risk.'

'I suppose so,' she said as she clung to him, dreading the moment when they'd have to say goodbye.

Their instructions were clear: to blend unobtrusively into the community, to maintain communications with headquarters and to carry out their missions without being arrested.

The most disappointing and frustrating thing was that communications, particularly their vital London link, frequently failed, which left not just Alice and Robin in the dark but every other Special Op too.

'The bloody Germans are getting too clever by half,' Robin told Alice. 'Their technique for tracking down clandestine Ops is more sophisticated than ours. Go carefully, my sweet.'

After Robin's warning Alice kept her wireless communications to the barest minimum. Fearful that the Gestapo might randomly pick up her location, she exchanged messages with London only at pre-arranged times then rapidly stowed her wireless set in the kindling box.

When her work was done there was nothing Alice could do but wait, and it was in the long boring hours that she decided to write a letter in encrypted code to Emily.

'Nobody but a Special Op will ever be able to read it,' she said into the silence of the flat. 'But it'll be the next best thing to talking to Emily and it might make me feel less lonely.'

She sharpened her pencil, opened her small notebook and began to write.

Dearest Emily,

How are you and Elsie, Agnes, Lillian, Esther and little Jonty? I miss you all so much. I miss Pendle too, and who would think I would ever say that? I'm in the south of France, which, as you know from all my endless fantasies, is somewhere I always longed to be. Well, I'm here in Marseilles, not teaching French and reading the French classics but decoding and intercepting radio messages from agents in the field. My days at the Phoenix paid off and I'm told I can assemble a bomb quicker than any female undercover agent in the area!

Not long ago Robin and I were given our first sabotage assignment; we were sent under the cover of darkness to blow up the main railway track out of Marseilles. I know I've handled

detonators and explosives before, but laying a bomb in the dark
with the Gestapo breathing down our necks was without doubt the
most terrifying thing I've ever done in my life so far.

I don't just fear for myself, Em, I fear for Robin too. I love
him so much. He's so clever and funny and brave and sexy. I can't
imagine life without him, yet here I am, employed in the most
dangerous occupation, madly in love with a fellow spy. A foolish
arrangement, given that life expectancy in the field can be less than
six weeks and

Her coded message was brought to an abrupt end when a blank piece of paper was slipped under her door; it was their pre-arranged signal to meet up. Alice stuffed the notebook under the newspapers in the kindling box, then quickly threw together a meagre picnic and waited for Robin. When she heard him down below in the courtyard ringing his bicycle bell, Alice skipped down the sweeping staircase with her basket. Hopping onto her bicycle, she set off with Robin, looking like the smiling young lovers that they were. They cycled out into the countryside where, instead of kissing and cuddling all afternoon, they planned their next explosion.

'All we ever do is talk war and destruction,' Alice moaned as they sat in a field full of swaying red poppies.

'That's why we're here, my darling,' he said as he gave her a kiss.

'So, tell me, what's our next assignment?' she asked as she tenderly twirled the blond moustache he'd grown since they were dropped into France.

'To take out a factory producing landing gear for the German Focke-Wulf 190 fighter,' he replied.

Alice stared at him thunderstruck.

'*What?*' she gasped. 'Blowing up a major railway line was scary enough but taking out a German factory . . .' She shook her head as words failed her. 'What on earth happened to our original communications brief?'

'I think the answer to your question, my sweet, is that, for some reason or another, there's nobody on the ground apart from you who can handle explosives,' Robin answered grimly.

Alice fell silent. She didn't need Robin to tell her that the Op she was replacing was probably dead or had been taken prisoner by the Gestapo.

'The tide's turning,' Robin said. 'We're on the attack and London says hit 'em hard and where it really hurts.'

Alice got straight to the point.

'I'll need more explosive material.'

Robin nodded.

'It's been arranged. I'll bring it with me.'

'Who's our contact?' she asked.

'One of the factory workers will guide us in,' Robin replied.

'When?' she asked as she wondered if she'd enough explosive for such a huge job.

'Tomorrow night,' he answered.

'So soon!'

'We'll leave the city immediately after the attack – the place will be crawling with the Gestapo.'

'Will we be together again?' she whispered.

'For a short time, yes,' he replied, then he added, 'Meet me at ten o'clock at the bandstand in the park opposite the factory.'

'What about the curfew?' she asked.

'We can duck and dive around that; we've done it before,' he said.

Then, seized by a sudden urgency, he started to load up her picnic basket.

'Sorry, sweetheart, I'm feeling edgy. Let's pack up and go home separately.'

Alice spent the next day nervously preparing for the attack. She had everything she needed: charger, detonators, some explosive, and Robin had promised to bring more. If there wasn't enough to take out the entire factory there was certainly enough to blow out the central walls and that would bring the roof down. Either way it would have a disastrous effect on the production of landing gear for the Focke-Wulf 190 fighter, she thought with a smile.

If Robin was right they'd be out of Marseilles by midnight and on their way to a safe house far away. Alice thought excitedly of the night train that would whisk them to safety.

In the hours she had to fill before meeting up with Robin, Alice took out her notebook and continued writing her coded message to Emily.

I often think of you in the digs. We had such happy times together. I wonder how you all are. Is the Phoenix still as busy? Do you still dance to Workers' Playtime *during your tea breaks?*

When I'm frightened I let my mind drift back home, and it's always to the moors, rolling away higher and higher, with the sun beating down, or the snow falling. In my fantasy I'm walking with you right to the very top, where we stand just like we did as

*children, staring across the vast expanse of the Pennine Way with
the wind lifting our hair.*

I love you, Emily. I always will.

All my love,

Alice

When it was time to leave Alice once again buried the little notebook at the bottom of the kindling box.

Wearing dark clothes and a cloche hat that covered her silver-bright hair, Alice left the flat. Avoiding the curfew meant scurrying through unlit back streets, hugging the shadows and freezing if she caught sight of a gendarme or, worse still, one of the Gestapo who patrolled the streets nightly. Alice carried a string bag of shopping, her 'bomb bread' as Robin jokingly called her explosive baguettes. Her pockets were stuffed with false identity papers and her false passport, which she hoped would protect her if she was caught prowling the streets during curfew hours.

Robin was waiting for her behind the bandstand in the park.

'The factory's guarded by soldiers,' he whispered as they crouched in the shadows. 'We'll have to hide and see how often they pass there.'

Silently, they slipped through the park, ducking behind trees and diving into bushes until they were opposite the factory. Avoiding the floodlights at the front of the building, they crept towards the high metal fence that ran along the side. Robin nodded towards a dense oleander bush and they wriggled into it.

'From here we can time how often the guard passes,' he hissed into Alice's ear.

With adrenalin coursing through their blood, they watched one armed guard walk the length of the fence, and as he did so he crossed paths with another. They stopped to exchange a few words and light up their cigarettes then went on their way.

With bugs creeping down her neck, Alice began to squirm.

'Shh!' hissed Robin.

'I'm being eaten alive,' she hissed back.

Ignoring her complaints, Robin timed how long it took the guards to circle the block.

'Nearly forty minutes,' he said. 'That's more than enough time to lay the explosives.'

After the guards passed them for the second time Alice and Robin waited for the footsteps to fade, then they scrambled out of the oleander bush and dashed to the metal fence, which Robin quickly attacked with metal cutters. Alice wriggled inside first followed by Robin, who secured the fence with metal strips so that the guards wouldn't notice the tear. Holding their breath, they dashed under the cover of some wooden crates where they waited, with their hearts in their mouths, for the worker who would guide them in. From the northern side of the building a small light flicked on and off twice.

'That's our signal,' whispered Robin.

Ducking behind empty crates and factory debris, they made their way to the worker who, in rapid French, told them that the best place to lay their explosives was against the wall of the loading bay.

'There's enough explosive material in there to wreck the place!' he said with a grim smile.

He led them between packing cases and crates to the darkest section of the loading bay, then with a quick thumbs-up he left them and was swallowed up by the shadows.

As Robin kept lookout, Alice planted the explosives packed with the timed detonators in strategic places along the loading bay. Once they were in place she and Robin ran towards the perimeter fence but, to their horror, they were stopped dead in their tracks by the sight of the two armed guards standing beside the fence smoking cigarettes.

'Jesus Christ, that's all we need!' groaned Robin as he pulled Alice down to the ground.

'What're they doing?' she groaned.

Robin listened for a few minutes.

'Can you believe it? Talking about some prostitute they've visited in town!'

Alice wondered how long their conversation could possibly go on for. Wouldn't they get into trouble dawdling about whilst on duty?

Crouched behind a pile of metal debris and with sweat pouring out of her, Alice checked her watch. She'd set the detonators for fifteen minutes, giving them what should have been more than enough time to make their getaway. But now with armed guards in their flight path they might be trapped inside the factory grounds when the blast went off.

'Please, God, please make them move on,' she prayed under her breath.

Stamping out their cigarette butts, the laughing guards finally moved away.

'Now!' she hissed.

But Robin held her back.

'They can't see us,' she muttered.

'They'll hear us – wait!' he warned.

Alice counted the minutes it took the guards' footsteps to recede.

'If we don't go in the next three minutes we'll be here when the place blows,' she whispered frantically.

At last they sprinted the hundred yards to the perimeter fence where Alice, with her heart at exploding point, watched Robin snip the wire. As soon as the hole was big enough they dived through it, just as the first explosive went off.

'Run, before the building catches fire and they can see us!' Alice cried.

With adrenalin pumping through their bloodstream, they raced back to the safety of the dark park from where they watched the explosives take the northern wall of the factory out and the roof too, the burning, falling debris igniting the loaded packing cases, which burst into flames. As the rest of the factory caught fire, Robin kissed Alice.

'I'm so proud of you, sweetheart,' he said with a smile. 'I'd say that was a job bloody well done!'

Alice tried to smile back but she couldn't stop shaking.

'I've never been so scared in my entire life,' she said as she leaned against him.

'Better get used to it, sweetheart,' he said with a soft laugh. 'You're wasted on communications!'

As Alice's heartbeat returned to normal, she felt weak with relief. Now they could leave Marseilles and get as far away from the scene of the crime as possible. As the factory fire raged, they crept away and hid in the side streets until dawn broke, then made their way to a café near the railway station where they planned to buy tickets to Amiens.

But as they sat drinking bowls of *café au lait*, Alice spotted out of the corner of her eye that the entire area around the station was crawling with Gestapo, who were on high alert after the factory explosion.

'We don't have to ask why,' said Robin as he nodded towards the flickering flames lighting up the pale morning sky.

'They're locking down the city,' she said under her breath.

'Dammit!' growled Robin from behind *Le Figaro*, which he was pretending to read. 'We'll never get out of Marseilles today.'

Alice's heart dropped; she felt like a child who'd been promised a treat that was immediately snatched away from her.

'We'd better go our separate ways,' he added quickly.

'Oh, Robin, no,' she said, nearly in tears.

'Come on,' he said sharply. 'We've no choice but to lie low till the heat's off.'

They hurried out of the café, but in their haste to get away they forgot to pay the *garçon* for their breakfast.

'*ATTENTION!*' bellowed the irate bartender.

His angry shout caught the attention of several nearby Gestapo, who immediately surrounded the café. Alice's instinct was to run but Robin stayed calm as he held her securely by the elbow.

'*ACHTUNG!*' they barked. 'What're you doing here?'

'We arrived on the overnight train and were just having coffee,' Robin replied in flawless French. 'We are so tired we forgot to pay. My apologies, *monsieur*,' Robin said to the sulky bartender as he dropped French francs into his hand.

'Where are your train tickets?' one of the soldiers snapped, not convinced by his story.

Alice turned her lovely eyes on him and smiled sweetly.

'I threw them away, sir,' she said apologetically.

'Your identity papers,' the same guard said.

Alice produced her papers, which the guard curtly nodded at; Robin's papers were not quite so acceptable. They'd been crumpled in his pocket and the forged signatures had faded. The guard passed the papers to his senior officer, who scrutinized them.

'Take them to Hôtel Canebière with the others,' he snapped.

Protesting their innocence all the way, Alice and Robin were herded into a hotel room, then they were separated and interrogated. Alice was pushed around and yelled at, but because her papers were in order she got off lightly. Robin, however, got the heavy treatment; he was dragged out of the room and coshed around the buttocks and calves then hit around the face. When they dragged him back with blood streaming from a deep cut above his right eye, tears stung Alice's eyes. The Gestapo started shoving prisoners out of the room and Alice tried to snatch Robin's hand.

'What's happening?' she sobbed in French.

As Robin and a dozen other men were thrown into trucks, Alice was unexpectedly set free.

'Get out of here!' Robin mouthed as the truck doors slammed on the prisoners.

Wild with fear, Alice grabbed a bike leaning up against the hotel wall.

'I'm not leaving you,' she screamed after him.

Cycling furiously along the dusty track she followed the van until it accelerated and disappeared into the distance. Falling from the bike she crouched on the ground and sobbed and sobbed.

'Oh, my love, when will I see you again? And how will I live without you till then?'

Chapter 34: D-Day

As Lillian, Emily and Agnes clocked on for their shift on 6 June, they had no idea that a momentous day in the history of the war was unfolding just across the Channel. As they sat in the canteen during their midday break, *Music While You Work* was interrupted by a flash news bulletin. The familiar calm voice of the BBC newsreader rang with suppressed excitement as he announced that under the command of General Eisenhower the allied forces had begun the D-Day attack.

The clatter and chatter usual in the packed canteen dropped to total silence as the munitions girls stared at each other in complete disbelief; could it really be true? Could the combined British and American forces be at this very moment storming the beaches of Normandy?

Then, unable to contain themselves a second longer the women leapt to their feet and started to shout and cheer as they punched the air with jubilation.

'D-DAY! D-DAY! D-DAY!' they cried till the windows shook with their wild exultation.

Grasping each other, the women hugged and kissed; smiling, laughing and weeping, they could hardly speak for the mixture of elation and apprehension that flooded through them, for nobody knew at that moment how the day would pan out.

'I don't know whether to laugh or cry,' Emily confessed.

'Laugh!' said Lillian. 'It makes a change from weeping!'

To the chirpy tune of Flanagan and Allen singing 'Underneath the Arches' they quite spontaneously broke into the conga. Singing at the tops of their voices, they danced out of the canteen and onto the cobbled street outside the Phoenix where they skipped along, kicking out their legs. Malc came rushing out to call them back into work.

'We've not won the bloody war yet!' he cried.

'No, but it's a step in the right direction,' several laughing women shouted back.

'Nobody said we don't need any more bombs,' Malc reminded them, with a smile he couldn't hide.

'Slave-driver!' the girls teased.

'Don't you want to be near the radio to hear the next news flash?' Malc deviously suggested.

Nobody could argue with that, and the women quickly returned to their lines, eagerly listening out over the clattering roll of the conveyor belt for more news of the invasion, which dribbled in slowly all through that long and fateful day. Their hearts sank as they heard of the beaches littered with mines.

'God help our lads,' Lillian prayed out loud.

'They're walking into a death trap!' gasped Agnes.

When the news finally came through that the Allies had secured the German beachheads and had begun marching inland the munitions girls were incredulous.

'They've got through!' yelled Emily. 'We've broken the line.'

Their shift came and went but nobody wanted to leave

the factory. As the next shift clocked on, Emily, Lillian and Agnes and many other women stayed gathered together, tensely waiting for more news from the BBC. As Emily looked at her fellow workers smoking and drinking tea, she thought of those thousands of soldiers landing on the Normandy beaches, rushing forwards with bayonets at the ready to kill the enemy or die trying, and wondered how many were husbands, sweethearts, sons and brothers of the women around her. Emily's heart suddenly skipped a beat. Bill, she thought. Where in God's name was he? She'd heard on the radio that all possible forces – Brits, Yanks, Poles, Canadians, anybody who could handle a weapon – had been utilized. Was Bill one of the boys on the beach, walking into the jaws of death with his bayonet at the ready?

To their amazement, Elsie came rushing into the canteen, pushing with one hand the big old Silver Cross pram that she'd picked up in a junk shop for a shilling and was immensely proud of.

'I couldn't stand not being here with you all,' she gasped, out of breath from running up the hill from Pendle.

It wasn't just Emily, Agnes and Lillian who loved Elsie; everybody at the Phoenix had admiration and respect for the little lass who had put herself in the line of fire, just like their loved ones were now doing in northern France.

'In't it wonderful?' Elsie cried as she grabbed a huge chip butty and a cup of scalding-hot tea.

'Bugger me!' Lillian exclaimed. 'Not even the D-Day landings take your appetite away.'

Elsie smiled as she bit into her butty.

'Eeh, I've been missing these!' she giggled.

They stayed together until exhaustion and Jonty's hungry cries for his supper sent them their separate ways, but not before they'd heard more heart-lifting news on the radio.

The Allied troops who'd landed that morning were already several miles inland of the Normandy beaches and were pushing steadily on.

'Nothing's going to stop 'em now," said Elsie gleefully.

'I'd say this was one of the best days of my life,' said Lillian happily. 'Well, apart from the day I met Gary – oh, and the day I first had sex!' she added naughtily.

'Ooh, Lillian, you can't say stuff like that,' said Elsie as she settled yawning Jonty in his pram.

'I can – and I do!' laughed Lillian.

They waved Elsie off then headed back to the digs; though it was evening, the night was summer-light and birds were still tweeting on the moors.

'Here we are, surrounded by peace and beauty, whilst just across the Channel all hell is breaking loose,' said Agnes with a sigh.

'God bless and save them all,' prayed Emily with all her heart.

Emily said a lot of prayers during the next few days after she heard from her mother that Bill's infantry unit had indeed been among the troops shipped over and deposited on the beaches of northern France. As soon as she could she hurried down the hill and into the town to visit Bill's mother.

When Mrs Redmond opened her door Emily immediately knew that something was wrong.

'What is it?' she gasped.

Mrs Redmond wiped a hand across her weary face.

'We don't know. You'd best come in,' she said as she turned around and walked into her tidy back kitchen that smelled of baking bread and soaking peas.

Emily looked around the familiar room where she'd so often sat with Bill. She remembered holding hands as they sat drinking tea – once they'd even had a cup of instant coffee, which she'd thought was very bold and exotic. They'd kissed in secret in the back kitchen and planned their lives together, she recalled with a gulp, but that was a lifetime ago when they were young and innocent.

'We know his division were sent out to Normandy,' Mrs Redmond said as she brewed a pot of tea. 'There's been a lot of fatalities,' she added nervously.

Emily bowed her head as she imagined lads even younger than Bill shot down as they ran off the boats or, if they made it to the beaches, blown up by one of the thousands of landmines.

Human fodder, she thought; but these words she wisely kept to herself.

'Some of the lads' families have had news, but we're still waiting,' Mrs Redmond continued as she put a china cup and saucer in front of Emily and a plate of carrot and coconut buns.

'Mrs Ryecroft round the corner has lost both her sons,' Mrs Redmond said as she picked up her cup and saucer with trembling hands. 'She heard the news this morning,' she added faintly.

Emily, who hadn't set foot in the Redmonds' house

since her split with Bill, stood up and walked around the table so she could put a hand on Mrs Redmond's shoulder.

'I know I did wrong,' she said quietly. 'There's not a day goes by when I don't kick myself for what I did . . . but I still love your son and I always will.'

'Aye, it's a pity,' Mrs Redmond replied sadly. 'You broke his heart and that's God's honest truth.' A knock at the door sent the blood rushing from her face. 'It might be a telegram,' she said faintly

It wasn't a telegram; it was a neighbour come to ask the same question as Emily.

'How's your lad?'

Emily bade Bill's mother farewell and then, feeling heavy-hearted, she made her way to Pendle church where she sat in silence praying for the soldiers fighting on the beaches of northern France.

She returned to the Phoenix in time to clock on for her shift, and as she was changing into her work overalls Agnes came rushing up to her.

'Great news!' she cried, flushed and excited.

Completely preoccupied with Bill and his brave battalion, Emily absent-mindedly answered, 'I just hope they make it home alive.'

'I'm not talking about the war!' Agnes exclaimed. 'Though I hope they are all safe too. But I've just got a letter off Stan. He's got a job interview on one of the local sheep farms and he's coming next week with Esther,' she finished excitedly.

'That's wonderful!' cried Emily, truly delighted for her friend.

'Oh, I can't wait!' said happy, smiling Agnes. 'Just think – if he gets the job we'll be near each other for the first time in five years.'

Every day more news dribbled in: the Allies were advancing on Caen, they'd taken Bayeux, Rommel was leading the Germans in a much-delayed counter-attack.

'It's emotionally exhausting listening to it all,' said Lillian. 'One minute you're up, the next you're down and worrying how many are dead, how many are casualties. I wish they could release names and put us out of our misery.'

'It's way too early for that, Lillian,' Agnes said realistically. 'All we can do is stay focused on the good news and pray for our boys over there.'

Emily nodded in agreement whilst at the same time she constantly wondered if Mrs Redmond had heard news of Bill yet, or would he turn out to be one of many missing in action?

When Stan arrived, Lillian and Emily made themselves scarce so Agnes could talk freely with her family – and there was a lot to talk about. Stan was determined that if he got the job he was going to live on the sheep farm, which was a five-mile hike over the moors from the Phoenix.

'But . . . what about Esther?' Agnes asked as she cradled her lovely daughter in her arms.

'She's still got to have treatment every month at the hospital in Keswick but one of us can take her up there on the train and bring her back again,' Stan said, then he added as he looked Agnes straight in the eye: 'Sweetheart, I've given this a lot of thought whilst I've been looking after Esther. We're a family who love and need each other very much, but because of circumstances, cruel twists of fate, we've been forced to live apart more than we've lived together. It's a miracle I got out of the POW camp alive. It's a miracle that Esther grows stronger every day. And it's a miracle you were evacuated out of London, well away from the Woolwich Arsenal. Don't you think that God's trying to tell us something?'

Blinded by tears, Agnes nodded.

'*If* I get this job I swear we're *never* going to be separated again,' he told his wife firmly. 'With a bit of luck we're going to be a family from now on.'

Agnes smiled through her tears as she said, 'But I can't leave here and live on a sheep farm!'

'And I'm not planning on turning into a Bomb Girl!' Stan joked. 'We'll only be a few miles apart, and that's nothing compared with what we've lived through.'

Agnes kissed her happy husband.

'Good luck with the interview,' she said softly.

'I'll need it,' he replied with a grin. 'I'm the world's best at driving London buses, but sheep . . . ? That'll be a steep learning curve!'

Due to the shortage of able-bodied men, Stan got the job as shepherd without any problems.

'They just want a fit man who's willing to work all hours,' he reported delightedly to Agnes a few hours later. 'In return they'll train me up, and give me accommodation. I start next week in the shearing shed, God help me!'

Agnes looked at her smiling, healthy husband.

My God, how he's changed, she thought.

Agnes wrapped her arms around Stan's neck and kissed him full on the mouth.

'We're so lucky.'

'The happiest family in Pendle!' he said as he picked her up and swung her in his arms.

Elsie, who'd been minding Esther whilst Stan had his interview and Agnes finished her shift, arrived with both Esther and Jonty in her big Silver Cross pram.

'They've played together all day,' said Elsie as she joined Lillian, Emily, Stan and Agnes, who were sitting outside the digs enjoying the lovely warm June evening.

'Have a beer,' said Stan, who'd managed to buy a few bottles of pale ale under the counter to celebrate his success.

Elsie, a complete teetotaller since her accident, shook her head.

'I'll settle for a pot of tea,' she laughed.

As Esther held Jonty's hand and led him very carefully onto the edge of the moors, where wild winberries grew, Agnes discussed their future domestic set-up.

'I'm sure Esther will get a place at the Phoenix nursery,' she said. 'She liked it there before.'

Elsie frowned at her.

'Why would you send her there?' she asked.

'She's got to go somewhere whilst I'm at work,' Agnes pointed out.

'Why wouldn't you let me look after her?' Elsie asked.

Agnes flushed; she had thought of that but she felt it would be too much for Elsie with her injury.

'I know what you're thinking, Agnes,' Elsie said quietly. 'I may only have one hand but I can manage two kids – look how I pushed the pair of them up the hill in that big old pram.' She looked her friend straight in the eye as she added, 'I would love to look after Esther. You could drop her off and pick her up before and after work. And if you're on late shifts, or lambing,' she said, nodding at Stan, 'Esther would be welcome to stay the night with us.'

'It's a lot of work, Elsie,' Stan said, though he was clearly moved by her love and generosity.

'Hard work's never bothered me, Stan,' Elsie replied with her usual candour. 'Having Esther about the house will be a joy, believe me. Jonty already thinks of her as a big sister.'

'What about Tommy's mum?' Emily asked. 'Will she mind?'

Elsie laughed out loud.

'Whatever makes Jonty happy makes Ma Carter happy too,' Elsie answered. 'Plus, she loves little Esther. We all do, Agnes,' Elsie said with tears in her honest, bright eyes.

And so it was settled: Elsie would look after Esther, Stan would become a sheep farmer and Agnes would continue to supervise her Bomb Girls at the Phoenix.

'Here's to one very happy family!' said Lillian as she raised her glass of beer. 'Cheers!'

Chapter 35: The Gestapo

Back at the flat that, only twenty-four hours ago, she thought she was leaving forever, Alice went to pieces. Where had they taken Robin? How could she find out what was happening? Why had those men been rounded up and driven away?

She talked to herself as she paced the flat like a caged animal.

'I have to get information. I'll go out of my mind if I stay a minute longer in this dreary place.'

Remembering her training at Helford House, she changed her dark clothes and rearranged her hair, which had got damp and flat under the black cloche hat she'd been wearing. The last thing she wanted was to be recognized as the girl who nearly got arrested at the Hôtel Canebière.

Leaving the flat, she checked in the shop windows she hurried past that she was not being followed, then she walked across the city to Robin's safe house. But although she rang the bell several times, nobody opened the door to her. Terrified that all the underground agents sheltering there had been arrested, Alice panicked. Her heart was pounding and she felt weak and sick from lack of sleep. Her instinct was to turn and run; instead she took several deep breaths then slowly and purposefully walked away. When she got back to her flat she found a note in her post box.

'Meet me in the bar on the corner, as soon as you can.'

Could it be Robin? Had he got away? Breathless and excited, Alice ran to the bar where she found not Robin but the Special Op who shared the same safe house as Robin. Steering her firmly by the elbow, he led Alice to a table outside where he ordered cognac. After drinking a double straight off he spoke quietly but furiously in French.

'*Never* do that again!'

Alice dropped her voice to a whisper.

'I had no choice. Robin's been arrested.'

'I know,' he muttered.

'You know?' she gasped incredulously. 'How do you know?'

'An insider's cracked under interrogation,' he replied. 'He gave a list of the false names we're using, and the Gestapo are rounding up everyone on the list.'

'So there's every chance they'll find us too,' said Alice weakly.

'If you go on the run they'll track you down, but if you lie low until the heat's off you might survive.'

Alice stared at him with her penetrating grey eyes.

'How can the heat ever be off if the Gestapo know our names?' she asked.

'In time we'll get new names, new papers,' he said as he rose to go. 'For now we're on our own,' he muttered as he walked away.

Alice did exactly as she was instructed: she holed up and waited for the storm to pass. But she was sick with worry about Robin. In between bouts of crying and trembling, she filled her time writing her coded diary to Emily.

My dearest Em,

I'm so scared. Robin's been taken by the Gestapo. I should be braver than this, my training taught me to deal with people who cracked and I'm ashamed of myself. Am I afraid because I'm on my own or am I just a weak woman who can't function without a man at the helm? I never thought I was weak until now, but the very moment I need to be strong and focused I fall apart. I have cyanide pills I could take; we were issued with them when we were dropped into France. We were advised to take them if we thought we'd break under interrogation. It's not that, oddly enough, that worries me; it's not knowing where my love is, whether he's alive or dead. How will I ever find out?

I hate this flat. It has become a prison to me. I'd love to get on a train and come home. Or would I? That would take me even further away from Robin. If I close my eyes I can imagine I'm home, in Pendle, on the moors, at the Phoenix, in the digs, laughing and happy, young and hopeful. Oh, Em, when will this terrible war ever end?

A sudden, terrible foreboding filled Alice and she was compelled to write of her darkest fears.

If I never come home, please look after Mum and be the daughter that I might have been. Try to find my Robin. Tell him I love him more than life itself and our love goes beyond the grave.

Take care of yourself, my dearest, sweetest Em, and every time you walk on the moors blow a kiss to heaven, where I hope I'll be when all this is finally over.

Find Bill, marry him, have babies, be happy.

I love you,

Alice

With tears streaming down her face, Alice closed the notebook. It would hurt to write more. She walked towards the kindling box then stopped dead in her tracks, filled again with a sense of foreboding. There were no more explosives left in the box because she and Robin had used the lot on the factory raid, but her wireless set along with the aerial and earth cable were still there. If the flat was searched again her radio equipment might be found, but she wanted her coded notebook, her last link with home, kept safe. Alice explored the flat; all she needed was a small place for a small notebook. Finally she shoved it up the chimney.

'It'll either be found or get burned,' she said out loud.

The next afternoon, whilst Alice lay wide awake on top of her bed, she heard loud footsteps thundering up the stairs and as she broke into a sweat of fear she knew with a heavy heart that this was what she had been dreading, yet half expecting, since yesterday. Within seconds the Gestapo broke down the door to her flat.

'PAPERS! Where are your papers?' they screamed in German.

Alice calmly presented her forged papers, which they threw on the floor before they dragged her into the street.

'In the truck, get in the truck.'

'*Why?*' she demanded in French. 'What have I done?'

'No questions,' they snarled as they bundled her into the back of a truck.

What Alice would never know is that many months later a British Op, newly dropped into enemy territory, would break into the safe house looking for any information he might find. As Alice had predicted, the Gestapo had taken the flat apart. Nothing remained in the kindling box, the mattress on the bed had been shredded, books ripped apart, floorboards wrenched up. But after much scrupulous searching the agent reached up the chimney and found Alice's coded notebook. Thinking it contained important information he passed the notebook on to a contact who was returning to England. The notebook finally finished up in Helford House.

Thrown into solitary confinement, Alice had plenty of time to go over her cover story. She was a French teacher, and she had papers to prove it. The school where she had taught in Amiens had been bombed and she was relocated to Marseilles, where she hoped to find a new position.

She'd practised the art of spinning a cover story a hundred times during her training in Helford; now she was doing it for real.

I won't crack, Alice vowed to herself. I WILL NOT CRACK!

Waiting alone in the darkness, it was difficult to know whether it was night or day, and impossible to keep track of how long she'd been held in prison. Every time she heard footsteps or the jangle of keys her heart leaped in hope, then she was filled with bowel-gripping terror. She was finally dragged before the Gestapo in the middle of the night.

'Why are you in Marseilles?'

In flawless French Alice repeated her cover story.

'I'm a teacher from Amiens.'

Unconvinced, they continued questioning her.

'Why was your name given to us by Claude Moirrot?'

Alice insisted that she'd never heard of Claude Moirrot,

though he was in fact the Special Op who'd shared the same safe house as Robin and had warned her off in the bar near her flat. Her heart sank as she realized that he too must have been arrested and interrogated.

After further questions, followed by Alice's rehearsed replies, the Gestapo grew impatient with her. They started to slap her around the face, then they moved onto shooting bullets in a circle around her feet.

'How do you know Claude Moirrot? Why did he give us your name? Why do you appear on several lists of resistance fighters?'

Terrified, Alice began to cry and sob.

Don't speak English, she told herself. Speak French, cry in French, weep in French! BE FRENCH!

A pain worse than any she had ever experienced in her life shot through her right foot as a German bullet shattered a bone close to her ankle. Falling to the floor, Alice tried to staunch the blood that pumped out from the gaping wound but the pain coursing up her leg was so unbearable she fainted clean away.

She came to in the dark of her cell, in a pool of blood; the wound in her foot was agony and there was no way of stopping the blood. Alice ripped up her underskirt and tied it in a tourniquet around her shattered ankle. Wracked with pain, she slumped back and instinctively felt for the cyanide pill sewn into her cuff.

It would be a quick death, she thought. And there would be no more pain.

But if she took it she would never see Robin again, she would never see his lovely, smiling face, never feel his hands or the soft touch of his lips.

'I can't die yet,' Alice muttered through the mist of pain that threatened to engulf her. 'I must wait for Robin.'

The following morning, crazed with pain, Alice was thrown into a truck along with dozens of other women and taken to Ravensbrück for further questioning.

'Why are they taking us all the way to Germany? Why not kill us now?' she whispered to a woman beside her.

'They won't kill us till they're sure we're not withholding information,' she whispered back.

'No talking,' snarled the German soldier. 'Quiet there,' he said as he raised the butt of his rifle, indicating he'd hit them with it if they disobeyed orders.

Alice slumped into semi-unconsciousness. In between the waves of pain that gripped her lower body, she dreamed of home: green hills bright with uncurling fern fronds, banks of fragrant bluebells under oak trees. The moors rolling away to Yorkshire, the song of larks and curlews, the taste of good food, a warm bed and a mother who loved her precious silver-haired daughter. Gasping in pain, Alice awoke with scalding tears rolling down her cheeks. How would her mother ever understand her daughter's dark secret? Alice would never be able to explain why she'd chosen to fight the war her way, living a life of secrecy and subterfuge, spinning a web of lies in the hope that her mother could be protected from the truth.

They arrived at Ravensbrück in the middle of the night. Screaming with pain as she was dragged out of the truck, Alice was stripped of her civilian clothes. She was then thrown into a hut along with hundreds of other female prisoners. Lying on a filthy bunk bed in a threadbare prison uniform already crawling with fleas, Alice wept as she realized that her cyanide pills had been taken away from her along with her civilian clothes. Too late, she regretted her decision not to take her own life earlier. She was in an all-women's prison in northern Germany and the only men in the camp were German soldiers. All hope of seeing Robin before she died was gone forever.

She never knew how many days passed before anything changed, it could even have been weeks, by which time Alice had become an emaciated cripple, hopping on improvised crutches.

I'll probably die of septicaemia before I'm shot for spying, Alice thought bitterly.

Then one morning she and many other women in her cell block were thrown into trucks and driven to Dachau where they were shoved and kicked out of the trucks like cattle. Too weak to stand and crying in pain, Alice slumped against the fence that separated the men's camp from the women's – was there a chance that Robin might be one of the men behind the fence? How would she ever spot him amongst hundreds of emaciated men in rags; for that matter how would he ever recognize her as the slender, silver-haired beauty he had loved a lifetime ago?

In despair, Alice turned as the guard pushed and poked her with his rifle.

'MOVE! WALK! NOW!'

Limping and bleeding, she followed the line of weary women to their hut, but not before she saw a tall, distinctive man behind the razor-wire fence.

'Robin . . . ?' she sobbed desperately. Then she shook her head. She was losing her mind; it couldn't possibly be him.

Still walking, she craned her head around to look again at the man in the crowd, a man with distinctive blond hair, taller than most and walking with an ease she remembered and loved. Now she was sure.

'Robin!'

As she stopped in her tracks, the guard, sick of her insubordination, butted her in the back with the end of his rifle.

'MOVE!' he screamed.

Later, under the pretence of going to the stinking latrines overrun with rats, Alice skirted the fence, her eyes scanning every man in the crowd. And then she saw him, running towards her. He'd watched the truck unload and recognized his love; though she was smeared in mud and blood and wearing rags, he'd spotted his silver-haired Alice and had been searching for her ever since.

'ALICE!' he gasped as he rushed to the fence.

Alice lifted her tired, bloodied face to him. Though the light had gone out of her wonderful eyes they brimmed with love at the sight of him.

'Robin, my love,' she said softly.

Robin pushed his arm through the fence and grabbed her hand, which he kissed and stroked.

'How did they find you?' he cried.

'We were all rounded up,' she said. 'One of the agents cracked under interrogation and they got a list of all our names.'

'They've hurt you,' he cried as she saw her mangled foot.

'It's a bullet wound,' she said lightly.

'Alice,' he whispered urgently, 'the war's nearly over

and we're winning, sweetheart. Paris has been liberated. We'll soon be free. You've just got to hold out a little longer.'

Alice gazed adoringly into his beautiful deep-blue eyes.

'We'll be free and together soon,' he insisted.

Before she could answer a female guard with a grip of iron yanked her by the shoulder and pushed her forward.

'MOVE!' she snarled.

Alice gripped Robin's hand.

'I love you, I always will!'

The female guard slapped her hard across the face.

'WHORE!' she snapped as she pushed and shoved Alice away from the fence.

The last thing she ever heard Robin say was, 'I love you, my sweetheart, stay strong.'

Then he too was grabbed by a guard and clubbed into silence.

Alice did stay strong; all through her interrogations she told herself over and over again that she had to stay alive, she had to see Robin just one more time.

Lying in her bunk one night, Alice heard fellow inmates passing news along the line.

'A group of Brits dug their way out – right under the sentry box!'

The following day several of the escapees were dragged back and shot on the spot. One of them, a tall, emaciated man, Alice recognized as the Special Op she and Robin had been dropped into France with, in what now seemed a lifetime ago. As the escapee was dragged by the Gestapo, he caught sight of Alice pressed against the fence. Though she was thin and bruised with a busted lip – hardly the dazzling silver-haired beauty that he trained with in Helford – he nevertheless recognized her. Pretending to stumble and fall, he dragged himself close to the fence where she was standing.

'Robin got out!' he whispered.

Before he could say another word he was kicked in the head and hauled away to be shot. Alice, nearly fainting with relief, gripped the fence as she gasped.

'Robin's free!'

It was the very last thought in her mind when, some days later, a lethal injection of phenol was administered to her at the end of her interrogation because – no matter what the Gestapo did to her – Alice refused to crack.

Chapter 36: The Visit

1945 brought great hope to the nation. The Allies were relentlessly advancing on Germany and the Soviets in the East had captured Warsaw.

But the world was soon to be shocked by newsreel footage showing skeletal prisoners being freed from concentration camps.

Emily, Lillian and Agnes had been to see Humphrey Bogart and Lauren Bacall in *To Have and Have Not* and they had watched the harrowing scenes on the Pathé News that accompanied the film.

'How can anyone hate a religion so much they'd want to wipe all its followers off the face of the earth?' Emily asked Lillian and Agnes as they walked home.

'And how could so many help Hitler achieve his ambition to annihilate the Jews?' Agnes asked.

'When they catch the murdering generals they'll string 'em up,' Lillian said wrathfully.

'That won't bring back the dead,' replied Emily sadly.

They were on a late shift the following day so Agnes took advantage of her free time to pop in and see Esther, who was thriving under Elsie's devoted care and Jonty's fawning adoration. Lillian decided to sleep in till she had to clock on for work, whilst Emily went to see her mum, who had heard news from Mrs Redmond about Bill.

'She said he'd written.'

Seeing Emily's tense face, Mrs Yates quickly added, 'The Lancashires had some heavy fighting near the River Rhine, wherever that is. But they've been singled out for their bravery and congratulated by Montgomery himself,' she concluded.

Emily didn't know whether to feel relieved or even more anxious. God, after all these months Bill's unit were still fighting, fighting all the way to Berlin, regardless of the thousands of fatalities on both sides.

'Oh, Mother,' she sighed as she put her head in her hands. 'Will it ever end?'

Mrs Yates gave her a comforting pat on the shoulder then dropped a large buff envelope on the kitchen table.

'This came for you,' she said.

Emily looked at the writing. She didn't recognize it, but she did recognize the postmark; it was from Helston in Cornwall.

'Looks official,' said Mrs Yates.

Trembling, Emily ripped open the envelope and pulled out several typewritten sheets of paper.

Dear Miss Yates,

Through a series of events, the details of which I am not at liberty to disclose, a notebook was delivered to me. It was written in code by Alice Massey. When transcribed, we discovered it was in fact a series of letters to you. For reasons of national security we found it necessary to censor some of the information, but the enclosed is an accurate transcription of what Miss Massey wrote personally to you.

Yours faithfully,

Brigadier Russell Kingsley

Frightened that her face would betray her emotions, Emily scooped up the package and said a hurried good-bye to her mother.

'I'd better get back, Mum. The girls will be waiting for me.'

Emily couldn't get back to the digs quick enough. She was relieved to find that Lillian was still snoozing and Agnes hadn't got back, so she would have the sitting room to herself while she read Alice's notebook, which Brigadier Kingsley's office had transcribed onto sheets of paper. The first thing she noticed was the date; Alice had written this months ago. Why had it taken so long to reach her? Who had handed it over to the Brigadier? Where was Alice now?

She began to read.

Dearest Emily,

How are you and Elsie, Agnes, Lillian, Esther and little Jonty? I miss you all so much . . .

. . . I often think of you in the digs. We had such happy times together . . .

. . . When I'm frightened I let my mind drift back home, and it's always to the moors, rolling away higher and higher, with the sun beating down, or the snow falling . . .

'Oh, Al, you'll never know how much I miss you, how much we all miss you and pray for your safe return,' Emily murmured as her eyes raced along the typewritten sheets.

When Emily turned the page her skin prickled; there was a dread and fear in what Alice wrote next.

If I never come home look after Mum and be the daughter that I might have been. Try to find my Robin. Tell him I love him more than life itself and our love goes beyond the grave.

Take care of yourself, my dearest, sweetest Em, and every time you walk on the moors blow a kiss to heaven, where I hope I'll be when all this is finally over.

Find Bill, marry him, have babies, be happy.

I love you,

Alice

Emily stared in disbelief at the letter then read it again.

If I never come home . . .

'You MUST come home, Alice, you must!' Emily said as she burst into tears. 'You've GOT to come back to me!' she sobbed.

'Em . . . ?'

It was Lillian, fresh from her bed, still with her rollers in.

Seeing Emily's tear-stained face and haunted expression, she hunkered down beside her.

'What's up, cock?'

Fed up with keeping secrets, Emily thrust the sheets of paper into Lillian's hands.

'Alice wrote to me. Half of it's censored but you can read between the lines,' she said bleakly.

'Sweet Jesus,' Lillian gasped as she read. 'I never even guessed.'

'I didn't until I went to stay with her in London,' Emily

said, relieved at last to talk openly about Alice. 'I promised I wouldn't say a word. She said it would be dangerous for her, so I kept silent.' She sighed as she leaned against Lillian. 'Would it have helped if I'd said something?'

'Of course not,' Lillian staunchly retorted. 'She took you into her confidence because she trusted you and you kept her secret.'

'Do you think she might still be alive?' Emily asked.

'It's possible,' Lillian replied. 'One thing this bastard war's taught us is to never give up hoping.'

When Agnes returned from her visit to Esther they showed her the letter too.

'All along I suspected she was doing something covert but I never imagined it was so dangerous,' she said. 'We'd better tell Elsie; she wouldn't want to be left out.'

Elsie was devastated.

'Why would a beautiful girl like Alice want to be a spy?' she cried angrily. 'She could have stayed here with us instead of running off to France and risking her life for others.'

Elsie's anger gave way to tears and Emily hugged her as she sobbed.

'It was what she wanted. And it was typical Alice: so small and delicate but underneath as tough as old boots and damned determined. She had to fight the war her way and we must respect that, Elsie, whether we like it or not,' Emily said sadly. 'Who knows how many lives she might have saved?'

The four girls swore a vow of secrecy.

'Nobody must know about this but us,' Agnes said

firmly. 'If Alice is alive and this got out she'd be in even more danger. All we can do is pray she'll come back,' she added wistfully.

As a cold spring set in, women began to leave the Phoenix. Bombs were still needed, of course, but the production lines up and down the country were coping so older women and women with families, all exhausted by the relentless work schedule, were allowed to go home. The goodbyes were both joyous and sad; girls and women who had worked, slept and lived alongside one another for four hard years wept as they parted.

'It'll be right bloody funny not sharing with a crowd of girls,' one of the cordite girls said as she sat in the canteen for the last time. 'I can't imagine not brewing up for ten lasses or queuing up for the lav. Us lot even had our periods in sync!' she laughed. 'Imagine the mood we were all in the week before we started. Believe me, we were ready for ripping each other's heads off!'

'There've been great days and sad days,' Agnes said.

'I'll even miss Malc,' the cordite girl said as she blew a kiss across the room to Malc, whose head was buried in a newspaper.

'We'll stay in touch. We won't forget,' the girls promised as they waved goodbye. But in truth, without the intensity of community living and sharing, without the driving force of the war effort, friendships would fade into fond memories.

Emily was delighted when she heard the Canadian airmen were leaving their base in the valley.

'Ontario's more than welcome to smarmy Freddie Bilodeaux!' she said. 'I might even burn the rude photograph I threatened him with,' she added with a laugh.

Even though German V1 and V2 rockets were still bombing London, news of the war continued to improve. The Allies took Cologne and built a bridge across the Rhine, the Soviets and the Western Allies were in a race to get to Berlin and Mussolini was in prison.

'Adolf's not shouting quite as loudly as he was,' mocked Lillian as she left the Phoenix one day with Emily.

She was chatting away nineteen to the dozen so didn't notice that Emily had stopped walking and was standing stock-still, her eyes fixed on a handsome young man with startling blue eyes and a blond moustache. Lillian looked over too and noticed he seemed to be carefully scrutinizing every girl that passed him. She heard Emily gasp in amazement.

'Could it really be?' she murmured, then turning to Lillian she quietly said, 'I think it's Alice's boyfriend.'

'I'll leave you to it,' Lillian said as she discreetly turned and left. Emily hesitantly approached the man, who was indeed Robin.

She smiled expectantly; maybe he was here with good news of Alice?

'Emily!' he cried. 'I must look highly suspicious standing here eyeing up women.'

Emily smiled but all the time her heart was hammering in her ribcage.

'I was hoping to see you,' he added gently.

Emily gazed into his face, scarred from gashes and cuts inflicted on him during his interrogations. He looked older too and his eyes were hollowed out with grief.

'It's Alice, isn't it?' she said.

Robin nodded.

Though Emily instinctively knew the news was bad she didn't want to hear him say the words; she didn't want to give up hope.

'Where is she? Is she hurt?' she blustered.

Robin took hold of her hands.

'Emily . . . Alice is dead,' he said.

Emily's eyes filled up with tears which splashed unchecked down her cheeks.

'NO! Please, Robin, no,' she begged.

'There's no way I can make it easy for you, Emily,' Robin said gently.

Emily, desperate for any hope to hold onto, blundered on.

'You got out and maybe Alice did too! She might be coming home. She might have been rescued, just like you,' she cried.

Robin squeezed her hands as he shook his head.

'No, Emily,' he said firmly. 'She was identified by somebody we trained with. He recognized her body when they were . . .' He struggled to finish his sentence as tears streamed down his face. '. . . When they were burning prisoners in the crematorium at Dachau. The Gestapo never got anything out of Alice . . .' He took a breath to steady his voice. 'They gave her a lethal injection then burned her.'

Emily's knees gave way, but before she could fall to the ground Robin grabbed her then half carried her back to the digs.

Malc was asked to go and pick up Elsie so she could hear Robin's tragic news along with her friends. She arrived white-faced and breathless. Ignoring the brandy Robin was pouring out for Agnes, Lillian and Emily, she sat tensely on the sofa, her lovely green eyes wide with fear.

Robin repeated what he'd told Emily earlier, and the silence that followed was long and painful. None of the girls dared to speak for fear of the emotion they might unleash.

'She was so brave; she was the best explosives Special Op Helford had ever come across. She was beautiful too and I adored her,' he said with a sob in his voice. 'We were so near the end of the war, I thought I'd go back for her, or the Allies would liberate the camp. I thought we'd be together again . . .' His voice trailed away as he became lost for words.

'Why would they kill her? Why wouldn't they just let her go?' Elsie wailed as she gave way to floods of tears.

'The Gestapo have never been generous about letting people go,' Robin said quietly. 'When they've got what they want out of you – or not, in brave Alice's case – you're disposed of.'

White-faced, he rose to his feet.

'It's time I told Mrs Massey,' he said.

'I'll come with you,' said Emily.

'What will you tell her?' Agnes asked.

'The truth,' said Robin. 'That her daughter was a hero who gave up her life for her friends and family, and her King and country.'

The whole town went into mourning for Alice, who

wasn't just a local hero but a national hero too. Her death and her sacrifice were written about in all the newspapers and the entire population of Pendle turned up for her memorial service in the parish church. There was no body, no coffin, but the church was full of spring flowers and the sun dappled the stained-glass windows and shone down on the mourners.

Robin and Emily sat on either side of Alice's mother, who had turned into a frail, trembling old lady almost overnight. She had collapsed on hearing Robin's terrible news and was heavily tranquillized in order to get through the service.

'Imagine being alone in her house with no hope of ever seeing her husband or daughter again,' said Agnes. 'Well, not in this life anyway.'

Brigadier Kingsley from Helford House came to the funeral and he spoke of Alice's unflagging energy and determination, her selflessness, her beauty and her bravery.

'She also had a cheeky, mischievous sense of humour, setting decoys to lead her fellow trainees on a merry dance that usually ended up in the Ladies! Being here in the town where Alice grew up, meeting Alice's friends and family, I can see where that humour came from and from where she drew her strength,' he said to the tearful congregation. 'You should be proud people of Pendle to have had such a daughter, one who loved and was loved and never gave up.'

By the end of the ceremony the entire congregation was in tears. After the final blessing they trooped out of the church and gathered around the memorial stone erected for Alice in the churchyard, where they laid wreaths of fragrant spring flowers.

As the mourners dispersed to the Station Hotel for strong drinks and sandwiches, Emily hung back; she was in no hurry to go anywhere. Resting her head against the memorial she read the words carved onto the grey Pennine slab.

ALICE MASSEY

Who lost her life in active service
in Dachau, Germany, aged 25.

Your sacrifice gave us our freedom.

Emily looked up into the vaulted blue sky.

'Catch this, Al,' she said as she blew a kiss up to heaven.

Seeing a figure approaching, Emily hurriedly took out her hankie and brushed tears off her cheeks. When her eyes had cleared she looked again, squinting, then caught her breath. Was she dreaming? The outline of the tall, slim figure in army uniform walking up the church path towards her took her breath away. Blinking hard, she looked again. Her Bill! Was it really him? As he got nearer, she saw the sweep of his dark hair over his forehead, the scar on his chin he'd got playing football at primary school, the soft smile playing on his lips. Wide-eyed, frightened and shaking in every limb, Emily gazed at him in total disbelief.

'Hiya,' he said in his old familiar way as he neared her.

Oh, the sound of his voice! How long since she'd heard it! How sweet it sounded, like a long-awaited caress. Holding onto Alice's memorial for support Emily swayed.

'Hiya,' she answered weakly.

'Need a hug?'

Weeping uncontrollably, Emily fell into his open arms, and then, pressed against his warm, strong chest, she sobbed herself dry.

'What will I do without her?' she cried.

Smiling gently, Bill wiped a finger down her wet cheeks and around her full mouth, which he kissed softly.

'Don't worry, sweetheart, I'll look after you,' he promised.

They stayed in the churchyard a long time. Moving her away from the memorial, Bill led a trembling Emily to a bench under an old elm where they sat holding hands. In between bouts of talking they gazed rapturously at each other.

'You're even more beautiful than I remember,' Bill said as he kissed each of her delicate eyebrows then traced her cheek with kisses.

'And you're even taller, broader and bonnier,' she said.

'It's not army grub!' he joked. 'Just a soldier's life,' he added dismissively.

'Fighting for six years,' she said as she carefully avoided adding, 'Killing and bombing, frightened, hungry, tired and lonely.'

'There's more fighting to come,' he said solemnly.

Emily closed her eyes as she leaned her head against his shoulder. She'd just got him back, only for him to be taken away again.

'Our regiment will be going to the Far East.'

Emily gazed up at him, her blue eyes wide and blazing with passion.

'I'll wait, darling. If it's twenty years, I'll wait,' she

vowed. 'I've paid for what I did a thousand times over. I was young, stupid – bloody vain! I'll never stray again, never! I thought I'd lost you, Bill,' she whispered. 'I'll *never* let you go again.'

'You lost me for a bit, Em,' he admitted. 'I was hurt and humiliated. I could've strangled the fella with mi bare hands!'

'Me and you both,' she said as she kissed him over and over again.

'Hell, Em, if there's one thing this war's taught me it's that life's precious. Love's what counts, not killing and maiming. When the war's over, what years I have left I want with you . . . Whether life's long or short I want you, Emily Yates, by my side for ever.'

Chapter 37: 8 May, VE Day 1945

One minute after midnight on Tuesday 8 May 1945, Victory in Europe was officially confirmed. Everybody knew the day was coming – Hitler was dead, Mussolini hanged and the Allies were in Berlin – but for all of that, the day they'd longed for and dreamed of started with a slow burn. Nobody could quite believe the news; there was simultaneously weeping and laughter combined with confusion, which Elsie summed up beautifully.

'What're we going to do now?'

'Six years . . .' Lillian sighed. 'Six long, long years of poverty, hard work, heartache and rationing.'

'And that dreaded knock on the door,' said Agnes knowingly.

Emily gazed around; she simply couldn't imagine not living with Agnes and Lillian, little Elsie too, who seemed to spend half her life running up the hill from town, pushing her Silver Cross pram overflowing with Jonty and Esther.

What would they do? Return to the same place, mentally and physically, where they'd been before the war started? Impossible! Millions of women had been part of Churchill's Secret Army, the special agents working underground; they couldn't just resume a life of drab domesticity, washing and cleaning, shopping and cooking. Here were women who'd made bombs, day in and day out; they'd been a vital part of the drive to destroy Hitler and prevent an invasion of their precious land. These women, Emily thought passionately, were a powerhouse not to be dismissed. Collectively they were an industrious, driven army who, out of necessity, had survived without their men. They'd made decisions on their own, forged new lives on their own, and how could that be reversed? Surely this war had turned the world upside down; surely the established customs and traditions of a pre-war society would be changed for ever.

Lillian interrupted Emily's deep thoughts.

'One thing's for certain,' she said. 'We can't stay in the Phoenix making bombs that nobody wants.'

'They're still needed in the Far East,' Agnes sharply reminded her.

Along with hundreds of other workers the Bomb Girls converged in the pouring rain on the town centre, where people were flooding out of their homes in the need to share the moment they'd been waiting for with the entire community. They stood in silence in the rain listening to the King's speech relayed through loudspeakers hastily strung up around the town hall.

'His stammer's so bad it's difficult to catch the poor man's drift,' Elsie said as she strained to hear him.

'He's saying the enemy's been overcome,' Agnes told her.

'Sshshh!' hissed several people around her.

'And now he's saying we've got to deal with the Japanese,' Agnes whispered to Elsie.

Lillian groaned as she rolled her eyes to the rain-sodden heavens.

'Just my bloody luck! Gary will be on his way over there when all the other fellas are on their way over here!'

A big woman in front turned to glare at the girls.

'I want to hear the King not you daft beggers – put a sock in it.'

The girls smiled at each other but did as they were told. When the King concluded his speech the crowd applauded and burst into a rousing chorus of 'God Save the King', then as the sun broke through the mood of cautious incredulity changed to jubilation. 'It's a Long Way to Tipperary' jangled out over the loudspeakers and the crowd quite spontaneously started dancing and singing. Children, who were let out of school for the day in celebration of peace in Europe, ran wild, the pubs stayed open and trestle tables were dragged out of church halls in readiness for a celebratory feast.

'I don't know what we'll be eating,' a woman cried. 'But we're sure to find summut!'

'Summut's not good enough on a day like this,' Emily replied.

The woman smiled at Emily.

'Then off you go, lovie, and come back like Jesus with enough food to feed five thousand!'

Emily persuaded the Phoenix cooks to lend her several portable gas rings and some great metal vats. Malc drove it all down to the town hall square where workmen connected the gas rings up to the mains. The vats were safely secured on trestle tables, then Emily asked everybody in the square to go home and return with their portion of fat rationing. As the vats filled up, Emily ignited the gas rings and the delicious smell of hot fat filled the air. Malc drove all round town picking up potatoes from anybody who had them. Emily and her workers peeled and chopped them, then the victory supper got underway. Bags of chips and bottles of beer hidden long ago under the counter were circulated all night long. Added to this, people brought out what they had stored away in their homes: corned beef, tins of fruit, pickles, meat pies, pasties and sausages.

'When we've finished all this cooking,' Lillian cried, 'I'd like half a bottle of gin then I'm going to dance my socks off!'

Hot, sweaty, but radiantly happy, Emily cooked until there was nothing left to cook.

Esther, who'd been pushing a chuckling Jonty in his pram around the square, approached Emily and saw she was starting to tidy away her improvised kitchen.

Knowing Emily's genius for inventive cookery, Esther said in a sweet, persuasive voice, 'No pudding, Em?'

Emily cocked her head as she thought.

'Fancy a pancake?'

'*Yes, please!*' cried Esther.

An hour later, after serving up dozens of pancakes spread with home-made jam, Emily called it a day. Drinking thirstily from a bottle of beer bought for her by Malc, she smiled with contentment.

'Thanks for everything, Malc,' she said. 'And I do mean *everything*,' she added pointedly.

Malc took a long pull on his bottle of beer before he replied.

'You lasses have led me a right bloody dance and there's no doubting we've had our up and downs,' he said nodding in the direction of Lillian, who by now was half-way up the flagpole. 'But you've worked hard and more than pulled your weight.' He raised his bottle in a salute to Emily and her friends. 'I shall always remember you Bomb Girls with respect and affection,' he said with a choke in his voice, then he added with a wink, 'Even if you were a set of little buggers at times!'

Emily's happy smile widened as she looked at the partying crowd dancing around the square. This was her community, which she loved with all her heart. All she needed was Bill home for good and her happiness would be complete.

Churchill's rousing speech brought the street-party revels to a temporary halt. When he congratulated the nation on how valiantly they had fought and how much they had endured there was hardly a dry eye in the crowd, as the Prime Minister's booming voice faded away, the crowd broke into spontaneous song.

> 'For he's a jolly good fellow,
> He's a jolly good fellow,
> For he's a jolly good fellow
> And so say all of us!'

And then the party started in earnest. Children dressed in red, white and blue paper ran wild in the streets waving Union Jack flags. Fireworks were set off and then, to everybody's astonishment, a beacon of fire fluttered into life high up on Pendle Hill. As it flared, another beacon further along the Pennines lit up, then another and another until the whole of the Pennine ridge was one long line of flaming beacons. For the first time in six years the night sky was lit up.

'No more blackouts!' the children cried as they danced up and down in disbelief. 'No more gas masks!'

Emily wiped tears away as a beacon flared on Witch Crag.

'Alice,' she said out loud. 'My sweet Al.'

They'd won the war but at what a cost. Millions dead, their lives snuffed out, taken too early. She and Alice should have grown into young mothers together, brought up their children together, shared childcare and birthdays; they should have grown old together and been buried in the same churchyard at the end of a long and happy life. But her lovely, delicate, beautiful friend was less than nothing now, her ashes blown by a stray breeze across some unknown part of Germany.

How could she keep Alice alive? How could she not forget?

A rush of emotion surged through her at these thoughts. There might be no body, no hand to hold, no smile to see, no words to speak, but there was love. All that finally remained was love.

'Just like the beacons burning on the moors I'll keep my love alive for you, Alice,' Emily promised. 'I'll never forget.'

Chapter 38: We'll Meet Again . . .

A few months later, just before Victory in Japan was declared, the Phoenix reopened as a cotton mill and the digs where Emily, Lillian, Elsie, Alice, Agnes and Daphne had lived for four years would soon revert to being a cowshed.

A terrible war was still raging in the Far East and the Lancashire Fusiliers were sent there, including Tommy, but not before he and Elsie had a wonderful few days' leave and Elsie fell for another baby.

'Honest to God, you two are like rabbits!' Lillian teased poor Elsie, who blushed to the roots of her hair.

Gary didn't come home – well, not to Pendle. He and his squadron were flown home to the States where Lillian, after the long years of waiting for her love, was shortly to join him.

Which is why the girls gathered one breezy day in their old digs. After collecting kindling from the moors they lit the old wood-burning stove just for old times' sake and prepared a farewell meal for each other. The food laid out on the table reflected their different tastes and their very different lives. Daphne had brought her favourite: foie gras and Bolly; Emily turned up with hot meat pies; Elsie had discovered black puddings in Bury market, and she could not get enough of them; Lillian settled for gin and chocolates, whilst Agnes arrived with lamb chops.

'Courtesy of Stan's sheep farmer,' she said.

As they cooked together and drank tea, champagne or gin, they discussed their futures.

'Well, we all know what you're doing, Lillian,' laughed Agnes as she turned the chops in the frying pan.

'At last I'm going to Ohio!' Lillian exclaimed as she boogied around the room. 'I'm going to get my hands on Gorgeous Gary and drag him into bed for a week. I don't care if I fall pregnant right away,' she added in a softer voice. 'I want that baby I never had.'

'Will we ever see you again, Lil?' Elsie asked sadly.

'Of course!' Lillian replied robustly. 'We're sisters and we stick together.'

'Cheers to that, darling,' said Daphne as she raised her glass of champagne. 'Though Ohio wouldn't suit me. Isn't it full of wagon trains and gun-punching cowboys?' she teased.

'You've seen too many westerns,' Lillian retorted.

'What about you, Daf?' Emily asked.

Daphne inserted a cigarette into her cigarette holder before replying.

'I'm getting a divorce.'

There was a collective gasp of disbelief.

'*Why?*' cried Elsie, who was shocked rigid. 'You've only been married a few years!'

Daphne blew out a ring of smoke.

'Rodders is a crashing bore!' she declared.

'I'd second that!' giggled Emily.

'I was hoping he'd be posted to Burma – somewhere I wouldn't have to see him – but, just my luck, he's got an office job in Whitehall, which means he's home most nights and I can't go out with my new lover.'

'You're not generally supposed to have lovers if you're married,' Agnes pointed out.

'Well, I'm not the marrying kind, I've decided,' said Daphne totally unconcerned. 'I like men and I like fun and Rodders is certainly neither of those!' she concluded.

'One thing's for sure – I'm going nowhere,' said Elsie predictably. 'When Tommy comes home, and pray to God he does,' she added as she crossed herself, 'we're going to save up and buy a little two-up, two-down near Tommy's mum.'

Lillian burst out laughing.

'You're joking!' she cried. 'Two-up, two-down? You'll need a six-bedroomed house for all your kids, the way you two are going!'

'Come on, let's eat,' Emily called before Elsie started hurling cushions at cheeky Lillian.

As they gathered round the table where they'd sat so many times in the past, Emily wiped away a tear.

'Alice should be sitting here with us.'

'Raise your glasses, ladies,' said Agnes.

As they did so, Emily made a toast.

'Blow a kiss to heaven where Alice said she'd be.'

After kisses were blown and the toast was drunk a sad silence fell.

'She and her like gave us our freedom,' Elsie said as she recalled the words on Alice's memorial stone.

Taking a deep breath, Emily forced a smile.

'Come on now, the last thing Alice would have wanted was sadness on a day like today,' she said.

'Absolutely right, darling,' said Daphne. Then, picking up on Emily's determined spirit, she turned to Agnes.

'What are your plans? Surely you're not staying on that ghastly sheep farm?'

Agnes laughed.

'Actually we're saving up to buy our own sheep farm. We love the life up here and the fresh air does Esther the world of good.'

'So you'll be a farmer's wife? Collecting eggs and baking scones on an old Aga!' Daphne teased gently.

'I'm planning to do more than bake scones, Daphne,' Agnes replied with an excited smile. 'I want to be Stan's partner and work alongside him rearing sheep.'

'Darling, rather you than me!' exclaimed incorrigible Daphne.

'So that just leaves you, Em,' said Agnes.

As all eyes turned on Emily, she smiled radiantly.

'When Bill gets back from the war we're getting married!'

Daphne lit up another cigarette.

'Has he bought the ring yet?' she asked.

Emily grinned as she took a big gulp of her fizzing champagne.

'No,' she replied. 'I asked for a chip shop instead!'

Read on for the first chapter of Daisy Styles's next book

The Code Girls

Due out August 2016

1. Ava

'Friday dinner time,' thought Ava as she tucked her long, dark hair under her cook's hat and checked her reflection in the small cracked mirror hanging on the canteen wall. Even smeared with grease the glass revealed the irrepressible sparkle in Ava's dark blue eyes, she beamed her characteristic wide, open smile, which revealed her small white teeth and a charming dimple in her left cheek. She was taller than most of her girlfriends, long legged and shapely with a full bust, softly curving hips and a willowy twenty-inch waist. Ava was fortunate: her strong frame and athletic build was down to hard work and years of horse riding on the wild Lancashire moors.

With her voluminous hair neatly tucked under her cotton hat Ava wrote the day's menu in white chalk on the canteen noticeboard; two years ago Friday's menu would always have been fish – cod and haddock freshly delivered from Fleetwood market. Ava had quickly learned how to skin and fillet fish, but that was two years ago before the outbreak of war and the start of food rationing. Nowadays it was impossible to buy enough fish to feed a family, never mind two hundred mill workers. As rationing got tougher and tougher Ava had tried variations: parsnip fritters, corn-beef fritters, fake-sausage fritters, and mince (very little) mixed with oatmeal and herbs made a tasty fritter too. But on a Friday the workers, predominantly Catholics, didn't eat meat as it was a day of abstinence. The best and most popular alternative to fish was Ava's delicious 'scallops', fresh local spuds washed, peeled and thickly sliced, then dipped in a thick creamy yellow batter, made from dried eggs combined with milk and water. Deeply fried in a vat of fat, Ava served the golden brown 'scallops' with mushy peas or butter beans and pickled red cabbage. It made her laugh when customers asked for chips as well.

'You'll sink like a stone with all them spuds inside you!' she teased.

'You've got to have chips on a Friday, cock,' one of her customers said with a wink. 'It's a bugger we can't 'ave fish like in't th'owd days but your scallops are bloody beltin'! Give us another, wil't?'

Ava smiled as she dropped a few more on his plate; she loved these people and she loved her strong, tight-knit, hard-working community. Half the people queuing up for their dinner lived within a block of Ava, in identical red-brick terraced houses, stacked back to back, row upon row reaching up to the foothills of the moors which dominated the landscape of the mill town. Everybody knew everybody else's business, it couldn't be otherwise when outdoor privies were shared and women gathered at the wash house to swop gossip and smoke cigarettes while they did their weekly wash, which they hung on washing lines threaded across the network of back streets where children played under wet sheets flapping like ships' sails in the breeze. The neighbours' over-familiar questions about her future had recently become both an irritant and an embarrassment to Ava.

'So when are you going to get yourself conscripted, our Ava? All't lasses in't town have gone off to do their bit for't war but you're still here. Can you not stand thowt o' leaving us?' neighbours and relatives alike teased.

Ava had self-consciously assured them she was definitely leaving, there was in fact no choice: female conscription was obligatory for women between the ages of eighteen and thirty. Women were being deployed all over the country, most of Ava's friends had already gone: some to munitions factories in Yorkshire and Wales; others had signed up to work as Land Girls in Scotland, but Ava had held back. She'd felt guilty of course. Would people think she was trying to duck out of war work, that she was unpatriotic? She was in fact fiercely patriotic and passionately believed in committing one hundred per cent to the war effort but she was determined to do something big, something bold that would take her outside of her comfort zone and push her to the limits in her sacrifice for king and country. Three months after female conscription had been authorized by the government, Ava was well aware that she had to do something soon otherwise the Labour Exchange would be on her tail and find war work for her.

'AVA! Check on them apple pies, lovie!' Audrey the

canteen boss yelled as the workers settled down on long wooden benches that ran alongside scrubbed wooden tables to eat their meal.

Ava dashed over to the huge oven where her pies were turning a soft golden brown, she was excited to see what the customers' reactions would be when they tucked into their puddings, which she'd added a surprise ingredient to. Last night she'd ridden her horse, Shamrock, across the moors to her favourite spot where wild winberries grew in abundance. Leaving the mare to crop clumps of tough grass, Ava had collected a large amount of small fruity berries that she'd mixed with baking apples then covered with a thick pastry crust. As she inspected the pies she could see rich purple juice seeping through the edges, they would taste delicious served with custard, but she'd have to warn Audrey to cut thin slices if every worker was to have their fair share of her pudding.

Ava loved the Lancashire moors, especially at this time of the year, late spring when the days were long and the nights were warm. Once work was finished and tea was cleared away at home she'd change into a pair of baggy old tweed trousers and head for the hills. Just a short walk up an old cobbled lane lined with oak and ash trees and Ava was on the moors, where most evenings she rode an old cob mare who belonged to a local farmer. He'd asked her if she'd like to take care of Shamrock, who needed exercising now that his daughter had left home. Not that Ava was an experienced rider but she was certainly not going to turn down the offer. Luckily Shamrock was willing and patient with Ava who took many a tumble as she learned the hard way how to walk, trot, canter and keep her seat over the bumpy moorland terrain. Ava and Shamrock developed a trusting, companionable relationship, both of them enjoying their rides over the rolling moors with only the skylarks and curlews for company.

It was while she'd been up at the farm the previous evening, tacking up Shamrock in readiness for a ride out that she'd caught sight of the local newspaper left lying around by the farmer in the tack room.

'WOMEN WORKING IN COMMUNICATION CENTRES'

Ava's heart had skipped a beat. She laid down Shamrock's reins and hurried over to read the article.

'As the war rolls on more and more women are required to fill the spaces left by men fighting on the frontline. Conscripted women are needed for training in communications, tracking, signalling, administration, interception and mapping intelligence in military command control centres. Training centres offering an intense six-month training are opening across the country to provide women with the necessary skills for this vital war work.'

Ava's deep blue eyes blazed with excitement. With her heart beating double time and her pulse pounding she let the paper drop into her lap as she gazed out over the open stable door at the arching blue sky.

'THIS is what I've been waiting for,' she said out loud. '*I* could be a code girl! That's the work for me.'

At the first available free moment she dashed into the Labour Exchange in the High Street and marched boldly up to the desk.

'I want to be a code girl,' she announced with a proud ring to her voice. The lady being the desk raised her eyebrows.

'Code girl?' she asked.

'I want to work in communications,' Ava explained. 'Please can I sign up?'

'What's your present employment?' the woman asked.

'Canteen cook.'

There was no doubting the shock on her face.

'Canteen cook!' she exclaimed.

Ava nodded.

'In Dove Mill, I'm second in charge,' she added with a proud smile.

'Cooking isn't exactly the right kind of background for a trainee in communications,' the woman retorted. 'They'll be looking for more academic lasses, them with a bit of schooling behind them.'

Ava's eyes flashed with indignation.

'Women are doing jobs nobody ever expected them to be doing all over England right now – why shouldn't I?'

The woman nodded.

'You're right there,' she replied as she handed Ava an application form and a pencil. 'Fill this in, when it comes to present employment you must state your job.'

'But –' Ava protested.

'You can add that you want to train in communications because you feel you have an aptitude for it,' the woman quickly explained.

Smiling happily Ava filled in the form, writing 'Canteen

Cook' as her profession but adding in big bold capitals that she wanted to switch to communications. 'I want to be a code girl as I believe it's far more beneficial to my king and country than cooking in the Dove Mill canteen in Bolton'. 'That should do it,' she said as she returned the completed form to the woman at the desk.

'Don't build your hopes up, lovie,' the woman advised. 'Be prepared to knuckle down to anything that's required.'

'I'll knuckle down to anything, just so long as it's not cooking!' Ava said with a winning smile.

The woman watched Ava walk away. There was no doubting she was a stunning girl but good looks didn't pay dividends, with a war on people got what they were given and did as they were told.

'I've enlisted as a code girl,' Ava proudly told her boss. Audrey looked up from the mound of pastry she was mixing and burst out laughing.

'And what's a code girl when she's at home?'

Standing by the massive industrial mixer stirring a mince and onion stew that was bulked up with root vegetables, suede, parsnips and turnips, Ava reiterated what she'd read in the paper.

'It could be anything from operations, tracking, signals, administration, interception or working in military command control centres,' she said with a bit of a swagger.

'Sounds bloody scary to me!' Audrey joked. 'Here, roll that lot out,' she added, as she pushed half the pastry across the table to Ava. 'Roll it thin, mind, we've two hundred hungry mouths to feed; a little must go a long way.'

As the two women at either end of the table rolled and cut pastry to fit into huge tin trays Audrey continued.

'How are you going to cope with all that brainy stuff?'

'I'll learn,' Ava said with conviction. 'I really want to improve myself.'

'Well good luck to you, lass, but I bet they turn you down,' Audrey said as she poured the cooled mince and onion mix into the trays now lined with pastry. 'It's not like you went to grammar school and got a good education, mark my words,' Audrey said as she slapped a pastry crust on top of the meat and neatly nipped in the edges. 'Them stuck-up communications toffs will be looking for brains, certificates and qualifications – none of which you've got Ava, love!'

Ava smiled confidently.

'Don't worry, Audrey – I'll be a good code girl. Just you see.'

A fortnight later Ava was packing her small, cheap suitcase, helped by her mother who was carefully folding her few dresses before laying them on top of Ava's freshly ironed blouses and new tweed skirt.

'Do you think you've got enough frocks?' Mrs Downham asked.

'They'll do for now,' Ava replied as she wrapped her two pairs of battered shoes which her mother had polished till they shone in newspaper.

'I wish I could have bought you a warm twin set,' Mrs Downham said wistfully.

'Mam!' Ava cried. 'Stop worrying; it's a communications centre not a fashion school.'

Seeing the tears welling up in her mother's eyes Ava took hold of her hands.

'I'll write every week,' she promised.

Mrs Downham nodded sadly.

'I wish you weren't going so far away, Norfolk's the other side of the country, miles away from here.'

'I have to go where the government sends me,' Ava pointed out. 'You should be thrilled it's only Norfolk; I could be in Scotland felling trees like Marjorie Carter from round the corner!'

Mrs Downham gave a bleak smile.

'I always knew this town wasn't big enough for you,' she said as she stroked her daughter's long dark hair. 'You were made for better things.'

'Mam, this isn't about day dreams, this is my contribution to beating Hitler,' she said with a laugh as she kissed her mother's cheek.

Before leaving Ava knew she had to say goodbye to Shamrock, something she'd been dreading doing since the moment she'd signed up; the old mare's excited whinny did nothing to lift Ava's spirits.

'Hey, sweetheart,' she said softly.

Shamrock nudged her gently in the chest.

'I haven't forgotten,' Ava murmured as she produced the mandatory carrot expected on every visit.

As Shamrock contentedly crunched on the carrot, Ava gulped back tears that were threatening to overwhelm her.

'I don't know how to say this, sweetheart,' she said. 'You see, I've got to leave you.'

Oblivious to the changes that were about to unfold Shamrock snickered before nuzzling Ava's arm. Even though

Ava had found a nice, local lass to replace her she still felt guilty about leaving Shamrock; how could you explain to an animal that her life was about to change for ever? Ava thought about the thousands upon thousands of young men who had joined up in September 1939 when the Prime Minister, Neville Chamberlain, had announced that England was at war with Germany. How many lives had been shattered by their departure? How many homes broken and families wrecked by the loss of a loved one who never came home?

Sighing, Ava bent to kiss Shamrock's soft velvety muzzle. Her sacrifice amounted to nothing compared to the soldiers, sailors and pilots who were risking their lives fighting the enemy in planes, ships and on land, in armoured tanks. Two years in and the war was not going well; Britain was ill-prepared and ill-equipped when compared to the organized might of the Third Reich. The Dunkirk evacuation had shown the true grit of the British, who'd launched thousands of boats into the North Sea on a hazardous, often fatal mission to rescue soldiers from the beaches, but the losses on that fateful day had cut deep as did the continuous bombing of Britain's major cities. The nation, no longer gripped with the irrefutable belief that they would win the war, began to fear the worst, an invasion.

'Which is why we all have to do our bit,' Ava said as she swiped away sentimental tears with the back of her hand. 'I'll miss you, sweetheart,' she whispered as she kissed Shamrock for the last time, then, turning, she briskly walked away leaving the old mare neighing shrilly behind her.

Ava's last day at home was fraught with emotion; her little sister kept bursting into tears and if her mum packed her case once, she packed it twenty times. Their last meal together was eaten in an awkward silence with none of the usual family banter and easy teasing. It was a relief when tea was over and Ava could busy herself with washing up while her parents gathered round the big Bakelite radio where they heard the grim news that Germany had marched on Russia.

'Bloody 'ell,' said Ava's Dad as he puffed hard on a Woodbine. 'There'll be no stopping the buggers now!'

'The Russians are bound to put up a fight. They're not going to take it lying down,' Mrs Downham insisted.

'Aye, but what guns and weapons have they got against the Huns?' Mr Downham pointed out. 'It could end up a bloodbath for the Bolshies.'

'Thank God it's the summer, at least they won't be fighting in five feet of snow,' Mrs Downham murmured.

Ava boiled up some milk and made cocoa for them all then sat as usual by the coal fire with her parents on either side of her.

'We'll miss you, our lass,' her dad said softly.

Ava took hold of their hands.

'I'll miss you too.'

She would miss them for sure but her heart skipped a beat when she thought of the wonderful new world waiting for her in Norfolk.

The next morning Ava settled her suitcase in the netted luggage rack of the compartment she was travelling in then leaned out of the open window to smile at her family, who stood on the platform with heavy, sorrowful faces.

'Write!' her mum pleaded as she dabbed away her tears with a hankie.

'Don't forget me!' wailed her little sister.

'Take care of yourself, lass,' her dad cried as the heavy steam train pulled out of the station.

'I love you!' Ava shouted through a belching cloud of black smoke.

As the platform receded Ava sat back in her seat and sighed. The goodbyes were over; her adventure was beginning!

Having never travelled further south than Rhyl, wide-eyed Ava peered out of the window at the ever changing countryside, the wild northern moors gave way to the Peak District with tidy grey stone farmhouses nestled neatly between green fields where sheep grazed.

'What wouldn't I give for one of them woolly lambs roasted with potatoes, Yorkshire puds, mint sauce and gravy,' said a young lad in a soldier's uniform on the opposite side of the carriage.

'That's never going to happen, lad,' said an older soldier, puffing hard on a cigarette next to him. 'Them animals will be made into mince and spread thin across half the county. I can't remember when I last had a solid piece of meat put in front of me,' he added as he took a greaseproof parcel out of his overcoat pocket.

'Fancy a beef paste buttie, sweetheart?' he asked with a wink.

'In exchange for one of my carrot buns,' Ava replied as she opened a small tin she'd packed with home-made buns.

'That'll be a rare treat,' said the soldier as he bit into the bun and nearly swallowed it whole.

'You too,' Ava said as she proffered the tin to all the soldiers in the carriage.

By the time it had done the rounds there was only one bun left but the soldiers all gave Ava something in return for her kindness: half an orange, a piece of chocolate, another soggy sandwich, a cigarette and cold tea from a bottle.

The cheery soldiers got off at Peterborough where Ava changed lines. On a slow train to Norwich Ava's heart began to pound with excitement, she had to keep reminding herself that this was war work, her sacrifice to save the country from Fascism. The only problem was it felt more like a great adventure rather than a painful sacrifice and she was having trouble keeping the smile off her face. A third and final train took her to Wells-Next-the-Sea on the north Norfolk coast. As Ava walked along the platform she felt the sea air blowing breezily around her and tasted sea salt on her lips. Her stomach flipped with nerves as she joined a few girls standing outside the station in the dark.

'Are you going to Walsingham Communication Centre,' a cheery, red-headed, young woman asked.

Ava nodded.

'Join the queue, we're waiting for a lift.'

The lift turned out to be a rickety old van.

'Hop in, ladies. I'm Peter, gamekeeper cum gardener from Walsingham Hall.'

As he piled their luggage on the roof the girls squeezed in. Instead of sitting beside each other they sat on benches facing each other which caused them all to fall sideways, almost into each others' laps as Peter cranked the gears and the van bounced forward.

'Hold on tight!' he warned too late.

Though the sun had set the summer light lingered in the eastern sky. Peering through the window Ava could see the town's people had dutifully pulled down their black-out blinds and Peter drove to the hall without any headlights to guide the way.

'How do you know where you're going?' laughed one of the girls.

'Instinct,' Peter replied without taking his eyes off the twisting road for a second.

Ten minutes later Peter took a sharp left-hand turn and swung into a drive flanked by elaborate metal gates gilded with an elaborate coat of arms.

'That's the hall,' he said as he dropped a gear to make his way up the drive that threaded through a deer park where even in the half light Ava could see fallow deer grazing under ancient oak and horse chestnut trees. They rattled over a cattle bridge then with a swoop Peter came to a halt in front of Walsingham Hall. Ava caught her breath; of course she'd expected a big place that would accommodate a lot of people but she hadn't expected *this*.

'It's beautiful,' she breathed as she stepped out of the van and gazed up at the majestic building that towered before her.

'One of the finest stately homes in the country,' Peter said proudly. 'Just wait till you see it in the daylight, it's a fine sight to behold.'

As the girls tumbled out of the van Peter called out,

'Make your way indoors, I'll follow with your luggage.'

With their feet crunching on the gravel drive the trainees pushed open the heavy front door and entered the elegant marble hall, which was decorated with ancestral portraits hung in huge, ornate gold frames.

'Nobody mentioned we'd be billeted in Buckingham Palace!' giggled one of the trainees.

Her laughter faded as a grim-faced women dressed from head to toe in black approached.

'Your accommodation is in the South Wing,' she said in a voice that bristled with contempt. 'Follow me.'

She quickly moved off as if she wanted no association with any of the newcomers.

'Who's she?' Ava whispered to Peter who was staggering along with as many cases as he could carry.

'Timms, the housekeeper,' he gasped under the strain of his heavy load. 'She doesn't like you,' he added with a wink.

'She's made that perfectly obvious,' Ava replied.

The make-shift dormitories in the South Wing had been built in what must have been a series of connecting drawing rooms all with high ceilings decorated with swirling stucco plasterwork and elegant floor-to-ceiling windows draped in blackout blinds.

'In there,' barked Timms before turning her stiff-as-a-ramrod back on the trainees and walking away with disapproval evident in every step she took.

'She's a regular bundle of laughs!' tittered the cheery red-headed girl.

'Don't worry, you won't be seeing much of her,' Peter assured them with a chuckle.

'Thank God for that,' thought Ava.

The yawning girls selected their bunk beds then made their way along the dark bewildering corridors to the bathroom, which had a line of sinks running along one wall and lavatories running along the opposite one.

'Oooh!' exclaimed an impressed trainee as she switched on a tap. 'Hot and cold water, more than we get at home.'

'Thank goodness!' joked one of the trainees as she dashed into the nearest cubicle. 'One minute longer and I would have wet myself!'

Ava cleaned her teeth, washed her face then dabbed her skin with a few blobs of Ponds Cold Cream, a parting gift from Audrey. Lying on a bottom bunk Ava pulled a blanket and a scratchy, starched single sheet over her body, then looked nervously up as the woman on the top bunk bounced around, causing the bed springs to sag and twang over Ava's face.

'Will I ever get to sleep?' she wondered as a few girls started to snore, a few even sniffing as though they were crying.

As Ava eventually slipped into a deep, exhausted sleep the smile that had been on her face all day remained there through the night; it was the smile of a girl who just couldn't wait to see what tomorrow would bring.